Miklós Vámos is one of the most respected and widely read writers in his native Hungary. He is the author of twenty-six books, including nine novels. He has taught at Yale University on a Fulbright Fellowship, served as *The Nation*'s Eastern Europe correspondent, worked as consultant on the Oscar-winning film *Mephisto*, and presented Hungary's most-watched cultural television show. Vámos has received numerous awards for his plays, screenplays, novels and short stories, including the Hungarian Merit Award for lifetime achievement.

The Book of Fathers is considered his most accomplished novel and has sold 200,000 copies in Hungary. It has been translated into eleven languages.

THE
BOOK
OF
FATHERS

MIKLÓS VÁMOS

Translated from the Hungarian by
PETER SHERWOOD

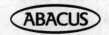

ABACUS

Originally published in Hungarian with the title
Apák könyve by Ab Ovo, Budapest, in 2000
First published in Great Britain in 2006 by Abacus as a paperback original
This edition published in 2007
Reprinted 2007 (three times)

A CIP catalogue record for this book
is available from the British Library.

ISBN 978-0-349-11931-1

Papers used by Abacus are natural, recyclable products made from
wood grown in sustainable forests and certified in accordance with
the rules of the Forest Stewardship Council.

Typeset in Caslon by M Rules

Printed and bound in Great Britain by
Clays Ltd, St Ives plc
Paper supplied by Hellefoss AS, Norway

Abacus
An imprint of
Little, Brown Book Group
Brettenham House
Lancaster Place
London WC2E 7EN

A Member of the Hachette Livre Group of Companies

www.littlebrown.co.uk

THE
BOOK
OF
FATHERS

I

THE WORLD COMES TO LIFE. WISPS OF GREEN STEAL across the fields, rich with the promise of spring. Tiny shoots push through the soil. Virgin buds uncoil at the tips of branches. Soft, fresh grass sweeps and swells across the meadows. Thornbushes blossom on the hillsides. The walnut trees have survived the winter, though their antlered crowns still stand bare. Fresh leaves reach longingly for rain from the sky.

The Lord be praised, we reached the village of Kos in the month of April in His Year of 1705. Five times in that year and in the year thereafter was the village laid waste, thrice by the Kurucz bands of the insurrectio Rákócziensis, twice by the Labancz troops of the Emperor. A third portion of the four-and-seventy houses burnt or fell to the ground, and another third were deserted by their tenants, who departed for more peaceful climes. Thus was the joyful tenor of life much diminished in this place; the lands lay fallow, the number of livestock about the houses did likewise decline. As we prepared for our first night there, my grandson Kornél asked, in German: Would it not be better at home? These were words we would oft repeat thereafter.

1

Thus began Grandpa Czuczor's story in the canvas-bound folio he was given by his daughter Zsuzsánna. Excellent though his spoken knowledge was of German, Slovak and Hungarian, he had so far written only in German. Having returned to the lands of the Magyar, he wanted to keep the story of their days in his mother tongue, perhaps because he wanted his grandson Kornél to read it when he grew up. The three of them had arrived by cart from Bavaria, whither Grandpa Czuczor and his brother had fled when the dust had settled over what was called, after its chief instigator, the Wesselényi conspiracy. Though the Czuczor brothers were strenuous in their denial of any involvement with the conspirators, some forgeries came to light which sealed their fate: their assets were confiscated and even worse might have followed had they not hastily fled. Over the border they soon acquired skills as typographers and compositors, and established a printing press, later making their mark as book-binders as well. In the guildhall of Thüningen their names were posted as the *Gebrüder Czuczur*.

Grandpa Czuczor never felt entirely at home in the windswept and rain-sodden lands of the beer-swilling Bavarians, whom in some obscure way he held responsible for the series of deaths that befell his family. Little wonder, then, that when he got wind of the Prince Primus's patent, he went running to the printing press, where his brother was working on the leads. 'We can pack our bags!' he yelled from the steps of the workshop. He pointed excitedly to his crumpled copy of the *Mercurius Hungaricus*, where a Latin text announced that a return to the de-populated villages of Hungary was now permitted without penalty.

No words of mine could win over my brother to the idea of going home with us. He preferred the comforts of Thüningen, newly acquired but at no small cost, where he wanted to pursue the crafts of printing and binding books. No news of him since that time. Zsuzsánna is troubled by the condition of little Kornél, her son, only in his fourth year of life, who in these straitened times suffers greatly from hunger, in want of meat and even eggs.

Returning by a circuitous route, they set up home in a house with a courtyard, put at their disposal at the edge of the village of Kos. Grandpa Czuczor immediately dug a hole at the bottom of the garden, by the rose bushes, and buried his money there, taking particular care not to inform either his grandson or his daughter of its whereabouts. Only Wilhelm, the servant they brought with them from Thüningen, knew of it, as he had helped with the digging.

'Wilhelm, *du mußt das nie erzählen, verstehst du mich?*' he warned Wilhelm, with an unambiguous gesture: drawing the edge of his palm across the front of his neck.

'*Jawohl!*' yelped the startled lad, as he did at every request or order. All he could manage in Hungarian was a fractured *Janapat*, 'Good day!'

Kornél endured much taunting by the other boys for his thin, straw-coloured hair, his oversized, floppy ears, and for the odd German word he would suddenly come out with. He picked up Hungarian quickly, even though these were not peaceful times conducive to study. Indeed, there was ominous news from every quarter.

The scrawny little boy was always hungry, yet never joined the noisy band of village youngsters who, despite a strict parental curfew, spent their days criss-crossing the fields and the forests, stripping them of anything remotely edible. Kornél preferred the company of his grandfather and would sit for hours in the yard where Grandpa Czuczor kept the printing paraphernalia he had brought back home. Kornél would try to make himself useful, but this generally turned out badly, as neither as a child nor later in

3

life was he particularly good with his hands. The blind leading the lame, thought Grandpa Czuczor, as his own ten little servants became ever more spindly and twisted, and acquired an ever more troubling tremor. He had let one of his thumbnails grow into a long, sharp implement that he used for prising type out of its storage boxes; nowadays, try as he might to take care, this nail would split lengthwise and would serve only to scratch his head.

'Off you go, play with your little friends!'

The boy did not move. 'I'd rather you told me a story!'

Grandpa Czuczor gave a sigh but was not unhappy to launch into one of his tales. 'Do you know how my dear late father, Szaniszló Czuczor of Felsőfenyves, was granted his patent of nobility by György Rákóczi I, for outstanding bravery in the Vienna campaign?'

'I do! Tell me about Mother, when Mother was small! And about Mother's mother!'

Grandpa Czuczor shook his head. It still ached often. In Thüningen he had married a smart and houseproud German woman. Hard-working but undemonstrative, Gisella had borne him six children, of whom all but the last, Zsuzsánna, the Lord had been pleased to take back unto Himself soon after their birth. The births had taken their toll on Gisella and it was not long before she, too, succumbed and joined her five little ones by the side of the Lord. Grandpa Czuczor's hair turned white when she died, and every morning he would clutch the bony little body of the three-year-old Zsuzsánna desperately to his bosom: 'May it please the Lord to let me keep you, my one and only!'

The girl would blink in surprise: '*Was ist das, Vati?*' She did not yet know Hungarian.

'*Ach, du mußt mir bleiben, Liebchen!*' he replied.

*

4

Zsuzsánna grew into a tall and slim young woman, and in due course married Péter Csillag, the son of another family that had chosen to return. Péter Csillag was granted the joys of married life for less than six months: he was out hunting when he was thrown by his horse and fell so awkwardly that he hit his head on a tree-stump and never recovered consciousness. After two weeks hovering between life and death, he expired.

'Grandpa! Why won't you tell me a story?'

So he began to tell a very old story, which he had himself heard in his childhood. Kornél's great-great-grandfather, Boldizsár Czuczor, was a skilful painter, a portraitist without compare in his time. He had an amazing eye for faces and detail, and he never needed a model: it was enough for him to set eyes on someone once to paint their portrait from memory. His wife Katalin was so beautiful that her fame spread to the neighbouring lands, and though she frequently sat for her husband, she was no leading filly in the matrimonial fidelity stakes. Boldizsár once caught her in flagrante with an officer quartered in the town, but calmly closed the door on them with an unruffled 'Do enjoy yourselves!' The couple were at a loss as to what to do, and when they had recovered somewhat, decided to do as they had been bidden. In the morning Boldizsár had a generous breakfast sent to their room and then invited the officer to the baths. There, he covered him, from top to toe, in green paint. News of this spread like wildfire. As the officer was quite unable to scrub off the layer of green, he lay low in his quarters as long as he could. In the end he had to send for Boldizsár and humbly ask him how to remove the paint, as he could hardly spend the rest of his life as a laughing stock. Boldizsár replied: 'My dear sir, you have covered me in shame that can never be washed away; it is right that you should share my fate!'

'Last time he painted the woman as well!' said Kornél.

'Pardon?'

'Grandpa, you didn't tell it like this last time . . . and the painter did not say they should enjoy themselves!'

'What did he say, then?'

'He said,' Kornél tried to lower his voice to a grandfatherly tone, 'may you take pleasure in each other!'

Grandpa Czuczor scratched the back of his head. 'Maybe I did, maybe I did . . .' This was not the first time his grandson had surprised him with the keenness of his mind. Only the other day the boy had been asking about numbers and remembered them up to a hundred on hearing them just the once, even drawing their shapes on the surface of his wax tablet. 'You take after your great-great-grandfather!'

'Yes, like him I never forget something I've once seen.'

'Indeed?' Grandpa Czuczor covered the boy's eyes with the palm of his left hand and asked him: 'Then tell me what you saw today on my worktop!'

Kornél began to list the items on the *regal*, as his grandfather called the worktop, clearly and faultlessly, as though ticking them off in his head, in a voice as clear as a bell: 'Two composing sticks, four balls of twine, one *handdruck*, one cutting machine, two paper planes, two awls, 30 metres of metal composing rule, two dozen spacers, three rack-cases for letters and spacing materials, seven books, hundreds of printed sheets, one pair of spectacles, two magnifying glasses, two round paper pill-boxes with your medicines in them, which you haven't yet taken today, the canvas-covered folio by the inkstand, four quills . . . and one fly!' He fell silent.

'How come you know what a composing stick is, or a composing rule, or a *handdruck*?'

'I've heard the words . . . and anyway you, dear Grandpa, have written them down in the folio!'

It took Grandpa Czuczor a moment or two to recall that he had indeed made a list of his printing equipment before packing up in Thüningen. 'Does that mean . . . that you can read?'

'Indeed I can!' said Kornél and, picking up one of the printed sheets, he began slowly but surely to articulate the words, with complete accuracy. Grandpa Czuczor put on his spectacles and followed as Kornél read the rather special text:

BY HIS SERENE HIGHNESS PRINCE FERENC RAKOCZI OF FELSŐ-VADASZ: On the unimaginable sufferings of our Nation and beloved Homeland under the tyrannical rule of the German Nation, and on the unworthy pains endured by his serene person.

A PUBLIC MANIFESTO, to be placed before the entire Christian world, concerning the innocent nature of the arms acquired by the Hungarians to liberate themselves from the oppression of the House of Austria. First published in the Latin tongue and now again in the Magyar language.

Grandpa Czuczor had picked up a tattered copy of the Prince's manifesto in a beerhall in Thüningen, from some visiting Hungarians. He meant to reprint it himself at some point.

Suddenly he shook his head. Lord Almighty, this little lad is not yet four years of age and can read fluently! 'Was it one of your friends that taught you to read?'

'No.'

'Well, who then?'

'No one . . . I just worked it out for myself.'

'No fibbing!'

'I'm not fibbing . . . I just kept looking at the pages until I could make out the different letters. Why do they put an *f* sometimes where there should be an *s*?'

7

'Only when there's an *ess-zet* ligature, for *sz*.'

'I see. But what about *Auftria*?'

'Well, that should also be with *sz* in Hungarian . . . they've left out the *z* . . .' Grandpa Czuczor was almost lost for words; he had read this Declaration many times yet had never noticed this misprint. Kornél could make an outstanding proofreader. He called out to his daughter: 'Ho, come quickly Zsuzsánna, see what this little pipsqueak can do!'

Kornél started to read out the document again: 'BY HIS SERENE HIGHNESS PRINCE FERENC RAKOCZI OF FELSŐ-VADASZ . . . Grandpa why is there no accent on the *A* and the *O*?'

'What accent?' asked Zsuzsánna, leaning closer.

'It's not usual on a majuscule, perhaps on an *A* or an *O*,' said Grandpa Czuczor.

'What does "major school" mean?' asked Zsuzsánna.

'Capital letter,' said Grandpa Czuczor sternly. This much she might have been expected to pick up over all these years. Despite all her father's efforts, Zsuzsánna had never learnt to read or write. Fortunately, it was not Zsuzsánna's brains that little Kornél had inherited.

My grandson Kornél read out what I have written here and I forbore to reprove him, so wonderful was it that he had learnt to read. In general he is very skilful with words. Perhaps he may become a man of the cloth or a university professor? Were times not so hard I should gladly take him to the college at Enyed or Nagyszombat, to see what the professors there made of him. But it is dangerous even to leave the village, let alone travel any distance. They say that only a day's walk away the Kurucz and the Labancz are preparing to do battle. Whichever takes flight will likely pass this way. And a defeated army knows no mercy.

8

It was suddenly light in the middle of the night. Grandpa Czuczor leapt out of bed and ran into the garden, looking round to see if the neighbours were also awake and, still half asleep, forgetting that the neighbouring houses were deserted. Down in the valley there were fires, lighting up the land in red almost as far as Varasd.

Zsuzsánna also came running out, the little boy whimpering on her shoulder and a satchel on her arm, ready with food, a change of underclothing, candles and other necessities she had fortunately packed some days before. 'Come on, Father!' she shouted. Grandpa Czuczor dashed back into the house, pulled on his kneeboots, snatched up his cape and hat, swept up his own satchel and the folio, and took a long last look at the house and his precious possessions. Will I ever see them intact again? He ran out onto the road that wound its way up Black Mountain.

The villagers were all heading that way – in times of danger it was sensible to hide in the Old Cavern. This lay deep in the cliffs above Bull Meadow and its mouth could be blocked by a triangular boulder in such a way that no one who did not know his way around would ever guess what lay behind it. The Cavern, its floor the shape of a flattened pear, had been in use since prehistoric times. It was with this dark hollow that mothers in Kos would threaten their unruly children: 'If you don't behave, I'll shut you up in the Old Cavern!'

By the time Grandpa Czuczor reached it with his daughter and grandson, the others had made themselves at home and they could barely squeeze in. The villagers still viewed the Czuczors with the suspicion that was normally the stranger's due. Zsuzsánna, like other widows, was the subject of salacious gossip, while of Grandpa Czuczor it was whispered that he consorted with the Devil, the chief proof of this being the extraordinary length of his left thumbnail. Half-a-dozen candles glimmered in the Cavern, assisted by two oil-lamps; clouds of soot rose to its rust-coloured roof. Two of the hired hands heaved the triangular boulder into place and the din gradually subsided.

'Where is Wilhelm?' asked Kornél.

'Isn't he here? He's always skiving off . . . I wash my hands of him,' said Zsuzsánna.

Kornél was soon overcome by sleep. He dreamt he was in a blinding white light, and saw an old man with talons like knife-blades on all ten fingers of his hands. He used them to carve animal shapes out of pieces of wood; these came to life and gambolled in the forest clearing. 'It's Uncle God!' he thought.

Grandpa Czuczor fell into conversation with Gáspár Dobruk, the farrier, who had a game leg that ensured his exemption from army service. The farrier informed him that in Varasd it was neither the Kurucz nor the Labancz that were wreaking havoc, but the irregulars of Farkas Balassi. These freebooters respected neither man nor God, all they wanted was to loot and scavenge.

'Then perhaps we should give them what they want!' said Grandpa Czuczor.

Gáspár Dobruk was aghast. 'Are you out of your mind, that we should freely give them all that we have sweated for years to gain?'

'They'll get it either way.'

A blast sounded from somewhere a little closer. Zsuzsánna began to cry.

'Quiet!' said Grandpa Czuczor.

What remained of the population of Kos was now gathered in the Old Cavern, holding its breath, praying, seeking comfort in each other's presence. May the Lord be merciful unto us, prayed Grandpa Czuczor. Meanwhile the advance guard of Farkas Balassi's irregulars was already roaming the village high street, going from yard to yard to the accompaniment of the dogs' howling. The drovers led their horses by their bridle, and used their drawn swords to pry open the doors of deserted houses, incredulous that not a soul remained. Axes and cleavers hacked off locks and hasps: they had been given a free hand by Farkas Balassi. But little of value remained in the buildings and they cursed eloquently as they flung cheap pots and pans out of the windows. The straw roofs of the houses burst into flame at the torches' kiss, and as the fire crackled along the housetops, the animals in the stables and pens howled and bleated, the dogs almost strangled on their leads as they tried to flee. Even far away in the Cavern Kornél could pick out from the distant rumble the throaty bark of Burkus, his grandfather's bushy komondor dog.

Zsuzsánna whimpered. 'Don't be afraid,' she sniffled into her son's ear. 'God will help us!'

'I'm not afraid,' grunted Kornél.

After a quarter of an hour, the noise of fighting died away.

'Perhaps they have moved on,' said Bálint Borzaváry Daróczy, the estate bailiff.

'I hardly think so,' said Grandpa Czuczor. 'They're up to something.'

'One of us should go out and look around.'

'Later,' said Grandpa Czuczor.

More and more lights went on in the depths of the Cavern. Grandpa Czuczor reached into his satchel, though he knew there was no point in looking for his writing implements – he had not brought them. He closed his eyes and tried to compose the lines he would have written had he brought pen and ink.

The First Day of April, the Year of our Lord 1706. The dogs of war are upon us and we know not if our homes still stand. We have supplies for three days, perhaps four if we are sparing. Zsuzsánna is tearful, but Kornél shows remarkable composure: further evidence of his mental capacity. If we live long enough, we shall be

11

very proud of him. May the Lord on High guide his steps and give
him the strength to take them.

Around midnight Bálint Borzaváry Daróczy and two of the
lads left the Old Cavern to take a look at the village. They
took lamps with them, but these proved unnecessary, as
several of the houses were still ablaze. The charred timbers
of the roof girders were all that stood, and the stench of
dead flesh was everywhere. Hardly a house was left standing. The church steeple had fallen in. Two bodies lay dead
in the street, Béla Vizvári and his wife, Boriska. They must
have taken shelter in the little winepress and been found by
the bandits. It looked as if they had been bayoneted to
death. The bodies, in their blood-soaked clothes, were
already bloated.

'Sir, oh sir!' said one of the lads. 'Best to just get ourselves
out of here, anywhere, double quick!'

'Quiet!'

Where could one go? he thought. There was no escaping
the dogs of war.

In front of the Czuczors' house they found another body,
which they took to be Wilhelm's; the young man's limbs had
been hacked off by the marauders. Scattered all around him
in the dust were Grandpa Czuczor's types, the casting
kettle, and the little type-case, shattered to bits. It looked as
though Wilhelm had tried to save the type foundry. The
bandits had not been interested in the type, and hoped
there might be money or gold in the type-case. A little farther off lay Burkus the dog; he must have gone to the
servant's aid. His side was slashed open, his guts spilled out
where he lay.

As he listened to these tales from the village, tears welled
up in Grandpa Czuczor's eyes. Poor Wilhelm: to come a distance of nine days' journey from his village, only to end his
days in such horror. Once peace reigned again, his mother

would have to be told. Grandpa Czuczor decided he would also send her some money and tried to decide how much it should be.

They thought Kornél was fast asleep, but the little fellow generally spent his nights half-awake. The scraps of sound that reached him contained no mention of Wilhelm or Burkus. He caught something about the fate of Béla Vizvári and his wife, though he was not yet aware of the meaning of death. He had seen, more than once, funeral cortèges winding their way to the cemetery, and had stared at the pinewood coffins, sensing the darkness of such times, hearing whispers and whimpers about the late so-and-so, but he could not quite comprehend that what lay in the wooden box was the body of a man or a woman. His mother had often told him the story of his dear father's death, and Kornél could see before him the fatal fall from the horse and hear the gut-wrenching crack as the head hit the tree-stump – indeed, he would often drive his own skull into anything hard. Having seen the tiny picture in his mother's locket, he always imagined his father as the very image of Grandpa Czuczor.

The men debated whether to return to their homes, or what was left of them, the following day. Bálint Borzaváry Daróczy was of the view that it was too early to return, as the marauding bands could return at any time, and it was even possible that their land would be the battleground for the Kurucz or the Labancz, or even both. Grandpa Czuczor was dismissive: 'We can't sit around here in the mountains till doomsday . . . Great is the mercy of the Lord, let His will be done.'

The debate dragged on. Grandpa Czuczor declared that he would go down into the village even if they all decided to stay where they were. At dawn he woke Zsuzsánna and Kornél: 'Time to go!'

They gathered their bundles, but the boulder at the

mouth of the Cavern proved impossible to move until one of the lads woke and gave them a hand.

A biting wind stung their faces as they made their way downhill. Not till the last turning would the village heave into view; Grandpa Czuczor used the time to prepare his daughter and grandson for the sights to come. But the horror that met their eyes far surpassed his imagination. Zsuzsánna sobbed and sobbed, her face a sodden pillow, despite her father's admonitions that this would hardly help matters. Kornél surveyed in silence the destruction of the burnt-out houses, the dead and dying animals, the vultures circling high above the village. Nor did he cry when he saw the earthly remains of Burkus. He sensed that this was only the beginning of something, though he could not put into words what that something was. He would not let go of his grand-father's warm and reassuring paw, and went with him everywhere. Grandpa Czuczor's first port of call was not the house – of which only the kitchen and part of the yard still had a roof – but to the bottom of the garden and the rose bushes there. These had not been touched by the bandits. He nodded and proceeded to douse them with his own water. Kornél's eyes opened wide in astonishment as he saw his grandfather's member for the first time, both in length and breadth the size of a very decent sausage.

Their furniture was in smithereens, their clothes and everything else had either been taken or else torn and tram-pled into useless rags.

'What are we to do now?' asked Zsuzsánna.

Grandpa Czuczor did not reply but drew a stool that was more or less intact up to the composing frame, sat down, and began sharpening the quills. He poured ink into the inkwell and began to write in the folio.

> *Day of mourning. We have lost Wilhelm, as we have most of the res mobilis. My equipment is largely gone and as yet I lack the*

14

*strength to scrape what remains out of the mud where it lies. Our
lives, too, are in danger. We can do naught but trust in our God.
Justus es Domine, et justa sunt judicia tua.*

He glanced sideways and saw his grandson crouching under
the composing frame and drawing with a lead pencil on a
scrap of paper, while resolutely clutching his grandfather's
trousers with his right hand.

'What are you doing there, Kornél?'

'Grandfather dear, I am writing.'

'Indeed?' Grandpa Czuczor gave a groan as he went down
on his knees to take a closer look at the scrap of paper.
To his great surprise the unsteady and imperfect letters
formed themselves into more or less readable script. 'Day
of mourning,' Kornél had written. 'We lost Burkus and
I'm going to bury him at the bottom of the garden, under
the rose . . .'

'Not there!' Grandpa Czuczor burst out.

The boy did not understand. 'I beg your pardon,
Grandpa?'

'No, not there . . . You have to bury him in . . . dry soil.
Let's do it together!' He led Kornél into the garden. 'Tell
me . . . where did you learn to write?'

'I watched you, Grandpa dear.'

By the fallen fence they found a casket of rotting wood.
In it they laid to rest the body of Wilhelm, placing it by the
shed, where the previous owner had planted a small pine
tree. For Burkus they dug a hole in the ground and buried
him in the purple tablecloth Zsuzsánna had made for the
big dining table. They had found it in front of the house,
torn and covered in puzzling brown stains.

By the evening the other villagers had also sneaked back.
The night was riven by sobs and cries, as each family
reached their front door.

*

15

It was well into the night when the sound of slamming and of horses' hoofs was heard.

Grandpa Czuczor swept up Kornél, still wrapped in his blanket, and headed out onto the road and up the mountain. Behind him came Zsuzsánna, her wooden clogs clattering as she ran. This second time round, only a third as many folk managed to reach the Old Cavern, mainly those who lived nearby. Bálint Borzaváry Daróczy was nowhere to be seen. Apart from Grandpa Czuczor, there were only two men: an old peasant and lame old Gáspár Dobruk, which suggested that even with his game leg he could run faster than most. The suddenness of their departure meant that this time they were short of food as well as light, and only a single lamp sputtered in the Cavern.

'If we have to stay here tomorrow, we shall all starve!' said Gáspár Dobruk.

'As long as we're alive, there is hope!' countered Grandpa Czuczor. 'Let us share out everything, like a family, until the danger has passed.'

They took stock. The only folk to express any unease were old Mrs Miszlivetz and her daughter, who had brought six round loaves, two skins of butter, a rib of salted pork, and several bottles of wine. Grandpa Czuczor rounded on them: 'You have no lamp of your own, yet you benefit from the light we share . . . if you begrudge us these victuals, get you hence! But if you stay, accept your fate as Christians! And let us now remember those we have lost!'

At this, the women's wails rose up in chorus. The wife (or more likely now, the widow) of Bálint Borzaváry Daróczy let out such a high-pitched shriek that there was concern that it might be heard outside. She kept bashing her head into the cavern wall until Grandpa Czuczor and Gáspár Dobruk wrapped her in a horse blanket and tied her up. Kornél watched all this almost with interest. He was still not afraid, although he suspected that the old world had come to a complete and definitive end, the world in which he had sat in the evenings, with a full belly and contented by the crackling fire, listening to the stories of his grandfather. He was sorry that they did not have with them paper, quills and ink, so that he might practise his newly acquired skills of writing.

His grandfather, too, was turning round in his head what he might have written in the folio by way of summing up the events of these chaotic days.

I understand not the purpose of our Lord in visiting these blows upon us; how great can be our sins that we deserve the destruction and loss of our homes and land? We must, none the less, we must believe in His almighty power, for we have sunk so low that hence the road cannot but lead upwards. Nemo ante mortem beatus.

Farkas Balassi had erred in assuming that the village was still the property of István Rigómezei Lukovits, who was thought to have made his fortune in Italy. Lukovits had in fact moved to Vienna months before, together with all his assets. It was the rumour of Italian treasure that led Farkas Balassi's freebooters to keep combing through the village of Kos; they would not settle for scraps and trash as booty.

At the fork at the top of the village, where the high road winds up the hill and the low road leads into the valley towards Varasd and beyond, to Szeben, a green kerchief of fine silk lay in a puddle. It was Jóska Telegdi, the quartermaster, who noticed it. Dismounting, he picked it up and sniffed it: a woman's fragrance tickled his nose. With some reluctance he trailed his hand in the muddy water in case there was anything else there. His fingers came upon a hard, egg-shaped object. He rubbed it clean. It was a decorated egg, made of some kind of metal. His initial joy dissipated when he bit into it and found it was not gold. He turned it

17

round and round in his hands, tapping it here and pressing it there, until the top suddenly snapped open. It was a delicate timepiece which showed the day, month, and even the year. It had stopped. Perhaps water had seeped into it? Looking at it closely, he saw that it showed the ninth day of October and the year 1683, a little after twelve o'clock. His face darkened as the date sank in: it was that of the Battle of Párkány, where his father had lost his life. He tried winding up the mechanism and shaking the metal egg, but it would not come to life. Could it have been lying here ever since 1683? Impossible – no trace of rust. But whoever had dropped it could have lost other items as well. So he cut off a couple of branches from the nearby bushes, fashioned them into a rough broom, and began to splash the water off the road's surface. He found nothing more.

On their second night in the Cavern, Zsuzsánna's skin broke out in blisters, and maggots began to plague her flesh. At one point, when the boulder was trundled aside to allow in some fresh air, she skipped out with a thick towel and a cake of soap. She went down to the stream intending to bathe and to wash her underclothes, thinking she would have plenty of time to return before the boulder was rolled back. Clouds crept over the heavens, neither moon nor stars illumined the sky. In the dark she grew afraid, since she could neither be seen, nor could she see much herself. Hardly had she removed her clothes when all the devils of hell pounced on her body; her limbs were seized by powerful hands which dragged her up to the grassy clearing, by which time she realized that these were vicious men, and she knew what they were after. Her mouth was sealed tight so that she could not cry out; indeed, it would have been of little use to do so. Searing pain rent her body as the first of the men pitched into her. The others then each took their turn. She bore it, limp and faint, her arms stretched like the arms of our Lord Christ nailed to the cross, reciting in her

18

head such prayers as she could recall, in pain and waiting for her suffering to end. When they had all relieved themselves and let go her arms, something even more vicious struck her body, like a bolt of lightning, quite taking her breath away.

Only in the morning did Grandpa Czuczor notice that there was no trace of his daughter. He could not understand how she could have got out of the Old Cavern. It took two men all their strength to shift the boulder.

'She went in the night,' said Kornél, 'when Grandpa and the other one had rolled the boulder aside!'

'Has she taken leave of her senses? And why did you not say anything?'

'I thought you had seen her go, Grandpa!'

There was nothing for it, Grandpa Czuczor thought. 'I shall have to find her!' He motioned to the old peasant to help him with the boulder. The old man demurred: 'Mr Czuczor, sir, it will be dangerous in daylight!'

'This is no time to be concerned with the safety of one's person . . . Come, push!' Soon Grandpa Czuczor stepped out into the light. Turning round, he addressed the depths of the cavern: 'Take good care of Kornél!'

It was the last time Grandpa Czuczor would see him.

Jóska Telegdi had a dozen men stationed at various lookouts. First one, then another reported that someone was approaching on the mountain road. They saw the modestly dressed, elderly man in felt boots, armed with a sabre in the Turkish style, whose matted hair and bushy beard the wind kept blowing into the shape of a turban. They waited till he came in earshot and then called out sharply, demanding his weapon. The old man would not obey and, drawing his sabre, fought his assailants valiantly until, bleeding profusely, he had to yield. Still, he managed to stumble unaided to the camp, where Farkas Balassi interrogated him. Failing to secure the answers he wanted, Balassi ordered him to be tortured. This also failed, and the old man ended his life on the rack.

One of the sharp-eyed men keeping watch noted a thin but steady wisp of smoke rising from Black Mountain. He reported this to Jóska Telegdi, who realized at once that the cliff face must have a cavern in it. He ordered a small group to go up and carefully survey the terrain, looking for any cracks in the rock face. Those in the cavern could hear their voices and the sound of their feet and held their breath, sitting stock-still.

His patience exhausted, Farkas Balassi wanted to move on. Jóska Telegdi begged permission for one last attempt. He had the smaller of their two cannon hauled over to the bend in the road and told the cannoneer to take aim at the rocks that capped the bald head of the mountain peak.

'Why in hell's name should we fire at rocks?' asked the cannoneer.

'Because I say so!' snapped Jóska Telegdi.

They bedded down the gun carriage, cleaned out the barrel, loaded up the shot and tamped it down. Then: 'Fire!'

The first ball overshot the target. The second fell just a little short, landing in the clearing before the Old Cavern's entrance.

'Lord help us!' screamed one of the servant girls in the Cavern. 'It is not us they are aiming the ball of fire at, surely?'

The third scored a direct hit on the top of the mountain. The expanse of rock cracked in several places and crashed into the Cavern. The thunderous noise drowned out every other sound. Instinctively Kornél threw himself flat on the ground and could feel as he fell the roof of the cavern breaking up above his head, while the boulder at the cavern mouth imploded, blinding them all with light. Then everything went black.

Farkas Balassi's men soon climbed their way up to the Cavern, now looking like an upset cauldron. Thick clouds of dust hung in the air. They clambered over the bodies of those who had died and past the little bundles of their belongings. Having examined the contents of a few of these, Farkas Balassi rounded on Jóska Telegdi: 'What a waste of decent gunpowder!'

Once the soldiers had gone, silence fell. In the afternoon, heavy rain began to fall, but the clouds of dust did not settle and from down below it looked as though the mountain was smoking a pipe. Now not only the village of Kos but its hinterland, too, was deserted; even the wild animals and birds had fled. The rain splashed on the rocks and stones, diluting the congealing blood to a shade of pink. A little later the advance guard of the Kurucz arrived. They could see the clouds of smoke and dust from afar and suspected a Labancz camp on the mountain, until reconnaissance reported not a soul alive. The troops travelled on to the west.

Kornél recovered consciousness on the third morning, feeling his body leaden and shattered in several places. He kept blacking out. In due course, as the night-time dew fell, he sat up unsteadily. He could not move his legs, which were wedged under a heavy slab of rock. There was a starry sky above, but uncertain images flickered and faded in his mind. He could remember that something catastrophic had happened, but could not recall what it was. Where was everybody? First tentatively, then with a full-throated roar, he shouted for help. His words ricocheted off the cliffs. He tried to inch his legs out, but the stab of pain this caused in his lower body quite winded him. He spent the night shivering and sobbing helplessly. He suspected that something serious had happened to his mother and grandfather, otherwise they would have come for him. He prayed earnestly to God to accept his prayers and free his legs, but above all, to bring the blessing of His dawn very soon; he was very afraid in the dark.

By first light, he could hear people coming along the forest road. Kornél thought that, whoever they might be, it would be better not to make any sound. Every part of his body ached. He closed his eyes. In a while he was startled to feel something hot and slimy licking his face. A furry muzzle, huge teeth, a rust-coloured tongue . . . He gave a scream.

'Here, boy, here, Málé!' said a deep male voice. The beast obediently loped back to its master. It was a dog, one of those Hungarian ones with thick, matted fur. Kornél could see three men. One was picking up with his pike a few items of clothing that still remained, the other two were in conversation. Kornél could not make out what they were saying. After a while, he gave a groan. The men reached for their guns. Then they noticed him.

'There's a lad here that's still alive!' said one.

'Yes, but I'm stuck . . .' Kornél was moaning as he said this, and had to say it again to be understood.

'Zsiga, come over here!' they said, calling the third fellow over. It took the three of them to roll the rock off Kornél's legs.

'Holy Mother of God!' exclaimed the one called Zsiga, seeing what was left of the lad's legs. The poor soul would not live to see the day out. 'Let's give him something to drink!' he said, squatting down beside him and, unscrewing his brown canvas-covered flask, placed it over Kornél's mouth. The slightly sour, watered-down wine dribbled down the boy's face.

'What's your name?'

'Kornél Csillag.'

'Your parents?'

Kornél told them what he could. He asked if they had seen his mother or his grandfather. He described their appearance in great detail. The three men hummed and hawed.

'They'll . . . turn up,' Zsiga lied. 'Don't you worry any, we'll look after you until they do. Now, would you be hungry at all?'

Kornél nodded. The most solidly built of the three, whom the others called Mikhál, took him carefully in his arms. Kornél gave a howl of pain. He realized only now that both legs were twisted the wrong way round and that the Turkish pants his mother had put on him back home had been cut to ribbons which were now glued to his skin by his own congealed blood. Overcome by despair he began to sob, childlike, in spasms, repeatedly gulping for air. As the man carried him, he could see limbs dangling from under lumps of rock. The older of the peasants was lying at what had been the cavern entrance, his skull neatly bisected by a sharp splinter of rock, his brains spilled out.

Mikhál made a fire in the clearing, while the third fellow, Palkó, was plucking a grey bird the size of a small loaf, throwing its feathers into the fire; their burning smell irritated Kornél's nose. He dared not ask any questions. His fingers began gingerly to explore his thighs. He detected some hard, sharp object lodged above his right knee. As he yanked it out, the pain made his heart skip a beat and he fainted again. It was evening by the time he came to.

Zsiga again made him drink a little and then fed him some meat, a mouthful at a time. 'Pigeon stew. You'll see, it'll build you up!' though he scarcely believed his own words. Kornél put all of his little soul's trust in this promise. When he had eaten himself full to bursting, he tried to get up, but Zsiga did not let him. 'First we'll have to bind up your wounds. Palkó is our medical orderly, he'll sort you out.'

'And then we must talk about what we are going to do!' said Mikhál.

They had been cut off from their regiment for a day and a half since they had had their horses shot from under them. They ran for dear life from the battle, down into the valley. As night fell, they took shelter in an old winepress. That was where they acquired the stray dog that Palkó, thinking of their guard-dog back home, had decided to call Málé. In the morning Zsiga set off to forage some food. He all but ran into Farkas Balassi's irregulars. He scampered to the winepress the back way, through the yards. 'Don't know who this lot are, but if we're sharp about it, we can get ourselves some horses!'

They crept out as far as the edge of the gully and could see how undisciplined this crew was. They waited until most of the band had gone past, hoping that there would be some stragglers bringing up the rear. Indeed, there were four such, whom they picked off one at a time, jumping on them from above and wrestling them off their saddles. They thus secured four horses, guns, clothing and the contents of the saddlebags. The most valuable item was a sword forged in Toledo, which went to Palkó. Mikhál asked for the cordovan leather topboots of the first soldier, who must have been of the nobility, for his pockets also yielded the egg-shaped timepiece that Zsiga took for himself. He thought it was silver. He did not manage to get the winder to work, but when he – God willing – got back home to Somogy, his brother, a jack-of-all-trades, was bound to be able to mend it. The timepiece recorded the day and the month, as well as the year: it showed a quarter past twelve on the ninth day of the tenth month of the year of our Lord one thousand six hundred and eighty-three.

In Palkó's view it was best to stay in this deserted village until they had word of how the fighting was going; there was little sense in running into the arms of the Kurucz, who were said to take no prisoners and gave those they captured the shortest of shrifts. With the various bands of freebooters

24

their chances were even less. Mikhál on the other hand voted for leaving at once and trying to reach their own troops as quickly as possible, trusting themselves to the mercy of God. The longer they took to catch up, the easier it would be to accuse them of desertion. Zsiga sucked on his empty pipe, throwing hunks of meat to Málé. He did not consider either approach entirely free of risk. 'Let's wait and see what the new day brings.'

'We must do something with this lad, though.'

'Goodness, is he still in the land of the living?'

Palkó had shied the remains of his pants off Kornél and tore one of the shirts they had appropriated into strips to bandage up his shrivelled legs. 'I'd be very much surprised if he ever ran again on those.'

In his sleep, Kornél was pursued by shapes in billowing black capes, who in the end wedged him tightly in a well. Starting awake, he could feel both his legs stuck in that well. He touched them and as he felt the thick lawn wadding, it all came back to him. He tried flexing his muscles one by one, and for the first time it occurred to him that perhaps his legs would never be the same again. Of the three men, two were sleeping the sleep of the just by the embers of the fire, the third was stroking Málé the dog, murmuring to him as if he were a human being.

Kornél closed his eyes. 'Grandpa, come back! Mother dear, you too! Come back to me! It is so hard without you!' he whimpered. His tears eased him into sleep once more, where again he was being pursued, this time even shot at.

Just before dawn broke, a Labancz patrol appeared in the clearing, cut off like the three men from the main body of their troops. They would have pitched camp had Zsiga and his fellows not started to fire at them at random. In the semi-darkness neither party knew who they were shooting at. As the newcomers were in the majority, they jumped on their horses and chased Zsiga's little band down into the valley.

Kornél woke with the golden disc of the sun high in the sky. The three men were gone. They had taken the four horses but little else; even the dog had been left behind. For a while Kornél listened to the pounding of his own heart and then began to yell. If no one came, he was sure to starve. He felt desperately weak, life barely flickered in the darkness of his soul. Days passed like this, or was it only hours? At times, Málé's rough tongue would lick him awake, into the land of the living.

On his second day alone, he managed to cling to the clumps of Málé's fur coat and so straighten up, lying on his back like a tired rider. With the better of his legs he managed to touch the ground and was able to push himself gingerly along on top of the dog, and succeeded thus in covering much of the ground in the clearing. He undid the various bundles and bags left behind by the three men. He took a fancy to the egg-shaped timepiece and hung on to it. After a longish rest, he also raked over the floor of the former cavern. What he saw there he would never forget. The dead bodies had since been ravaged by wild animals. There was no escaping the stench of decomposing bodies, even if he held his nose. Grandpa Czuczor's folio was nowhere to be found; perhaps it had ended up under a ton of rock.

The dog took him back to the clearing. On both sides of it the trees and bushes had donned their lushest and finest. Kornél was dizzy with hunger. One of the branches of an acacia reached almost to the ground and Kornél took its tip into his mouth. The tiny petals tickled a little but tasted amazingly sweet, and he chewed off as much as he could in the position in which he lay. Later he also found some myrtle berries, a little sour, but still edible.

As the evening dew fell, he shivered as he rolled on the grass, stripping the clothes off his body and picking clean clothing from what Zsiga and his companions had left behind. On his legs the dried blood had turned the bandages a rusty colour; these he did not dare touch.

On the third day he ventured even further afield, down the mountain road to the first winepress, the one they had set on fire. Among the battered and broken flagons thrown into the garden he found two still intact, but could not manage to prise their stoppers out. He also found a few dried-up seed potatoes, which he gobbled up, raw, straight away. Eventually he managed to jam the neck of a bottle between two pieces of rock and thus break it at the neck. Though he lost some of the wine to the dry soil, most of it he was able to gulp down from the broken stem of the bottle. He was soon nodding off, no longer cold. Perhaps . . . somehow . . . it will be all right . . . in the end. Perhaps . . . somehow . . .

As he felt the strength returning to his legs, he was able to make longer excursions. From the ruined yards around he gathered up every scrap he thought could be eaten. Near the clearing the buildings were mostly winepresses, and Kornél soon acquired a taste for wine and spirits. At first they made him feel nauseous and often he would gag and vomit up the liquid, but it did not take him long to get used to it. The alcohol helped him through the cool nights. His hair grew and became as matted as the coat of Málé the dog. The better Kornél got, though, the worse Málé became, not able to find enough food to his liking. Reduced to lapping up the mountain's nectar, he would get unsteady on his feet and go cross-eyed, providing Kornél with no end of amusement. Then, at night, he would snore like Grandpa Czuczor, a sound that Kornél loved.

In company, Kornél's way with words had always struck everyone as suprisingly advanced for his age, but now, on his own, he had virtually stopped speaking. When he told Málé what to do, his words resembled the noises made by the dog more than those of his own language.

27

He learnt how to catch the silvery dace in the upper brook. He lay on his stomach dangling his arm in the icy water just where the fish used to come to bask in the sun. When one swam over his carefully positioned open palm he would close his fingers around it gradually, imperceptibly slowly. Provided he managed to make this last an age he would suddenly feel the fish in his grasp. With a jerk he would throw it out on to the rocks, wait until the wet little body thrashed itself to exhaustion, and then crunch it between his teeth, spitting the fishbones back into the stream.

This is how he lived, his existence growing hardly distinguishable from those of the small wild creatures of the forest. His leg, which had healed crooked, made it possible for him to take firmer, more complicated steps, and even to run, if necessary, though his loping gait recalled that of a scavenging dog with three legs.

Málé's nose would not stop bleeding; his teeth were loose, one or two had even fallen out. The skin under his coat had begun to fester and tiny parasites crawled around the wounds. Then one morning he could no longer get on his feet. Kornél called out to him gently: Woof-woof! Woof-woof!

The dog did not raise its head; it wanted to be left alone. Kornél could not understand this and kept stroking and shaking him by turns, barking at him with ever-greater tenderness.

The bushes and hedgerows in the village, which had perhaps never offered such a dense canopy to the fences, lost their flowers by the wayside. The air did not cool down at night. Even without having to drink Kornél managed not to feel cold. The noonday sun rose high in the sky and the hot cupola of the heavens hung over the landscape; only the sound of the church bells at noon was missing, and of course the sound of other people. Málé's tongue hung dry from his mangled jaw. As he watched the half-shut eyes of the dog Kornél was seized by an uncertain dread that a fate worse than anything that had happened up to then awaited him. His breathing came in spasms and he continued to bark obstinately, with a childlike belief that this would somehow stay his doom.

Though it was only noon, the sky unexpectedly turned dark. Kornél gave a roar like a wounded animal. He could feel that this was the end: a blow more terrifying than any before would strike them and they would die like his mother, grandfather and every other creature. There was nowhere for the emaciated dog to flee, and he too had no future. He lay on his back, clasped his two dirt-stained little hands together in prayer, but the words that once he could say even in his sleep would not come, and all he could utter was: woof-woof . . .

In the sky that rapidly turned dark, the corona of the light-ball of the sun darkened by degrees, as if another, black sun were thrusting itself across it, each lilac-blue flame a tiny javelin stabbing the little boy in the eyes, which he then shut, as did the dog. It was the end, they both thought. Under Kornél's eyelids were rings of fire, behind them shades of images from the past which he had never seen but which still seemed somehow familiar. Had he the time, he might be able to unravel their meaning, but thick and fast there came the throb of nothingness.

The doctor with the goatee washed his hands and proclaimed the verdict:

'The end is nigh!'

Mrs Sternovszky buried her face in her kerchief. 'What will become of us if . . . ?' She did not finish the sentence. Her sister embraced her tightly, as if afraid that she might crumble into small pieces.

She drew away. 'Doctor, how much longer . . .'

'I cannot foretell the future, but . . . not very long.'

'But how long . . . Days?'

'Days or hours. Who knows? I'll be back at nightfall,' he said, and left. His fee was handed to him in a buff envelope by the maid in the entrance hall where the flowers for the patient were arrayed in vases of various size, their fragrance lying heavy upon the air.

The dying man was gasping for air. His wound had not healed one jot, though the doctor had doused it thoroughly with some yellow powder for the inflammation. He could see no reason to apply a bandage, but he did so none the less, just to comfort the relatives. In any case, it was better if they did not see the wound itself. The blade had penetrated just above the ribcage and below the collar bone, at an unfortunate angle, so that it pierced the lungs and very likely reached the pericardium. At this stage science can do no more, and all is in the hands of the heavenly powers.

Mrs Sternovszky returned to her husband's room and leaned over his bed. 'My dear husband is thirsty perhaps? Some fresh lemon juice? Should I have the maid squeeze you some?'

He shook his head.

'A bite or two to eat? A light soup, perhaps?'

Another shake of the head.

'Does my dear husband have any other wish?'

A smile formed across the sunken cheeks: 'Thank you, no.' And he closed his eyes. If only they would leave him alone in the throes of his death, he thought. There is no hope. If his misfortune were not the result of his own stupidity, it would perhaps be easier to accept. What will happen to the glassworks once he offers up his soul to his Maker? Will his wife be able to look after it and make it prosper? He heard news that the smelting ovens were not working, and this distressed him. Just because I'm dying there is no reason to let the fire go out! But the master

30

glassmaker, Imre Farkas junior, who should have had charge of production in the glassworks, was then sitting in irons, in prison, because he had attacked the inspector. This Imre Farkas had been a difficult man from the start, too quick to anger and too quick to act.

A painful sigh rent his throat. His wife was once again trying to tempt him with food and drink and kind words. Once again he did not tell her to go. It is the right of one's wife to be there when . . . yes. He tried to work out what day it was, the twentieth or the twenty-first of March, but he was confused about the time and the day. All his life he had been acutely sensitive to the year, the season, the week, even the day and the hour. He often amazed his wife and children by his accurate recall of – say – the date of the great fall of snow in Felvincz: the nineteenth day of January in the year of our lord 1738, and he even knew they had been snowed in until the twenty-eighth.

The memorable days of his life he was wont to recall with particular pleasure in the bosom of his family and friends. His acquisitions, his marriage, the birth of his children, the setting up of the glassworks, his successful career and growing wealth, his election as town councillor – these were the tales he told most gladly. What preceded these glories, it was best to forget. But with the ability to forget he had not, alas, been blessed. He had once read an Italian canticle which said that at the boundary of the Lower World there flowed not only the waters of oblivion, the river Lethe, but also its twin, Eunoe, rising from the same source, the waters of good remembrance. As an infant it must have been of Eunoe that he had been given to drink, though this is the one thing that he cannot recall.

His strength continued to ebb away and soon he could no longer even sit up. Yet how gladly he would have entered in his folio all that went through his head in these dread times. It would have served to guide his wife and three children in

31

the days ahead. In adulthood it had been rare indeed for him to end the day without writing copiously on the large pages of the thick album he had brought from Italy for this purpose. It was said to have been made in a famous bible scriptorium and originally intended to bear the Holy Writ. Kornél always wrote in this folio with due respect for its distinguished history. If his descendants desired to know how he had spent the time allotted to him on this earth, they could read all about it in there.

He had no means of giving an account of the last few hours of his life. He could not write at the top of the page: Chapter the Last: My Decease. Fortunately he had made his last will and testament the previous year, and in a leaden casket sealed with three seals it awaited the attention of the appropriate authorities. And he had copied the will into his folio.

Though he had gone over it in his head a hundred, a thousand times, still he was assailed by doubt. Was he right to leave the glassworks to Bálint? Perhaps the lad is not adult enough to manage twenty men, to meet the weekly, monthly totals, to haggle with the tradesmen, to tug his forelock at the nobles most likely to place substantial orders. But he was still young, he had time to grow up.

Bálint did not take after him. Kornél Sternovszky (Csillag) was of very small build, his limbs thinner and weaker than they should be. Though his legs had remained crooked, so skilled was he at using them that the untrained eye would not have detected that he was lame. No amount of meat and drink would give him a pot-belly, and his face had preserved to this day its pleasant, oval shape. Physically he was more or less hale, only the hair over his unusually arched brow had begun to thin, though still only tinged with grey. His moustache and beard had never thickened into a grown man's, and to his eternal regret resembled more the sprouting hairs of an adolescent.

How he would have loved to go on living! If only he could hear, just once more, the three smelting ovens bellowed up, the carefully dried wooden logs catching fire with a sudden zizz; then the heat would start its work, the wondrous heat that produced the specially hard-wearing yet splendidly pellucid glassware. Even in the windows of his own house he had fitted lead-framed panes of glass produced in his own works, and would proudly point them out to visitors. Now he saw sadly how the light of the sun beat down through them. Born in the heat of the fire, they loyally continued in the service of warmth: during winter they sealed it in, but let it in during summer, all the while keeping the winds without.

Turning these thoughts over in his head, he did not notice that Bálint had entered the room and knelt down on the ground by the bed, his face radiant with pious concern. He, too, was aware that soon . . . The dying man's eyes filled with tears. God will surely provide. The image of Grandpa Czuczor came into his mind, the person whom outwardly Bálint most closely resembled: though still growing, he was already big and strong, a veritable colossus. The only respect in which his first-born son resembled him, his father, was his phenomenal powers of recall. Any text he heard or read, even casually, he was able to repeat exactly and without error, and never ever forgot. Yet the boy did not think this an unmixed blessing as had his father in his own younger days. Bálint revelled more in other talents he possessed, above all his ability to sing and dance like none among his school peers. All it needed was the sound of music and his muscular feet would set to tapping. What a splendid night it would be, the night of the wedding feast, when he would dance till dawn with his betrothed, holding her delicate body again and again to his brawny one. How infinitely sad that he, Kornél, would never see that girl, would never be her father-in-law. It could not be far off, a few years at most, as Bálint was a mere two months short of his seventeenth birthday.

My last will and testament

I have done all that I was able to do; more or better I could not have done.

Let my wife Mrs Sternovszky, born Janka Windisch, take care to ensure that the glassworks, the Sternovszky lands and estates, including the horses, the town house in Felvincz, and the woodlands registered under my name, remain together in the manner hereunder described. Let her take care that they do not become run down and as far as possible let them be maintained and expanded, and let her look after my earthly assets as if I were still by her side.

My first-born, Bálint Sternovszky, will come into his inheritance when he reaches the age of one-and-twenty. He will take over the glassworks and those woodlands marked one to seven in the register. At this time also he will come into possession of my folio and sundry other writings.

My second-born, Zoltán Sternovszky, will at the age of one-and-twenty come into ownership of the family estates together with the horses, provided he undertakes to take good care of them and manage them.

Should he fail to undertake this, the ownership of the family estates will devolve upon my youngest son, Kálmán Sternovszky, who additionally inherits the woodlands marked eight to twelve in the register, as well as my share of the ore mine in Tordas.

In the event that the estates and the horses devolve upon Kálmán, however, the share of the ore mine and the woodlands marked eight to twelve in the register will become the property of his elder brother Zoltán.

The house in Felvincz and all chattels appertaining

34

thereto, including its gold and silver plate, jewellery, and the sum of 12,000 florins, of the whereabouts of which she is fully cognizant, remain the sole and unconditional property of my wife.

Written while of sound mind, of my own free will, and in full possession of all my faculties.

I should have married younger, then I would have grand-children around my deathbed. His difficult and troubled childhood and youth had prevented this. His childhood was a dance between life and death. Three times at the least only divine providence had saved him from certain death. The third time he had had cholera: given up for dead, he was carted out to the far end of the cemetery and thrown in the communal pit. It was midwinter and by dawn he was frozen stiff, but somehow the pulse of life began to pound again in his veins. He had to escape, to a place where they did not know that he had the plague; back home he would surely have been beaten to death.

He came from nothing and nowhere; until the age of fourteen his life was not worth the price of a bottle of wine. He was found by Gypsies, spent some time with them, then helped out men wandering the forest, or charcoal-burners, in return for food and lodging. In his heart of hearts he knew he was worth more than this and that the time would come when he would prove it. All this while he was lower than a footclout, his fate to endure humiliation and suffering. And, with his astonishing memory, he forgot not a whit of this when later, with God's help, his fate took a turn for the better.

At one time he was working as a stable lad on the estate of General Onczay, where he found satisfaction in caring for the horses. The General began to pay more attention to the keen young man once it turned out that he was fluent in the German tongue. He tried him out first as groom and then as jockey, a position for which his weight and his crippled, bandy legs made him ideal. In the races arranged by General Onczay, Kornél, riding Arabella, was without equal. He toured Austria and even England, countries where he would come in a respectable second or third. A number of foreign nobles made him tempting offers but he remained loyal to General Onczay, who on their return rewarded him with one of his three stud farms, the one on the Galócz plateau. This was called the Sternovszky puszta, after its first master of the horse.

Under Kornél the number and the value of the horses went up in leaps and bounds; no one had a surer eye than he when it came to weighing up a foal's potential after proper training. On the clayey soil he grew oats and alfalfa imported from England, selling on any surplus at a goodly price to the other studs. In time he took Sternovszky as his surname.

It was rumoured that General Onczay had betrayed the Prime Prince. Kornél would have none of it. Such a good man would certainly be incapable of such a thing. Now a patriarch with snow-white hair, the General to his dying day treated Kornél as in every respect his equal. When he reached the age of 22, he had called him in for a word. They took wine on the first-floor terrace. The General did not beat about the bush: 'Well now, my boy, have you given any thought to marriage?'

Kornél blushed. 'So far I . . . I have not considered it timely.'

'It is. You have land, you are held in high esteem, there is nothing to prevent you from starting a family. Years unmarried are years fallow. Time you wed.'

Kornél lacked any experience in this field. He had all his life been ashamed of his crooked legs and would never, if he could help it, undress in the presence of another. Racked by temptations of the body, he often felt his sap rising, especially at the break of day, so that it was enough for him to lie on his stomach for it to spill forth. It happened to him on horseback, too. Yet he had not touched a woman. Just once, in England, after much wrestling with his conscience he had paid for a whore, only to change his mind after all and snatch back half his money as he chased the cursing, wailing wench from his rooms. He rarely sought out society – not that on the Galócz plateau there was much society to be sought – while in town he was still given the cold shoulder; behind his back, his rolled German *r*s were mocked unmercifully.

The next time they met the General suggested one of his nieces, who came with a decent dowry. Kornél did not feel that he could say no this offer, and in any event trusted his patron implicitly.

'Well then, when can I take you to inspect the young lady?'

'There is no need. She who pleases my good master needs must please me.'

The wedding was held later in the year. General Onczay was best man. Janka Windisch certainly pleased Kornél, her pale skin, especially, and the thick bunches of flaxen hair. The Windisches were barons of Austrian stock, whose alliance with the Onczays, initially displeasing to both sides, now dated back a century. The notion of Kornél Sternovszky as groom met with hardly a murmur of dissent, in part because General Onczay's recommendation carried a good deal of weight.

The honeymoon was spent with the Windisches' kinsmen in Tergestum, the Adriatic Trieste. They spent some uncomfortable days jolting in the carriage and arrived exhausted at the manor house on the hillside, which in virtually every direction offered a wide and wonderful panorama of the sea. Kornél was so spellbound by the endless body of water that he spent their first night in a deckchair on the canopied balcony. His newly-wed waited for him all night. The following night Janka took her husband by the hand and led him to the bedchamber's four-poster. Kornél halted uncertainly, eyeing the fireplace ablaze with thick logs. Janka turned her back and removed one layer after another of her outer- and then underwear. Her naked back had an ivory sheen that glinted with the reflected light of the flames. She slipped under the Venetian lace sheets. 'Husband mine, what is keeping you?'

Kornél stood stock-still. Desire flared within him, yet he did not follow his bride into the bed.

'First put out the light!'

'You are ashamed in front of me?'

Kornél did not reply, but himself turned down the wick of the oil-lamp. The chief difficulty posed by his crooked legs was how to wriggle out of regular trousers, which is why for his everyday wear he chose the lawn pantaloons sported by the stable lads. He rolled over to Janka, the duvet cool to the touch. He was on fire, trembling. He had no idea how to proceed. No one would have thought him so wet behind the ears. General Onczay's parting words had been: 'See you take care of the main thing!'

Janka had been vouchsafed a certain amount of information by her mother and her aunt, the gist of which had been that it was up to the man to take the first step, she had but to endure and to manoeuvre herself into the best position possible to alleviate the pain. So she waited, patiently. Quite some time passed. She could hear sharp intakes of breath from her husband. Summoning up her courage, she touched him on the shoulder. He responded in kind, and their hands began, slowly and hesitantly at first, an age-old dialogue of discovery, surprised at encountering this part or that of the body, as if one part said: 'Goodness, is that what that's like?' and the tenderly touched part responded: 'Indeed, come and get to know me better!'

The tinder within caught fire, veins and arteries began to pound, simmering streams of air commingled, astonished sounds split lips asunder. Kornél was almost beside himself. And then it happened.

Images, living dioramas. Scenes not unfamiliar, scenes he seemed to have seen somewhere before, a long time ago. The wedding night of some others. In the first tableau a lumbering figure nervously fingered the precious red stone inlay of his belt buckle and Kornél simply knew he was seeing his father, long dead, on his wedding night; the young woman with the masses of curly hair could be none but his mother, that crooked smile having given birth his own. There followed a man with a deformed spine and jet-black eyes and hair, certainly his grandfather: only the furniture was different, the expression on the face and the hesitancy were exactly the same. Then his grandmother Gisella, hitherto glimpsed only in a locket as a young girl. It was her death that had turned grandfather's hair white. And now it was his great-grandparents, in their hastily built wooden cabin, high in the snow-covered hills, their troubled faces lit by the billowing flames of the open hearth. And so it went on, back through great-great-grandparents, and their parents, and theirs, back to unknown ancestors, back twelve generations. Kornél stared and stared, the images of the past burning themselves into his memory.

'Something the matter?' asked Janka.

Kornél's smile was reassuring: 'Never in my life have I had such a moment of grace.'

He was dimly aware that he had lived through such a deluge of images at some earlier time, but he could not remember when. He committed what he had seen to the pages of the folio.

In the course of their married life Kornél gave his wife unsparingly of the joys of Venus, but that descent into the realms of the past was never to be repeated. Why was it on the second day of his honeymoon that this world was illuminated? It was a question to which he was never to find the answer.

Later, a young man and skilful, as he rode with his flintlock for the first time into the depths of the forest he had just inherited, he was equally unsure what made him announce in the middle of a clearing, with great solemnity: 'In this sacred place we shall set up a manufactory for glass.' He repeated these words, changing only 'this' to 'that', when he reached home.

'Why?' asked Janka.

'So that we can trade in light,' he replied, his face transfigured.

Neither his wife's sensible arguments nor his estate manager's facts and figures could dent his resolve; still less the fact that even tinted spectacles could not protect his weak eyes from the glassworks' incandescent furnace. He imported two master glassmakers from Saxony and within a year the first glass panes for wooden windowframes were in production. After these came glass bottles, containers for shipping wine, wine decanters, and countless other glass products. The goods sold well, orders came in from all over the country. Janka asked him a hundred times: 'How on earth did you know?'

He dared not admit that his knowledge was unearthly. Now, on his deathbed, when he could no longer communicate what he could see to his wife and three sons, the flow of images unexpectedly began anew. Finally he understood what it was that, at the age of thirty, and as a successful studfarmer, had made him build a glassworks in the middle of the forest inherited from his wife's kinsmen. There unrolled before him in a series of drab tableaux the history of the clan of the Csillags. He could see his father Péter Csillag, and his father's father, Pál Csillag, who had ended up in Bavaria and made his living as a shoemaker, but had previously owned a prosperous glassworks in the Slovak Highlands destroyed by the Ottoman Turk. He saw his paternal great-grandfather János fleeing his home as a youth and then being killed in one of the Turkish campaigns of the legendary Miklós Zrínyi: a cannonball tore him apart as he was scraping the mud off his boots.

He could see himself, as a boy, clinging onto a starved dog with matted fur. Yes . . . then, a long time ago, there in the clearing he had had a vision, until he lost consciousness, but he had not realised that he should have preserved on paper these seemingly chaotic images. And now he saw Grandpa Czuczor, burying some kind of casket at the bottom of the garden, under the rose bushes.

'The treasure! Grandpa's treasure! The roses . . .' he wanted to cry out. No words issued from his lips.

His grieving relatives heard a rattle from his throat and thought Kornél Sternovszky was no longer for this world. Someone placed a damp dressing on his brow; the cool droplets ran down his temples. Exhausted, he closed his eyes. He could hear his loved ones whispering, the swish of skirts and coats on the wooden floor; this troubled him. He thought again what a blessing it would be if they just let him alone. He saw the dog Málé, then his sole companion, dying in his arms. Perhaps Málé, too, would have preferred to take leave of the world by himself.

He had been scared to death when the sky had darkened in the middle of the day, when the sun was swallowed up by blackness. Later he was told that there had been an eclipse. His eyes never recovered from that burning; thereafter they watered frequently and were always weak.

The final tally, then: in the course of my life I received from God the wondrous gift of the Vision no fewer than three times. It is no use sorrowing that the third came so late. Boundless is His power, inscrutable are His ways. Might I hope that His kindness will extend to my children also?

He felt a leaden tiredness in his limbs. He arranged his arms across his chest as he had seen on sarcophagi. My time is done. I give myself into His hands. *Fiat voluntas tua Domine.*

Why did he go and throw that boiling tea in the master glassmaker's face? And why, to cap that, did he go and draw his sword on him? After all he, Kornél Sternovszky, was hardly a distinguished swordsman, whereas the brute of a master glassmaker was said to be a veteran of a dozen duels. At the first clash of blades, the glassmaker had wrenched the weapon from his hand, with the same downward movement stabbing him deep in the chest. He could feel distinctly the foam of blood spatter across his chest.

When he was four, he had been found by good people – travelling Gypsies – with barely a sign of life in his body. As he recovered, there were days when he could only howl and scowl, and it was weeks before he was speaking again. Now, as he is laid out, he can no longer make the smallest sound. Now there comes to cover him again the odious dankness of the dark.

II

THE BURNING ORB OF THE SUN BLAZES A PATH ACROSS the heavens, like some truculent sovereign sultry on high. The crops are chiffon scarves waving in the wind. The air is pale blue and restless with flurrying things: a broken twig, a fluttering feather, small scraps of cloth, grains of sand, fallen rose blossom, as if Mother Earth sought to shake off whatever she deemed superfluous. As the air warms up, so the countryside fills with the joyous sounds of nature. From the stalls and stables sounds of braying and grunting and neighing fill the air at all hours of the day. Birds burst into song, as do the children in many a house.

That year estate manager Károly Bodó was determined that the maypole would be of quite outstanding height. He took the trouble personally to select from the thick of the forests of the estate the tallest of their magnificent maples, which took the foresters hours to fell. Four of his men had endless trouble hauling it out onto the track, where they could at last manoeuvre it onto a cart. For displaying the maypole, manager Bodó had picked a spot on the gentle slope in front of the tiny artificial lake in the park of Castle Forgách. There were groans aplenty from the men: there was no

43

stonier ground in the entire estate and they would have to dig extra deep if the winds were not to bring it down on the gardener's lodge or, on the other side, the delicate tracery of the wooden bridge's balustrade. All in vain. Manager Bodó brooked no opposition: his word was law.

Manager Bodó knew what he was doing in insisting on this site. Planted here, the maypole could be seen with equal ease from the road, from the garden, and from the spacious first-floor terrace, the venue for most of the festivities.

The delicate curly leaves of the estate's renowned two-hundred-year-old walnut trees had turned a deep green and, as every autumn, manager Bodó had had the crop carted down to the plain where they fetched a very acceptable price. The trees yielded walnuts the size of smallish hen's eggs. Their shells were so thin they were almost transparent, and it was the work of a moment even for a small child to crack them open. Manager Bodó himself was particularly fond of walnuts and could hardly wait for them to ripen, sometimes having them shaken down as early as July and delightedly consuming his share of the crop dipped in honey or crumbled onto strips of pasta, or even raw, keeping a handful stuffed in his pocket. He liked to have something to chew on: pumpkin seeds, a sweetmeat of some kind, or even the stem of a pipe.

Manager Bodó had served the Count's estates for many a year. A distant relative of the Countess's mother, he had been taken on after her premature death, more or less out of kindness, but with his industrious nature and sharp mind for business, he had quickly proved he needed no favours. He presented just one enduring problem: he could not stand music. He had been born cloth-eared – in both ears. Count Forgách and his wife, however, could not live without the sound of music, and their many visitors and guests were entertained by concerts, amateur operas and choral singing every weekend, especially around Whitsuntide and in the Christmas season.

On Tuesday mornings manager Bodó would meet with the master of the Count's music, whose proper title was 'maestro', to learn of the programme planned for the weekend, and invariably argued against performances by visiting musicians, as he hated to spend money needlessly – even other people's money. The Count had in his permanent employ no fewer than seventeen musicians, including two singers; why could the caterwauling not be done by them, for the not inconsiderable annual sum they were paid? However, it was the maestro who tended to win the argument, as the Count was invariably on his side.

'I am all ears,' began manager Bodó.

'The pianoforte needs attention. I've already sent word to master Schattel. It will be 80 dinars plus the cost of transport,' said the master of music.

'So be it. Anything else?'

'Accommodation to be arranged for the scholars from Rimaszombat, coming for the choral singing.'

'Number of persons?'

'I have not yet had word.'

'Round figures: Five? Ten? A hundred?'

'Perhaps fifteen. Expected Friday night.'

Manager Bodó nodded grudgingly. 'And what can that lot do that the village lads' choir cannot?'

'Polyphony. Madrigals, on sight.' As the light of understanding failed to dawn on manager Bodó's face, the master of music began to explain: 'They will perform from György Maróthy's psalter, we shall accompany them. They know the music by heart, the bass will accommodate to the tenor, the alto and the treble . . . you will hear, master Bodó, what a glorious sound they make!'

Manager Bodó was sure only of one thing: that he would not hear. As soon as the concert began he would slip out into the kitchen, saying that he had to oversee the preparations for supper.

By the time the master of music left, the lads had raised the maypole. It lifted up manager Bodó's heart to see the colourful ribbons on the branches dancing and shimmering in the dew-laden breeze. The master of the Count's music was also watching the scene from the garden. The air is too damp, he thought, the instruments might be damaged if the air's not dry. But why should it not be dry? We have a whole week to go.

'Maestro!' Count Forgách was gesturing from the terrace.

The master of music bowed low towards him.

'A word, if you would be so kind. Broken your fast yet?'

Sweeping up his papers in his arms, the master of music loped over to the Count. 'Indeed I have, your grace,' he panted. He could see that the Count had just risen from the breakfast table: at the end of his moustache there hung a small piece of egg-yolk.

'What will be the leading attraction at the ball?'

'May it please your grace to recall that we have invited the choir of the Rimaszombat Collegium.'

'Ah, yes. What is it that they will be singing?'

'Psalms, most splendid psalms, with orchestral accompaniment.'

'Psalms, yes . . .' the Count nodded, a little unhappily. 'Any soloists?' He was remembering the pleasure he had taken last time in the performance of that Polish soprano.

'Not on this occasion . . . Manager Bodó is none too pleased with this visit as it is.'

'What does that matter? It is I who pay, not manager Bodó! See to it at once.'

'Your grace's wish is my command.'

The master of the Count's music hurried back to the manager to report the good news. Though he took some pleasure in getting his own back on the manager, he truly had no idea where to turn for a decent singer at such short notice. He asked the manager for a conveyance, and was offered, with some diffidence, his carriage and pair. By the time the maestro reached Várad, it was late evening. He roused the conservatory's gatekeeper, who recognized him and opened up the visitor's lodge and even sent up a cold supper. The maestro had spent eight years at the conservatory of music. Early the next day he presented himself at the dean's office. The bespectacled clerk failed to recognize him and made him wait a good quarter of an hour, which earned him a royal dressing-down from his employer:

'Making master Titusz Angelli kick his heels, eh? Our most distinguished scholar and musician? The deputy head of our old boys' association?'

'Begging your gracious pardons, your honours,' he said, bowing and scraping in fear to all points of the compass.

The maestro and the dean embraced, each patting the other gently on the back.

'Well, my dear Titusz, how goes it? What brings you to these parts?'

'I have come to find a soloist, a solo singer.'

The dean ushered him into his office where, as for the last 26 years, the scent from a pot of basil filled the air. The dean had a weakness for delicate fragrances. The maestro settled himself on a stool and recounted the Count's wishes, which he had somewhat misunderstood, for the Count certainly had in mind a female singer. The dean shook his head: trained singers do not grow on trees, and there was no one currently studying at the conservatory whom he would dare recommend as worthy of the distinguished guests at the Count's ball.

But he did have an idea. The wandering minstrels of Árpád Jávorffy had recently come to town; perhaps in their ranks there was someone suitable. The bespectacled clerk was at once dispatched to make inquiries. The company

47

had already set up their tents in the market place the previous evening.

It was around noon by the time Árpád Jávorffy presented himself at the dean's office. Despite a great deal of bowing and much sweeping of his headgear across the floor he was unable to help, as his company offered only circus-style entertainments. He was about to propose his equestrienne Lola, who sang earthy Italian songs while playing the mandolin and riding a dapple-grey, but the dean would not even let him finish the list of her accomplishments: 'Out of the question.'

As the disappointed Jávorffy departed – he had been hoping to get at least a luncheon out of the invitation – the secretary suggested they ought perhaps to consider Bálint Sternovszky.

'Goodness me. No,' said the dean immediately.

'Who is this Bálint Sternovszky?' inquired the maestro.

'He's a landowner in this area. A curious figure. Even his house is not exactly run of the mill . . . It were best to show it you. You will not have seen its like.'

They climbed into the conservatory's brake. Two and a half hours' riding in the puszta brought them to the narrow path where a carved sign informed them:

CASTLE STERNOVSZKY – KEEP OUT

'He is not noted for his hospitality,' remarked the dean. He instructed the driver to wait for them and set off along the path, using both hands to raise his cape high, as in places the grass was spattered with mud. The maestro followed doubtfully. Soon the building came into sight. The maestro had to rub his eyes. An Italian turret in the shape of a five-pointed star stood in the thick of the forest, but without ramparts. It was as if storms had ripped it from a fortress elsewhere and dropped it in the middle of this wild terrain.

Instead of windows the grey walls sported only embrasures, slits for shooting arrows. A long ladder as to a hencoop led up to the first-floor entrance, which was more like the narrow opening of a cave than a door. They climbed up. A copper bell dangled at the end of a cord; they gave it a pull. There was nothing to indicate that it had been heard within. The dean, a noted bass in his day, boomed out: 'Anyone within?'

'Who may that be?' came the reply.

The dean gave both their names.

'What business have you in these parts?'

'We have come to see milord Sternovszky, our business being singing!'

A deal of shuffling could be heard behind the wooden structure barring the entrance, and soon this moved aside to let them enter the turret. There was total darkness, so at first they could see nothing. Two flambeaus blazed on the walls. A hump-backed figure with a soot-lined face led the way up the spiral stairs: 'Sorr's steward. Sorr will be with yer honners presently.'

To the maestro it was like climbing inside a beehive. They reached a level where there was some planking, a bare, unadorned dining area, with two long benches lining one corner and a dining table between them, the table supported on four thick pillars of the hardest oak, with wide footrests which in that region they called 'swelpmegods'. At the head of the table was placed a large armchair similarly furnished with a footrest; it was practically a throne, with the family coat-of-arms carved in the wood of the back: a precious horn-shaped stone splitting a rock in twain.

The steward offered them seats and then disappeared. They remained standing. The three sooty oil-lamps barely made an impression on the semi-darkness. On the far side of the dining room there was a large fireplace, burning a sizeable fire. Two foxhounds lounged before it, their

49

tongues lolling; one of them gave a bark as the strangers entered.

As Bálint Sternovszky entered, the floorboards creaked under his feet. He was a well-built man, with pale skin and luxuriant chestnut-coloured hair brushing his shoulders; a thick but untrimmed beard covered much of his face. He wore ceremonial garb, with lavishly embroidered hose.

'God grant you a good day.'

'And you also,' they responded politely.

After introductions they settled down, Bálint Sternovszky taking the armchair. Though he sat very much at his ease in the chair, he still towered above those sitting on the benches below. The dean sang the praises of the maestro, who in his turn elaborated the nature of the performance which he had the honour of inviting his honour Sternovszky to participate in, should he be willing.

'What makes you so convinced of my skills as a singer?'

'It's the talk of the county,' said the dean. 'We thought you would very kindly give us a demonstration.'

Bálint Sternovszky gave a mellifluous laugh. 'I might and I might not.'

'What can your honour sing and in what part?'

A watch-chain dangled from Bálint Sternovszky's trouser pocket, which he proceeded to withdraw; at the end of it was a deerskin-covered timepiece in the shape of an egg, the top of which he flicked open and then said: 'Night is drawing on. You gentlemen will be my guests for dinner. We shall resume this conversation thereafter,' and he clapped. Two servant girls entered and quickly laid the table for four. The dean did not forget his coachman, whom Sternovszky gave orders to be provided for in the lower kitchen.

Soon there appeared the lady of the house, Borbála, who at the sight of the visitors showed neither pleasure nor displeasure on her face, which reminded the maestro of a knotted breadroll. The dinner was superb. The two servant girls piled everything high on the table in the Transylvanian manner. There were loaves made with hops, beef with horseradish, fowl au poivre, and pasta with lashings of butter. The red wine, from the vintage three years back, went very well with the meal and was much praised by all.

'Your honour,' began the dean, 'how is it that you built your lodge so much out of the way and not in some secure town?'

'I don't trust people. They are capable of the utmost evil. It is better to withdraw. If you are not in the public eye, you will not attract trouble.'

'I see what you mean,' said the dean, though his eyes showed otherwise.

'And where did you learn to sing?' asked the maestro.

'From my grandfather.'

On hearing this reply Mrs Sternovszky rolled her eyes towards the rafters, as if her husband were claiming something nonsensical. The pewter plates had been removed by the servant girls and they brought coffee in the Turkish coffee pot.

'Where do you perform?' asked the dean.

'Rarely . . . sometimes on family occasions.'

'Your repertoire?'

'Seven hundred and fourteen songs and arias.' Bálint Sternovszky left the room, returning with a thick, much-thumbed tome which he opened towards its end and pointed: 'This is the folio in which I have written all their titles. The ones with a cross I can also play on the virginal.'

'No small achievement. Your grandfather must have been a well-trained musician.'

Bálint Sternovszky nodded sagely. A tremor passed across Borbála's face, which it was impossible not to notice. The two visitors caught each other's eye.

Bálint Sternovszky elaborated: 'My paternal grandfather, Péter Csillag, was a tanner who also played the pianoforte in

51

the town orchestra of Thüningen. He also wrote songs to the words of Otto von Niebelmayer, the orchestra's first violin.'

The lady of the house guffawed, and planted a fist in her mouth.

The dean cleared his throat: 'Might I be so bold as to ask why . . . Did you deem my query impertinent?'

'It is my answer she deems impertinent,' replied Bálint Sternovszky, 'for my grandfather Péter Csillag departed this life in the year of our Lord 1702. My good lady is doubtful that I could have learnt my musical skills from my grandfather if I was born 24 years after his death.'

The two visitors again exchanged glances. Sternovszky continued: 'I see that you gentlemen also doubt my words. Yet I must tell you that my German speech, for example, which is quite fluent even though I have never studied the language, is also wholly inherited from my grandfather.'

Borbála tried to control her laughter, and stared intently at the floor. 'That could as well have come from your father.'

'True. Only my dear father kept a lifelong silence about his knowledge of the German language. Furthermore, my younger brothers speak no German: how am I to explain that? And I also speak Turkish, of which my father knew not a word, whereas my grandfather was brought up with two Turkish playmates. *Per amore Dei*, my father was wholly ignorant of music.'

The maestro looked round carefully: 'So . . . how was it possible to learn from someone who would . . .'

'Indeed, I do not understand that myself. From time to time I have the ability to go back into the past and at such times I feel quite clearly what my forefathers felt and know what my forefathers knew. Never have I had any musical training, yet the music that my grandfather Péter Csillag knew, I am able to play and sing myself. I could, if the opportunity presented itself, conduct an orchestra the way

52

he did. I can feel exactly, with eyes closed, the tune, the phrasing, and . . . Do not imagine that I have taken leave of my senses!' He stood up and almost ran to the corner of the stone steps and, whipping off the brocade covering the virginals, began to play. The melancholy chords echoed around the bleak stone walls, which amplified their volume.

The dean closed his eyes and the maestro's feet began to tap in time to the beat. Bálint Sternovszky's performance of the piece was flawless.

'What is the name of this piece?' the visitors asked.

'It was composed by a young organist who went to school with Péter Csillag in Luneburg. Bach is the name.'

'Bach? Johann Sebastian?' asked the dean.

'His Christian name I have not been vouchsafed.'

'He has distinguished himself considerably. I had news only the other day that he was on his deathbed. I have a good friend who is a choirmaster in Leipzig; he mentioned it in a letter.'

There was a moment's silence.

'Does your honour read music?'

'To some extent. What I sing or play on the virginal I can certainly follow in written form. But I have little practice, rarely do I have music to read.'

'So,' said the maestro, going over to the instrument, 'your honour did not learn to play this, you know it only through the memory of your grandfather?'

'Something of that sort.'

'It's quite unbelievable!'

'Yes. Yet that is how it is.'

'And your honour also learnt the arias in the same . . . ?'

Sternovszky nodded.

'Terrifying,' said the maestro.

'Were others able to avail themselves of this . . . technique, our craft would become quite pointless,' mused the dean.

Sternovszky's face broke into a smile. He suddenly launched into a song. His voice was mellow and powerful, though able to reach a higher register than could most men. The words of the Italian lyrics seemed unclear in places and some he certainly elided, but neither the dean nor the maestro noticed, so powerfully did they fall under the music's spell. As he came to the end they both burst into spontaneous applause.

'Whence comes this aria?' asked the maestro.

'Also from my grandfather Péter Csillag.'

'Yes, but who is the composer? Monteverdi?'

'I do not know. My dear grandfather was unsure.'

'Let us have a look at the music.'

'I have told you: there is no music.'

'But then where are the words from?'

'Have you not been listening? I just remember what my grandfather knew; that is how it is with me!' he said, impatiently slamming down the lid of the virginals.

The two musicians voiced no further doubts. The maestro asked if his honour would be willing to perform at the ball to be held in Count Forgách's castle, and what he would like to perform to the accompaniment of the orchestra. Bálint Sternovszky accepted the invitation. Though showing no interest in the fee, he remarked that he had never in his life performed with an orchestra. The maestro deemed none the less that two days' rehearsal would suffice.

They thought Sternovszky would try to prevail upon them to stay the night, but as he made no remark to this effect, they packed their things. As they were saying their farewells, the dean asked Sternovszky: 'With such a voice you could have gone to the top of the profession. Why have you not tried?'

'I am not even sure that it is right for me to sing before an audience, especially for money ... My kinsmen will curse me left, right and centre. My father, God rest his soul, might have disowned me.'

'Then it is fortunate indeed that he . . .' The maestro fortunately bit his tongue before reaching the end of his wayward train of thought.

'Our grateful thanks for your hospitality,' said the dean. 'God bless you.'

As darkness fell Bálint Sternovszky watched through the window slits while the two men set off uncertainly along the forest track. They are afraid, he thought. Even in daylight this part of the world is none too friendly, never mind at night. Wolves howl by the reed-beds; but as long as there is such a rich supply of pheasant, quail and hare, they will not hunger for man flesh. Even the hen-coops in the servants' houses behind the turret were in no danger.

When Bálint Sternovszky had first come to these parts not every trace of the old village had been carried away by winds and thieves. The ruins of the houses had sometimes been covered by mounds of blackish dust. The area was largely in thrall to the young trees that had sprung up, forming a new forest. Where once the church had stood there were now reed-beds, as if it were the shore of a lake. High above the rock face the peak loomed lonely, the colour of rust, and rivulets of rainwater by the hundred bubbled down through the rocks, sweeping everything into the valley. The tiny traces of the life lived here by the people of old had crumbled away; there was, in any case, no one here to pick them up as souvenirs.

In the clearing alongside the rocky cliffs where he wanted to build his home, the brushwood and the undergrowth had first to be cleared away. Somewhere in the middle, mouth downwards, embedded in the soil, lay a copper mortar with a hole in it. Bálint Sternovszky had it cleaned and polished, and had treasured it ever since.

It took two years to build the turret, to his own design, in that clearing. 'This is where it has to be!'

No one was clear why he wanted it built in just this spot or why he wanted this kind of structure as his home. The cost of the works regularly exceeded the budget. Bálint Sternovszky was unconcerned. 'What has to be done, must be done.'

The family despaired when it learned that he had bought himself property many hours' ride away from Felvincz, and that it consisted of two wholly ruined villages complete with the woods and meadows they shared. Nor could they find any explanation for where he had found the money for this purchase and for the building works. Income from the glass-works had declined steeply since Kornél Sternovszky had given back his soul to his Creator. His son Bálint was less successful as a businessman and devoted to it little of his time or energy. He was never very happy to be working; he preferred to sleep or to lie around dreaming of castles in Spain or Transylvania. However, he would have neglected the glassworks even if he had been of a more industrious nature. He hated the glassworks. In the absence of close supervision the master glassmakers who followed one another in rapid succession had little of his interest at heart and rather more of their own. The matriarch Janka summoned the family council with increasing frequency, but to no avail: neither carrot nor stick had any effect on Bálint Sternovszky.

His two younger brothers shrugged helplessly: they had no say in the running of the glassworks.

When the debts were such that they made the production and sale of the glass products no longer viable, Bálint Sternovszky received with equanimity the news that the glassworks would soon come under the hammer. 'The Lord giveth, and the Lord taketh away,' he said quietly.

Borbála was pregnant with their third son (whom the

56

Lord would later be pleased to call to Him while he was still at the breast) and held her swollen stomach before him: 'Do you not see that we shall be thrown out of our own house? Where will I go with my two infants? Where will I give birth to this third one? Have you not thought of this?'

'I have. Be of good cheer. I have done everything that I could.'

More than this he was not prepared to say. Only when they had loaded what remained of their belongings onto the oxcarts and everyone had clambered up on top of them, was he willing to vouchsafe the following: 'Take the road in the direction of Kos.'

'Kos? Where on earth is Kos?'

'Westwards. Keep going west until I say the word.'

The caravan set off. For several months Bálint Sternovszky and his family had fallen off the edge of the world as far as his relatives, friends and creditors were concerned.

He was born so small that the midwife did not think he would live to see the dawn of day.

Bálint Sternovszky came into the world at about nine of the clock in the evening. He did not cry, only after hot and cold baths did he give a little squeal. His head had turned blue from the strain of the birth but it was already covered in unusually thick coils of hair. By the next evening his skin colour had become more normal and his face had assumed the dreamy look that it was to bear all his life.

From a very early age his talent for music amazed his parents and teachers. He had only to hear a tune once – just once – and he was able to repeat it, immediately, note for note, even weeks later. Whenever his father sat him on his knee, he hummed Kurucz songs in his ear, despite his wife's oft-repeated warning 'You'll get us into trouble one of these days!'

'Janka, don't go on! Surely one is allowed to sing!'

Allowed and aloud: certainly, Bálint did not stop all day. When he was not singing he would be humming a tune, and when he wasn't humming a tune he would be whistling like a blackbird.

One day when he was eight he woke up hardly able to breathe. The little air that was getting through his throat was producing a dreadful, harsh wheeze. The doctor in Felvincz diagnosed diphtheria and with a resigned shake of the head by the skinny little lad's bed said: 'There is nothing more that I can do.'

Mrs Sternovszky sobbed and howled, begging the Lord to have mercy on her son and imagining what curses she would heap on him if, God forbid . . . For days Bálint produced no sign of life other than a barely perceptible heartbeat. While he was unconscious he made great journeys, in regions unknown to him. When he recovered he was able to recall exactly what he had seen and heard, though for a long time he ascribed little significance to what he had come to know as he lay on the border between life and death.

Years passed, and years. When he reached sixteen he was chasing butterflies one afternoon with his brothers by the side of the brook. His younger brothers Zoltán and Kálmán were often left in his care by his mother and he always looked after them conscientiously. Since both of them seemed much shorter and more fragile than he, and than they should have been, he would not allow them to sit on grass that was wet with dew, say, or to play too close to the water.

Across the brook grazed the family's sheep. Despite the summer sun, the shepherd did not take off his thick sheepskin coat, and his thick-coated puli dog kept yelping at the brothers, who noisily barked back. Farther up, where the stream curled away to the right, ancient willows swept the water, the branches lightly slapping its surface again and again. The boys had tired themselves out and lay down in the shade to eat the luncheon in their saddlebags. The monotonous little noises soon made them nod off.

Bálint stirred and turned to see suddenly beauty that made his eyes ache. A girl was bathing on the far bank, almost stark naked. Her faultless skin was as white as swan's down. Her luxuriant hair, wound around her head, was the colour of blackest coal. She was splashing in the water with the abandon of a puppy. At first he thought he must be dreaming and that the slightest movement on his part would make the image dissolve.

In the evening he found out that he had seen Kata, the only daughter of the new glassmaster, Imre Farkas II. His excitement knew no bounds. He could not sleep a wink all night: he kept seeing the girl again and again, her slightest movement came to life, every curve and crevice of her body was deeply etched in his brain. The following day he spent in a moonstruck daze: he would neither eat nor drink; in his usual summer pastimes, whether hunting or ninepins, he took no pleasure at all. He was pining, pining for the bank of the stream where he might again glimpse the figure of Kata.

His mother drew him aside: 'What has got into you, my son?'

In his excitement Bálint could barely blurt the words out: 'Morr dear! Morr dear! My heart's afire! I lover! I wanter! I'll avveraswife!'

'Who?'

'Kata Farkas! I want Kata Farkas, Morr dear!'

'Who is Kata Farkas?'

The master glassmaker's daughter had arrived only a week earlier from Vásárhely, where she lived with her mother. She was to spend a month in Felvincz. Mrs Sternovszky had not yet seen her. She lost no time in finding

59

Imre Farkas, but he knew nothing of the matter. Farkas summoned his daughter.

She shrugged her shoulders. 'I have never set eyes on the young sir. I wouldn't even know if he was blond or dark or pug!'

'Pug?' Mrs Sternovszky did not understand.

'That's what we call a bald man back home.'

'But my son Bálint has a wonderful head of dark hair!'

'That's as may be, but as I said, I don't know him.'

The master glassmaker gave a nod. 'Right. You may go for now.' Turning to Mrs Sternovszky, he said: 'As you see, my good lady, no need to pay heed. This love affair is your son's invention. But then he is of an age when these things happen. And besides, Kata is only rising thirteen, too soon to think of church and children.'

And that was how they left the matter. A great weight had fallen off Mrs Sternovszky's shoulders. Though her husband was of humble origin she, Janka Windisch, came from a line of Austrian nobles. True, her branch of the family had fallen on hard times and had only narrowly escaped ruin, but why should we rake up the past? Suffice it to say that thanks to the stables and the glassworks, they had made enough to be comfortable. Why should they allow their firstborn to marry a peasant girl? And so she told him, as soon as she caught up with him. Bálint said nothing, but in his heart he had decided otherwise. He did everything he could to catch another sight of the girl, but as she was determined not to be seen, for two days he found no trace of her. For Bálint these two days seemed like two long years. At times he felt that heavy, glittering flakes of snow were falling on his head. He was lost in a forest of dreams, desires and images in his mind.

He made far-reaching plans. From his father's gun room he appropriated the field glasses Kornél Sternovszky used at the horse races, and spied from every conceivable angle on the house of the master of the glassworks. No trace of Kata. He wrote her a letter in which he lavished extravagant praise on the amazing beauty of every part of her body, from the hair on her head to the tips of her toes. He begged for an opportunity to present himself formally. He folded the letter into a triangle and sealed it with his father's ruby-coloured sealing-wax. On the outside he drew a heart pierced by an arrow, but he was so unhappy with the shape of the design that he was tempted to tear the whole thing up. In the end he did not, and concentrated on how he might get the letter to Kata. He guessed that she would be at Sunday morning service at the Great Church in Felvincz: that would be an opportunity. But he did not see her there.

The reason being that Imre Farkas II suspected the worst and after the departure of his wife would not let their daughter leave the house. He did not bother to explain his decision and Kata received her father's command without emotion. She would work at her embroidery, read, help out in the kitchen, and sing and hum the bittersweet songs of her native Transylvania.

At dawn on Sunday the rain began to fall. The wind tore into the thatch on the roofs, the sky thundered darkly, the lightning creating broad daylight for a moment as it flashed. Kata was petrified. She kept wondering whether to flee the room they had made for her in the loft down to her father, but she did not want him to mock her. Trembling, she buried her face deep under the pillows, praying at the top of her voice. She begged Jesus not to be angry with her for obeying her father's command not to go to church. She was sure that devilish creatures were abroad and in her room, and she rattled off her prayers at ever-increasing speed.

Suddenly she felt a cold hand on her arm and was about to shriek had its fingers not been clamped at once over her mouth. She heard some rustling that the next roll of thunder drowned and at the next lightning flash she had a glimpse of the creature of the devil. It was certainly human in shape. Oh no, it's the master's son . . . And now there were words, too:

'I pray you, please, don't scream, not a finger will I lay on you, all I beg of you is that you hear me out!'

She sat up in the bed. Her eyes gradually adjusted to the gloom. The little window was wide open and rain was falling on the parapet. He came up a ladder, she thought. Bálint stood by the side of the bed, soaked to the skin, trembling much more violently than was she. Kata took pity on him: 'Hurry up and say your piece, then out, before they catch you here!'

Bálint fell on his knees but no words would come. He gripped her arm, as if that were his greatest joy on this earth. And it was then, in that extraordinary state, that the cavalcade of images began, images familiar from the past, those he had already experienced a long time ago, when he was ill, yet their meaning then had been obscure.

A half-naked man is painted green by a painter or artist in some bath-house; the man is quite unable to wash or scrub off the paint. The painter must be one of the ancestors, he thought, that his father had told of before.

A red-bearded old man in foreign parts, pack-horses and carts piled high. A large house Bálint had never known, where he could clearly see the furniture, the mysterious drawers and tools, out in the yard. The patriarchal figure must be Great-Grandpa Czuczor, who had been done to death by either the Kurucz or the Labancz. Bálint's father had never mentioned his first name but always called him 'Grandpa Czuczor'. He could even make out the inscription on the cover of the great folio book lying on the worktop: *Bálint Czuczor his notes, made by his own hand*. Now he knew he had been named for his great-grandfather.

He knew, too, that Great-Grandpa Czuczor had had to flee from Bavaria to Kos with his daughter and grandson, so it followed that this was how their house had looked. He feasted his eyes on the scenes as the lid lifted on the past.

He saw his great-grandfather busy at the bottom of the garden, behind the rose bushes, assisted by a lad no bigger than he was now, though with hair of a startling colour, as yellow as the yolk of an egg. They dug long and hard and eventually lowered into the hole a black iron casket, which they then proceeded to cover up carefully.

'*Wilhelm, du darfst das nie erzählen, verstehst du mich?*' he warned, shaking his spade at the lad.

'*Jawohl!*'

The sad end of his grandfather, too, came to life before him, a story he knew well from his father. His broad-chested dapple-grey throws Péter Csillag while he is out hunting, and as he falls he smashes his head into a tree-trunk, never to recover consciousness.

'Are you unwell? Speak to me!' Kata was kneeling on the bed, the blanket drawn about her like a shawl.

Bálint gave a heavy sigh and was about to launch into his carefully prepared speech, a paean of praise for the girl's beauty which would have culminated in a formal request for her hand. But before he could say a word fists battered on the door.

'Kata, open up! Open up at once, I say!' boomed the voice of Imre Farkas II.

'If you hold your life dear, run for it!' shouted the girl, jumping out of bed and half-pushing, half-tugging the lad in the direction of the window. He seemed not unwilling to comply, but could not bear to take his eyes off Kata's face and the snow-white skin of her arms and legs left uncovered by her night dress. This was no time to worry about modesty, it crossed Kata's mind. 'Coming, father dear!'

By the time Bálint reached the ladder outside the window, the door had yielded to the shoulders of Imre Farkas, who was holding a three-pronged candlestick in one hand and a drawn sword in the other. He took everything in at once. He leapt to the window and in the light of the candles saw Bálint Sternovszky scuttling down the ladder. 'Stop!' he cried, and when there was no response, he flung the heavy candlestick after him. As they fell the candles flew in three different directions and went out. Down below a shadow flew by, then came the sound of footfalls dying away.

Imre Farkas wasted no time in questioning his daughter, but to little avail: whatever Kata said he would not believe. He even slapped her across the face, just to be on the safe side. 'You will get a hundred times that if I ever see him hanging around you again!'

Imre Farkas stormed round to his master's first thing and demanded to be seen. Secretary Haller did not let him in. 'Later, master glassmaker, he is just breaking his fast.'

'So what?' said Imre Farkas, pushing the wizened old man aside and bursting in.

Kornél Sternovszky was just stirring his tea, which he had reinforced with a tot of rum. 'What is your business here?'

Haller was hovering in the background: 'I did say to him, master . . .'

'I found your son Bálint in my daughter's bedroom last night.'

'How do you mean?'

'I demand an explanation.'

'Haller, you may go.' Kornél Sternovszky placed the palms of both his hands on the table. He waited until the secretary had closed the door after him. 'I find it hard to believe that my son would leave my house in the dead of night.'

'Is your grace suggesting that I am a liar?'

'That is not what I said. What I said was that my son Bálint is not in the habit of leaving my house without permission.'

'Yet that is what he did. Ask him.'

'I shall. Presently he is still abed, as indeed I believe he has been all night.'

'I tell you: he has not!'

'What is this tone that you take with me? Remember whom you are addressing!'

'It were not easy to forget.'

'And what is that supposed to mean?'

'Suppose what you will, it does not change the facts. But I will not allow the smallest blot on my daughter's reputation!'

'How much longer do you expect me to tolerate your impertinence?'

'Let us not stray from the topic: if ever again I see your son hanging around my daughter, I swear he will bring home his head on a plate!'

'A threat? Are you threatening me? What an outrage!' Kornél Sternovszky rose from the breakfast table, knocking over as he did so a cup filled with tea which rapidly soaked into the white damask tablecloth. 'You are dismissed herewith! Leave at once!'

Imre Farkas II broke out in a cackling laugh of such vehemence that Kornél Sternovszky thought he had taken leave of his senses. He edged back, trying to reach the bell to summon his servant or Haller. Farkas was quicker off the mark and pushed the bell out of his reach as he bellowed: 'You can't get rid of me, I built the glassworks from the ground up, it will never function without me!'

'It will function if I will it to! You are not the only master glassmaker in the world. You will be amazed, Farkas, how quickly your name will be forgotten! Get out of here!' And Kornél Sternovszky took a step towards him.

The master glassmaker snorted like a wild boar: 'Master thinks he can do with me what he will? Thinks his offspring can dishonour my daughter by way of amusement? That you can just throw me out, like some used toerag? That I will put up with anything and everything?'

'I have nothing more to say! Out!'

Kornél Sternovszky gave his master glassmaker a push in the chest. Imre Farkas II was in good shape and his chest barely registered the gesture. He began to shout out at the top of his voice unconnected words like 'compensation', 'contract', 'complaint', 'courts', and the like, until Kornél Sternovszky grabbed hold of the teapot and threw its hot contents in his face. For a fraction of a second the master glassmaker could not see. Then he drew his sword, as did Kornél Sternovszky his own, but the glassmaker was quicker on the draw and at the first clash of the blades wrenched Kornél Sternovszky's weapon from his grip and with the same movement plunged his blade deep into his chest. For this Farkas was some months later duly hanged in the main square of Felvincz. By then Kornél Sternovszky lay in a copper-plated coffin six feet deep in the soil of his homeland. Kata's mother came to take her away and Bálint never saw or heard from her again.

Three years after his father's funeral Bálint Sternovszky took over from his mother the running of the glassworks. He also inherited Kornél Sternovszky's papers and folio. His brothers were jealous, coveting especially the glassworks, for which they would both have given their eye-teeth. Yet Kornél Sternovszky himself truly hated the glassworks, as well as all master glassmakers, every one of whom brought Kata to mind. He married as soon as he could. The daughter of the miller of Felvincz brought less in the way of a dowry than a gentleman of his station was entitled to expect, but when his mother raised this topic, Bálint silenced her with the words: 'She will make a good wife. That is what matters.'

The decline of the glassworks began as the young couple were enjoying their honeymoon. One night the drying kiln burnt to the ground. Bálint dismissed the news with unconcern: 'It could have been worse. At least we shan't have to dry the glass for a while.'

Haller, who had retained his post, clapped his hands to his head; 'But sir, that's impossible. It will crack!'

'Less fussing, Haller! Some of the glass will, some won't.'

No one could understand how Bálint Sternovszky could remain so indifferent to the rapid decline of the glassworks. He would spend long mornings in the forests he had inherited alongside the glassworks. He told his wife he was looking for mushrooms.

'How is it, husband mine, that you are always looking for mushrooms, yet never find any?'

'Find them I certainly do! Only they are poisonous, like your good self.'

In fact, mushrooming was not how he spent his days. The moment he found himself in the thick of the forest, he would sit down and eat his rations. Then he would burst into song. He sang all day long, as the locals could testify. When he was in full flow he could be heard many miles away.

Betimes he would wander so far that he would not return home for the night. He preferred to sleep under the open sky rather than seek the hospitality of others. He liked to lie in the dark on the grass or on the sand and examine the stars, as he ground his memories ever finer in the windmills of his mind. It was during such reveries that it dawned on him that he had to make the trip to Kos to find the house of Great-Grandpa Czuczor, or rather the garden with the rose bushes where he could dig for the iron casket and get hold of the treasure he had buried. He was certain there was a reason that God had blessed him with the rare gift of seeing into the past. It was compensation for all he had endured.

So when one afternoon he came upon the forest that had grown over the old village, he recognized it at once. Ankle-deep in black dust, he knew that the rains and the snows had still not washed the soil clean of the black ash which was all that remained of the houses burnt to the ground all those years ago. He looked first for traces of Great-Grandpa Czuczor's house. In a landscape almost entirely reclaimed by nature he found it hard to make out the building that had so vividly appeared to him. The road up the mountain was overgrown with scrub; the only sure sign of the route was the jagged cliffs. Bálint Sternovszky was almost beside himself with excitement as he hacked his way through the prickly bushes and fought off the trailers twining round his legs, careless of the bloody scratches from the spines and spikes of the vegetation. He did not mind. He knew that no one can blunder into the past without paying the price.

Another clue presented itself in the form of a fragment of wall no more than waist-high, a remainder of the church. It had been overgrown by a bed of reeds that would have made the average visitor think that there was a lake or river behind it, but there was no trace of either. Bálint followed the twists and turns of a line where the vegetation was somewhat less lush, thinking that perhaps it might once have been the road. As he slowly reached the top of the mountain, night was falling and he sat down by a tree-stump and cut himself some bread and salami from his shoulder-bag. He fell asleep as he sat, and dreamt of his ancestors. Great-Grandpa Czuczor was throwing rocks into the stream, to dam the water in order to have a bath. He called out to Bálint, who was reluctant to join him, thinking the water too cold, but when he eventually did so, it turned out to be lukewarm and silky. Great-Grandpa Czuczor was stroking his brow, his wet fingers felt rough.

He woke to find a dog licking his face.

'Get out of here!' he said, chasing it away. The animal went a few steps, then stopped and turned back. In its eyes there burned a fire, a light of longing. He's hungry, thought Bálint, and threw it a piece of salami. The dog gave a snort

68

and wolfed it down greedily. Bálint threw it some more pieces and got to his feet. He was in a clearing covered with boulders and rocks and overgrown with scrub and trees that had grown up wild, some the height of a man. He heard years later that this clearing was called Bull Meadow. Long, long ago the bull belonging to Gáspár Dobruk, the local farrier, had got free and it was here that they caught up with the unruly creature, eventually.

'Here,' said Bálint out loud. 'Here and nowhere else!'

He wondered if it would not be a good idea to seek out the scene of all the memories that had come to him in Kata's room. But the only place with a name had been Kos. If He who had revealed to him all this wanted to direct him to another place, surely He would provide the means.

That same afternoon he happened upon the outlines of his great-grandfather's garden. The rose bushes had long been strangled by weeds. He hacked off a willow withy and marked out in the soil the area where he suspected the iron casket lay. Who was the trusty servant he could return with to dig up the treasure? Who could be warned – as did Great-Grandpa Czuczor – with the words:

'*Du darfst das nie erzählen, verstehst du mich?*'

'*Jawohl!*'

There was no one. It was an act of criminal folly to let that boy into the secret. Were they to survive the catastrophe, the German lad would surely loot the treasure. You must never trust anyone but yourself.

Thanks to Grandpa Czuczor's valuables, he would never be short of money again. This was a secret he shared with no one, any more than he shared the buried treasure. At times he was troubled by his conscience. Perhaps his brothers should have had some of it. In his mind's eye he often heaped up into three piles what he had found, or rather what was left of it. But he kept putting off the time he would reward his brothers.

In any case, they would not believe where and how I had come by the money. They think little of me as it is. Let them think they have the better of me.

On Saturday afternoon the wind picked up again and began to whip the ribbons on the maypole. The slim trunk of the tall maple began to sway perilously, sometimes seemingly at breaking point. The broad courtyard of the castle rapidly filled up with carts and sprung carriages, indifferent to the careful raking of the gardeners. The visitors alighted and paused when they saw the giddy swaying of the maypole, its colourful ribbons swishing sharply in the wind. Four of the ground staff also rode in, to keep order. Two posted themselves at the double oaken gates of the building, while two secured the entrance to the stairwell.

Castle Forgách had been decorated in readiness for the ball. The famed avenue of walnut trees was hung with lanterns whose candles, to say nothing of the vast array of lights on the stone balustrades of the first-floor terrace, could hardly be lit if the wind did not abate; indeed, the lanterns themselves were in some danger. The ornately carved sides of the bridge across the artificial lake had been garlanded with flowers.

Manager Bodó was regulating the arrival of the carriages, having planned well in advance how they might all fit into the courtyard without ruining the lawns or the flowerbeds. In his agitation he was crunching away furiously at the walnuts he had stuffed in his waistcoat pocket. He needed this ball as an oxcart needs a ditch.

The maestro had had the first-floor terrace in mind for the evening concert, but had to report to the Count that in such a wind neither musicians nor audience would feel comfortable; so they moved to the grand hall of the castle – the Count called it the *sala grande* – in plenty of time. The servants were already offering drinks in the foyer.

Bálint Sternovszky had been quartered in the end room on the second floor of the U-shaped building, from the window of which he was able to follow with interest the folk streaming in. He had brought his binoculars with him. These, too, he had found in his great-grandfather's iron casket, and although he had never shown them abroad, he was of the opinion that they were made of gold. He could see his wife and two sons alighting from a black carriage. Little János was pushing his way forward as he clung to his mother's frilly skirts. István, his firstborn, strode along with all the soldierly pride of a four-year-old, his miniature mantle ornate with frogging, his right hand resting on a tiny sword.

So they've come after all, Bálint thought. Borbála was not in the least inclined to be present when her husband sang. 'Must you again make a fool of yourself?'

'What do you know about it?'

He imagined the feeling of seeing his sons in the audience. He did not know whether they had inherited even a little of what he had had as a gift. István was not prepared to sing even simple songs all the way through, though he never stopped talking: a chatterbox if ever there was one. Little János, on the other hand, would not say a word, and they were regularly having anxious exchanges with the doctor. Though it is no use being impatient; everything in its time.

Wheels creak down below as the guests stream onto the terrace and the foyer. Count Forgács had not yet appeared and manager Bodó welcomed the guests. The Count's four children – all of them girls – were larking about on the lawn in their finest. Bálint Sternovszky knew that his family would not be lodged with him and was thankful; this was not a time he wanted them around. Again he went through in his head the pieces he had several times rehearsed with the maestro, first with the latter at the virginal, then with the castle orchestra. The maestro nodded approval, judging

71

both the melody and the measure to be just right, querying only the Latin text here and there. 'That's not exactly how it is written.'

'That's the way I know it.'

'But if you look on the sheet you will see the text . . .'

Sternovszky broke in: 'There's no time now for learning something new. Let it be as I picked it up.'

The maestro yielded with a nod. Had he insisted, Bálint Sternovszky would have had to declare that he had no choice. Which the maestro could in no way have understood. Not if it is beyond even me, he thought.

Outside the wind had whipped up the dust into whirling cornet shapes and the panes of the wide windows rattled in their frames. Sternovszky registered in passing that they could not have come from his former glassworks, as they never produced glass of such thickness.

There was a knock on his door. A liveried servant bowed: 'Your excellency is awaited for dinner.'

The round and oblong tables were set up in three rooms that opened into one another. The gilded candlesticks radiated a bright glow even though it was still light outside. The noise of wind could be heard within. Bálint Sternovszky greeted Borbála and the children kissed his hand. They did not speak through the five-course meal of cold pigeon pâte, lamb broth, grilled sturgeon in grey liquor, beef ragout with dill and walnut roll.

As they took their places in the sala grande the musicians, sitting in two rows facing one another, were already tuning up, as the maestro looked through his sheet music by the pianoforte. The boys' choir was lined up against the wall, in three rows.

Pál Forgách was in the front row, discoursing with his most distinguished guest, Count Limburg. Quite suddenly he nodded in the maestro's direction without turning to face him. The maestro, in turn, gave the signal to the orchestra, and the concert had begun. The two counts nodded in time to the rhythm, but without once interrupting their conversation. Until the madrigals of the choir drowned their words, their discussion was audible to all: the leader of the Felsőlendva threshers had lodged an official complaint with the county council, alleging that Count Forgách had unjustly and contrary to the terms of their contract withheld from them a payment of eighty florins.

Bálint Sternovszky was due to sing the third, the fifth, and the closing numbers. Helping hands had provided him with a music stand, though he had no need of such. When the time came, he stepped up to the stand and waited for the maestro's signal after the opening bars. Other singers would at this point be floating on the surface of the tune, ready to begin; Bálint Sternovszky knew that when the moment came, there would issue flawlessly from his mouth, in a single movement, all that he had inherited. He thus had time to look around. He saw the flushed cheeks of the ladies, the fluttering fans, the ceaseless play of the candlelight, the bored expressions on the faces of the liveried servants propping up the walls, enjoying a moment of relaxation.

His mouth was just rounding out into the opening sound when he turned pale and froze. The maestro knew that the bars would recur and gestured again, but for Bálint Sternovszky nothing existed any more except the snow-white face, the dark eyes, the dark hair combed into a chignon. In his numbness he was unable to move and so could not run and fall on his knees before her. Meanwhile the maestro had told himself a hundred times that he should not have had anything to do with this madman of the turret; you should never have dealings with eccentrics and odd men, he knew that, but needs must. He was furious with the dean for embroiling him in this farce. No use crying over spilt milk. Heavens, it could cost him his job.

Head bowed, he continued to play, the players bore up well, and even without the song the piece billowed its way to an affecting climax.

Bálint Sternosznky had no other role in the first half of the performance that evening. At the interval the maestro turned on him with a face like death: 'What on earth was that?'

Sternovszky walked off without a word, as if in a dream, towards the creature whose very sight had blotted out all. The maestro did not follow, but hurried over to Count Forgách and bowed deeply: 'I earnestly beg your grace's pardon for this deeply embarrassing episode with his honour Bálint Sternovszky. I have no idea what got into him.'

The Count's consumption of punch had been sufficient for him to take a lenient view of the business, and with something of a grin he said: 'Well, we managed to survive, what? The others laboured tolerably well, wouldn't you say?'

Nods and approving noises from his circle.

'Next time organize a woman to sing, eh?' the Count added.

The maestro again bowed deeply and hurried back to his players. 'Where on earth am I going to get a woman?' he steamed. They are as rare as hen's teeth.

During this time Bálint Sternovszky hunted high and low for Kata Farkas, but without success. He kept the distance of a bargepole from his wife and two sons. People whispered behind his back, some thinking he had gone unexpectedly hoarse, others suspecting he had succumbed to witchcraft. There were already rumours aplenty in the county about the noble who lived in the turret. Bálint Sternovszky offered no excuses or explanations, but for the second half of the concert did not take his place with the players. He hovered at the back by one of the doorways, scanning the audience with mounting agitation. Kata Farkas had disappeared into thin air. Bálint Sternovszky felt he was losing his mind. He was shivering, and sweating so much that damp patches began to form on his clothing. He now perceived the world around him only in broad outline. He could hardly control the trembling of his knees or maintain himself upright. He slid down the wall and on to the highly polished floor.

Two servants standing nearby pulled him unobtrusively out into the corridor, where they brought him back to consciousness with a glass of plum brandy, and then helped him to his room. As he recovered he asked them where the lady Kata Farkas had been seated. He was informed that no guest bearing this name was to be found anywhere in the castle. Some while later his wife and boys asked to be admitted but he turned them away, saying he felt too weak. It was no lie: his fiasco had distressed him just as much as had the sudden sight of Kata Farkas. Though now he was no longer sure that he had really seen her.

Mrs Emil Murányi had been lodged in two interconnecting rooms with her husband and three little daughters, of whom the youngest, Hajnalka, was a source of continued concern, beginning with her birth, when the umbilical cord had wound itself around her neck and would have strangled her had the midwife not managed carefully to untangle it. By the time she did so, the newborn had turned as blue as a forget-me-not.

'Lord a-mercy,' the mother whispered, 'will she live?'

The midwife gave no reply, splashing the newborn baby who had, worryingly, not yet uttered a sound, with warm water. To cap it all, the baby's left eye was sky-blue but her right corn-yellow, and this perhaps betokened some illness. Within a day or two, however, Hajnalka Murányi had picked up and was cheerfully sucking away at her mother's breast, behaving in every respect as any other child of her age. But once a month, quite unpredictably, she would have an attack: she had trouble breathing, bubbles foamed from her mouth, her skin turned as blue as at birth, she thrashed about with her limbs, or lost consciousness, and for short periods her heartbeat would also fail. At such times they would send the maid running for the doctor quite in vain: invariably, by the time he arrived Hajnalka was happily sucking her thumb with a peaceful smile and quite unaware of the panic that she had induced in those around her. Mrs Murányi never travelled anywhere without Dr Koch: better safe than sorry.

She was not minded to accept Count Forgách's very kind invitation. Her children were still too small to be going to balls and concerts. Emil Murányi thought otherwise: one had to get out of these four walls sometimes, and Count Forgách might take it amiss if they declined. Naturally they would take Dr Koch with them: there would be no worry on that account.

At the eleventh hour Emil Murányi received bad news: *Your father has had a stroke* – wrote his mother – *and has no movement in the left side of his body; come at once!* So he could not join them in the carriage. Before galloping off on his black steed, he promised to meet them at Castle Forgách the next day, if at all possible. Mrs Murányi had a feeling that this little trip would not pass off without incident and made sure Dr Koch brought with him the entire contents of his medicine chest. Her foreboding was fulfilled some one-third of the way through the concert, when Hajnalka's eyes swelled up and her breathing became laboured and turned into a hiss. As she began to froth at the mouth, her mother and Dr Koch bundled her up and made a dash for their room, where they put her to bed, placed a bandage on her forehead, and held down her arms and legs to stop her doing herself an injury.

'We have caught it in time, madam,' whispered Dr Koch, as the girl's steadied breathing showed that the danger was over.

'God be praised.'

Mrs Murányi would not have been unhappy to have her husband burst into the room. She knew hardly any of the guests, and hated nothing more than to be the focus of attention in strange company. She thought all eyes were on her as they ran from the sala grande with the limp little body; her cheeks were crimson with embarrassment and the excitement of the day. On these occasions her husband always knew how to calm her down with soothing words and the broad, cool palms of his hands. Emil Murányi was always the subject of somewhat condescending smiles for the slowness of his speech, which was almost a stutter. Born with a harelip, he was able to disguise this with a lavish growth of facial hair, but the manner of his speech gave the game away. Kata was quite untroubled by this; with no other man did she feel so completely safe, including her own father. Emil Murányi held some 90 Hungarian acres of land, of which he took exemplary care; people came from far and wide to admire it. His estate manager was a Saxon, who had the hayricks constructed in the cylindrical style of his homeland; this was enough for an expert eye to tell that the lands belonged to Emil Murányi.

Dr Koch's room was in one of the castle's outbuildings, with those of the other guests' servants. He kissed Kata's hands as he left: 'I cannot imagine that there will be any problems, but if you need me, just send!'

As soon as she was on her own, Kata removed her ball-gown. Despite her husband's protestations she did not want to bring her maid for just the one night; she was quite able to undress by herself. Had she worn a corset, she might well have needed assistance; but she had not. She put on her silk dressing gown and red slippers, sat down in the armchair and listened to the music filtering through the half-open window. The concert was over, and there remained only a Gypsy band giving its all on the terrace. Kata closed her eyes. This music reminded her of her childhood, when her father woke her daily with the sound of the violin. He had knelt by her bed, the instrument lodged firmly under his chin, and the melody came meltingly from the strings as her father crooned the words: 'Wake up, sleepy head, sunshine's on your bed . . .' This was the most wonderful thing he ever did for his daughter. Though Kata's husband did not serenade her or the children with such morning music, in every other respect he was a better man. She forced herself not to think of her father's sad end, but of her husband's face instead. I'll croon for two. If only Emil were here!

There was a timid knock.

'Yes?' she said, making for the door with a spring in her step.

From the opposite direction there came: 'Please, don't be frightened, I'm . . . it's . . . I'm . . .'

A dark shape framed by the glass of the window. Mrs Murányi let out a scream.

'Don't . . . forgive me for . . . do you not recognize me?'

The woman shook her head. She picked up the candlestick and took a step towards the door. But she now knew, even without the light. She had seen the name of Bálint Sternovszky in the programme and was surprised that he was singing here; she was curious and somewhat concerned about how it would feel to see him again. But Hajnalka's fit had driven all of this out of her head. 'You are incorrigible! Haven't you heard about doors?'

Bálint Sternovszky eased himself into the room. 'I know . . . I am lodged two rooms away . . . I had only to climb over the balconies and . . . you haven't changed at all!' A beatific smile lit up his face. She looked exactly as she had all those years ago, in the loft room of Kata Farkas.

'Please don't!' Kata had no illusions about the ravages of having given birth, which her silk dressing gown generously shielded from view. She was 28 Viennese pounds

78

heavier than when she married. It did not bother Emil, who often said you cannot have too much of a good thing – or a good person. 'But you have indeed not changed at all,' she lied. The vast amounts of hair had transformed Bálint from a boisterous puppy into a suspicious hedgehog. 'None the less, I must insist that you leave. It is not done to burst into the room of a married woman under the cover of night.'

'It's still only evening,' mumbled Bálint Sternovszky.

'Leave at once! Or I shall scream!'

'I beseech you, please, don't scream, not a finger will I lay on you, all I beg of you is that you hear me out!'

Kata could not help but smile. The words were deeply etched in her memory. She responded with another quotation: 'Hurry and say your piece, then out, before they catch you here!'

Bálint Sternovszky gave a little sigh of relief and bowed as he knelt. In the years since that scene, the scene that Imre Farkas II's bursting into the room had shattered, had flashed before him a thousand times. A thousand times he had rehearsed all that he could have said to Kata to soften her heart towards him. He had even thought up clever words he could have said to blunt the anger of her enraged father, instead of scurrying away with his puppy tail between his legs. Every time he thought of these things he came to the conclusion that it was no use crying over spilt milk. He had never imagined that another occasion would arise when he could be with Kata, years later, a scene lit only by candlelight and the twin stars of Kata's eyes, just as it had been then.

I'm not going to get it wrong this time! He could hear the sound of loud cracking and realized it was his fingers. Come on! Out with it! But the words would not come.

The marble paving of the corridor floor resounded to steps that suddenly they could both hear: metal-heeled riding boots neared rhythmically. 'Surely, it can't be . . .' thought Bálint Sternovszky. Kata's father had long ago ended his days in the main square of Felvincz.

There was a knock. Kata shivered and firmly pushed him in the direction of the window.

'Kata, my dearest!' said a velvety voice in the corridor.

'Emil! How wonderful! I'm coming!' she said loudly, but pushed the window wide open. Her eyes commanded him with such steel that he obediently stepped out onto the parapet.

'No, it can't happen again, just like last time, no, please, no!' he thought in desperation. If they caught him like last time, Kata would hate him for ever, to say nothing of the scandal, the duel . . . He readied himself to swing over the wrought-iron railings of the balcony next door.

The night-time dew had wetted the metal rail and he slipped, latching on to the wooden shutter with his left hand as his right arm desperately reached out for something – anything, and then he fell, at first upright but then head-first onto the ground. An almighty thud as he struck, his back cracking on the stone flags of the pathway around the building. Complete darkness.

Slowly the mists cleared. Up above, the light of a few square windows shimmered in the dark. Here and there candles were lit, heads turned towards him from every direction. He sought only Kata's face, an apologetic smile planted on his own, but Kata was nowhere to be seen. From down here he was not entirely sure which window he had fallen from, so he could not pick out Emil Murányi from the many men blinking at him incredulously, unable to comprehend what he was doing down there, with his body and limbs in such a curiously twisted shape.

The pain came only later, by which time the world had turned grey and images and sounds were fragmenting into smaller pieces. Behind his brow the many ancient faces began to stream forth; scenes, landscapes, time rolled backwards for him, the torrent of images seemed as if it would never end.

First on the scene was manager Bodó, lantern in hand. He clapped a palm to his face when he saw the twisted body. Is there never going to be a moment's peace in this accursed estate? What on earth has happened to this man? Is it not enough for him that he came to grief at the concert? What a mess! He hunkered down and touched him on the shoulder. Then he saw that the grass was red with blood. 'Holy Mother of God!' he said, straightening up. 'Get Dr Kalászy! At once!'

Dr Kalászy had, however, consumed so much alcohol at dinner that there was no reply when they hammered on his door, except the sound of a rasping snore. But Dr Koch hurried over on his own initiative, a cape thrown over his long nightshirt and a capacious doctor's bag under one arm. A brief examination later he whispered into the manager's ear: 'Summon a priest.'

By then Borbála had arrived, weeping and moaning, throwing herself on the body of Bálint Sternovszky, who thought that this was the last straw and that he must die. The gut-wrenching shrieks of the woman could be heard far away. 'Oh, dear husband, sweet husband, do not leave us, my dearest, don't do this to us, oh my God, please save him!'

Count Forgách arrived just as manager Bodó was having an unused bedframe brought over to serve as an emergency stretcher, onto which his men heaved the massive body. Just like a peasant, thought Count Forgács, then, out loud: 'What has happened here?'

'He fell out of a window.'

'Oh my dear husband, what will become of us without you?' wailed Borbála.

Dr Koch's efforts to drag her from the body of her husband were in vain. It needed two people to grasp her by the

81

arms and take her to one side. Bálint Sternovszky was quickly taken to a sheltered spot. At this juncture the Count realized that the victim of the accident was the singer who had failed to sing. I should check with the estate manager if he has paid him yet for the performance – he certainly does not deserve anything.

The body was carried to the small house in the garden, so that they did not have to brave the throng. Dr Koch kept feeling for Bálint Sternovszky's pulse, listening to his heart, but he felt and heard nothing to make him change his mind, and when Borbála was not looking, he shook his head in response to manager Bodó's questioning glance. However, Bálint Sternovszky clung on: a movement of his leg or a twitching eyelid gave notice that he was still alive. Borbála clutched his hands encouragingly (something he could not feel as he teetered on the brink of death). An acidic pain throbbed in his head, cascaded into his chest, bludgeoned every part of his body.

He saw, as of old, as in Kata's loft room, times past. First it was stations in the life of his father and then of his father's father and, beyond that, his great-grandfather. He sensed these might be his final hours and that he was seeing the images for the last time, unable to do anything about them. He regretted that he had spent his years in such sloth and without purpose. For the thousandth time he realized that he had been the cause of his father's premature death, something for which he could never forgive himself. And now came the painful realization that he had deprived his own brothers of something which perhaps, though they did not know of it, rightly belonged to them also. It makes no difference now.

He had spent most of his time without noticing its passing: lolling about, singing, in the self-satisfied manner of a married man, doing nothing, enjoying being served and enjoying that he did not have to serve. God! Why did I not make more of an effort? Why did I not pass on to my sons the knowledge I managed to glean? I could have written it all down in the folio from my father, had I thought about my offspring. Yet I only made notes on music. How selfishly I have lived! It's all too late now.

Everything went dark within.

He had no idea how much time had passed when he began to recover his senses. He was in the sleeping quarters of the turret, in the hastily knocked together contrivance he used as a bed. His head and all his limbs rested on wooden laths. He tried to lift an arm; the muscles did not obey. Ah . . . well . . . never mind. He sank back into the past, where he felt much more comfortable, where fate had not condemned him to immobility.

In the few days that remained to him Bálint Sternovszky could not sit up, or move, or speak. Still, he was restless. He explored his family's history, a tireless traveller of the mind, and tried without cease to think how he might pass on the substance of his visions. If only he could lift just one finger he might be able to do it, might be able to give a sign. He agonized in vain; there was no way.

Borbála tended to him faithfully, asserting to the very end that she could converse with her husband and divine his desires from the fluttering of his eyelids. But Bálint Sternovszky did not recover precisely because he no longer desired anything.

III

NO END IN SIGHT TO THE TEEMING RAINS. THE pastures lie deep under water. On higher ground the mud is ankle-deep, in places knee-high. Just when all hope of summer seems gone, it bursts of a sudden upon the land, swelling the corn and nourishing the plants. As the sodden terrain dries out, the crusting mud crumbles to a yellowish dust that covers every surface, fills every crack. As if afraid to be left behind, the corn ripens fast to a rich golden hue. Natterjack toads and gorged grasshoppers inform their kind that they have had their fill. The sudden wave of heat cuts a swathe through the stock; the bloated bodies of sheep and swine putresce in the acrid air.

The windows of the county assembly stand wide open. Both within and without, the dog days of June have brought everything to a standstill. The languorous members were not even inclined to indulge in the amorous trifling that was a regular feature of life in this building at other times. The exchanges were fuelled by little more than a general exasperation at having to rot here in the chamber. They were debating the proposals from the county administrator, alispán Sándor Vajda, regarding the repeal of legislation passed in the course of the reign of His Majesty Joseph II. The alispán blinked in disappointment at the complete absence of the noisy glee that might have been expected to welcome this topic. What a contrast with the clamorous reception accorded these laws when originally promulgated! It was the monarch himself who had now withdrawn them from his deathbed. A cause for celebration, one might think, for the repeal of the Habsburg legislation imposed upon us means we can return to our ancestral ways. The alispán's proposals began with a preamble in convoluted language which urged us to take the action that all the other counties had taken already. He went on to list the decisions that had to be taken by means of a vote of the members of the assembly.

To the high lords of the estates and others with privileged status the laws entitling them to the exercise of the power of life or death over evildoers under the terms of the ius gladii: be it known that this power is again restored to them, likewise the right to hold their manorial court, in accordance with the exercise of their rights and privileges of old.

The numbers painted by order upon the walls of houses shall everywhere be removed, likewise there shall be dug up the signs that mark and note the number and name of every village, and the measuring sticks inserted in every field in the land.

Furthermore, to ensure that those manipulators of the measurements of the land, meaning thereby those of foreign nationality and not of the nobility, shall no longer be able to enforce payment of taxes, nor in any other wise mislead the people, such manipulators of the land are hereby given notice to leave this noble county within the eight days next, whereafter if they should be found therein, those suitable for the purpose shall be obliged to enlist in the army, while those unsuitable shall be expelled forthwith from the territory of the noble county.

In all the business of the noble county and in all correspondence the German language that has been imposed upon it shall cease to be in use but in its stead the Latin tongue, neglected of late years but formerly in traditional use, shall be reinstated.

In the schools known as normal schools the syllabus lately instituted shall be abolished and the youth of the noble county shall be taught not in the German language, but in the former Hungarian tongue that was established of old.

The assembly was slow to stir, with only a few rumbles of '*Vivat!*' There were hardly any objections and voting took place in virtual silence. Only the abolition of the house numbers managed to raise some whoops of approval. István Stern added his voice to the chorus with a degree of reluctance, the words of his former father-in-law still ringing in his ears: 'High time His Majesty Joseph II set about cleaning these Augean stables we call Hungary.' In any case, the turret had received the number '111', which warmed István Stern's heart. Thrice a first, and a palindrome to boot.

The section decrying the manipulators was greeted with thunderous applause. Everyone hated the arrogant officials imported from outside by the powers that be and with little or no Hungarian, who hammered shoddy little stakes into the ground, resolving at a blow decades-old boundary disputes, and demarcated the boundaries of fields, meadows and even the manors without so much as a by-your-leave. Even with these István Stern had no quarrel – the boundaries of his lands had already been marked off with stakes which, after mooting a few measurements here and there, the three assessors decided to confirm. The abandonment of the German tongue received an even greater ovation from the assembly. A number of the older nobles proceeded to make mock of the way German had come to dominate in every sphere, and one, Ádám Geleji Katona, even demonstrated how his guard dog now barked in German.

Speaker Sándor Vajda had trouble keeping order in the boisterous assembly as he declared the proposals approved in toto. He ordered a break for luncheon, which provoked some booing, as the members had no intention of spending the afternoon in the house and every determination to dine on the more substantial fare awaiting them at home.

'What work is there left to be done?' queried Ádám Geleji Katona.

The alispán read out the agenda. Mihály Baróti, a teacher of Latin at the town school, petitions for relief from his taxes, as he is unable to survive on his salary. The chief constable's report on the current state of the legal dispute between the lessee of the abbey and the county. Pál Hamburger's petition, claiming that the Emperor in Vienna had personally allowed him to freely carry on the trade or calling of tapster. A review and possible adjustment of the tithe. A number of appeals from prisoners in the county jail. And so on and so forth.

Amid mutterings the members reluctantly agreed to send word home that they should not be expected for lunch. In groups of various sizes they ambled over to the Fényes taprooms on the far side of the square. István Stern preferred to rest his bones on one of the blue benches in the courtyard of the council building. What weather! I'm melting, he thought, wiping his face, crab-red in the heat. In recent years he had found it harder to take his breath. He loosened his collar.

One of the town attendants turned into the courtyard, carrying folded papers in a wooden basket, and dropped them on the ground.

'What's he up to?' wondered István Stern – he could see that these were official documents. By the time he realized what was happening, the man had put another pile on top of the first. He wondered whether to shout at him; by then the third batch had arrived. The attendant was bringing them from the archive. 'I say!'

'At your command, sir,' said the man.

'What might be your business with those papers?'

'They have to be burned.'

'*What?*'

'The alispán's orders, sir.'

'That cannot be true!'

'It certainly is!' came the words of Sándor Vajda, leaning out of a window.

'Why do they have to be burned?'

'These are the papers relating to the original orders of His Majesty Joseph II.'

'Books and papers should never be thrown in the fire . . . you never know when they might be needed.'

'Get along with you! Just carry on, János!' Sándor Vajda reassured the attendant, who had stopped in his tracks.

'Don't!' István Stern hurried over and prevented the man from emptying his basket again.

'István, why poke your nose into this?'

'Books and papers should never be thrown in the fire,' he repeated obdurately. To the man he commanded: 'Pick them up!'

The man was young but already balding, with an enormous Adam's apple, which now slid down his neck and disappeared below the collar of his embroidered shirt. He looked at the alispán questioningly. Sándor Vajda came out into the courtyard, took the basket and emptied the documents, followed by the contents of his smoking pipe, straight onto the heap. The dry sheets immediately caught fire. Enraged, István Stern tried to stamp out the fire and kick the documents away. The alispán took him by the arm and dragged him off: 'Come now, don't make such a fool of yourself, Stern!'

Stern pulled himself free and again tried to put the fire out, but most of the sheets were now well and truly ablaze, giving off acrid fumes.

'Books and papers should never be thrown in the fire!' István Stern roared for a third time, kicking clear of the embers the few sheets that could still be saved.

The Smorakh family had moved from Lemberg to Prague and then again to Vienna in the hope of improving their lot. They reached the imperial capital just as Queen Maria Theresa was giving expression to her convictions about their kind in a phrase that was to be widely repeated throughout her lands: 'The Jews are worse than the bubonic plague.'

Though she made this declaration in German, they understood it perfectly; there had always been at least three languages spoken in the family. The Queen's was no empty phrase: with strictly enforced edicts she banned Jews from Vienna and Prague. The Smorakhs reached Posonium, the Queen's Pressburg and the Hungarians' Pozsony, on the back of a cart, in the hope of establishing themselves in the furniture business there, but they were not granted the necessary permit by the council. They loaded up again and went south, as Aaron Smorakh, the head of the family at the time, put it: 'on the highway of hardships'. Their wanderings around the heart of Europe, punctuated by frequent stops, lasted some eight years. During these they suffered many hardships and disasters, of which the most painful was the death of Elisha, Aaron Smorakh's wife, mourned by her husband, her mother, her three daughters Helga, Eszter and Éva, and her two sons Jacob and Joseph. In these eight miserable years Aaron Smorakh tried desperately to keep the

family together by making what he could by trading. Asked
what was his occupation, he would say with a crestfallen
smile: 'I buy and I sell!'

It was the autumn of their eighth year when they came to
Hegyhát. The lord of the manor here in the Tokay region
was looking for someone to take over his village general
store, following the death of the previous leaseholder,
Ármin Kertész, who had ingested poisonous toadstools. The
contract was held by the Smorakh family in great respect
and a gilt frame, which in the stone house they subse-
quently built for themselves had pride of place above the
mantelpiece. Every member of the family knew its words
by heart, like a poem.

On the sixteenth day of January in the year of our Lord
1759 the general store of the lord of the manor in
Hegyhát is hereby leased to the Jew Aaron Smorakh in
accordance with the points of the contract agreed as
stated hereunder.

1mo. The said Jew will stock in the general store all kinds
of goods, iron and other necessities, to ensure that as and
when the lord of the manor desires to purchase tools,
equipment, or other goods for husbandry, they will not be
wanting in the general store, and also so that the poor
should not be obliged to walk long distances for every
small thing.

2do. It will be permitted to the said Jew to trade in and
sell salt, tobacco, candles, pipes and other such small
necessities.

3tio. If the lord of the manor himself or his officers or ser-
vants have need of some particular item and that item is
wanting in his general store, the said Jew will be bound to
obtain it and offer it for sale at a price that is meet.

4to. Under the terms of this contract the Jew shall pay the
sum of one hundred Rhenish florins by way of rent every

year, and shall according to custom pay it in two parts, one part every six months.

5to. The said Jew shall be obliged to keep to the terms of this contract to the letter and if he should be disinclined so to do, it will be permitted to his lordship in person to take such steps concerning the general store as he deems necessary. Provided only that the terms of the contract are duly observed in peace, and that he behaves as behoves an honourable man, his lordship will provide him with due care and protection and will not permit any party to harass him unjustly. This contract will have force for a period of two years and if in the second year the Jew should be minded to extend it or surrender it to his lordship, he will be required to give three months' notice thereof.

Stamped and dated in the year of our Lord stated above, on the day of the month and in the place there stated.

Bertalan T. Vámbéry

Aaron Smorakh was thirty-two years of age when he signed this contract, his hair already white, his face furrowed and worn. He knew that for their rapid change of fortune his family owed particular thanks to two powerful men who wished them well, namely Bertalan T. Vámbéry and His Majesty King Joseph II, who only a year after his intolerant mother's death ordered that the Jews were to have the status of a 'tolerated minority', as they were 'in this wise more useful to the state'. Aaron Smorakh even adopted as his own the favourite saying of the only uncrowned king of Hungary: '*Es geht, wenn man's nimmt!*', 'it goes – if you take it.'

His Majesty Joseph II had ten years earlier, while still co-ruler with Maria Theresa, determined that the Jews choose 'proper' surnames. To this end they were to appear in the offices established with the aim of noting down the date of birth or death of every single subject of the Empire. Since the official language was German, it was expected that the Jews would choose German names. As a dutiful citizen, Aaron Smorakh duly rode into the town of Eger to find a new name for his family. His first act was to place two jeroboams across the ink-spattered desk (the family had by then obtained permission to cultivate a vineyard on a sharecropping basis), and then he asked the bespectacled official: '*Wie heissen Sie, Herr . . . ?*'

'*Wilhelm Stern,*' came the reply from the surprised official.

Aaron Smorakh drew himself up to his full height and announced solemnly: '*Dann wird Stern unser Name sein.*'

'*Sind Sie sicher?*'

'*Ja, ja.*'

'*Also, Stern?*'

'*Gut.*'

Aaron Stern jiggled and jolted his way home to Hegyhát, with the deed poll in his saddlebag. Up went the new shop sign without any more ado: *Stern and Son.* Jacob, his firstborn, was already his right hand in the store.

Éva, now of marriageable age, these days often busied herself with her trousseau, assisted by two servant girls. Aaron Stern had laid by a crate of special, sparkling wine from the region of Champagne for the wedding feast. She had a dozen or more suitors vying for her hand in the next few years, but found none to her liking. By her age her older sisters had long tied the knot. Aaron Stern was more and more concerned: 'You are certain? Not this one either?'

Éva would give a nod. She trusted that her father would have as much patience as she to wait for The One.

She met István Sternovszky in the burgh of Debreczen, whither she had gone with her father to buy supplies. A harvest ball was being held in the grand hall of the hotel. Aaron Stern was so pleased with the advantageous terms on which he had secured his purchases that he surprised his daughter with an evening gown decorated around the neck with the most delicate Brussels lace. The event was patronized chiefly by the nobility of the area, the only outsiders apart from the Sterns being the debonair Sternovszky boys, magnets for the fan-shielded eyes of every girl's mother. István and János stood a head taller than the mass. Their glances kept returning to Éva, whose coal-black curls bounced and fluttered like dark little birds around her ivory shoulders. They both put themselves down on Éva's dance card. Though they spent the same amount of time in the girl's company, it was clear from the outset that István's intentions were of the utmost seriousness. The Sternovszky boys were on a two-month tour of the kingdom, thanks to their uncle's generosity. A few days later István abandoned the tour to ride to Hegyhát to see Éva again, leaving his younger brother in the hostel at Csaroda. Unable to see her, amid the utmost secrecy he sent her three brief letters. He received but one reply: 'The road to me leads through my father.' The higher the wall, the harder it is to conquer, thought István Sternovszky, his ardour only further inflamed by the delicate pearly script of her dear hand.

Éva forbore to inform him that she had told her father: István Sternovszky is the one. Aaron Stern flew into a rage, his white hair billowing as he stormed: 'Have you taken leave of your senses? The Sternovszkys of all people . . . Does that man have any idea who we are?'

'He does, rest assured, father dear.'

'Do you think his family will let him take a Jewish girl to the altar? How on earth could anyone imagine that?'

'Let that be his business.'

For more than a week István Sternovszky delayed making the announcement. His mother had a weak heart, he knew that if he now said his piece, it might be the end of her. Borbála no longer resembled the girl she had once been: in recent years she had put on a deal of weight, so much so that she was now out of breath after taking just a few steps, wheezing as if she had run halfway round the town. The doctor had put her on a strict diet that she only pretended to keep. Sometimes she would even slip out in the dead of night to feast on something from the larder.

When István Sternovszky finally steeled himself to speak to his mother, Borbála was lying in the deckchair, her feet raised off the floor, digesting her modest breakfast which consisted merely of a bacon omelette, a jug of cream, two green peppers, a cup of Turkish coffee, and a few prunes that did not really form part of the meal but were taken, rather, for the benefit of her digestion. Hearing that her son wished to speak to her, she closed her eyes in weary anticipation of news of further debts amassed by István at the card table. 'How much this time?'

Her son's attempt to explain that this was about something else, that he wanted to marry, made simply no sense to Borbála. 'Who is this Éva?'

'The girl I want to marry.'

'You?'

'Yes, Mother, me, not the Pope!'

'But you are still a child.'

'I'm in my twenty-third year.'

'Yes, but even so . . . just like that? From one day to the next?'

István Sternovszky patiently explained that such things always happen from one day to the next, and sought his mother's blessing on the union. He did not receive it. Borbála insisted first of all on knowing who this girl was, where she came from, what was known of her family, and how much dowry came with her. István Sternovszky considered the dialogue increasingly irrelevant. 'I had hoped you would rejoice at the news.'

'Rejoice at what? That you have been ensnared by a grasping woman?'

'I am the one who is ensnaring her!' he spluttered, gritting his teeth, knowing that the worst – Éva's origins – was yet to come. He began a dozen times to say that his betrothed was Jewish, but the words stuck in his throat. For him the word 'Jew' was a sharp knife twisted in his spine, though he himself knew only one Jew, old Kochán, the village grocer, who would give credit to anyone who asked. But he had no doubt that the darkest of evil fates dogged Éva's ancestors and all her family, which he must perforce share if he really were to marry the girl.

'But why this Éva, of whom we know virtually nothing?'

'Because she is my twin, born to other parents.'

'Why would you want to marry her if she is already your twin?'

'Mother, I beg you!'

It did not take long for Borbála to unearth the location and origins of the Stern family. She declared, tearing at her hair, that she would not under any circumstances acquire them as kin. By then István Sternovszky had made several visits to Hegyhát and had decided beyond a shadow of doubt that he could not find happiness except by the side of Éva Stern. He regarded it as a sign from heaven that the beginning of his surname was the same as that of Éva's. The situation at home had deteriorated to such an extent that he and Borbála were no longer on speaking terms and communicated only via his brother. 'Tell him, János, that dinner will be served shortly!'

István Sternovszky saw that things could not go on like this. One night, when the turret's inhabitants were fast asleep, he and his servant, the lanky Jóska, quietly carried down the two chests and six large leather bags in which he had packed all of his belongings. Into his calfskin satchel he placed everything that he wanted to preserve in case of disaster – as much money as he could, a few family mementoes, and above all his father's and grandfather's folio, to which he gave the title The Book of Fathers. He considered that this was certainly his property.

Below the oxcart waited, with his dapple-grey, as he had ordered. He sat Jóska up by the driver, and they set off into an ominous night. By dawn next day they had reached Hegyhát and lodged themselves in the guest cottage that stood in the garden of the house, amid the raspberry bushes. Her husband-to-be could hardly take rooms at the hostel, for all to see. He unpacked, sent the cart back, and sent Jóska to fetch pen and paper. As soon as these were brought, he opened The Book of Fathers and in it inscribed these words:

> *The course of my life has taken a new turn. Leaving behind the parental home, the famed five-pointed turret, perhaps for ever, in order to find here, in the hilly country, a wife and happiness. Though I am not without fears, I am bold enough to put them to one side, as I believe the Almighty guards my steps. Omnis dies, omnis hora, quam nihil simus ostendit.*

Aaron Stern sent word to Borbála, assuring her that her son was hale and hearty. 'I am humbly at your disposal!' he added at the foot of the letter. The reply was addressed not to him but to István Sternovszky. 'Return at once or I shall disinherit you!' Whereupon he replied: 'Let your will be done!' and stayed. Chaperoned by Aaron Stern, he was able briefly to meet Éva every evening. They exchanged awkward, hesitant words. Once Éva spoke of her mother, whom she had lost at an early age. István Sternovszky nodded: 'Yes . . . tuberculosis.'

The girl's jaw fell. 'Have you been making inquiries about our family?'

'Suffice it to say that I know.'

Or Aaron Stern would reminisce about their long years on the road and the difficult times in Vienna and Prague.

'On the highway of hardships,' added István Sternovszky.

'Where did you hear that?'

'I . . . well . . . you won't believe this . . . but sometimes I can see into the past.'

Aaron Stern bombarded him with questions about their history and every answer proved absolutely right. As if the young man had had them investigated by the secret police. Aaron Stern scratched his head. 'Would you mind if I took you to see our Rabbi?'

'Not in the least.'

Rabbi Ben Loew had arrived from Prague a year and a half earlier. His destination was Odessa, but he had not taken the most direct route. He lodged for a few nights at the Sonntag hostel, in the bend of the stream. He asked after his co-religionists in somewhat broken Hungarian – with soft *h*s behind his *t*-sounds. He was pointed in the direction of Hegyhát. There the first house he knocked at happened to be the Sterns'. He was made to feel very much at home and asked to stay for the meal. The Rabbi, however, wanted to see only the local house of Jewish prayer and was much astonished to learn from Aaron Stern that there was not one in this neck of the woods.

'No-o? Then where do our people gather for Shabbos?'

'Well . . . here, in the garden.' Aaron Stern was reluctant to admit that they did not gather at all. The Jews here are just glad they have a hole in their arse and can work hard; they have no wish to antagonize the nobility by building a synagogue.

Rabbi Ben Loew could read between his lines. 'I tell you there is synagogue here. Today.'

'How do you mean?'

'We shall build one, all of us together. Just meet me all of you this afternoon, by the bank of the stream.'

The Sterns alerted their friends and acquaintances. As they reached the site, Rabbi Ben Loew was already stripping the eight acacias he had felled with a handsaw and tying their ends together. The eight-cornered shape thus obtained had then to be covered with wattle and daub. Only above the ark of the covenant did they hammer together a roof when – as Rabbi Ben Loew's generous gift – the ark was unloaded from his cart and put in its place. Later the members of the community raised the building a little higher and added a layer of thatch.

The service that first night was somewhat protracted, as the congregation's grasp of the Hebrew language and ritual was rather uncertain. Rabbi Ben Loew was tense and tore at his beard: 'Not ever I have seen such a thing! You are not knowing anything!'

'Don't screech! Teach!' hissed Aaron Stern.

And so it came to pass that the Rabbi stayed longer than planned on the banks of the Hegyhát stream, where his congregation soon built him a house so that he would always remain there. News of his wisdom spread rapidly, and Jews from far afield came to him for advice, for teaching, or even simply to touch the fringes of his caftan, which was widely thought to ensure a life of plenty. It became the custom for couples about to wed to make his house their first port of call before the wedding ceremony. The nobility of the county tried more than once to have the synagogue closed down and to withdraw the right of assembly, but the Rabbi managed to frustrate their plans every time, by persuasion or guile or courage. Nor was it a disadvantage that one of the two landowners in the area, Baroness Sigray, took the Jews under her wing: 'What harm does it do to anyone if the Jews praise their god? Especially if they make such excellent wine!'

Rabbi Ben Loew was able to continue to preach his faith unmolested.

Aaron Stern knew that he would not find it easy to gain access to the Rabbi's person; the queue wound its way from the garden all the way down to the willows on the bank. Aaron Stern had helped to build the Rabbi's house and knew the layout well: he led István Sternovszky directly to the back door. He made as if he were heading for the tiny servant hut but at the last minute veered right into the kitchen of the big house. István Sternovszky followed him hesitantly. In the kitchen the Rabbi's Polish servant Igor was making coffee on the stove. He shook his head, but motioned with his eyes that Aaron Stern should go ahead. Inside the Rabbi had just completed a session with his visitor, a small, plump, doddery old fellow.

'I don't understand either,' whispered Aaron Stern. 'It's Yiddish.'

István Sternovszky nodded; in his excitement he had not even noticed that they were speaking another tongue. As soon as the old man bowed and left, Rabbi Ben Loew offered them a seat. Turning his face towards Aaron Stern, he asked: 'And what can I do for you?'

'Rabbi, this young man can see into the caverns of the past; he knows things that he cannot have learnt from us, either in whole or in part. I would be glad to know what you think of him.'

Rabbi Ben Loew looked István Sternovszky up and down with great thoroughness. Finally he said: 'Is it as Mr Stern said?'

'In essence, yes.'

'Well then, tell me how I came to live in this part of the world.'

'I would not know. I can only see the past of those who are close to me.'

Rabbi Ben Loew looked even more closely at the young man. István Sternovszky stood his ground unblinkingly. The Rabbi gave a nod. 'That's fair enough. And are the Sterns close enough to you?'

'As close as can be, almost.'

'Would you be aware of a contract that they might hold particularly dear?'

István Sternovszky nodded and began to recite: '*On the sixteenth day of January in the year of our Lord 1759 the general store of the lord of the manor in Hegyhát is hereby leased to the Jew Aaron Smorakh in accordance with the points of the contract agreed as stated hereunder—*'

'*Stimmt!* Word-perfect!' said Aaron Stern.

'Right.' This interpellation disturbed Rabbi Ben Loew. He placed a hand on Aaron Stern's shoulder. 'It does not matter if there are those who know more than you do about your past. There is no cause for concern. You may believe this fine young man. But do not shout it from the housetops that he has such extraordinary powers.' With these words and a determined shake of their hands he bade them farewell. They were outside the house when he called after them: 'Next time you have a question for me, use the main entrance and wait your turn.'

'Yes, Rabbi,' said Aaron Stern bowing low from the waist. Arm in arm with István Sternovszky they walked home. 'A real wonder rabbi,' he said in a low voice.

It was thus decided that István Sternovszky could marry into the family. But the negotiations concerning which house of God was to be the venue took a great deal longer. Aaron Stern insisted on the synagogue, but István Sternovszky was Calvinist and wished to employ the rites of his faith; moreover, he intended that his future offspring also be brought up in that faith and therefore sought from his intended as part of their nuptial vows the usual *reversalis* to this effect. While Éva was inclined to sign a reversalis, her father threatened to disinherit her if she did.

'Now that truly is excellent,' István Sternovszky exclaimed. 'This wedding will mean that both families disown us.' He had not seen or heard from his mother and younger brother since he had taken himself off to Hegyhát.

They might have argued for years if the Calvinist minister of Tokay had not declared that not for all the gold in the Erzgebirge would he marry a Jewish girl to such a fine upstanding Christian as István Sternovszky.

'All right, reverend sir, you will not have to do any such thing!' István Sternovszky said, leaving the minister standing. He galloped back to Hegyhát. Bursting in once again through the back door on Rabbi Ben Loew, who was in the middle of his evening meal, a batiste napkin tucked under his chin, he exclaimed: 'Rabbi, how can you make me a Jew?'

'This second? Or can you wait until I have taken my dinner?'

István Sternovszky was covered with embarrassment and began to back away, but the Rabbi cordially invited him to join him and share his stuffed neck of goose. By the time they had consumed the delicacy, they had agreed on how István Sternovszky might join the Jewish community of Hegyhát. For half a year he visited the Rabbi's house three times a week to learn all that a good Jew must know. Of course, Ben Loew explained, he could not become a Jew in the eyes of the secular world, but the law was not everything.

The house on the hillside that was Aaron Stern's gift to the young couple was readied in time for the wedding. In the garden of this building, furnished with every comfort, there was not only a pavilion suitable for concerts and other entertainments, as well as a fountain, but also a comfortable bathhouse. István Sternovszky's eyes clouded over with tears when his father-in-law conducted them and the wedding party on a tour of their new residence – he had managed somehow to keep the building works secret from the couple. István Sternovszky could not think what he might offer in exchange. In a voice trembling with emotion he declared: 'From today in your honour I shall shorten my name to Stern!'

This declaration was applauded by all the relatives present (all the Sterns, that is, since no one came from the family of the groom).

In the mornings István Stern always bade his wife farewell with the words: 'Have a happy day, my darling!'

Éva planted a rose bower in the garden, and along the fence bushes of lavender. Their tickling fragrance penetrated the whole house and there was always a bunch or two in the vases on the table. István Stern put great effort into his work selling the white and red wines of his father-in-law. He managed to secure markets for them in places so far away that the Stern family had not even heard of them. He was masterly at talking the tradesmen into contracts, and when they had signed on the dotted line and drunk on it, they often remarked: 'Huh! Never get involved with a Jew!' István Stern pretended not to hear such talk.

Once, as a substantial shipment was setting off for Lemberg, Aaron Stern shook his head incredulously: 'How in the name of all that's holy can this be? They hounded our people out of there and now they'll pay a good price for our wine? It's a crazy world we're living in!'

István Stern was inordinately proud of the fact that the family wine business had prospered since he made himself useful in it. He wrote only one letter to his mother, most of it on this topic.

I have not, with the greatest respect, fulfilled my dear mother's words of ill-omen, that I shall be a masterless man and will beg on bended knee to be taken back at home. With the work of my own two hands I have provided for my family. I hope that your anger will in time lessen and that you will kindly visit us. If my good fortune should hold, I expect that by then there will be three of us at least to welcome you.

After Lemberg it was the turn of palates in Tarnopol, Odessa and Vitebsk to make the acquaintance of the Stern brand. In earlier times it had been difficult to carry wine of quality such distances, or only in barrels. István Stern had special crates made with thin wooden laths separating the 24 bottles and holding them secure. The crate lids had a huge S, for Stern, burnt into them with an iron like those used for branding animals. To István Stern this was a glittering snake which haunted his dreams.

At the end of their first year of marriage Éva found herself with child. The birth was difficult and protracted, with the midwife as concerned for the life of the mother as for that of the child.

István Stern recorded the birth of his offspring in The Book of Fathers as elsewhere they might in the family Bible.

Our Richard was born on the seventh day of July in the year 1775, one month earlier than expected. He was very small at birth but proved to be a good child; even as an infant he cried only when racked by pain. His small body was well-proportioned and flawless, like a statue. His only weakness, perhaps, is his eyes, which were prescribed eye-glasses by Dr Rákosfalvy as early as primary school . . .

Our Robert was born on the last day of the year 1777, much more easily than we had feared. My Éva is in bursting good health . . .

Our little Rudolf was born on the twenty-third day of March in the year 1779. Like Robert he perhaps takes more after me, at least with regard to build. My wife Éva had a particularly painful time with him. After the birth she recovered the slender figure that she had when I came to know her at the Debreczen ball. Those who do not know often take her for our sons' older

103

sister. I wish everyone the enormous joy that it has been my good
fortune to share. Truly, my cup runneth not over only because I
have not secured my mother's forgiveness, and would dearly like
to see her and my younger brother. I think of them often. I
wonder if they ever miss me.

Twice István Stern rode over to the five-pointed turret,
fondly imagining that he might simply knock on the door, but
he shrank back each time, fearing Borbála would order him to
leave. Around the turret lily-of-the-valley had burgeoned
wildly. This caused him a special kind of pain.

On Friday afternoons the extended family would gather
in Grandfather Aaron's house, spending the evening and the
following day together and passing Shabbos free of work, as
prescribed. The three girls – all married by now – took turns
to bring dinner in pans, jugs and dishes whose number
increased with the size of the tribe. The food was laid on
the table and the candles were lit early in the afternoon, so
that when they returned from the synagogue of Ben Loew,
there would be nothing left for them to do. After dinner the
grandchildren would beg Uncle Aaron to tell them about
the old days. These tales had only one listener more attent-
ive than the children, and that was István Stern. He had
preserved in his memory many fragments of the past of the
Stern (Smorakh) family, whose meaning fell into place only
very gradually. Grandfather Aaron revelled in the telling of
the tales, with frequent digressions, and returning again and
again to certain details. He etched in vivid colours the
Smorakh home in Lemberg, which had burnt to the ground
when hotheaded scoundrels threw flaming torches onto the
half-tiled roof. This was a scene István Stern had seen many
times, but only later was he to discover why.

The children could not understand who those scoundrels
were and why their heads were hot.

'It was a pogrom,' said Aaron Stern.

'What's a pogrom?'

'It's when Jews are attacked for no rational reason. People can be very wicked.'

'What does rational mean?'

There was no answer to this. The room fell silent, only the crackling of the wood in the grate.

Éva grasped the shoulders of her older sons (the smallest had fallen asleep in her lap): 'Don't you worry, there will never be a pogrom here.'

After the children had gone to bed Grandfather Aaron told his sons-in-law how the family's library of books, collected over four generations, went up in flames in Lemberg's Haymarket. 'Two of the curs threw the books out of the window, the pages sizzling as they flew; another two made a bonfire and shovelled the knowledge of the world on to it, literature, holy scripture, everything. The paper quickly caught fire; the bindings burnt more slowly, giving off thick smoke, and the choking smell penetrated our clothes; we could smell it for days. Elise's mother herded everyone behind the house and took them over to the Market Place where a cart was waiting for us . . . Yes, that's how it was. I have never since felt like buying books, as my first thought is: what if the fire gets it . . . stupid notion.'

Indeed, Aaron Stern's house contained very little reading matter: his library consisted of yearbooks and almanacs. The Torah rolls that had been Rabbi Ben Loew's gift, he kept in a locked chest.

Though regularly invited, the Rabbi was not a frequent visitor to the Sterns' house. But he was a weekly institution at the István Stern household. The latter had never been called the Stern house: after the avenue of trees before it the house was always called the Chestnuts. The Rabbi's preference for István Stern was all the more curious because – in the words of Grandfather Stern – 'He isn't really a Jew, we just sort of took him in.'

In fact Aaron Stern was beginning to take offence at the Rabbi, who had, when all was said and done, him, Aaron, to thank for settling there, but preferred to give his attention to a person who had also him, Aaron, to thank for settling in Hegyhát. István Stern was aware of the tension and even mentioned it to the Rabbi, who replied: 'I am not in the debt of Aaron Stern, nor of any other local, just as they do not owe me anything either. We all of us owe thanks only to Him whom we cannot mention by name.'

Conversation flowed easily in the Chestnuts, at the ash table with wine bottles and peeled fruit, in the reed armchairs lined with soft lambskins. Rabbi Ben Loew told parables from the Talmud which István Stern, who still considered himself a tyro in matters of the history and traditions of his chosen people, was happy to make notes of in his head. In the company of the Rabbi he became unusually loquacious and found himself gabbling, as he had in his childhood. Often he would disrespectfully interrupt the Rabbi, of which he was much ashamed.

Not infrequently he would complain how hard it was to assimilate into their community. In the synagogue he was never sure whether he had to bow or stand and some of the Hebrew texts had never been explained to him, and he mouthed them without knowing what they meant. The long and short of it was that he still felt himself a stranger among the Jews.

'Everyone is a stranger in this world,' said the Rabbi. 'Above all the Jews. The pharaohs drove them from their ancient homeland, they dispersed to all points of the compass. They are to this day not allowed to buy land in many places. If, after all that, you have asked to join them, why should they not accept you?'

'Perhaps it's not their fault. Maybe I have no talent for something that you have to be born for.'

'And what might that be, that you have to be born for?

Look around: which Jew lives a life more Jewish than you? You do not have to tell me. Many of them eat forbidden meats, for example Aaron Stern does . . . they fail in kashrut, mixing milky and meaty plates and cutlery, they are strangers to the synagogue. It is not a very attractive thing, being Jewish, you may be assured of that.'

Another of their recurrent topics was István Stern's miraculous gift of memory. The Rabbi wanted to understand exactly how the past began to stream for him. Could it be induced or accelerated by any particular type of behaviour? Could he influence the periods that unreeled? István Stern could not supply satisfactory answers; all he could say with any confidence was that when he was agitated or excited, the images came more frequently and in greater numbers. If he was calm, say after a good meal, he could not even remember what he previously wrote in the Book of Fathers.

Rabbi Ben Loew asked to see the Book of the Fathers. He wanted to borrow it, but István Stern would not let him take it. 'Begging your pardon, but I don't want to be parted from it for a moment.'

'Understandable. May I look at it here, in your presence?'

'As long as you please.'

The more the Rabbi read, the more questions he asked. As if he were writing a history of the Sternovszky/Csillag family. István Stern readily responded to every query, thinking ruefully meanwhile that neither his dear mother nor his younger brother, nor even his good wife, had expressed so much interest in his forebears. Nor his own sons, though perhaps their interest would develop later; after all, even the oldest was just coming up to seven.

'My dear Stern, I wonder: have you ever tried to look ahead?'

'Ahead?'

'Into the future.'

István Stern stared at Rabbi Ben Loew in astonishment. After a while he said: 'That perspective is the privilege of Him whom we do not call by name.'

'Let me be the judge of that, and answer my question.'

'No, I have never looked into the future.'

'You cannot or you will not?'

'I would hardly dare to try.'

'Pity. What pain and suffering you could spare yourself and all your loved ones!'

This remark set István Stern thinking. That night, after the Rabbi had departed, he stayed on the veranda as darkness fell, watching the shadows lengthen along the avenue of chestnut trees and by the three small silver firs that he had planted when each of his sons was born. The chestnut trees had grown taller than the average man (not as tall as István himself), while the firs, like organpipes, were respectively only a few inches ahead of his Richard, Robert and Rudolf. How tall would the chestnuts be in ten years' time? Twice this height, perhaps. And the firs? We shall see. Hopefully . . .

Were he able to do what the Rabbi suggested, he could find out now what awaited him – awaited them all. The thought made him break out in a cold sweat. He recalled the Gypsy who had told his fortune in Tokay. The entire family had gone by cart to the fair and everybody got a souvenir. Richard got the little monkey that a large Gypsy family was exhibiting for a fee; it was no bigger than a medium-sized hare. Aaron Stern thought it must be a baby monkey, but the Gypsies swore it was twelve years old and called it Aster. After this, only the haggling separated Richard and the frightened little creature, which had now settled on his shoulder and clung to him like a baby to the breast. Aaron Stern gave up the haggling more than once, but each time István Stern resumed it and in the end it was he who paid. He was ashamed to admit that he was taken with the little monkey perhaps even more than was his son. From that night onwards, despite his mother's protestations, he slept with the little creature in his bed, cuddling and kissing it constantly through the day, calling it Aszti, my little Aszti.

The oldest female member of the Gypsy family, a vast rotund creature dressed in red silk from top to toe, inhabited the darkness of the tent and would read one's fortune from one's palm, using cards, or her glass ball. To general surprise Aaron Stern paid for all the male members of the family to have their fortunes told. István Stern was the last to reach the fortune-teller's table, which was host to a lazy black cat curled around the iron base of the magic ball.

'What's it made of?' asked István Stern, thinking of the mysteriously shining ball.

'Just show me your palm!' said the Gypsy, grasping his hand and drawing the palm into the pool of light under the oil-lamp suspended close to her head. For a long time she studied the various lines and grooves, touching here, prodding there. István Stern thought her stocky fingers were sticky and wanted to draw back his hand, but the fortune-teller would not let it go. 'I see great fires,' she declared at length with some solemnity.

'What sort of fires?'

'Blazing fires, flames as tall as a human being.'

'What is ablaze? Stubble? Logs of wood? Or a roof?'

'Snow-white, square birds tumble into the flames, burning to death.'

István Stern could extract nothing more from the Gypsy. Later he asked his father-in-law: 'What can it mean?'

'Nothing good.'

'I still don't understand it.'

Aaron Stern grimaced: 'And for this I paid good money!'

István Stern imagined the scene a hundred times. He saw the snow-white birds as doves; it was his own house that had burst into flame, the wings would be trying to extinguish the fire – that's why they dive onto it in suicidal frenzy, the smoke darkens the tapestry of the heavens. But he kept coming up against one thing: who has ever seen a rectangular dove?'

One summer night, when a seasonal storm burst over the house with ear-splitting rolls of thunder and heavy rain, the past was again summoned up in István Stern's mind and when he had again lived through what he had lived through so many times before, the Rabbi's question occurred to him, as well as the Gypsy's prophecy. Now, he thought, now or never! Eyes shut, he waited for the superhuman powers to launch in him the visions, this time the visions of the unknown regions of tomorrow. As his heartbeat accelerated, so it grew louder and began to shut out the roaring of the heavens. Then, then, oh, there came shreds of the first tableau, which eerily resembled the Gypsy's prophecy: vast flames leapt from somewhere and white blotches flew about, which perhaps resembled scraps of white lawn more than birds. But he had no chance to make them out properly. He could not even be sure that what he had been vouchsafed was indeed some tiny fragment of the future and not just images of the Gypsy's prophecy.

Rabbi Ben Loew hummed as he listened to István Stern's account, as if he both believed it and did not. 'Was that all?'

'That's all I saw.'

'Don't give up hope. Whoever gave you this will give you more, when the time comes.'

The profit from the vineyard that year was especially bountiful. The late summer heat had ripened the grapes to bursting and the mountain yielded a superlative nectar. Orders for István Stern's S-branded containers came pouring in from every quarter. Aaron Stern winked happily at his son-in-law: 'If it goes on like this, we might even get rich!'

With István Stern it was not only his family, but the entire Jewish community of Hegyhát that was extremely satisfied. He was a model husband, who gave his wife the respect and material security that was her due. A strict but warm-hearted father, for whom his sons would give their right arm if necessary. A generous patron of the poor in the whole region. An assiduous visitor to the synagogue. At the forefront of those who observe the law and maintain the customs. Intelligent, comfortably off, yet without putting on airs. There was little evidence that he was none the less . . . in actual fact . . . to put it bluntly: that he joined the community of his own free will. He was equally respected by the Calvinist tenant farmers: in matters viticultural he would be the first they turned to; his word was widely respected even when the issue was the taste of the wine. Some tenant farmers would cheat by sugaring their wine or even watering it: to deal with them the Wine Protection Union of Hegyhát and Tokay was formed, with Tivadar Frank as its president, after István Stern had categorically declined this high office – whereupon he was elected deputy president, by acclamation.

Éva Stern was proud of her husband and liked to say that she was the only woman who gained her own name on marriage for a second time. She admitted to only one weakness in respect of her husband's activities: his visits to the marital bed were not as frequent as she would have liked. This weakness she ascribed to her husband's excessive devotion to the successful business; he often came home late and it was commonplace for him not to join the family at dinner. Éva did not even suspect that it was not always overwork that kept István Stern from the bosom of his family. Not infrequently he spent his evenings in the house of a widow of substance whom he had encountered in the course of plying his trade, since from her late husband she had inherited one of the finest model vineyards of the Tokay region.

It was one of Éva's regular pleas to her husband that they should shed the daily yoke of labour and go somewhere where they could take their ease for a while. István Stern was not minded to have his bones shaken on the way to some far-off place. But slowly the whole family came round to Éva's view, and even Grandfather Aaron urged them to take a rest: 'Off with you! Years have passed without your taking a rest from your bottles!'

A suitable opportunity arose in the form of a warm invitation from Tadeus Weissberger, a merchant from Lemberg, for István Stern, together with his whole family, to visit him in his castle. 'We are but a quarter of an hour from the town, by the shores of the lake, you can swim, sail, enjoy the sun!' he said in his broken German, their common language since István Stern was not able to speak Yiddish.

There were extensive preparations before cart and carriage were filled with the five members of the Stern family, two coachmen, three footmen, a chambermaid, nine travel trunks, six bundles of clothing, three hatboxes, and the small monkey. Éva sat with her two younger sons in the direction of travel on the carriage couch; facing her sat István, Richard and his little Aszti. There was a footman by each of the coachmen up on the coach-box, the third had to squeeze onto the cart with the chambermaid, among the trunks which they had to constantly watch out for, in case they fell on top of them. The journey took four whole days, the nights spent at unmemorable lodgings.

Tadeus Weissberger received them in the garden of the T-shaped mansion, with a huge bouquet for Madame Éva. Agnieska Weissberger, the lady of the house, did her utmost to ensure that their guests from Hungary enjoyed themselves, her solicitousness going so far as to secure suitable aliment for little Aszti from the tsar's zoological gardens. The Weissbergers' six daughters – the youngest still in swaddling clouts, the oldest highly marriageable – attended to the Stern boys with very similar broad smiles, which did not however make the boys feel entirely comfortable, since they were unable to understand their kind and generous hosts.

'At least now you will appreciate how useful it is to speak other languages!' their father pointed out, though in truth even he sometimes had to guess what his hosts had to say. He determined that on their return he and his sons would all take lessons from Rabbi Ben Loew. It was Éva who proved the best conversationalist, as she had a smattering of Yiddish from Elisa, her adored mother, who had perished at one of the stations of the highway of hardships. Her earthly remains were later finally laid to rest in the Jewish cemetery at Hegyhát, thanks to Aaron Stern.

Tadeus Weissberger arranged some kind of amusement for every night of their stay. Either musicians filled the salon with dance music, or a round of cards would be organized for István Stern. Up to this time he had known only the games that could be played with Hungarian cards; here he learnt how to play the tarot, and proved exceptionally skilful at the game. After a substantial win Tadeus Weissberger would raise his glass and cry: '*Mazele!*'

His long-suppressed passion for playing cards came upon István Stern like a bucket of boiling water: he was on fire from the crown of his head to the soles of his feet. He revelled in getting the better of the others by adopting a wooden, expressionless face. He was much less taken with the notion of winning money. Perhaps, if he had not been so carried away by the game, he might have attended to what the local men were whispering about between the deals, and if he had, he would almost certainly have understood. In the streets of Lemberg young hooligans were looting the shops and coffee houses, throwing all the goods of the Jews out into the street, daubing the walls with the vilest slogans. The card-players' consensus was that it was not a good idea to make too much of these events. Such excesses by hot-headed youngsters were likely to wane as suddenly as they had waxed.

Tadeus Weissberger was in the minority. He could not understand how the gentlemen could be so sure of themselves. Once emotions have burst to the surface, no one is really safe. But to the question of what was to be done, he no more had a sensible reply than anyone else. Be prepared, then you won't be scared – that was his motto.

'Very well then, let us be scared,' said a voice. 'How does that improve matters?'

István Stern meanwhile shuffled the pack and dealt everyone a hand.

'It would be better if we packed and went home!' whispered Éva in his ear at the breakfast table the following morning.

'What's got into you? You were the one keen to travel!'

'I didn't imagine we would end up just where the goyim want to kill us.'

'Kill us?' spluttered István Stern, as if surfacing from under water.

Éva told him what she had heard from Agnieska. István Stern could feel his heart beating faster. Have these people gone mad? They destroy the property of others simply because they are of a different faith?

He went running off to Tadeus Weissberger. His host was in the smaller greenhouse, watering his plants. 'Why did you not tell me about this before, Weissberger?' he asked in his best German.

'But we talked of nothing else all evening!'

'Should we not start packing?'

'The vandals have never bothered us in this house . . . on the other hand, who knows what the morrow may bring?'

István Stern found himself on the horns of a dilemma. One part of him thought it ungallant to flee like a coward, another part of him felt a strong responsibility towards his family, so . . . The longer he thought about it, the less he knew what to do. If only Grandfather Aaron were here, or Rabbi Ben Loew.

That afternoon, of the gentlemen invited to play cards only one, Samuel Bratkow, managed to reach the card table. His clothing was torn and, as he explained it, torches had been flung at the roof of his house and his family had fled to Tarnopol. He was heading after them and would be glad to take anyone who wished to go. Tadeus Weissberger hurriedly ordered his daughters, wife and mother-in-law to take to the carriages. There were Weissbergers in Tarnopol who would look after them. He would follow as soon as he had taken care of the valuables. Alas, the carriage springs were dangerously overstretched and Samuel Bratkow begged their pardon for being unable to take all the ladies. Agnieska volunteered to lighten the load, as, with a little gentle prodding, did her mother. The carriage raced off, to the tearful cries of the Weissberger girls. István Stern at once offered his cart, which Tadeus Weissberger declined with the words: 'We have our own carriage; in fact, we have two.'

Éva wanted to be off at once, but István Stern first had everything quickly packed up, so it was half an hour before they were embracing their hosts, commending one another to the care of the Almighty. By then the Weissbergers were also ready, and the horses harnessed to the carriages were fairly pawing the ground in their impatience. Let us go while we can, thought Éva. They climbed into the carriage. István Stern lowered the lids of his bloodshot eyes.

The pounding of hoofs, from somewhere in the distance.

Stern was sure it would be Samuel Bratkow, coming back for something he had forgotten. But it was more than two score horsemen, wearing only animal pelts and skins, reminding István Stern of the original Magyars who rode into the Carpathian basin. In the carriage little Aszti gave a sharp little shriek and everyone realized that they were on the brink of catastrophe. The riders had reached them.

István Stern jumped down onto the carriage step and drew his sword, but in vain: he was the first to be speared through the neck by a lance and thrown under the carriage. The noise around him seemed to abate, the outlines of things became hazy. Before he finally lost consciousness he saw fire engulf the entrance of the house and there, falling from the first-floor windows, were the by now familiar white birds. Only later, on his sickbed, did he understand that for a fraction of a second he had witnessed the Weissberger family's justly famous collection of books being consumed by the flames.

Thinking that he was dead, the attackers let him be. Night had already fallen when he came to. Some local peasants provided him with shelter and care. Richard also turned up, wandering among the pine trees of the park, as was little Aszti, whose crazed screeches drove István Stern out of his wits, so that several times he took aim at the creature. Richard always protected it.

In a foreign land, without acquaintances and helping hands, lacking the language and money, István Stern was unable to discover where his wife's and two sons' final resting places – if they indeed had such – might be found. Grandfather Aaron lambasted him with hate-filled letters, cursing him for ever for not taking proper care of his daughter and two grandsons. Had Richard not been with him, István Stern would have thrust his dagger into his heart.

The Sterns never forgave him. Disowned first by one lot, then by the other.

In the end he took himself off with Richard and little Aszti and, abandoning his property at Hegyhát, asked permission to live in the five-pointed turret. The Sternovszkys tolerated their presence but never fully accepted them. No day passed but he toyed with the idea that he would end his days of suffering in this world. So burdened was he by the weight of his conscience that he was virtually bent double. In the years that remained to him he gave few signs of being alive. He passed his time mainly playing cards. His right hand played his left; they fought battles of life and death. He was unwilling to play with anyone else.

When the Sternovszky family's influence secured him a seat in the county assembly, he would sometimes attend the sessions, but he rarely made a speech. It was thus a surprise to all when he objected to the burning of the documents and papers relating to the abolition of the decrees of His Majesty Joseph II. It needed six people to hold him down, such was the passion this had ignited in him. He raved as he bellowed: 'Papers and books must not be thrown into the fire!'

They locked him in an office in the assembly building. As soon as the key turned creakily in the lock, István Stern calmed down and his face once again wore the indifferent expression it generally had. The guards who looked in through the peephole reported this to the alispán, who ordered him to be set free.

István Stern walked home. That night he wrote in the Book of Fathers: *Audi, vide, tace, si vis vivere in pace*. He kept his word in the Book, and died quietly a year later. There was no surprise in the turret: they were used to the heads of families saying little or nothing as they took their leave of this world.

IV

EVEN ON NORTH-FACING CLIFFS HITHERTO BARE, SIGNS
of life, ruffs of green. The fruit-trees' boughs sweep the
ground, so swollen are they with their crop. Few whoops or
cries from the fowl of the air; hens are busy brooding on the
nest. Water lilies carpet the surface of the lakes. The tillers
of the soil rejoice: there will be a rich harvest. Those short of
food and drink are spurned less often now by those who are
not. At times even in daylight an ever-waxing, ever more
yellow moon rises in the sky.

They will have their work cut out to gather in this harvest,
thought Richard Stern. He raised himself to the iron bars of
the cell and let himself dangle as long as his strength allowed,
in part by way of exercise, in part to see something of the
world outside. Ever since being brought here from Spielberg
he had prayed for a cell in the far corner of the tower, whence
he might observe the slope which, his cartographic studies
led him to deduce, would have a crescent shape.

Already, despite the distance, he was able to identify
some of the local farmers and their lads. When all's said and
done, better a cell giving onto a hill in the fortress at
Munkács, under the Carpathians, than any cell in that

Austrian eyrie, Kufstein; at least Munkács was in Hungary. The horrors they told of the hell of Kufstein! Inmates in irons day and night, no letters in or out, and up to six months without being allowed a turn in the yard. To cap it all, consumption was rife, scores took to the bare boards they had for beds, and the bodies were not released to the family but tossed into the moat in sacks with hardly a sprinkling of lime, let alone a decent spadeful of soil.

Richard Stern never expected a pardon; he thought he knew that the thread of his life, though it might be spun out for quite a long time, would finally be cut in the prison of the fortress of Munkács. So he could work only with what he had. Whenever his eyes could bear it, he spent his time writing; otherwise he hung from the window's iron bars and feasted them, so that he might take not the bleak cell but the world outside, the summer cavalcade of nature, with him to the bourn whence no earthly traveller returns. He knew in his bones that the heavenly ones would never admit him. As a child he had been brought up in the faith of the Jews, but nowadays he would strain his memory in vain for their word for 'devil' or 'salvation'. Did the Jews have devils and angels at all? It hardly matters now . . . It makes not a bean's worth of difference.

He let go of the iron bars and dropped down onto the rough-hewn stone floor; a twinge of pain shot through his kneecaps. The warmth of the month of July had brought little relief for his aching limbs. He could no longer bend his arms and legs without stabs of pain. It has not taken me long to wear them out, he thought. But that, too, hardly matters now; I expect them to perform little in the way of service to me. He sat down at the rough and splintery table which served two of the functions that mattered to him most: writing and eating. The third was met by the wooden bucket in the corner, whose ill-fitting lid ensured the constant companionship of noisome smells.

He opened the Book of Fathers, of which no more than thirteen folios remained blank. Richard Stern was an industrious diarist, filling more pages of the book by himself than all his ancestors combined. And this was despite his cells, especially the one in Spielberg, being severely deprived of light; sometimes he thought the goose-quill found its own way in the dark. He was given a single candle every other day and learnt how to be sparing with it.

Earlier in his life it had not occurred to him that he might himself write in the pages of the Book of Fathers, even though in his younger days he had turned to it more often than even the Bible.

'This is another of the sins of the Sterns: that you don't even go to the synagogue! Mark my words, the Creator will punish you for this!' came his grandmother's refrain; she would have preferred him to revert to Sternovszky as his surname.

Richard Stern was not in the least inclined to do this. 'Please, Grandma Borbála, spare me these reproaches and rest content with the first half of my name. I owe it to my poor brothers and my mother, and my father, too.'

'Leave your father out of this!' cackled Borbála, who had by this time come to resemble the witches of the fairytales. Her huge bulk could hardly be eased through a normal doorway. True enough, this was rarely required, for she would spend days on end in her round-backed armchair, specially made for her by the turret's overseer András, who was something of a jack-of-all-trades. Richard Stern loved his grandmother, little good though she did him. Whenever he had the chance, he asked her to sing. When Borbála fully unleashed her voice, the song would carry a long way indeed: *The way before me weeps, the trail before me grieves* . . . Richard Stern's eyes at once clouded with tears when his grandmother began to sing; all the songs she knew were melancholy ones and he, her grandson, was at such times

120

able quite clearly to conjure up the face of his late mother, which had otherwise quite faded. The images of Robert and Rudolf were lost even more deeply in the mists of time.

I have no need of fine words; I will have only words that are true!

With these words Richard Stern began his chapter in the Book of Fathers. He was especially prodigal in the period following his arrest, even in the temporary prison, while awaiting trial. He was fortunate to have it delivered to him at his request, with other books.

There being no looking-glass at my disposal, I am employing my fingers to examine my face for the ravages of time. Since I have been imprisoned I have not shaved off the hair of my face, which thus covers up the random scars left by the childhood pox, of which I was then, as now, very much ashamed. Because of it I was unwilling to show my face to others and always preferred the comfort afforded by solitude. The hair of my head is falling out in clumps and is now very thin. On my chest growth continues apace, even as, here and there, it is turning white.

When I was arrested I was still a young buck, but here one grows old more quickly, since there is little else to do. The angle of my nose is more pronounced, my brow is furrowed much like the rind of muscat melon. I am lanky in build, yet the little flesh that remains has none the less begun to droop, especially at my hips and also under my chin, where there has developed a dewlap resembling the collar of a cape, which I find so repulsive that several times a day I claw at it with my nails until I draw blood. Even less am I able to endure the two somewhat feminine little mounds that have developed on my chest, which, especially when I sit, fold themselves onto the upper half of my stomach. Compared with the proportions of my other parts, my hand is on the small side and my left thumb is missing, a victim of the

121

quack after our tragedy at Lemberg: he claimed that gangrene would have set in after the sword-cut and that, had he not removed root as well as branch, it might have cost me my hand, my arm, or even my life.

Whenever he thought of his lost thumb, he relived the pain of its loss; a more agonizing experience he had never endured, though his interrogators had tortured him mercilessly with prickings and brandings that pained him still and which perhaps his body would not get over until his dying day. At seven years of age, he had awakened to see two men armed to the teeth ripping off the carriage door. His mother was dragged away by her hair, shrieking; his brothers were sliced up with scimitars, his brother Robert's head flying off his body like a tossed ball and Rudolf's bloody guts spilling onto the carriage step and flooding Richard's only escape route. By then the other door of the carriage had opened and from that side a blade pierced his back even as it seemed also to strike his neck and left hand. In his final glint of consciousness he saw a series of images: a very familiar-looking young man, in irons, in a prison.

As he grew up, he gradually understood that provided he bore the suffering that accompanied his memories of the past, he would be given some taste of the future awaiting him. Once he divined that the young man was himself, he was certain there was no escaping the bitter fate of imprisonment. He was a student at the Sárospatak Collegium when his visions first gave him access to even more curious sights. He could see his own marriage feast, then his wedding night and the birth of his six children, all of them boys. If this prophecy was to be believed, his bride would be a lady who spoke an alien language, with skin the colour of honey, hair as black as night, and a triangular birthmark on her breastbone. Though fearful of his visions, yet he trusted them.

As a young man he resisted stubbornly all Borbála's aggressive efforts and machinations at matchmaking. He stood his ground at her litany of the most incredible dowries and socially most desirable matches and told his grandmother: 'You will see that there will come someone who is finer and more lovely; someone right for me.'

At the Sárospatak Collegium there were two subjects – geography and grammar – at which, in his teachers' opinion, he surpassed even the best of the students. He found that his extraordinary memory was particularly useful. By his third year at the college he had already mastered eight tongues. His favourite teacher, a Frenchman called de la Motte, urged him to try his fortune in the outside world. He wrote for him a letter of recommendation to Academician Carmillac, the distinguished French linguist at the University of Paris, who replied by return that if the Hungarian student had no more than half the talent that de la Motte claimed for him, he was assured of a place in his seminar. Thus did Richard reach the French capital despite the fulminations of Borbála.

'If you go, you must not count on our support!'

'I wouldn't dream of being a parasite.'

No question, I had no idea how I would keep myself in the city of Paris. Professor de la Motte strongly supported my visit and his parting words to me were: Dieu choisit le courageux! Or as we would say in Hungarian: Fortune favours the brave. I did not feel very brave however when I stood in front of the famous cathedral of Lutetia, Notre Dame, without a sou in my pocket. Fortune did favour me shortly, however, when I secured some students to tutor, three in Latin and two for Greek grammar.

Richard Stern – Risharre, as the French had it – continued his spectacular progress at the University of Paris and was able to join as early as the second term the comparative grammar seminars of Academician Carmillac. Carmillac, whose academic status at the university entitled him to be addressed as Maistre, was engaged in a project to demonstrate that the evolution of the French language was closely linked to the general condition of particular regions. He had selected three regions which he deemed most advanced from the point of view of handicrafts, agriculture and cultural matters; three which he thought the most underdeveloped in these respects; and a further three which he considered middling. His thesis was that those parts where the network of highways and travel is most advanced, where the wells and other buildings rise highest, where more people purchase newspapers and almanacs and admission to entertainments – these are likely to be the places where people's usage of the sacred French language, in the Maistre's view the eighth wonder of the world, will be the most cultivated. Richard Stern concurred, though he was able to make comparisons with only seven other languages, whereas Academician Carmillac could boast knowledge of fifteen, including such rare birds as Basque and Breton – the latter admittedly the Maistre's grandmother-tongue. The end of March found Richard Stern in the village of Francaroutier, at the foot of the Pyrenees. On the Maistre's lists, Francaroutier very much brought up the rear.

'Risharre, you will collect the data down there by yourself. Make sure you follow my instructions.'

Richard Stern had made himself a copy of the shorter catechism of Academician Carmillac: 77 numbered points. The size of four folios, he slipped this into the Book of Fathers, in consequence of which he was able to read it often even in the hard years of his imprisonment. In Munkács it prompted him to reflect thus:

124

What arrant nonsense! To imagine that where they dig more wells, the use of the past subjunctive is more subtle! Knowing what I do today it is well-nigh impossible to understand why I failed to point out that my Maistre's theory of comparison lacked any solid foundation! Doubtless the unquestioned respect I had for him prompted me to suppress my commonsensical view, fearing that my arguments would be crushed by the weight of his vast erudition and that I would be humiliated. The lesson is that one must speak up if one is convinced something is right, whatever the cost, because not standing by one's beliefs is also a defeat and the thought of it will gnaw as much thereafter.

In Francaroutier Richard Stern's careful budgeting had made it possible for him to employ two young men as clerks: one to note down random dialogues in the village market-place, the other to scour the notices in the village and in the inns and taverns and wherever else he found any writing, noting down both correct and incorrect examples of sentences, as instructed. They would have looked at the local newspaper, too, but in this case there was none. Richard Stern visited in turn the mayor, the notary, the doctor, the fire chief and other officials, putting to them the questions devised by Academician Carmillac. Of the answers he had to record only those that were outstandingly good or quite imperfect.

There being no hostelry in Francaroutier, he accepted the hospitality of the curé, who offered not only lodging but also evening meals, in return for suitable payment to the thickset woman who appeared to be his housekeeper. She lived on the far side of the church with her husband and three children and presumably had her hands full with her house, the vegetable garden and the chicken run, but seemed to spend a deal of her time, from a very early hour, around the rectory. Sometimes even late at night, when the scholar came home from his labours, he could hear the rapid gabble of the good lady, of which at first he could not pick out a single word. The curé enlightened him: 'Do not be concerned, Domine, this woman broke her jaw as a child, hence her distorted speech; one gets used to it after a time.'

During one of his endless reveries in the cell it dawned on him that the 'housekeeper' was no doubt the curé's lover. At that time it did not occur to him for a moment. He was a complete innocent in these matters. If during the humid nights he was troubled by wet dreams, he would keep a voluntary fast for several days, thinking that he might thus cleanse himself. Women he merely admired, always and incurably in hopes that he would come across that woman who spoke no Hungarian – honey-coloured skin, hair as dark as night, a triangular birthmark above her breastbone – and who would bring him the blessing of six boys. These were his dreams as he lay on the musty-smelling sack of straw on the guest-bed of the parish curé, tolerating *alta pace* the bites of the cockroaches (these sleep-preventing creatures were somewhat smaller than their Hungarian cousins, but all the more hungry for blood).

The inhabitants of Francaroutier looked forward with especially keen anticipation to the first Sunday after Easter, when there was traditionally an open-air entertainment, the biggest for many miles around, on the field in front of the Grotta. The Grotta was an opening into the depths of the cliff-face above the village. It was so narrow that a grown man could scarcely penetrate it if he crawled into it slowly – if he dared. In the dark crevices of the Grotta lurked evil spirits whose appeasement was secured at this time of the year by means of sacrifices, prayers conducted by the parish curé, and a torchlight procession followed by dancing until dawn. It was whispered that in the old days even newborn babes were sacrificed, but not even the oldest inhabitants could confirm this; these days a ram roasted but still blood-red would be cast in to the crack, with two round loaves, a few bottles of the local wine and fruit brandy, all crowned by wreaths of water lilies.

As the two assistants had categorically refused to work on the festival day, Richard Stern was at a loss as to what to do on this day of general jollity; he felt he had not been sent there to enjoy himself. But he was unlikely to find himself a sober companion to converse with. In the milling crowds of the fair, though, he was likely to hear turns of phrase not heard elsewhere. With his notebook in his satchel, goose-quills and inkpot secured to his belt, he set off behind the red-cheeked locals on their way to the Grotta. As he arrived in the field, the ball-throwing competition was well under way. Boys and young men in rolled-up sleeves stood by the white lime line drawn on the grass, to throw the iron balls as close as they could to the red-painted stake. Anyone whose ball was hit and rolled too far was out of the competition, as were those whose balls went in the wrong direction.

By the edge of the forest the butchers were roasting an ox. One could buy honey cake, Spanish tapas, freshly baked pot-loaf, and the delightful dark maroon nectar of the nearby vineyards. Music played as women in clogs swung into the jumping dance with lads in black waistcoats and curly-brimmed felt hats. The spectacle held no interest for Richard Stern, and he pushed his way through the crowd to the mouth of the Grotta. He delayed his meal until later – he liked to save up his pleasures, always leaving the tastiest morsel to the last – so for himself he took only half a pint of wine.

The basalt blocks had been scoured rough by wind, rain and snow. They looked like untanned hides. The opening had already been garlanded with lilies; Richard Stern's nose was irritated by the heavy smell of the flowers. He felt a sudden wave of homesickness wash over him, for he knew, not only from the Book of Fathers but from the streams of his own memory, that back home the turret had similarly been built at the site of a cavern; indeed, the builders had used fragments of rock from the explosion. He saw before him Borbála, draped on her deckchair. Next came the famous copper mortar found by his grandfather Bálint Sternovszky after he cleared the bushes away: it was now used by Borbála, since the doctor forbade her sweetmeats, as a container to hide her delicacies. She had a particular fondness for those egg-shaped lumps of starch sugar.

Richard Stern was reminded of the egg-shaped timepiece he had received on leaving Magyarland, as a good-luck charm.

The ornate timepiece was found by my great-great-grandfather, when he lived like a wild dog on the clearing known as Bull Meadow. When it came into my grandfather's possession, he had it repaired. From him it passed to my father, István Stern, who had to repair it himself on a number of occasions, so that it could once more show the day, the month, and even the year. Now it is mine. But it remains a temperamental little creature, as if it were not a timepiece but a traveller adrift in time. It loses a month or two now and then; on occasion it can be a decade in error.

At the edge of the stalls set up at dawn, a whey-faced peasant was selling quiche lorraine from under an awning fixed to his cart. Tied up nearby were his two little shepherd dogs, their fur trimmed back to an unnatural shortness. Richard Stern was unsure if he should try the quiche lorraine. He often had trouble with his stomach and had just had a bad night, perhaps the result of the previous evening's bouillabaisse, liberally doused with the home-made wine of the parish curé's housekeeper. Richard Stern by no means disdained the fruit of the sea and enjoyed everything that grew or bred in salty water, even if this black fish soup from the south of France contained many varieties of crab and shellfish, to say nothing of some edible algae too.

The smell of the fresh-baked quiche lorraine overcame that of the lilies and Richard Stern began to lick his lips. Perhaps they might give him half a slice? As he was hesitating, the crowd behind him fell silent and parted to let through a black-fringed carriage, driven by a grim-faced liveried coachman in charge of plumed horses. The road turned toward the valley at the point where the whey-faced quiche-seller had parked his cart. The carriage slowed to take the turn. From the carriage window there looked out a veiled lady of noble bearing. The moment she saw the two bald dogs she let out a cry: 'What immodesty! Drive on, quickly!'

The coachman applied his whip to the horses, which suddenly quickened their pace, giving the carriage a mighty jolt. The front wheels lost their grip on the road and began to slide in the direction of the chasm. The liveried coachman bellowed at the rearing horses, but they were unable to check the momentum of the carriage as it veered sideways. Richard Stern jumped in front of the carriage and would have pushed it back on the road, but he could feel his strength ebbing away as the carriage careered towards him, its passenger compartment listing dangerously. A ghastly rattle rose from his throat as he flexed his body against the wooden spokes, as if he were being broken on the wheel; the lady's terrified screams were accompanied by the cracking of his bones.

According to eyewitnesses I fell under the carriage wheels, the carriage rolled over me, and it was my chest with its broken ribs that prevented the carriage and its noble occupant from plunging into the chasm. Everyone who saw it assumed I had died on

the spot. A catastrophe was averted only by a hair's breadth. It
seemed little short of a miracle when only a short while later I
was able to stand up, despite appalling pains. Thus were we
both reborn, I and the Marquise des Reaux: we were married at
year's end.

The Marquise des Reaux was the eldest daughter of an impoverished baron; her excessive piety was the subject of gossip even several counties away. Richard Stern knew nothing of this. The veiled lady jumped out of the carriage and leaning above him asked, greatly agitated: 'Sir, are you alive?'

Richard Stern said only: 'At last.'

The Marquise did not understand. 'A doctor! Send for a doctor!' she shouted, and fortunately there was a barber-surgeon in the crowd. Richard Stern closed his eyes but saw still the lady's honey-coloured skin, her hair dark as night, and the triangular birthmark on her breastbone. He shed tears of joy, whereupon the barber-surgeon made him drink a pain-killing decoction.

As soon as his broken ribs were healed he sought out the Marquise des Reaux on her estate and delicately inquired whom he might ask for her hand.

'Me, Monseigneur; I am an orphan in this world.'

In the end there did appear a portly uncle, one Jean-Baptiste des Reaux, who was her guardian until she came of an age to inherit the little that remained after the gambling losses of her late father. The uncle readily gave his blessing to the union, he and the rest of the family having been privately concerned that she might be left on the shelf. The last barrier to the marriage – the des Reaux were Catholics – was surmounted when the husband-to-be agreed in the marriage contract to convert as well as to permit any offspring to be brought up in the Roman Catholic faith. Even if he had started life as a Jew, he reflected, what reason was there now to cling to his grandparents' faith?

They were already engaged when Richard Stern inquired: 'Mademoiselle, may I ask what you found so immodest in the quiche-seller when we first met?'

'My dear Monseigneur, do you not think it immodest to shear dogs naked? Nakedness sullies the mind!'

The Marquise des Reaux was a *précieuse* through and through. She forbade all discussion in her presence of male undergarments, of any aspect of the workings of the gut, or of any similarly scandalous topic. She did not tolerate Richard Stern eating in her company, nor would she dine at the same table as her husband-to-be. In accordance with the Marquise's wishes, their wedding was held in Nîmes cathedral, the bishop officiating. For the ceremony Borbála arrived in the company of several dozen distant relatives, in a caravan of carts that seemed never to end. When it was announced that the Mademoiselle would henceforth be known as the Marquise de Stern – mar-keys dö störn – from the direction of Borbála there could be heard a full-throated gurgle of Hungarian laughter.

There was but one matter in which Richard Stern would not submit to his wife's demands: he felt not the slightest inclination to lead the life of the minor gentry in the south of France. Ideally he would have liked to return home to Magyarland, but he saw no possibility of the Marquise accompanying him there. But if it had to be Francaroutier, well, it would be through his own skills and efforts that he would support himself and the six sons that he promised, to general applause, to the well-wishers gathered at the wedding breakfast. He wanted to continue his grammatical studies irrespective of whether they brought home the bacon, for a real man does not live by bacon alone. To the chiding of the Marquise he responded with a bon mot from the Paris salons: Do you expect me to sacrifice Holland for

131

the Netherlands? As the lady showed puzzlement, he was obliged to explain the euphemistic word-play: Holland referred to expensive lace fripperies, while the Pays-Bas stood for the body's nether regions. The women of the streets offer the latter for the former.

In addition to his grammatical projects, he also had more lucrative plans, based on an account by one of his Dutch fellow students. The lad described how in Holland there were countless windmills, used not only to grind corn but also to generate some kind of electricity which made possible their use to drive machinery and to produce lighting; in places it had wholly replaced the manual labour of the weavers. Richard Stern did not hold out much hope for the support of this project in Francaroutier; the select few to whom he confided these ideas had burst out laughing. Undaunted he decided to build, beside the hundred-year-old watermill on the des Reaux estate, another, with sails to catch the wind. He had the books needed for the design brought over from Holland; in order to read them he managed in the space of six weeks to become passably proficient in Flemish. He then bought the necessary materials and stood daylong instructing a select few of the more intelligent labourers on the estate in the construction of the sails. He imagined that the New Mill – it was so christened by the villagers as soon as the foundations were dug – would be used alternately for grinding and for generating electricity, by means of an ingenious switchgear of his own devising.

To this day I fail to understand how I came to be so humiliated. My machinery was incapable of even beginning to harness the force of the winds, even though I had spent many hours beforehand carefully considering the matter and working everything out with the precision for which I am known, checking all the calculations several times over. I became the object of general mockery, which the Marquise was never to forgive me.

Richard Stern kept up a lively correspondence with Academician Carmillac and other distinguished scholars that he had met at the University of Paris, as well as with his contacts at the Sárospatak Collegium, particularly Bálint Csokonya, who had gained his laurels as a poet while still at the school. It was from the latter that Richard Stern learnt of the dire straits in which the Collegium now found itself. Never had the governors of this prestigious school had to face such a difficult situation: not only books, but even writing paper and ink, were becoming barely affordable. The field of Hungarian culture is a fallow field visited by drought, he wrote; no one considers it of any importance; the intellectual elite of our country read in German, if indeed they read at all; it would seem that they are loath even to speak Hungarian. The few with the talent and means to cultivate our sciences or our arts prefer to pass their time abroad. The character of the nation is fading fast.

The reproach he read between the lines prompted Richard Stern to think of returning, sooner rather than later, to the land of his birth. He sought out by the most delicately circuitous means the views of Academician Carmillac. The Maistre urged him by all means to visit Magyarland and to travel the length and breadth of the country. While doing so he might usefully take advantage of the opportunity to collect data to see if the Carmillac theory also stood the test in a backward land such as his. This sentence stung the patriotic sentiments of Richard Stern. What French arrogance . . . and in any event we have not yet proven that the Carmillac theory is applicable anywhere at all. He would gladly have shared his dilemma with the Marquise, but the lady had, since the ignominious affair of the windmill, taken pains to avoid his presence and indeed in recent weeks had denied him access to her bedchamber. Richard Stern was not excessively troubled by this; even in better times his wife permitted only one means of amorous dalliance: through a carefully placed slit in her nightwear.

On the eve of their wedding anniversary Richard Stern was called on by Jean-Baptiste des Reaux, who with a great deal of circumlocutory hemming and hawing finally let it be known that his wedded wife had against him a gravamen that was indeed grave.

'The Marquise? *Mon Dieu*, not that blessed windmill business still?'

'O no, my dear sir, it is a matter much more serious. The Marquise desires a congress . . . *Vous comprenez?*'

'I certainly do not!'

'Monsieur Störn knows not what means this congress? I tried in vain to dissuade her, but she will not listen to me; she will lead us all into the vipers' nest of gossip. I have told her: be patient, the good Lord will *assurément* bless you with child . . .'

'Is that the problem? That she has not yet conceived by me?'

'*Exactement*. She has taken it into her head that she wants a proof of her husband's *impotentia*. Whoever heard of such a thing? We are having no congress here for almost fifty years! I know what you are feeling now, Monsieur Störn. Perhaps she will think better of it.'

Richard Stern reeled off in one uninterrupted sequence every curse he knew in the French language. He knew he was mired in the deepest trouble. The Marquise had never in her life been known to change her mind. Since he knew little of Hungarian law and even less of French, he needed help, in the form of good advice. He chose as confidant the reverend curé, who explained to him that in essence a congress was the ordering by the ecclesiastical court of an act of coition to be held in the presence of expert witnesses.

134

'If that is all she wants from me, she can have it!' swore Richard Stern, blushing crimson. They were on their second bottle of wine. Alas, his confidant did not keep his confidence. By the next day the whole village knew that the Magyar Monsieur was soft in the organ. Sniggers dogged his every step. He affected a lofty indifference in the face of his misfortune.

The Marquise de Stern had indeed petitioned the ecclesiastical court. So convinced was she of the justice of her case that in her application, instead of the statutory four experts, she begged for 'ten doctors of medicine and midwives with expertise in such matters'. Richard Stern would have liked to discuss the matters, but his wife barricaded herself in her wing of the building. Richard Stern composed a lengthy letter in which he eloquently pointed out that the Marquise could not be in the right, if only because, until she denied him her favours, normal coitus had taken place on no fewer than twenty-four occasions.

The chambermaid returned his letter in shreds. 'Madame protests that she will not be the recipient of such immodest remarks.'

'She did not even read it?'

'No.'

'Then how does she know the remarks are immodest?'

Stern wrote her another letter, which also came back in shreds. On the back of one scrap were the words: 'LET THE LAW DECIDE!'

The preliminary examination of the Marquise took place in one of the bath-houses of Nîmes. The conclusion of the medical experts was unanimous that the Marquise had 'without a shadow of doubt been deprived of her virginity'. Richard Stern was jubilant. His jubilation was, however, short-lived. The Marquise de Stern claimed that what the doctors of medicine had observed was merely the 'result of a *rapprochement* by her husband that was vulgar and incompetent and not in the manner deemed appropriate'. The taverns of Francaroutier rang that night with the latest news: 'The Magyar can only dig with his digit!'

The congress had the couple summoned to that same bath-house. On the advice of Academician Carmillac, Richard Stern submitted a particular request: 'Ensure that my wife is bathed thoroughly. It may not be beneath her to employ one of those cramping tools employed by the women of the streets.'

Wonder of wonders, the Marquise consented to bathe before the witnesses, fully covered from top to toe, but remarked to her husband: 'Monsieur appears to be rather well informed regarding the habits of street women!'

Richard Stern downed the yolks of four new-laid eggs before turning to the Marquise on the bed, whose curtains the court bailiffs had discreetly drawn. 'I will make her a boy, the first of the six,' he swore, clenching his fists. Sweat poured off his body, but down below there was no sign of movement. 'Impossible! I'm going to have six male offspring! Six boys! Six boys!' he said, in his mother tongue, panicking.

'Your summons here was not for prayer!' hissed the Marquise.

Time went on. One of the shrivelled little midwives peeked behind the curtains from time to time and reported to the assembly: 'Nothing, not a thing.'

'I'm lost! ... I've been bewitched!' he croaked bronchially, adding a few choice curses for good measure in the Hungarian that neither the committee not his eminently pious wife would understand.

The citizens of Nîmes, and those who had gathered here from Francaroutier, had laid substantial bets, some on the husband, some on the wife. Those who had voted for Richard Stern lost their stake when the committee's decision was made public. The marriage was speedily annulled,

136

the Marquise reverted to being known as des Reaux, her ex-husband was forbidden to set foot on the estate, and his belongings were carted over to the parish curé's, where he found temporary lodging for a second time.

'Accept the dispensation of providence,' said the reverend.

'I would appreciate it if you kept at least God out of this!'

He spent three days in Paris, saying his farewells to his friends and teachers. As he recounted the details to Academician Carmillac, the latter shook his head in disbelief. This time Richard Stern added the story of how he knew, beyond the shadow of a doubt, that this was indeed the woman he was destined to marry.

'Perhaps you were mistaken, and she is not, after all, the one.'

Richard Stern shrugged his shoulders and again listed the attributes, like lines of a poem: 'Foreign tongue, honey-coloured skin, hair as black as night, a triangular birthmark above the breastbone.'

As he packed his bags in Francaroutier he saw that he had acquired almost nothing apart from books. He bought a cart with four reliable horses, so that he would not have to depend on the nags of the post-houses on the way. Before he finally turned his back on his life in France, it happened that he ran into the Marquise des Reaux in the marketplace. The woman was on the arm of a gentleman with auburn whiskers and a tall top hat and was tripping among the stalls with a lack of inhibition that made one doubt that it was truly she. An even more striking change was that her hair had become a light chestnut colour, the one the French call brunette. Richard Stern cried out: 'Marquise!'

The woman did not look up. Coolly she continued on her way. The same day Richard Stern discovered from one of the coachmen on the estate (in return for a ten-franc note) that as a result of scarlet fever in her childhood the

Marquise was to all intents completely bald and had worn a perruque ever since. 'I am surprised that this is news to Monsieur Störn ... in Francaroutier it is common knowledge!'

To Richard Stern the passage of his time in prison seemed like the progress of a rotting boat floating or, rather, just drifting with infinitesimal slowness, somewhere in the outside world. He pondered the mysterious nature of time, as he hung in his cell window, clinging to the bars, made slippery and slightly warm by his sweat. He tried to grip them at a point as high as possible, but sooner or later his fingers began to slither downwards and he landed on the rough stone ledge, gashing his lower arms which bore traces similar to the raw wounds left by the rubbing of the leg-irons.

Sometimes it seemed that even a quarter of an hour would not pass, and writing about the endlessness of his days seemed even harder than living through them. None the less, somehow, the seemingly unending, snail's-pace crawl of the mornings, afternoons and evenings began to add up to weeks and months, and when the prisoner least expected it, the first year had passed. In the Book of the Fathers he regularly and carefully marked with little strokes the calendar of his days of imprisonment. It was as if the boat, having been stuck fast on a reef, at last pushed off and gathered speed, only to become stranded on a sandbank, with no movement again until who knows when. Somehow, lo and behold, the second year, too, was gone, with a sudden impetus at its end like the lightning swoop of an eagle on its prey, after what seems like an eternity of stillness with its wings spread wide.

Richard Stern was still in Spielberg Castle prison when time's eagle captured its most succulent prey: the century itself. The midnight tolling of the church bells found him kneeling by his bed; in the absence of a table this was also the position in which he wrote in the Book of Fathers. Will anything out of the ordinary happen? After all, it is not every day that the calendar turns the page to a new century.

Nothing.

Well, at least the century is over, he thought. He spent the night awake, first exercising his mind through prayer, then by counting. He stopped when he reached nine thousand nine hundred and ninety-nine: some unnameable fear gripped him and would not let him utter the figure with four zeroes.

In the early hours of New Century's Day one of the prisoners began to sing in a low, dark voice: *The way before me weeps, the trail before me grieves* . . . Richard Stern broke down in tears. It was the end of the century in which he was born and the one just beginning was likely to hold in store nothing more than damp cell walls. In Spielberg the window was so high that he was not able to look out at all.

Still, something did happen. For the first time since the Marquise had tossed him aside, his loins had stirred. He thought that was something to which he had long since bidden farewell. The erectness was palpable. For some time he did not take the trouble to grasp his manhood and would have had it decline. In vain. He was constrained to take it firmly in hand and enjoy it until it yielded relief.

Borbála had taught him that whatever one does on the first day of the New Year, one will be doing all year long. Ah, if this was true for the first hours of the century . . . then I shall have no end of trouble. And from that day few were the mornings that he did not bedew. Because of this he was racked by guilt. In his childhood, in the years in the turret, the reverend priest would visit them to celebrate mass and to teach the children. At his bidding, Richard Stern duly reported how he played by himself. The reverend priest shook his head and hissed: 'You must not practise self-abuse! It is the work of the Devil! It will rot your brain!'

In the semi-darkness of the cell, stewing in his own juices, he consoled himself by saying that there was no more rotting left for his brain to do. In the crawl of his days this was the only event of note. The space allotted him in Spielberg was very small, only half the amount he had afterwards in Munkács.

'MY TIME IS TOO MUCH, MY SPACE IS TOO LITTLE!' he wrote in the Book of the Fathers, in capital letters. He pondered whether he had chanced upon some philosophical truth. Could it be that to him whom God had given such a small space – his cell was no more than five paces by five – He would allot a great deal of time? And vice versa: he who is blessed with a vast open space will have only a limited amount of time? Indeed, his ancestors had travelled over much of their land and over the world, and none of them had a very long span. And while he Richard Stern was travelling around France the weeks and months had galloped by; yet here, entombed in a dark, stone box, it was as if, alongside him, they had also captured time.

Looking back upon his youth, he now saw that his childhood had been neatly bisected by the Lemberg tragedy. The smell of the warm nest during one's first years in the Stern family is hard to forget, even more so the heady honey smell of the vineyards at Hegyhát! His skin remembered still the rough yet soothing touch of Grandfather Aaron's beard, and he could hear still the Jewish prayers, whose words, left unexplained, the children were made to learn by heart in the Talmud class on Sunday. Some of them Richard Stern could still recite under his breath, if he closed his eyes: *Baruch ata adonai* . . . Odd, it does not work with your eyes open.

For the children the world of the Sterns was a veritable paradise, which he wept for in the cold turret where Borbála used a willow withy to punish smaller infractions, using a riding crop for graver ones. Little Aszti, Richard Stern's little monkey, found it even more difficult to endure the regime and soon after the Lemberg catastrophe began to show signs of breakdown, climbing into the most impossible places for the night. He squeezed himself through the larder's tiny ventilation flap and by morning the floor was awash with honey, fat, jam and broken pieces of crockery. Borbála demanded that István Stern get rid of 'that monster!'

Richard Stern clutched his father's palm, sobbing: 'Daddy dearest, don't, please! Daddy dearest, please don't let her!'

Little Aszti escaped that time. Next time, however, he insinuated himself into the oven, which was being fired up for baking, managing to singe his arms, brow and stomach coal black, and ran up and down half-mad and shrieking with pain, wreaking further havoc among the plates and pans and glass; then, as he was being pursued, he squeezed himself through one of the embrasures onto the outside wall of the turret and jumped onto a ledge, ripping down a shutter on the way. His desperate howls were outdone only by Borbála's ear-splitting ravings.

'My dear boy,' said his father, 'we have no choice but to return little Aszti whence he came.'

In vain did he sob and plead, and the little monkey disappeared from his life for ever. The story went that they managed to find the Gypsies and returned him to them. Now, thinking back, he was sure that somehow or other they had done away with Aszti, though obviously his father was not responsible. István Stern's heart was too gentle for that.

The first fiasco stemming from my looking into the future was my marriage in Francaroutier; the second my liberation from Munkács. I believed that my prison gate would never open, that my imprisonment would last until the end of my days. It was in anticipation of this that I wrote about myself and my experiences in so much detail in this book. No longer might I hope that the prophecy that had miscarried, alluring me with thoughts of six fine sons, could ever come true. I suspected I would not have issue who might have the benefit of my admonitions and counsel. But it seems God had second thoughts and decided to do otherwise with me. I was set free as unexpectedly as I had been arrested all those years ago.

Richard Stern put his signature to the German-language document that set him free; he gave it only a cursory glance, as he knew what it was about: in connection with his imprisonment he was not entitled to make any claim of compensation, whether now or in the future; furthermore, in future he undertook to respect without fail the legal system of the Austrian Empire.

Respect! That I did in earlier times, too; yet here I am. My crime amounted to no more than the fact that I corresponded concerning the grammatical problems of the Hungarian language with a few worthy literati, unaware that they were members of the Freemasons' lodges. To this day I have no clear notion of the aims of that secret and secretive society; all I know is that my intention was no more than to attempt to stir up the stagnant waters of the Hungarian arts and sciences. If that is against the law, the law is an ass.

At the time of Richard Stern's arrest the case against the main perpetrators of the Jacobite conspiracy had been concluded. Ferenc Kazinczy, the distinguished littérateur with whom he had corresponded while in France, was sentenced to death. This enraged Richard Stern and he composed, jointly with Bálint Csokonya, a letter to His Majesty begging for a royal pardon and had it countersigned by many former students of Latin at Sárospatak. The case concocted against him was based chiefly on this letter,

142

which had not even been sent: the court ruled that the line of reasoning employed by the signatories was tantamount to treason.

When he was released, he had no idea which way to turn. He had received the sad news of the death of his grandmother Borbála at about the time he was sentenced. At her request, she was laid to rest in the garden around the turret, next to her son, István Stern, who had gone to his Maker while Richard was a student at Sárospatak. His first pilgrimage was to these twin graves, though he knew that the turret now belonged to strangers, as his punishment had included the confiscation of his property.

Grandmother Borbála had then moved to Debreczen, her way of life becoming extremely circumscribed. His uncle János had disappeared without trace. One of his drinking partners claimed he was living in Vienna as a captain of dragoons, under the name Johann Sternov. But to his letters of inquiry to the various military command posts he received identical replies, consisting of a single, if complex, German sentence: 'Following exhaustive inquiries carried out in response to your written request, we have the honour to inform you that, in relation to the person you seek, in this division of the army of His Majesty there exists neither in armed nor in non-combatant service any person bearing the surname Sternov, Stern, or Sternovszky.'

Richard Stern placed bouquets made of lilies of the valley on the graves of his father and grandmother and knelt there from noon until sunset, mourning, remembering, praying. Then he commended himself to the mercy of God, cut himself a stave from the tree behind the graves, and set off into what seemed like endless space, of which he now had plenty. I wonder how much time I have left? He no longer dared believe in the images of the future, which had returned to haunt him even while he was on his knees, chiefly in the form of a wife and six sons. But the bride

143

always resembled the Marquise des Reaux, whom not the least fibre of his being desired, so he shook himself free of the vision with a shudder.

He began to enjoy having not a penny to his name and no particular aim, and chose the carts to travel on according to the warmth of the carters' invitation. By a long and round-about route he came to Sárospatak, where the gatekeeper at the Collegium, glancing at his dress and unkempt beard, had no hesitation in leading him to the modest shelter maintained for the gentlemen of the road. Here he was also given a bowl of gruel and a jug of fresh milk. The following morning he opened his eyes to find a man sitting on a stool next to him, half-lit by the slanting rays of the morning sun. The man was watching him. He seemed familiar, at least the dark eyes with their suffused glint.

'Richard! Richard Stern!' the man exclaimed.

'Good God, Bálint Csokonya!'

'Richard . . . what has become of you? Where have you been?'

They embraced but could not speak; they wept with the soundless sobs that lie deep in men's hearts. A while later they were calmer and each gave the other an account of his sufferings in prison, the disasters that had befallen their families, and exchanged news of others. Bálint Csokonya had been held throughout in Kufstein, compared with which Spielberg or Munkács was a spa resort. This was the first news that Richard Stern had of Kazinczy, whose death sentence had been by the King's grace commuted to life imprisonment; so he was in gaol still, though shortly after Richard's release he had been transferred to the prison at Munkács which Richard Stern knew so well. Was Kazinczy able to look out onto the hill, he wondered, or did he get one of the cells on the side of the slope? To this question, Richard Stern received an answer only many years later, when he read Kazinczy's diary of his years in prison.

Bálint Csokonya was an assistant instructor in Greek and Latin at the Collegium. He had been free for some nine months. He warned Richard Stern that spies and informers were everywhere and that he should comport himself bearing this in mind.

'Sometimes even the walls have ears!' he whispered.

He promised Richard Stern that he would have a word with the eminent Professor Telegdy, head of the faculty of grammatical studies at the Collegium. And thanks to Bálint Csokonya's influence, Richard Stern gained employment in his alma mater as an assistant in French. It fell to him to keep the French books of the library in proper order and to revise the catalogue. He found this work congenial, and as soon as he secured suitable reading glasses – his eyes had been much weakened by the years in prison – he would crouch or kneel all day among the precious books in his care. Rarely did he pick up a volume without reading at least some part of it. He settled quickly to this way of life and had no difficulty imagining that he might spend the rest of his days as a bespectacled bookworm.

He took Bálint Csokonya's advice and would not let his guard down when conversing with anyone. But he could not, or did not want to, resist renewing his correspondence; in prison it was perhaps this that he had missed most. He wrote on the yellow-veined paper of the Collegium and sealed the couverture with a purple wax seal. He sent news of his liberation to Academician Carmillac, but the terse reply from the University of Paris said only that the Maistre had retired two years earlier and soon after that had departed this life. The curé at Francaroutier informed him that where his windmill had once stood a house of ill-repute had been opened by an exotic dancer from Toulouse, of whom it was rumoured that she had been expelled from all the major towns of southern France. The Marquise was in good health; she was childless still; and her second husband had gone to his grave as the result of a devastating illness which some said was a variety of African syphilis.

He also picked up the threads with his literary friends. His most faithful correspondent was Endre Dembinszki, who had married Bálint Csokonya's sister and moved to Debreczen to teach at the faculty there. In cooperation with two other professors at Debreczen he was working on a revision and new edition of the pioneering 1795 Debreczen Grammar. In this connection Richard Stern addressed a long memorandum to them, taking issue with the Debreczen triad's fundamental beliefs, which he considered excessively beholden to traditional views.

> Not only is it legitimate to form new words regularly from old, on the basis of analogies borrowed from other languages not alien to the spirit of Hungarian; we must actively encourage writers and scholars to create such words; and word formations that appear in literature and are adjudged to be useful should be made available to all in the form of lists and dictionaries.

Bálint Csokonya was resolutely opposed to this view, as was his brother-in-law. 'The language of our fathers is sacred and inviolable. It is not meet to patch and mend it under the slogan of modernity, like some torn item of clothing!'

In the evenings the debates in the rooms in the Collegium would become so heated that their fellow teachers complained about the noise. This was the time that Ferenc Kazinczy was set free from prison, a person they both esteemed as an authority, and as soon as they obtained his address they turned to him in a joint letter with their questions. No reply ever came from Ferenc Kazinczy; it may be that the couverture for some reason failed to reach his hand.

Richard Stern was surprised at the suddenness and the intensity with which he felt the absence of his parents, having assumed that such feelings had long died in his heart. He had dreams and images, more of them and more often, of his mother, both at night and by day. The image he held of her in his mind was but enchantment by the passing of time: gradually the crow's feet disappeared, the warty growth was smoothed from her brow, and the manifold chins shrank down to one. Her figure became slimmer in her son's imagination. Her stubby fingers lengthened and grew thinner, the heavy ankles became trim and delicate. The same kind of magical transformation affected his father, István Stern, and to a lesser degree his two brothers Robert and Rudolf, who would not grow old as he had grown old, not even in his imagination.

These wishful thoughts prompted him to write to the Sterns, his relatives in Hegyhát. He weighed carefully every word committed to the writing paper; he did not know who was still alive of those he remembered, and how much remained of the hostile feelings with which Grandfather Aaron had cast out his son-in-law after the Lemberg tragedy. The reply came with unexpected speed, from Grandfather Aaron himself, who – as the opening lines informed him – on account of the tremor in his hand was no longer able himself to write and had dictated this letter to his great-granddaughter Rebecca. Rebecca was the second child of his grandson Benjamin, the son of Aaron's daughter Eszter. He, Aaron Stern, registered with astonishment that he was in his seventy-ninth year and the whole family was making fevered preparations to celebrate his eightieth birthday. They think reaching such a ripe old age is something of an achievement, but it is more a burden, he wrote, as the number of tormenting memories just grows and grows. At this point in the letter the great-granddaughter inserted a bracketed comment: Uncle Aaron

147

loves to complain, but at this rate he will live to be a hundred.

Letter followed letter, and soon Richard Stern received a cordial invitation to pay his respects to Uncle Aaron on his eightieth birthday, on which occasion there would be a gathering of the clan, from near and far. He thanked them warmly for the invitation.

I set off on the third day of September. I begged lifts on carts. Nightfall found me in a field, but the following day I reached Tokay. I set off thence on Shanks's pony for Hegyhát, arriving a day earlier than I was expected.

As I reached the village, the sun was high in a sky decked by puffy clouds. My heart was in my mouth as I skirted the serried ranks of vines laden with clusters of swollen grapes. It would be a good year for the vine-harvest.

The road turned sharply, like a man's elbow, and there on the hill was the cemetery. He stepped into the garden of the dead with head bowed, donning his hat in accordance with Jewish custom. From behind his brow there rose from the dregs of a distant past the forms of the Hebrew characters, as he traced with his index finger the incisions on the grey-brown stones, gleaning the names, more or less. His insides were quaking and he dreaded the pain that would follow if among these ancient symbols he were to stumble upon someone who was family or friend. But he found none such. Later he heard that Grandpa Aaron had wanted to raise a memorial to those who perished in Lemberg, but Rabbi Ben Loew – then still very much alive – had not allowed it. The Rabbi's own headstone, in accordance with his will, bore only an ancient Jewish blessing.

Richard Stern pushed on, further and deeper into his own past. In the sharp bend of the stream, the old Sonntag hostel still stood, now boasting an extra floor and an additional wing; on the sign, freshly painted: *Rabinowitz and Burke*. A smaller notice declared: *First-class koshere food and drink – Do not aske for credit*. Richard Stern felt an urge to correct the spelling on the notice, but suppressed his teacherly instincts and continued along the steep path. The synagogue seemed considerably bigger. It had been rebuilt using large slabs of stone. Behind it a section of the river bed had been widened and a few granite steps now linked it to the bank. Four very elderly men sat hissing and clucking in the swirling cold of the water, eyes closed, their white beards floating on the surface like rafts of wood-bark. A ritual bath, thought Richard Stern, recalling vaguely sharing one with his father and grandfather and feeling the flow of the icy water on his skin.

'Richard! Richard Stern!' cried the voice of one of the Methuselahs as he rose from the stream, a hand waving towards him like a shivering bird.

'Grandpa Aaron,' said Richard Stern, stumbling out the words, deducing rather than recognizing. His grandfather had been a strong, powerfully built figure; this old gentleman was more like a child, his skin dried around his bones like parchment, his loin-cloth revealing parts of parts turned grey; Richard Stern had to force himself to look away. 'I must go over, embrace him, kiss him!': the feelings from the past came welling up, and as he enclosed in his arms the ancient, time-worn body, as he touched the damp, goose-pimpled skin, as he heard again the high-pitched voice repeating his name again and again, laughing and crying, he knew, he suddenly knew, that he had at last come home.

In the house where he was born there now lived his aunt Eszter. Everything was so familiar, yet somehow alien.

Aaron Stern took the evening meal with his grandfather Aaron. The news of his arrival had brought over, that same day, all the relatives living in Hegyhát, one after the other.

At first Richard Stern was unable to put faces to the names, though the latter he did manage to note. Without anyone ever mentioning it, his newly rediscovered family knew, just as Richard Stern knew himself, that in the future he would be living here, with them, for them. At the end of the academic year he bade farewell to the Collegium in Sárospatak and moved to Hegyhát. At first he enjoyed Grandfather Aaron's hospitality, but the following spring the male members of the family joined together to build him a house on the hill above the cemetery.

He continued his work as a teacher, bringing to the pupils at the Hegyhát yeshiva his aptitude for foreign languages, while remaining unremitting in his own pursuit of knowledge. He studied the Hebrew language, particularly exploring the Talmud, and at the same time he did not abandon his studies of Hungarian. He played an important role in the countrywide efforts of the writer and editor Ferenc Kazinczy to cultivate the language. Six words that he created for the Hungarian language passed, in time, into general use, and he lived to see them admitted by the dictionaries. His income was spent entirely on books.

When he discovered that Kazinczy, on his marriage to the Countess Sophie Török, some twenty years younger, had found himself in financial straits and therefore sold his books to the Collegium at Sárospatak, Richard Stern was furious. He wrote a thunderous letter to the poet. *It is not meet to profit from the Collegium, may it be blessed a thousand times.* To this letter, too, he never received a reply. This prompted Richard Stern to draw up his will: on his death his books and writings would go to the Collegium, gratis.

His aunt Eszter often shook her head: 'Better you were wed.'

'It's too late for that.'

'Stuff and nonsense!' Eszter began to list grooms from Hegyhát's present and recent past, all of whom were about his age. The triumphal list went on until Richard Stern broke in: 'No more, dear aunt . . . Remember, I have had a taste of marriage and I didn't like it enough for a second helping!'

'Once bitten is not twice shy, it just needs a second try! We will find you a treat of a girl who will have you licking your lips!'

Richard Stern wanted to bring this exchange firmly to a close: 'My bride must have skin the colour of honey, locks as dark as night – real ones, not a wig – and a triangular birth-mark on her breastbone. And to cap it all, she must speak a foreign tongue. That is how I dreamt it. *Dictum, factum, punctum!*'

He was sure he was asking for the impossible and was very much bemused when he was introduced to the mar-riageable girls of the region, all of whom spoke a foreign tongue, such as Slovak, Ruthene or Yiddish. Nor was there any shortage of skins the colour of honey or genuine black hair – only the triangular birthmark was lacking. The women of the Stern family put their heads together: we can make a birthmark, all we need is a little ink! But before they could carry out their plan, there came to visit them from Prague a very distant and very poor relative, Yanna. The moment he set eyes on her, Richard Stern was thunder-struck.

In the person of Yanna I came to know someone more wonder-ful, both within and without, than I could ever have imagined. The description fitted her perfectly: her skin like this season's honey, her hair the colour of ebony, and she could manage only broken Hungarian, her mother tongue being Czech. True, when on our wedding night I parted her from the shimmering bridal gown, I found no birthmark on her alabaster body; but I at once hung around her neck a triangular stone, black, on a gold chain, which I had bought her. Thereafter she would not be seen

151

without this precious stone, day or night. Thus was the prophecy fulfilled, the vision which I, of little faith, had not for years dared hope to live.

In due course their first child was born, a son, hale and healthy. He was christened Otto. He was followed, at intervals of approximately two years, by Ferenc, Ignác, Mihály, József and János.

Richard Stern lived to a ripe old age in the bosom of his family.

Perhaps now at long last the seven lean years have passed. My ancestors and I have had our share of suffering; from this day forward let years of happiness beckon. If we had a star, it would last for eternity, or even longer.

V

DESPITE THE RISING WAVES OF WHITE HEAT NOT A LEAF stirs; time seems to slow to a halt. Like shimmering aspic the heat dribbles down even into the depths of the cellars. The wine is on the turn, viscous, its fire and its bouquet slowly evaporate. Languid bees lazily loop the sweet mal-vasia grapes. In the fields ever-widening fissures in the ground, which the oldest mavens think it unwise to inspect lest their faces be singed by a blast from hell. The song of the whitethroat, the crested lark and the titmouse is heard rarely in the land. Only the cry of the cuckoo breaks the silence now and then, and the persistent tap-tap of the woodpecker on the desiccated trunks.

The gentry regularly visited the Nagyfalu hostelry to seek, and find, amusement. Benedek Bordás had started out as a common tapster in Varjúlapos, but as the years went by he realized that the more moneyed the class of customer, the better he fared. He sold his wayside alehouse and had a hostelry built in Nagyfalu, close by the lock-keeper's cot-tage. Here the best of Gypsy bands played for all they were worth, the finest cooks from Transylvania bustled about the kitchens, and eye-catching wenches from Ruthenia served the oaken tables. The full-bellied gentlemen were able to take their ease and recover from the orgy of culinary delights in the hostelry's spacious guestrooms. Benedek Bordás took care always to keep freshly filled the china lavoirs of the mirrored washing table, with a crisp napkin on the side; and on the bedside tables a bowl of fruit, with knotted rolls fresh baked that dawn.

Keen young wenches frequented the hostelry by the dozen, some without the knowledge of their families, others – particularly from the wrong end of Basahalom and Kazárbocor – with their heads held high. A particularly dissolute group of regulars liberated Benedek Bordás's heavy bunch of keys and took off with it to the Lesser Tisza, intending to throw it in the river, declaring that 'Henceforth the Nagyfalu hostelry will never shut its doors!'

And it never did. The finest wine drained unceasing from the barrels into the wineglasses, while in the fire they grilled and roasted vast quantities of game and fowl, in the belly of which the Transylvanian cooks always liked to conceal some surprise: perhaps a smaller bird roasted whole, or a pierced apple stuffed with heart and liver. But the gentlemen did not always demand such masterpieces of the cook's art; simpler, home-made delicacies regularly featured on Benedek Bordás's bill of fare and enjoyed great popularity: pork crackling served lukewarm, for example, or fried dough with bacon.

In the entrance hall a wooden board proclaimed: 'Any dish prepared on request, if ingredients available.' Visitors sometimes put Benedek Bordás's claim to the most severe of tests, but he almost always managed to keep his promise. The only guests who shrank his stomach to a walnut-sized dumpling were the Vandal Band. These rough fellows were the terror of the neighbourhood. The Vandal Band feared nothing and no one and rarely did a week pass without stories of their duels or revels or other adventures reverberating round the barstools. One August, after a night of drinking and carousing, they painted the Nagyfalu calvary red and – God forgive them their sin – stuffed a lemon in the mouth of the Christ on the cross. Another time they forced the Gypsy band to strip and hung them upside down from the branches of the oak tree by the hostelry entrance and ordered the mortified musicians to play their favourite tunes as they hung. The mirrored great saloon they smashed up almost every month. Though their moneyed parents invariably paid for the damage, Benedek Bordás could not abide them. Every time he heard their horses' hoofs thundering in the puszta – his ears were keenly attuned to it by now – he prayed: 'The pox consume you all!'

But the pox had other matters to attend to, and never did consume the Vandal Band. They rode in every week; sometimes, to the owner's chagrin, every day. Those who had already had the pleasure avoided them at all costs; in the bar-room no one ever sat at their table. Their cordovan knee-boots redound roughly on the floor as they enter, and the last one slams the door behind them. Reaching the corner table, they slap down their riding crops and Otto Stern, the senior Vandal, with mane of reddish hair like a lion, immediately bellows: 'Wine! White! The roughest!' His powerful voice commands respect: the bar-flies fall silent, and only the hum of the fat kitchen flies can be heard.

Old Örzse, whose job it is to keep the tables clean, rushes over with the dishcloth, but without turning her back on them, else she is bound to get slapped on the rump. The six goblets are empty in a flash and Benedek Bordás can bring over the second round. And very soon the third. The Vandals know how to drink, no two ways about it. Little János, the youngest, constantly wants to dance with all the waitresses, sometimes even dragging Örzse round the tables. The other visitors dare not laugh; they have learnt the unwisdom of getting involved with this lot; bloodshed is never far away. Following these visits, Benedek Bordás nearly always found it necessary to take to his cart and seek out their parents with the handwritten bill, often several pages long, which offered a history, indeed a blow-by-blow account, of the particular night's revels. Their father, Richard Stern, was a keen historian of these accounts. 'It completely passes my understanding what they find so amusing about smashing up an inn,' he grumbled to himself as he rummaged in his leather pouch.

'They are but young and giddy-pated!' Yanna purred.

Benedek Bordás reflected that if these Vandals were his own, he would break them in two, but he kept his views to himself. Richard Stern was a bookish man held in great esteem in the locality and was therefore forgiven the antics of his six sons. The Sterns managed the region's most highly respected firm of vintners and retailers of wine, though it seemed that it was mostly the women who did the work to enable their menfolk to spend the money on their whims. The office with its solid, weathered floor was in the hands of Nanna Eszter, a bent old lady rising eighty. With her pebble glasses she had to peer so closely at the folded sheets of the accounts that she often had ink on the tip of her nose.

It was said among the travelling wine merchants that until you have tried to make a deal with Nanna Eszter, you do not know what haggling is. Behind her back Nanna Eszter was known as *Jew ultimo*, this being the term at the time for the Pagát, the first card in the Hungarian tarot pack. No one dared cast her ancestry in the face of this sharp-visaged old woman or her family since she had all but blinded a Romanian trader with a whip for insulting her. She had been only about seventy at the time but her strength had diminished little since. Her grey, waist-length hair was always carefully coiled into a severe chignon; whenever her temper rose, a lock of hair would break free and begin a life of its own, fluttering like a miniature pennant.

Yanna, Richard Stern's wife, now close to completing her fifth decade, retained her original colours, the complexion and hair for which her husband would have walked all the way to Pest-Buda; neither the honey of her skin nor the silky ebony of her hair had faded, only little crow's feet around her eyes suggested the passing of the years. Yanna became the right hand of Nanna Eszter. She picked up the mysteries of viticulture with such natural ease it was as if she had been born a Stern. These two women understood each other without recourse to words. There was no man that Richard Stern was jealous of, save Nanna Eszter, who seemed to require Yanna's services for very considerable periods of time. If he protested, Nanna Eszter would stop him short with the words: 'Not a word, Richard. Someone has to mind the shop while you bury yourself in your books in the ivory tower.'

Yanna was responsible, in Richard Stern's name, for the formulation of the rules of conduct for the vineyards on the entire hill, which subsequently gained the acceptance of all the producers. The charter, affirmed by the initials or marks of all, hung in the office of the Master of the Guild of the Hill's Vineyards and its text was drummed out once a month. The Vandal Band would even sing it, accompanied by the Gypsy band, at the climax of a night out, to the tune of the subversive Kurucz song 'Csínom Palkó'.

Since the creation of too many paths is damaging to the vines, it is hereby ordered that everyone will keep to their traditional paths. If a stranger walks the paths, the Master of the Guild shall arrest him and whatever is taken from the stranger is his to keep.

If anyone steals of the grapes and takes them to his cellars, upon proof of theft he will lose those grapes. If it

157

be a child stealing but without the father consenting, the above punishment may be excused.

Affray on this hill will result in a fine of 18 florins, 5 to accrue to the municipality, the rest to the owner. If there be damage in consequence, it will be assessed and a further fine levied.

If swords or flintlocks be carried in a hostile manner, the Master of the Guild will arrest the party and lock him in his house. Those with fences who fail to maintain them and in consequence let cattle stray shall pay due compensation.

No one may sell their grapes directly, nor transfer his lease, except with the knowledge of the Master of the Guild. Those who do so none the less will pay a fine of 20 florins . . .

Yanna felt proud to have her words sung. Richard Stern, however, was beside himself: 'Wretched curs! You hold nothing sacred!'

It was generally every two months that he completely lost his temper with his sons. He would line them up in the dining hall filled with heavy, dark furniture and give them more or less the same dressing down each time. Well now, what on earth do you think you are doing? Why did they think they could do as they like? That they owned everything including the walnut trees? How many more times would the family have to pay for their frolics? Would they ever grow up?

The boys listened to the speech with eyes firmly fixed on the ground. When their father had unburdened himself, Otto acted as spokesman for them all. 'Father dear, may it please you not to be too upset; we were just amusing ourselves!'

By then they had drawn the sting of Richard Stern's words and he excused them with a shaking head. 'For

Heaven's sake, do something useful!' he said and disappeared into his study. That year he was translating some Hebrew prayers into Hungarian, so that those without knowledge of the Old Testament language could also pray when they would. (He was also the first to produce a Hebrew-to-Hungarian glossary, of which the printing house of Izidor Berg printed 150 copies almost nine years later. As he surveyed the clarity of the printed page and the quality of the binding, Richard Stern could not help thinking that this would have gained the approval of his ancestor, Grandpa Czuczor.)

The six Vandals were back in the Nagyfalu hostelry that night. Otto Stern demanded a virgin and when he was offered one, chased her out of his room at the point of his sword, bellowing that if this whore was a virgin, he was Pegasus. Eventually his brothers managed to calm him down. Little János suggested a game of cards. Otto Stern was reluctant: 'Why should I take the shirt off my own brothers' backs? Let's play with others!' But no one really wanted to share the green baize table with the six Vandals. 'I am bored!' boomed Otto Stern. 'Let's ride down to the Greater Tisza and have a swimming race!'

'We've done that twice already this week ... and you always win!' said Mihály.

'A fencing competition then!'

'You always win that as well.'

'Then tell me a story!'

But his brothers were not as skilled at the storyteller's craft as he. They could guffaw, and guzzle wine and spirits, but in the end it was Otto Stern who told a story to the others, about all that he saw in his visionary moments about the past and the future. His brothers were unsure whether to believe him or not. The most inclined to believe him was the fourth-born, Mihály, who was still in short pants when he declared that he was going to be a famous general or statesman. His hero was

Alexander the Great. He hoped that in his career he would encounter a knot like that of Gordius, which he would be able to cut with his sabre at a single stroke. He was taken aback when Otto Stern informed him: 'You will not be a general, but you will be elected a senator in Parliament . . . next century there will be a street named after you in Pest-Buda . . . that is to say in Budapest.'

'Budapest?' All five young men burst out laughing. In fact all six, as the word had an amusing ring for Otto Stern as well.

The prophecy was the cause of endless banter from the other four brothers, who thenceforth called him Nobby Nobody. Otto's claims were not taken seriously. The only thing he himself could not understand was why it was his eyes that had been chosen by the heavenly powers to be opened to the flow of time. In his childhood he had thought that the past and the present were visible to all, at least sometimes. He wanted to convince especially his brothers that this was no laughing matter. If only he could have offered to prophesy something in the near future that would soon have come to pass! But no such opportunity arose.

Of the six, Nobby Nobody was the most serious, most industrious and the most intelligent. The two lads who were his elders, Ferenc and Ignác, were in the same league as Otto as regards physical strength, but not in respect of their mental power. They rarely spoke, and if they wanted something they simply took it by force. The girls went in fear of them, even the humblest. With Mihály, however, it seemed as if some other kind of blood had transfused into the family, and little Józsi and János, who followed him, were more in his image than in Otto's. Though the three youngest lads joined in the amusements of the brothers, the destruction and violence was nearly always wrought by the others.

Otto Stern organized the activities of the Vandal Band with military precision, brooking no opposition when he gave an order: 'We shall swim the Tisza and ride to the fair at Eszlár!'

They all suspected that at the fair there would be some rumpus for which their greying father would once again have to reach into his pockets and give them a telling-off, and rightly too. During these ritual reproofs it often occurred to Otto that it was perhaps time to bring down the curtain on this revelry, or at the least to spare Mihály and little Józsi and János this wastrel way of life; in their case it was worth educating their minds. 'They could be sent to the Collegium!'

Yanna would not hear of it. 'Far better they roister about here. The vineyards will come into their hands sooner or later, and the ins and outs of that life are best learnt round here.'

Richard Stern did not agree, but by this time he had lost much of his ability to concern himself with the ways of the real world. It seemed that none of the six would ever get a decent education. This sometimes vexed Otto Stern, but he flicked the thought away, as an animal's tail might a fly.

Otto Stern brought his clenched fist down on the solid wood table of the Nagyfalu hostelry: 'Reveille! What are you waiting for?'

Benedek Bordás scampered up. 'What can I do for you, sir?'

Otto Stern ordered dinner, for twelve, as usual. And new women. The owner delicately inquired whether he had any money. Having received some from his mother the other day, Otto Stern haughtily snapped back: 'I shall not be in your debt!', like one who regards such questions as being completely uncalled for. He never let his brothers pay, nor anyone else. It did sometimes cross his mind that it was indeed someone else paying: his parents. He shrugged. With the advance on my inheritance I do what I will.

He ordered the Gypsy to come over. The band followed

161

behind their leader, crouching humbly. Otto Stern launched into: *The way before me weeps, the trail before me grieves* . . . This was their father's favourite song. He was always moved by it. Otto had seen a few times the scene from the past in which Borbála (his father's grandmother) taught her grandson this song. His five brothers immediately joined in: they had all inherited their talent for music from their great-grandfather, Bálint Sternovszky. By this time the next course on the menu had arrived. Otto Stern examined them one by one, grasping them by the chin. The girls were either too thin or too young, none of them likely to be experienced in the bedroom. 'I said women, not children!'

Benedek Bordás gulped, suspecting the worst. 'Sir wanted chaste ones . . . I cannot answer for the chastity of the older ones.' He wished Otto Stern in hell. If only this booby knew how hard it is to find fresh whores! The women of this sort had already been used by the Vandals. The penniless families, whose daughters can be bought for small sums, keep racking up their prices. And it's the poor old landlord who has to pay for it all in the end.

Meanwhile Otto Stern urged his brothers to take their pick of the girls, but they dragged their heels; none of them was in the mood. Nor was Otto. He could not understand what was wrong with him. One's youth is for eating, drinking, dallying with women and one's fellows. Could I have left my youth at home this morning?

While he was pondering this, Mihály said: 'Let us go from here in peace. Let us devote ourselves to nobler things.'

It was clear that the other four were of the same mind and they began to get their things together. Otto Stern exploded in an impotent rage and with a sweep of his arm sent the bottles and glasses on the table crashing to the floor and set off after his brothers.

Benedek Bordás barred his way: 'And who is going to pay?'

162

Otto Stern threw a shower of notes on the floor and elbowed the owner, who smelled of onions, out of his way. As he reached the gate the others were already in the saddle. 'Hey! Wait! Where now?'

'Back to Hegyhát,' said little Józsi. 'There is a meeting in the synagogue.'

'What kind of meeting?' There was no reply. The brothers were already heeling their horses round and Otto Stern followed them. His mood had taken a turn for the worse. He was hurt that his brothers seemed to be slipping out of his control. While they were growing up, the five younger brothers had accepted him unconditionally as leader; now the halo of their boundless admiration was slipping. But he resolved generously to give his approval to this particular excursion. Why should they not, for once, go where Józsi and the others wished?

The stream was in full spate and had surely risen while they were in the hostelry. On the way there the water had come up to the horses' flanks; now they had to lift their boots out of the stirrups to keep dry. Otto Stern's horse shied back when the stream swept a dead cat by; he kept it calm by squeezing the animal with the inside of his thighs.

They reached the yeshiva, where some thirty horses were already sniffling around the grass. As many people must have come on foot: the two interconnected rooms were filled to capacity, with some standing in the narrow corridor.

'We are too late!' said Mihály.

'Come on!' said Otto Stern, taking the initiative and, instead of entering by the door, strode to one of the arched windows and climbed in. His brothers followed. They were hushed and hissed by those within. On the platform one of the Sterns' distant relatives, Miksa Stern, was reading from a sheet of paper to which he held a candle so close that Otto Stern thought it might at any moment catch fire.

Miksa Stern's reedy voice kept halting; he was so moved that tears came to his eyes. 'Whereas our Magyar mother tongue has for centuries on end languished in the slough of imperfection, we have here gathered together this day, inspired by our love of the tongue of our motherland and at the instance of our highly respected and learned Mr Lajos Bullock, teacher of the Hungarian language at the yeshiva of Hegyhát and Doctor of Philosophy and the Fine Arts, to form a Magyar Society . . .'

The audience clapped. Lajos Bullock sat in the front row, and on being repeatedly prompted, rose and awkwardly bowed. As the noise died down, Miksa Stern continued: 'We desire, on the altar of the homeland, to unite our humble thoughts and efforts, in so far as our modest abilities allow. Let our Magyar Society strive for the cultivation of our language, for the flowering of philosophy and belles-lettres. Let the guiding spirit of our efforts be the great God of the Magyars, so that, reaching our desired goal, we might rejoice in the sight of the fruits of development in ourselves and in those who come after us.'

Applause rang out once more. Miksa Stern bowed repeatedly, his right palm stretched out pointing to Lajos Bullock.

'Vivat! Vivat!' came the cry from all around, the voice of Otto Stern rising above the chorus.

There was pandemonium for several minutes. The audience, mainly the cream of the youth of Hegyhát, tossed hats into the air, embraced each other, shook hands vigorously. The enthusiasm was catching and caught the Stern brothers, who felt they had been part of an exceptional moment of history.

On the platform a ruddy-faced boy of about 14 with dark hair was clearly waiting for his turn. Miksa Stern began to make hissing noises and tried to curb the passions of the audience. As this proved ineffectual, he urged the boy to start. But he was a long time getting ready.

Mihály leant over to Otto and whispered in his ear: 'But seeing as we are Jewish, why are we setting up a Magyar Society, rather than one that is partly Magyar and partly Jewish?'

Otto Stern pondered the question as the next one came: 'And why is it only the great God of the Magyars that is our guiding spirit? What will happen to our faith?'

'Magyar tongue goes with Magyar God,' said Otto Stern.

At length the dark-haired boy had the stage. He was declaiming a poem by the man they called the Hungarian Horace, Benedek Virág:

> While youth smiles still,
> With strength of will,
> The path of glory you should tread:
> The Muse doth hold
> No silver, nor gold,
> But laurels and life ere we are dead.

Otto Stern's mood unexpectedly changed. Indeed, how noble a task it was to concern oneself with the mother tongue, philosophy, belles-lettres, the sciences . . . Father devotes his life to such things, why should we not make sacrifices for their sake? He could hardly wait for the recital to end. Scarcely had the applause subsided before he elbowed his way into the middle of the throng and in his booming voice declared: 'In the name of the family Stern I pledge one thousand florins in support of the noble aims of the Magyar Society!'

For a moment there was complete silence and then an eruption of hurrahs fairly raised the rafters; Otto Stern, too, was raised shoulder-high and tossed in their direction by the founders of the Society. (His brothers were concerned that they might drop him, as they knew only too well the true weight of that body.) Sigismund Beleznay asked for the floor; at one time all the land on the hillside had belonged to his family. 'If the Jews are going to be so generous, we shall give, too, as much as we can!' He pledged two thousand.

Their example was followed by many others: the figures came thick and fast so that Miksa Stern could barely keep track. To celebrate the triumphant establishment of the Hungarian Society, a toast was proposed. Otto Stern proudly displayed the swell of his massive chest; he was pleased to have turned this evening, too, to his advantage. They were riding back at a comfortable canter when Mihály asked: 'And where did that thousand come from?'

Otto Stern harrumphed. 'It will surface somehow . . .' and his throat constricted at the thought of having to ask for money yet again. Surely Father will give to a cultural good cause! He has devoted his whole life to it, after all. It would of course be more sensible to turn to Mother, whose heart is softer in matters of money. But a thousand florins is a veritable fortune . . . perhaps five hundred would have been enough . . . or three hundred . . . well, it's too late now. He decided to leave the matter to another day. He might as well leave worrying about it until the morrow.

As he was getting ready for the night he scoured his memory for anything that would help him discover what lay in the future for the Magyar Society, to see if he might find arguments to support his plea to his father. But when it was at his request, nothing ever came; only his own memories, and what had occurred earlier, swirled around his head. He lay on his stomach. He thought of girls, as always when sleep would not come, of those he had enjoyed in Benedek Bordás's hostelry, not those that he was wooing as a suitor. His most committed suit lay in the direction of Rakamaz, the middle daughter of Baron Hadházy, Clara, but that family did not think much of approaches from nobodies like the Sterns.

Nor was Otto Stern entirely certain that he could spend

the rest of his life by the side of the always pale Baroness with the bloodless lips, though the substantial dowry that came with her did increase somewhat his interest in a union. How wonderful it would be if there were a marriageable girl within his circle of acquaintance, who might kindle his passion in the manner of the little strumpets with their rags reeking mustily of the forest yet with marble skin of immaculate smoothness.

Yanna was keen for Otto to marry as soon as possible, and Nanna Eszter urged him likewise. 'I want six boys, as many as your good mother bore, and while I am still able to enjoy them.'

Of course, his mother and grandmother imagined some well-to-do Jewish girl by his side. Otto Stern knew – he could see – that he would have only one child and it would not be a Jewess who brought it into the world. But he had no wish to dishearten Yanna and Nanna Eszter.

The following morning he gritted his teeth to bring up the thousand florins at the breakfast table, but Richard Stern was unwell and did not come down to breakfast. The following day Otto Stern spent at Rakamaz, so again support for Hungarian culture went undiscussed at the Stern residence. Richard Stern, Yanna and Nanna Eszter learnt of his magnanimous gesture from the columns of the Magyar Society's Gazette, which was sent to all the generous patrons of the Society. Otto Stern's morning greeting received a whiplash response from his father: 'Have you taken leave of what little sense remains in your skull? What makes you think I am going to reach into our coffers for this latest idiocy of yours? Have you no shame? Are you glad to lose your self-respect before everyone? Because you will! Because we are not going to pay! You have waded waist-deep in the family fortune for long enough!'

Otto Stern held up his arms to shield his head from the blows raining down on it. 'But Father, how can the sorrowful state of the Hungarian language and the arts leave you cold? You, of all people!'

'Hungarian language and the arts, my foot! Did you swallow all that eyewash? Did you read, at all, what you have put your name to? Why should you squander money on that? A few hotheads getting all worked up will not lead to the cultivation of the language! If you want to support culture, you should give your money to the poor Collegiums, which are on their last legs! What did I do to make you such a prize idiot? And this is the example you set your brothers! Out of my sight, you useless piece of . . .' he bellowed, lashing him with the whip right, left and centre.

Otto Stern held him down. 'That's enough, Father, because I cannot vouch for myself!' He was a head taller and quite a bit wider than Richard Stern. For a while, as they both panted, they tried to stare each other down; then the son turned and walked out. He went up to the library and lay down on the bearskin before the fireplace. Thoughts whirled round his head. If his father did not pay up, he would be branded with an indelible mark of shame and have to leave the area. On the other hand, in terms of the future that he had foreseen, there was room for him elsewhere, somewhere new, where his son would come into the world, a son whose name would be – if the signs were to be believed – Szilárd.

He heard his father arguing with his mother, before Nanna Eszter joined in, and then the door slammed as Richard Stern rode out to work off his anger. I wonder where my brothers might be?

Silence reigned in the house, only the sound of the brook burbling outside could be heard. Lying on the floor, Otto Stern could see out of the leaded window: the crown of the garden willow had grown so huge that someone trim could easily have climbed out onto it. But perhaps vice versa, someone could get in with evil intent; he should have a word with his father about having the branches lopped. A sweet spicy smell tickled his nose. Honey bread ... his favourite delicacy. He hesitated: should he go down the creaky stairs to ask for a slice? But it could just as well be his senses playing tricks on him. Outside the sun beat down fiercely. If Clara smiles with the sun at me, a fine crop of apples there will be, he thought – it was Clara's name-day the following week. I shall take her flowers. And a case of the best vintage, if Nanna Eszter lets me. If not, I shall just filch a case myself.

He turned on his side. The floor under him gave a creak. One of the floorboards rose perceptibly. What is this? The top floor had been added by his father the previous year; the tipple-prone builder had made many mistakes and Richard Stern had held back some of the payment, some temporarily, some permanently. Otto Stern folded back the bearskin. One of the floorboards was warped and was on the verge of slipping onto the joists. He was about to adjust it when he noticed that it was loose. He lifted it up, revealing a long gap padded with pieces of felt. There was a large metal cask lying there and two books wrapped in white lawn. He could see that one of the volumes was French, a Bible of some considerable age. The other was ... well, well ... the Book of Fathers. He knew of its existence from any number of sources, but he had never been vouchsafed a look. Any such request was decisively rejected: 'You will have it when the time comes!'

Otto Stern hesitated. Dare he open it? If his father found him here poking about in the stuff hidden under the floorboards, he would surely strike him dead. But he was unable to resist the temptation. With trembling fingers he opened the battered folio, at the very end. Three hundred and twenty numbered pages had already been filled. Richard Stern had even scribbled over the inside covers.

From this day on Otto Stern took every possible opportunity to hang around the library and secretly read the Book of Fathers. Richard Stern was uncomprehending: 'What has got into you, my boy? You never read anything before!'

'I have taken a decision, Father,' he lied. 'I shall pull myself together and apply to go to the Collegium.'

'Well said!' Richard Stern compiled a long list of basic works that he had to know without fail.

Otto Stern placed a few of these around him on the floor, but the moment he was on his own, he took out the Book of Fathers. He felt that the most important knowledge lay within its covers. He made slow progress, able to concentrate only when there was no danger of being caught book-handed.

He had little difficulty with the neat script of Kornél Csillag, though he had to make a guess at many of the Latin tags. Kornél Csillag must have been a meticulous person: not only was the date clearly given, but he had produced a balance-sheet of his assets and liabilities every year. Otto Stern found his last will and testament just as he found his views on the more important affairs of the world, as well as a summary of everything that Kornél Csillag knew or professed to know about his late father Péter Csillag and the Grandpa Czuczor who had brought him up, including the latter's keepsake volume, of which the contents followed on 24 pages under Kornél Csillag's title: *Committed to paper to the best of my recall*.

Bálint Sternovszky filled fewer pages and his spidery scrawl was much harder to decipher. It seemed that he was interested only in music. At the bottom of one page he had doodled a bouquet of musical notes in a circle.

István Stern had recorded his family's tragedy at Lemberg in impassioned detail, as if the successful depiction of these horrendous scenes in the Book of Fathers would ensure that they haunted him less thereafter.

Otto Stern sobbed all the way through the diary of Richard Stern's imprisonment, biting his lips to ensure he did not let out a sound.

When he had read every word, he understood why Richard Stern would not allow him to open the Book of Fathers before the time was ripe. Not only his father but also his grandfather had described their suspicions of the future and from this he knew that he would not have a long life himself: his death would be sudden and quick. At the same time the prophecy of István Stern regarding Otto was the same as that which he had foreseen himself: that he would have but one son, named Szilárd. The danger was still a long way off, he thought to himself, since I have not even married and a child would be conceived only after that. He tried to recall whether in his own visions his wife-to-be had made an appearance, but he found no trace of such a person. Would it be Clara? Or someone quite other?

He slid the Book of Fathers back into the hollow and replaced the floorboard. He stared blankly ahead. It was as if something had come to an end with the filling of the folio, which, as Kornél Csillag noted, had been specially brought from Italy. Said to have been made in a famous bible scriptorium and originally intended to bear the Holy Writ, for some reason it was never used for that purpose and became instead the personal bible of this family. Only now it was full, and this somehow seemed an ill omen. As if the story had come to an end.

Otto Stern resolved to have another folio brought from Italy, a faithful copy of this one, and one in which he would be the first to write. Thus could the end become the beginning of something new. But he had to act in the strictest secrecy, lest Richard Stern immediately guess that one of his sons had read the Book of Fathers – suspicion would be certain to fall on him. Weighing all this carefully, he thought it best to order a large-format folio from the Szerencs Paper

Manufactory, with cream-laid paper suitable for handwritten script. This was perhaps one-fifth bigger than the original Book of Fathers, but of the same thickness. The deerskin binding bore on its cover an ornament: the snake in the shape of an S that had become well known as the seal on Stern wine-bottles and cases. The gold paint on the S soon rubbed off, however.

> *Shalom aleichem. I am starting again, or rather, continuing on this day the Book of the Fathers, in my own name and by right. As the firstborn of this generation of the Stern family, I beseech on behalf of my family and my household the protection and support on our path of Him whom it is not possible to name.*
>
> *With these lines I bring to a close my dissolute youth and formally pledge that in the time that remains to me I shall put away my childish things and will instead serve the public good. First of all I must earn by dint of my own labour the one thousand florins I have promised the Magyar Society. Therefore I vow to devote myself with all my strength to the family wine business.*

Yanna and Nanna Eszter thought they had seen a ghost when amongst the carters arriving for the morning work-roll they spotted Otto Stern, whose build and height were certainly a match for theirs. 'What are you looking for? Or perhaps I should ask: for how much?' said Nanna Eszter in lieu of a greeting.

'Work. All day.'

Amid gasps of incredulity he was assigned to copy bills of lading. Otto Stern's grip on the goose-quill was initially awkward, but in a short while he produced reasonably legible documents despite his stubby fingers, which like his trousers became so spattered with inkblots that Yanna finally dug out an old leather apron for him to wear. By afternoon Rebecca, followed later by Richard Stern himself, had wandered into the office to see for themselves that it was no mirage or trick: their eldest son had of his own accord put his shoulder to the wheel.

His brothers were at a loss to explain Otto Stern's volte-face, and over supper bombarded him with questions. Otto Stern replied only: 'The time of the Vandal Band is done.'

As night fell, Ferenc and Ignác were in the Nagyfalu hostelry; Mihály and little Józsi and János were not with them ('If Otto is staying, we are not going. We painted it red enough last week!').

Otto Stern suspended his visits to Rakamaz also. In his industry and stamina he reminded the oldest generation of István Stern in his prime. Otto Stern also began to resemble his paternal grandfather in his looks, particularly his face, and the way he trimmed his hair and beard.

The first snow had fallen when Nanna Eszter and Yanna had the chief accountant produce the annual balance sheet for the business. By then most of their turnover had been achieved, and the contracts made it possible also to calculate the amounts outstanding. The Stern Wine Emporium had had a year that surpassed all previous years. Everyone had to grant that this was in large measure thanks to Otto Stern, and Nanna Eszter pushed the iron-bound cashbox on the table towards him: 'Take as much money as you see fit!'

Otto Stern took out two hundred florins and then, after some hesitation, another hundred. That evening he counted it all out into Miksa Stern's hands and asked for a receipt. 'To be continued,' he said. He had worked out that in three years he would be able to honour his undertaking. With luck it might be sooner. From time to time he would disappear for a day to no one knew where – Nanna Eszter and Yanna hoped that he was secretly wooing some marriageable girl, like that one in Rakamaz.

After Hanukah, Mihály bade farewell to the family and

moved to Debreczen where the Collegium – thanks to the intervention of Endre Dembinszki – had given him a place. Richard Stern slapped his back proudly: 'Don't you dare bring shame on me ... many people there know me.' Leaning closer to his ear, he whispered: 'There's no need to advertise what family you come from ... understand?' As the boy looked blank and blinked at him he added, even more quietly: 'We are Jews but that is our business, right?'

Otto Stern encouraged little Józsi and János to follow Mihály's example while there was still time, but a family council resolved that the two boys should not yet leave the family home. Ferenc and Ignác, on the other hand, were hoping to travel to Vienna and with someone's influence ask for admission to the cadet school. Richard Stern broke out in a cold sweat at the thought of his sons as army officers of the emperor whose secret service had deprived him of so many years of his life. But he voiced his opposition only once, and even then it sounded more with melancholy than command. Ferenc and Ignác responded that times had changed.

Otto Stern shrugged his shoulders: 'If the grapes are ripe, they have to be picked.' Nowadays he expressed himself solely in viticultural metaphors. When his father asked him to explain this gnomic utterance, he elucidated: 'Let them play at soldiers if that is what they want.'

The spring brought much rain and brown, muddy liquid swirled down the hillsides, swelling the rivulets into streams, the streams into rivers. The vintners watched with sinking hearts as the water poured down through the lower-lying vineyards. They dug trenches to divert the water, built sandbanks, and emptied the tool sheds. While Richard Stern's house was safe on a hilltop, the old Stern house was almost encircled by the swollen stream and the rising waters had burst into the cellars and were lapping the supporting walls outside. Those were made of the local red stone, but the rear walls, of sun-dried brick, virtually fell apart in the water. Carpenters were summoned to prop up the ends of the timbers with supporting beams. None the less the situation was dangerous; if the blessed waters from above did not cease, more serious problems were on the cards.

The whole of Hegyhát, from youngest to oldest, was preoccupied with the floodwaters when there arrived, incognito, Graf Franz Neusiedler, a member of the Governing Council, and took lodgings in the Nagyfalu hostelry. He made the county council building his first port of call. He had his calling card sent in to Ádám Geleji Katona jun., the alispán, who received him without further ado. Graf Franz Neusiedler announced, in a sing-song German that made little effort to disguise his Tyrolean origins, that in his capacity as a royal commissioner he had been charged with the confidential task of investigating a report made to the police by one Lipót Vinkó, an inhabitant of Tokay. According to Lipót Vinkó there had been established here some kind of secret society, with subversive aims, whose members have declared themselves a citizen's militia and carry out training with arms and in uniform. The ringleaders are Miksa Stern, unemployed jurist, and Nándor Wimpassing, apothecary. In every matter relating to this case the alispán will be kindly subject to the commissioner's instructions.

Ádám Geleji Katona jun. was open-mouthed. To the best of his knowledge no such organization existed in the area. The office workers he summoned assured the gentlemen that no apothecary by the name of Wimpassing was to be found either in Tokay or in Hegyhát; the locals had to send for their medicaments to Szerencs, where the apothecary was one Győző Ferenczy, an elderly widower of a sedentary disposition who lived on his own and could hardly be suspected of such activity. Miksa Stern had indeed founded a Magyar Society for the advancement of Hungarian culture,

175

but had obtained permission in writing to do so. The document was duly presented to the commissioner. Graf Franz Neusiedler gave a knowing smile: 'Because you are not aware of something, it does not mean that it does not exist. Have Miksa Stern sent for at once.'

The bailiff had not located Miksa Stern by nightfall, so the interrogation was postponed until the following day.

That night Miksa Stern was to be found in Szerencs, in the Tulip House. This modest building was concealed behind a high stone fence and centuries-old oak trees; it was known only to those who had heard about it by word of mouth. It owed its name to the four-petal tulips crowning its wrought-iron gate. The house had only a single storey, its thick walls rising to arches, its roof tiled, and its windows and doors so ungenerously proportioned that candles and lamps needed to be lit even during daylight hours. It consisted of six square rooms, a kitchen, a bathing room and a privy. The rooms were identical and could be made into one enormous space by opening the interconnecting doors, at the cost, of course, of privacy. This arrangement was suitable for the Tulip House's current use: a card-playing saloon in which the gentlemen played for quite hair-raising sums.

Otto Stern was counted among the regular visitors, Miksa Stern came less often, preferring to be the kibitz, if they let him. Otto Stern played with clenched teeth and if he did not leave with his money trebled he would be most dissatisfied. Miksa Stern played for smaller stakes, which he none the less managed to lose in the end. He never asked for loans or credit; at such needful times he would rise from the card-table, offended, and watch how the others battled on without him.

Otto Stern was having little luck that day. He was surrounded by four tobacco merchants at the table, people used to playing together and capable of understanding each other from the droop of an eyelid. When the amount that he had allotted himself for gambling had migrated over to his partners, Otto Stern struggled to his feet, departing with a click of his heels and the accompanying of his spurs. Miksa Stern followed him like a puli dog. 'Where now?' he asked when the iron gate had slammed behind them.

'What is that to do with you? Mind your own business.'

'Be not angry with me, I was on your side. I find it touching, your effort on the Society's behalf.'

'Not the Society's; my own. I keep my word.'

They walked on towards the centre of town, where they had tethered their mounts. No one ever tied up a horse at the Tulip House, lest the act reveal that their owners were within. Otto Stern gave a round stone such a kick that it flew some two hundred ells, hitting a post with a sharp crack.

It was well past midnight when the two riders reached the first bend in the Hegyhát stream. The low-lying field was waterlogged, the water up to the tired horses' knees, their hoofs slipping dangerously. Otto Stern turned back. His cousin thought he was looking for a ford, but Otto Stern had decided to head for the Nagyfalu hostelry. Climbing down from his horse, he gave the wooden door a resounding knock. No answer. He then battered on the door with both fists so hard that at every blow the wood visibly bent inwards. An old woman wearing a black kerchief looked out of the spyhole; she must have tumbled out of bed – a grey feather fluttered on her hair. 'Stop that row!'

'Since when have they been locking the door?' asked Otto Stern.

'Holy Mother of God!' The old woman mellowed as the key rattled and turned in the lock. 'A good while since Sir last honoured us with his presence!' Wordless, Otto Stern aimed for the bar. Only two drunkards lay in a stupor across the tables, fallen together by the ears. The instruments of the Gypsy band were piled up in one corner, wrapped in layers of rags. Otto Stern let out a bellow: 'What on earth is this? A condemned cell?'

The two drunks started awake and blinked at him in confusion. By then Benedek Bordás had scuttled out, a gown hurriedly wrapped about his night-shirt. 'Mr Stern, sir, . . . at such a late hour?'

'Just so. A pint of your best red!' he glanced at Miksa Stern: 'Same for him!'

'Thank you, but I would rather . . .' he began, but an angry flash from the eyes of Otto Stern made him swallow his words.

When the wine arrived, Otto Stern tossed his off in a single gulp and then pulled the landlord close by his leather apron: 'Have you any girls?'

'I do.'

'What sort?'

'What sort does Sir wish?'

Otto Stern considered his reply. He had not touched a woman since time out of mind; desire rose afresh within him. 'Full bosomed, tight-rumped, and one who washes often!'

Benedek Bordás ran to the serving girls' quarters behind the hostelry. There were only two left now, the others having moved on. Borcsa, the fiery Gypsy, and Fatimeh, who had fetched up here from some distant shore. Benedek Bordás wondered which one to wake up, and chose Fatimeh, as her door was closer. Fatimeh, dressed in accordance with the customs of her village, looked as if she had wound a Turkish prayer-mat around herself. She asked tremulously from within: 'Who is that?'

'Open the door. I have a job for you.'

Fatimeh's dark iris was clouded still by the mist of sleep.

Benedek Bordás felt sorry for her. 'It is no joy for me either, at a time like this . . .' and he yawned.

'Let us go!' said Fatimeh.

Otto Stern was waiting in the back room. He was staring out of the window, wondering if those really were the first faint rosy fingers of dawn outside, or if his eyes were simply deceiving him.

They knocked. Otto Stern let the girl in.

'At your service.'

'What's you name?'

'Fatimeh.'

'I have no memory of you here before.'

The girl did not reply. She was twisting and tugging at the material of her dress, her eyes fixed on the ground. Otto Stern took her chin into his hand and studied her more closely. Then, quietly, he asked: 'Are you a Jew?'

'Of course I am not a Jew!' Fatimeh's indignation raised the pitch of her voice so high that it offended Otto Stern's ears.

'Well then, where were you sprung from?'

'Isn't that all the same to you?'

Otto Stern bawled her out: 'Answer my question if I ask you, or I will . . .'

But before he had a chance to strike her, Fatimeh began to undress, and as her soft nakedness shone out, there was more light than when the double candlestick was burning on its own. Otto Stern threw himself upon the girl in the way he thought a man is supposed to find pleasure in a woman. Fatimeh took him by the arm: 'No, good sir, not like that. Let me undress you properly. Lie down, close your eyes, and leave the rest to me.'

Otto Stern's anger – if he is paying, no little whore should be telling him what to do – unexpectedly dissipated, and warm feelings of childhood spread within him and for a few moments he was a suckling babe in the arms of his mother, Yanna. And then he received from the girl something he had never before experienced. For him hitherto the securing of pleasures of the body was a struggle: the more stormily he conquered the female of the species the more he felt himself the conqueror, and his pleasure came from this source too. Fatimeh tamed him, coaxed the feral beast within into a sweet household pet.

By the time he awoke in the morning the girl had gone. Otto Stern was staring at the ceiling, musing on the events of the night, when two bailiffs burst into the room and ordered him to the bar, and, since he resisted, they whistled for two more of their kind so that together they overcame him, tied him up, and led him through the corridor into the large room now bathed in sunlight. Already sitting there, every muscle of his body trembling and also with his hands tied behind his back, was Miksa Stern, face to face with Ádám Geleji Katona, jun., and Graf Franz Neusiedler, member of the Governing Council. Who proceeded to wipe his moustachios – they had just been drinking wine – and began, in the official language of the empire: 'Do you speak German?'

'Yes . . . as much as I have to,' replied Otto Stern.

'Quite a fellow! While I have people looking for you everywhere, you are hiding in the hostelry, a stone's throw from my bed for the night.'

'I am at home in these parts.' He bellowed at Miksa Stern: 'You will shake yourself to death if you don't stop! They are not going to eat you!'

'Speak only when you are spoken to!' exclaimed Graf Franz Neusiedler.

Otto Stern threw him a murderous look. The royal commissioner, leafing through his papers to begin the interrogation, was untroubled by it.

What were the aims of this particular Society? Why was the primitive Hungarian language more important to them than use of German or Latin? Where does the Society store its uniforms and weapons? Denial is useless: the truth will out. And so on, relentlessly, for many hours. Otto Stern

180

sometimes lost his self-control and bawled or uttered threats, but the alispán always called him to order and because of the offence to a person of his rank he held out the prospect of monetary fines or imprisonment. Otto Stern felt worse and worse, sweat poured off his brow, but he could not wipe it away; the rope dug deep into his flesh; his spine had acquired a crick on the hard-backed chair; but most of all he was consumed by sheer fury: on what grounds were they interrogating him like a criminal? He was afraid that he would share the fate of his father, who in all innocence and in the prime of life was cast into the prison of the Austrian emperor and Hungarian king. Come to think of it, what right does he have to rule over us? Why is Austria not enough for him? And why don't we have a Hungarian king of our own? One who speaks our language, knows our customs, has our interests at heart . . . When he reached this point it dawned on him that what they should have done is precisely what he was being unjustly accused of doing: donned uniforms, taken up arms, and gone to war against the tyranny that tells us what to do from far-off Vienna, with rough hands and the injudicious exercise of power. He felt a growing knot in his head and in his ribcage; he was wheezing like a blacksmith's bellows.

'Are you unwell?' asked Ádám Geleji Katona jun., and motioned to one of the bailiffs to give the accused some water. Otto Stern would have reached for the cup but forgot that his hands were tied behind his back. He tripped forward on the chair and knocked his chin on the table with an almighty crack that made even the councillor shudder.

Miksa Stern gave a high-pitched shriek that sounded like a girl's: 'Otto!'

Graf Franz Neusiedler slipped out from behind the table. 'We shall have a pause. Bring him round as quickly as you can.' Grasping the wine bottle and his cup he went out into the hostelry garden. In summer it was possible to dine out

181

of doors, at X-legged tables painted green. He sat down on a bench at one of these.

Benedek Bordás hurried out to wipe down the wooden table as the Graf sat down, and instantly conjured up a blue-and-white tablecloth. 'Nice day we are having!' he said to the Graf, in Hungarian.

Graf Franz Neusiedler looked straight through him. Thanks to his mother, Annamária Lórántffy, he was fluent in the language but considered that when representing the Austrian emperor he could not stray from the official language.

It proved quite impossible to obey his command and beat some life into Otto Stern, though they even tried to do so literally. In the end they had to seek new orders from the Graf, who had both suspects taken to the prison cell of the county assembly, where they were manacled hand and foot and chained to the walls. Otto Stern was in a sitting position on the cold stone. Miksa Stern's chains were close enough to Otto Stern's to allow him to reach his head with the palm of his hand. He kept putting his fingers in his mouth and with the moisture thus gained he would stroke Otto Stern's face, though the latter continued to show no sign of life. Miksa Stern sobbed and wondered what his elderly parents would say if they knew.

Golden honey from the comb rolled softly on some flat surface, the bees buzzed soothingly above him. Otto Stern, in swaddling clouts, watched as Nanna Eszter spread the honey with practised movements. Now Otto Stern could see that the pale surface was the rolled-out pastry of the strudel and covered the entire table, like a tablecloth. After the honey there came the sprinkling of poppyseed, sultanas and chopped walnuts, and finally a dusting of fine white sugar – this was the Sterns' recipe for strudel.

Otto Stern was clear, however, that he was merely remembering this. In the background the stone flags of the prison cellar, black with damp, confirmed that this was the dream, not the other. The images of the past were followed by a token vouchsafing of the future: he could see how there was a flood, then a conflagration, and the foaming of much blood: difficult years lay ahead of us. He could see the birth of his son Szilárd. He could see in the light of many candles on a glittering wooden podium wildly gesticulating men saying their piece as the now-adult Szilárd quietly whispered the odd word to them . . .

His pain increased and again he fell into the well of the unconscious.

When he next came to himself, night had fallen, and he was very cold. Someone nearby was snoring with something more like a croak (on the basis of his family history, his guess was that it was a dog). He could feel that the time-piece was missing from his pocket, the egg-shaped watch, his most treasured possession! He tried to reach for his pocket in so far as the irons permitted and could feel that the chain, too, was gone – someone had torn it off. The henchmen? Or that girl? What was her name? Fatimeh . . .

This loss pained him more than all the physical suffering. His teeth were chattering. Had he not been able to look ahead, he would have been quite unable to quell his baleful foreboding that this was undoubtedly the end. But he knew he would have a son, and that was possible only if he survived this filthy prison, this filthy business, this filthy time.

Graf Franz Neusiedler was still at the breakfast table when news was brought to him that one of the suspects had expired during the night.

'Pity. That means he will not be able to undergo interrogation.'

Some hours later he discovered from the sealed package brought to him by mounted courier that he had travelled so far from Vienna in vain. The Hegyhát where Nándor Wimpassinger (not Wimpassing) and Miska (not Miksa)

Stern had secretly founded a citizen's militia was another Hegyhát, at the far end of the country and no more than a day's ride from the imperial capital. The councillor immediately issued instructions to Vienna to have the copyist who had committed the error dismissed from his post.

'What shall we do with Miksa Stern?' asked Ádám Geleji Katona, jun.

'Is he a noble?'

'No. He is part of the local vintner fraternity.'

'The lash.'

'How many?'

'Five and twenty.'

'In public?'

'Please yourself.'

Graf Franz Neusiedler was the last person to leave the lower part of the village on four wheels, raising his feet onto the seat opposite, as the water in the carriage rose knee-high. There were no other outsiders there. A third of the houses, chiefly along the low-lying banks of the stream, were in danger of collapse. The cellars had turned into baths, the walls were wet through and on the point of disintegrating. The following day the waters rose again, drowned some domestic fowl, and all manner of objects were swept away by the swirling stream.

Along the stream it was possible to do little more than move what could be moved to higher ground. All the boats, rafts and other useful equipment that could be found or made proved inadequate. Those who lived higher up also thought it best to carry away their goods piecemeal; those who had carts of some sort used them; those who did not pushed or dragged trolley-like contraptions.

The flood had damaged 23 houses, of which 14 collapsed. The embankment was breached. The water did not start to subside for another week. Those who had lost a great deal included the Sterns; though their homes fortunately did not fall, most of their goods were gone. In the confusion and chaos the death of Otto Stern passed with little notice; even his burial they did not get round to until a month later, and even then it did not go at all smoothly. His body had by then swollen considerably and a much larger than usual coffin had to be made.

The water table in the cemetery had risen so high that it was not possible to dig a grave; even a moderately deep burial pit immediately turned into a duckpond. The earthly remains of Otto Stern were laid to rest only by lining the sides of his burial chamber closely with rocks and using buckets, for hours before the burial, to empty it of the thin sludge that steadily seeped into it. When the gravediggers threw the earth on the coffin, the mourners feared that the clods of earth would float off at once, before their very eyes, as the water welled up again.

'We have done what we could,' mumbled Nanna Eszter, as she placed her own pebble on the mound. She kept thinking how this dear boy loved to swim. Her eyes burned, without tears, as she recalled how the six Vandals would swim across the Tisza, each urging the others on, like a pack of dogs let off the leash, with Otto Stern at their head, his muscular arms splashing and swirling in the river, his red hair blazing like the biblical burning bush.

VI

THE FIRST BREATH OF DECAY BRUSHES THE FACE OF the land: autumn is here. Colours, fragrances, delectable tastes there remain aplenty, but the grain is now piled high in the barns, and the barrels are brimming with must. The bushes and trees sigh as they are relieved of their burdens. As soon as her treasures have been harvested, mother earth can afford to attend less to her outward appearance. The greens are mollified by yellows that pave the way for the russet browns to come. The dogs are now less tolerant of the feline cabals than hitherto. The latter flee from before them with hissing squeals and caterwaulings to the far end of the yard, the top of the fence, into the lofts or up chimney stacks.

'The good Lord surely did not make you with childbearing in mind, my dear,' said the midwife, perspiring profusely, to the delicately built young woman, when at last the throes of labour came to an end and the baby's rather swollen and unusually bloody little body emerged.

'Safe and sound,' said the midwife.

The baby gave a little cry. Sparrow cheeps, thought the exhausted mother, barely able to keep her eyes open.

The child was christened Szulard. In the part of the

country whence her mother hailed this was a favourite name for puppy dogs. With his bright eyes, a permanently furrowed, receding brow and fragile-looking limbs, Szulard indeed resembled a retriever puppy in many ways. Even in adulthood his face recalled the muzzle of a well-fed dog. And for this reason he was rarely taken seriously. As he grew up there were few children more obedient and gentle than he; perhaps the only respect in which he stood out from his companions was that he never stopped talking. He spent his childhood in a village by the sea in the care of his grandmother.

The most wonderful years of my life were those before I knew either my cross or my misfortune. My existence differed little from that of the beasts of the field. I could play as an equal with the other boys, and through my physical prowess I was able even to earn a measure of their respect. I excelled at running, swimming and in catching fish by means of trap or rod.

When he came of an age for education, his grandmother took him to the local school, where all four classes sat together in one big hall, and the teacher took turns at feeding them knowledge.

That same week, his mother came to take him away. The two women's difference of opinion concerning the immediate future of the boy became so heated that the neighbours wondered whether to intervene. The grandmother, whom Szulard addressed as Babka, regarded it as a crime against heaven to pluck the boy out of his normal surroundings. 'You say you have finally settled down, but how many times have you said that before? Who knows when you will next get an itchy arse and then he will be in your way again! This is a little human being, not some object you leave in pawn at your mother's whenever you feel the urge!'

187

'I swear those days are over! I have made a home – little wonder that I should want my child with me! It's time he had some discipline at last.'

'And you are just the one to give him some, eh?'

'Yes, me! Yes!'

'Well, I am not letting him go.'

'What gives you the right—'

'It isn't a matter of rights!'

'Yes it is!'

Szulard listened to this altercation in the kitchen and was scared. He was perched in the inglenook with the black cat in his lap, both of them basking in the warmth of the crackling logs. It was the first time this year that Babka had lit a fire in the morning. Szulard remembered that every time his mother visited, she and Babka always fought like cat and dog; you could hear the grinding of their teeth. His child's trusting soul trusted with all his might in Babka and his mother, whom she called Matushka. He knew that it was his future that was at issue but he was not worried. Neither of them could possibly wish him ill.

An hour and a half passed and Matushka opened the door. 'Get dressed, my boy, we're going to visit your grandfather.'

The two women in black walked with the boy between them, holding his hands on the bumpy road that led to the cemetery on the hill. Szulard had never known his grandfather. When he was first brought here by his mother, Uncle Pani had already lain in his grave for some time. He had never seen Babka in anything but mourning dress; when he was younger he thought all women dressed in black all the time.

At the graveside peace suddenly broke out between mother and daughter. Like some well-rehearsed couple they used a little spade to do some weeding, and cleaned up the gravestone where – Szulard could not yet read it – just a

188

few words had been engraved in old-fashioned Cyrillic letters: *Pane Vikulich Boldin, died in the year 1825. May the grave burden him not.* They lit the two candles in their cardboard sleeves and prayed for a long time, sometimes silently, sometimes out loud and in a duet of mourning, Babka's deep, booming prayers entwined, liana-like, with Matushka's higher-pitched chant. Szulard knew Our Father and Hail Mary and to these he added his thin little piping.

Two days later they were in the post-chaise, all three of them. Babka wanted to see with her own eyes where her grandson was going. All Szulard's worldly goods fitted easily into his grandfather's army chest, which had been rubbed clean with a rag dipped in vinegar. For the journey Babka had prepared Szulard's favourite food: pork tenderloin fried in fat on sliced white bread. Matushka did not want any: 'Makes me feel bloated.'

'Bloated my foot!'

They were at each other's throats again. Szulard was unconcerned; all the more for him.

Matushka would not cease elaborating on their idyllic future. Szulard should not imagine some God-forsaken little one-horse place; he would be moving to a proper big city, where the roads are paved, a brass band plays in the main square on Sundays, and the dramatic society, of which she, Matushka, is a founding member and cashier, performs twice a week in the grand salon of the Golden Lamb hostelry. 'But that's not all. We have our own house, thank God, in the Lower Town; we shall plant violets and forget-me-nots in the garden in the spring! You will see how glorious it will be!'

'Kitchen garden?' barked Babka sternly.

'At the back. But we no longer need it.'

'Don't you get too full of yourself! Don't forget there will be lean years.'

Szulard was sorry to leave behind only one thing: the

black cat. Babka held the view that cats belong with their houses and waste away if parted from them. Szulard wept bitterly, stroking the shiny black fur with great affection.

'We will come back for a visit no later than summer!' said Matushka. As this had no effect, she promised Szulard a brand-new cat and he, with many sniffs and whispers, was at length assuaged. The black cat did not bat an eyelid as the boy bade farewell.

This was only the first of his mother's promises not to be fulfilled. It was to be followed by many more. No younger brother or sister was born. He was not educated in an expensive school. He did not become a well-to-do landowner. He did not become a respected member of the community. He did not live to a ripe old age.

After several days of being tossed about in the carriage, they arrived, in the middle of the night and a violent storm, in a town with cobblestones that made the post-chaise's wheels clatter so loudly that it awoke Szulard from his slumber. They clambered out in a square surrounded by terrifyingly tall houses on every side, yet a biting wind swirled through them as the coachman unloaded their baggage. Matushka leaned over to Szulard and pointed out their new home: 'There it is!' she said, her scarf fluttering like a flag.

Szulard, still half in the realm of sleep, could not understand why his mother was saying this. Leaving the chests and coffers on the cobblestones, they set off, leaning into the wind, as the first streaks of dawn brought some light. They turned in the direction of a crescent that opened from the square. A loud knock on the wooden door of the third house brought a servant in a shawl to the door and, with noises resembling the bleating of goats, she welcomed them through the arch, whence the path led to the courtyard and then through several doors to the rooms. A man also emerged; he too began to bleat, but this Szulard found less odd, since he wore a goatee. He also wore a pince-nez, like the teacher back home. He picked up Szulard and lifted him high, in the direction of the oil-lamp. He burst into tears, and his mother took him. 'There, there. It's all right. He says he is pleased you are here!'

'Who says?' asked Szulard.

'My husband, that's who!' replied Matushka.

'Good God!' said Babka. 'You have a husband?'

'Of course I do! I told you so!'

'You say so many things . . . And it has to be such a lard-tub?'

'He is not in the least a lardtub, he is Béla Berda, town clerk of the Noble County!'

Hearing his name, the man became more animated, shaking Babka by the hand and rattling away in goatish.

'I don't understand . . . what language is he speaking?' asked Babka.

'What do you mean what language? It's Hungarian of course!' Matushka replied.

'You didn't tell me that either.'

'Oh, mother! We are in Hungary after all! What language do you think they speak here? Romanian?'

Szulard was still in tears and the man, Béla Berda, town clerk of the Noble County, could not fathom why. He had expected scenes of joy unconfined to greet the arrival of the woman and the child, the child he had most generously consented to have in his home. Béla Berda was fond of giving his own names and nicknames to things and people. He called his wife countress (with reference to her role as cashier) or artress (in view of her other roles), and considered these terms outstandingly witty. He had decided well in advance that he would call the boy Frisky Rabbit, which he thought highly amusing. Only for his mother-in-law could he not find a suitable nickname; he had supposed that one would occur to him the moment he saw her. Later he heard Frisky Rabbit address her as Babka, so he playfully derived from this Babotchka, 'Little Bean', which was not in the least appropriate for that particular lady.

Frisky Rabbit failed to stick as a nickname, and the slight twist to the more standard Szilárd by his classmates in the school proved more lasting. He spent the first day there in a state of shock: he could not make out a single word the teachers – there seemed to be quite a number taking classes in turns – were saying. He felt he was for ever banished from the cacophonous noise that united the Hungarian children. He did not speak to strangers gladly, even when they spoke his language. Matushka made reassuring noises: 'You'll get the hang of it soon enough, don't you worry. If I could do it, with my thick skull! You will also hear Hungarian at home.'

The boy sobbed through every night; his pillows traced his tears in veiny blotches. After Babka went back, he felt very much alone. When he could, he spent his time hovering around the yard behind the now-wilted lilac bushes, where Béla Berda had laid out his dovecote, with its hundred or more black birds. Szilárd was much happier learning their language, spending hours billing and cooing with them. Naturally Béla Berda also tagged his birds with sobriquets, his favourite layer being designated Icarus, for example; Szilárd preferred the male called Pilinga, whose unusually long, straight bill did truly resemble the knifeblade that the word denotes in Magyar.

Forbidden it may have been, he none the less soon mastered the art of climbing up to the dovecote. His mother would summon him down because of the cold autumn wind; but Béla Berda was more concerned about the exemplary order he maintained up there: 'If you foul up the fowl, you will have to clear up yourself!'

Despite these threats the boy happily spent his time in the dovecote. Unsurprisingly Béla Berda in due course dubbed him the Ace of Doves, playing on the name of the highest card in Hungarian tarot, and every time he uttered this sobriquet he would chortle at his own wit. When no one else adopted it, Béla Berda noted yet again how others seemed to be deaf to sophisticated verbal humour.

Szilárd went in fear of his stepfather, never knowing where he stood with him, and kept out of his way as much as possible. He also avoided his mother, as she was invariably on the side of her husband. Szilárd never got close to his mother; he much preferred Babka and her absence pained him greatly. Nor did he find any support among his school friends; he was relentlessly mocked for the way his Hungarian *a*s curled into *á*s and for his splashy *s*s. He was racked by a vague memory that this was not the first time this had happened to him. Only in the company of the doves did he find peace of mind and satisfaction. He held their warm little bodies close and was thus no longer cold; he imitated, successfully, the little noises they made with their beaks. If he was sure no one was looking he would stand up quite straight on the steep roof of the dovecote and stretch out his arms, as if flying. At times like this warm little birds of joy fluttered up in his soul.

He must have made a startling sight as he stirred the autumn sky with his spindly arms, eyes closed, head to one side, raising one leg again and again, like a dove. Those in the building paid him no heed, while on the courtyard side he was shielded from view by the tall poplars. He firmly believed that there would come a day when, as a result of all his practice, he would be able to rise into the sky, circle the yard a few times and then fly off, far away, to the distant village where Babka lived, near the sea, the place where he last remembered being happy. Since he had lived here, he was sure that even the number of stars in the heavens was fewer.

Even rain could not keep him away from the dovecote; he welcomed the little fat drops falling on his face. At such times there pounded in him even more powerfully than usual the desire to fly south, on the trail of the migratory birds. He stood up on tiptoe.

'Get down at once!' his mother shouted at him, when she saw the boy, soaked to the skin, from the kitchen window.

The cry came as a shock to Szilárd and for a moment he lost his balance, the soles of his shoes seeking but failing to find purchase on the wet planks; he slid down to the edge and although he reached out with his arm, it was in vain and he plunged head-first into the air. As he fell his knee hooked itself around one of the dovecote's supporting beams and for a fraction of a second it seemed to hold, only for the rotten wood to snap in two, and down came the bracket as well, right on the boy's head as he landed on the ground, the doves spraying out as he flew.

The medical orderly who lived near by came running over in his apron and slippers and promptly gave up on him. 'Look, town clerk Berda, the skull has split wide open, the brain's damaged, I will be bound; what could I do?'

His mother was hysterical and had to be dragged away from the blood-stained ottoman on which he had been laid. There was a gentle smile playing about Szilárd's lips. Now, at last, he was able to do what he had so long been preparing for: to fly away.

He saw Kornél Csillag being teased and mocked for the German accent of his Hungarian speech.

He saw Bálint Sternovszky as a child and a young man, falling out of a window, twice.

He saw István Stern at the time of the Lemberg catastrophe.

He saw Richard Stern on the wide double bed, struggling in the presence of the congress – of this and of so much else, he understood little.

He saw Otto Stern with a wreath of tiny yellow flowers – buttercups? marigolds? euphorbia? – about his neck. He felt peculiarly drawn to this huge-eyed man with the flowing hair.

He saw Matushka, her hair let down, scantily clad, giving her favours to total strangers. What is this? He felt a sharp, stabbing pain as he saw this and how the men touched his mother.

The living dioramas cascaded and swirled around him. Fragments of present time would surface, too: the honeyed light of the curtains glittering on the windows, his mother's tear-soaked cheeks, a man with mutton-chop whiskers and hairy hands – the professor of medicine summoned from the hospital who in the end decided, against his professional judgement, to sew up the inches-long gash: 'We can but hope.' Szilárd bore the intervention – which the doctor said was particularly painful – without a murmur, so captivated was he by his sojourn in the past. He found out about the Book of Fathers, and was able to observe even its where-abouts: the completed folio was in Richard Stern's library, hidden in a gap between the floorboards; the one begun by Otto Stern lay in the offices of the Stern & Stern Wine Emporium, on the top shelf, buried under stacks of old bills.

Months passed without the boy regaining consciousness. One day there came through the town Dr József Koch, who had been elevated to the post of court physician by the Emperor in person, and whose ancestors, going back seven generations, had all been distinguished medical practition-ers; three of his brothers, too, had chosen the same career. He lodged in the Golden Lamb. Matushka begged him on bended knee to take a look at her little boy as he hovered between life and death. Town clerk Béla Berda hovered in the background with a servile smile, repeating: 'Money no object.'

'But it would be, were I greedy for money,' remarked Dr Koch. 'However, one asks for only as much as is right.'

Dr József Koch's fee equalled one month's emoluments

for town clerk Béla Berda, but it was no use; not even he knew the remedy for Szilárd's condition. 'If ever he were to get on his feet again, which I do not think at all likely, he would certainly be feeble-minded.'

'We had managed to reach that conclusion all by ourselves,' commented Béla Berda.

'Silence!' hissed Matushka, livid.

Béla Berda was quite certain his bankess had taken leave of her senses. She temporarily gave up her theatrical activities to devote all her time to her son. Where was that proud artess of old, who was not prepared to give up the stage even for his sake?

'I would leave any man for the stage, but there was never a man born that I would leave the stage for! That is not something you would ever understand . . . you . . . clerk of the town!'

It was through the theatrical company that they had met. A three-member delegation visited the county assembly to seek the support of the Noble County for their petition, which had been declaimed in ringing tones by the delegation's female member. Béla Berda put his weight behind their proposals, though in fact he wished to put his weight only upon their spokeswoman. A committee was established for the purpose of considering what might be done in the town to promote theatrical activity in the Hungarian language, to raise its status, and to ensure that performances in the Golden Lamb enjoyed the support of a select public.

The lilac bushes were in bloom by the time Szilárd was able to sit up in bed, and it was the grape harvest by the time he was able to leave it. He could have fitted into his clothes twice over, and his mother had to tie his trousers with string at the waist. He was to remain anaemic for the rest of his life, even if he was fed to bursting with the richest foods. He went the rounds of physician after physician, being prescribed fortifying concoctions and the oils of salt-water fish, or urged to spend summers by the sea and in the mountains of the High Tatras; nothing was any use.

'This boy's bones seem for some strange reason unable to retain flesh on them,' remarked the doctor in the mountain sanatorium.

Little though he may have borne in terms of flesh, he carried an enormous burden in his soul. What he had seen and almost touched at the opening of death's door remained with him for ever, and as he grew older he felt with increasing urgency the need to unravel their meaning. The first sign came as he was innocently rummaging around in his mother's writing desk: he chanced upon a broken gold necklace from which was suspended a very small gold locket. Szilárd felt that compared with the other glittering items, this one radiated warmth, and he held it tight in his hand for several minutes. Whenever thereafter the opportunity presented itself he would head for his mother's desk and at once seek out the locket and clutch it tight. The warmth that seemed to emanate from the locket he took as a message from days long past. He fingered and fondled it so much that suddenly the tiny lid sprang open. The image of a familiar face met his gaze.

The picture of Otto Stern had been made by a goldsmith in Debreczen. Yanna had ordered sketches of all her children, but only three were ever produced, as the goldsmith had lost his life in a robbery on his premises. Otto Stern had begged for the one of himself, thinking he would give it to Clara, but in the end he thought better of it.

Szilárd also turned up the egg-shaped timepiece; this came as no surprise, as he had seen it often enough in his visions. He longed to know more, but his mother was implacable: 'Leave off with all that ancient history; what little I knew I was only too glad to forget.'

'All right, but why will you not say who was my father? And my grandfather?'

197

'Your father now is town clerk Béla Berda and that is all there is to it. You unfortunate creature, rejoice and stop moping! Now that fortune is smiling upon us, why keep twisting that dagger in my heart?'

Szilárd sighed and left it at that. Once mother puts on one of her performances, truth flies out of the window. Only one sure source remained: the wellspring of the past. But how to launch again the kaleidoscope of images? He pondered this, night after night, sensing that thick blackness was the most likely part of the day for the longed-for wonder to occur. But for a long time he had nothing more to occupy his thoughts than the images he had been vouchsafed when he was so seriously ill with his head wound. He could feel still the little trough in his skull, the place of the imperfectly healed gap; his hair grew rather sparsely over it. His mother was ashamed of her son's gash and was constantly trying to cover it with a cap or hat or by combing his locks over it. For Szilárd it was not a problem; it made him unique. His fingers often found their way to the indentation and delicately mapped every tiny landmark in minute detail. He found much pleasure in carefully scratching his little trough, and would play with it just as other boys of his age enjoyed their penises. And he was told off in much the same way when his mother caught him: 'Stop fiddling with it!'

But in vain. In the caverns of the night when he was on his own and he could insert all five fingers in the uneven gash, his thoughts became more focused, as if his nails scratched the surface of the brain, waking whatever slept within. At such times he came closest to achieving the unfolding of everything that he longed so passionately to discover.

Meanwhile his mother paid him little attention – bigger things were brewing. The town was in turmoil. The Hungarian nobles were less and less inclined to comply with the

Emperor's wishes, finding his orders increasingly outrageous. There was a notable scandal when the Emperor's personal envoy was welcomed in the main square with a speech in Hungarian, the translation of which was not forthcoming. In a matter of minutes this crystallized into a slogan, which was soon on everyone's lips, indeed became the headline of the local newspaper: 'He who does not know our language cannot truly understand us!'; the crowds began to cheer and clap. The Emperor's envoy, a paunchy, goatee-bearded little fellow, misunderstood the situation, rose and began to bow low in all directions. He was met by booing and cries of 'Off, off!'

That evening in the Golden Lamb the local playwright Gáspár Szerdahelyi's tragedy *The Unhappy Hungarians* was being performed by the company. The action was set in the period of the Tartar invasions in the thirteenth century, yet the evil Tartars wore Austrian army uniforms, and their lines were peppered with words of German. The play was such a success that it held the audience in the Golden Lamb until well past midnight, and the company had to encore the fifth act. Szilárd's mother played a heroic sutler wench to universal acclaim, with her hair billowing and in a skirt so short that not only her ankle but sometimes also her shins flashed into view. Szilárd, who had been forbidden by Béla Berda to view the tragedy, partly because of the lateness of the hour and partly because he had not covered himself with glory at school, watched from behind the back row in the company of the other children. Here it struck him for the first time how beautiful his mother was and how much she was admired by the menfolk. It was an odd, tingling sensation, which kept him awake for nights on end.

The following day the Noble County unanimously voted for the resolution. Béla Berda took a copy home with him and proudly read it out at the dinner table. Szilárd's mother learnt it by heart. She often recited it, even if there was no obvious reason or audience, and even while doing the housework. It stuck in Szilárd's memory, too, he heard it so many times.

Under the chairmanship of Royal Councillor his Honour Endre Jagasics of Bátormező, Judges of the County Court Messrs József Morocza and Ferenc Dániel, Chief Constable Antal Varasdy, and Town Clerk Béla Berda, as members delegated by the Noble County to establish in its bosom the National Theatre Company, having met in the matter of the advancement of Theatre in the Hungarian language, humbly and respectfully beg to bring the following further proposals to the attention of the Estates of the Realm.

The aid which the Company shall need, over and above its other income, to consist partly of capital moneys raised, partly obtained by subscription from the Noble County, is hereby guaranteed. It is however deemed necessary to engage in discussions jointly with neighbouring Counties concerning the need to support the Theatre Company performing in the Hungarian language irrespective of the Noble County in which it is performing, since the Company can serve as a barrier and dam against the Germanization that is flooding us from the direction of Austria and Styria.

Further aid may consist in harnessing the support of a subscribing audience for 21 performances of the Hungarian Theatre Company over a period of five years. In addition, there should be established a Fund, of which the standing capital would assist the Company's goals and endeavours. Finally, in every district of the land all chief and deputy constables are to call upon all owners of land, men of the cloth, and nobles of quality and quantity, to contribute to the advancement of the National Theatre Company.

One night Szilárd had the sudden and absurd notion that if he were to climb up into the dovecote again, he would be able to imbibe some of the opium of the worlds long past. He pulled a gown over his nightshirt and stole out into the yard. Streaks boding ill lined the sky, veiling the full moon. From somewhere the desperate barking of a dog unable to sleep could be heard. Szilárd was shivering, the cool of the evening grass made his bare feet tingle. The dovecotes loomed huge in the dark, seeming much bigger than in the light of day. With considerable difficulty, he managed to shin up. He had grown recently and was heavier than in those days; the pole bowed under his weight. A few birds startled awake, cooing in righteous indignation.

'Only me,' he reassured them. He drew his palm along the feathers of the closely packed birds. It felt like the fur of the black cat they had left behind; goodness, how long it has been since he thought of her. Or of Babka; it was almost more difficult to summon up her face than those of the Sterns, whom he had encountered only in his visions.

He stood out on the edge of the dovecote, closed his eyes, and, using his right hand, inserted his fingers in the gash on his skull. And there, on the creaking plank, swaying this way and that like a reed in the night wind, a hair's breadth short of plunging into the deep, he finally got what he wanted.

The onset of his antipathy towards his mother began on this night. His unrelenting questions more than once convulsed Matushka with tears which only potent medicaments could stanch. Béla Berda categorically ordered Szilárd to cease this torturing of his mother, but he was no longer prepared to be ignored. In vain did they beat him, threaten to send him away to board, lock him in the cellars, make him kneel on maize cobs – nothing helped. As soon as he was within earshot of his mother, he would begin his litany: 'My father was called Otto Stern, was he not, and he had a heart attack in prison? My grandfather was a writer, was he not, who completed the Book of Fathers? You were a strumpet in hostelries, were you not, and allowed men to have their way with you for money? I could have had two brothers or sisters, had the angel-maker not freed you of your burden? Is that not so?'

Answers came there none. Béla Berda used a horsewhip or a riding crop to harry him from the house if he discovered that Szilárd had been harassing his mother again. The woman began to lose weight, coming to resemble her son in stature.

'Do you not see that you are killing her? You will be the death of your mother, you idiot!'

Szilárd nodded in sympathy: 'Of course, it is I who will be her death, not she who will be mine, by denying me any information about myself!'

'Very well! Ask me; I will answer your every question!'

Except that town clerk Béla Berda knew almost nothing about his wedded wife's past. Szilárd's appalling accusation, that Fatimeh was some kind of strumpet, he had no hesitation in rejecting. Completely out of the question. But the seed of suspicion had been sown in his heart. When he had first got to know her she was already in the troupe of actors, living with them in the Golden Lamb's seediest garret rooms. Even him she was not prepared to enlighten about her past: 'What has been is gone; if you want me, your desire must be for what there is now!'

But of course it is well known what women in the acting profession are like, mused Béla Berda now, staring deep into Szilárd's eyes, which were like those of an exhausted hound. And now both of them were pained by the past. But while Béla Berda was gnawed by a growing jealousy, in Szilárd Berda – he had adopted him officially – it was what he knew for certain that throbbed as an open wound.

On the sixteenth anniversary of the day of his birth,

Szilárd Berda slipped away from the house of his mother and stepfather. Apart from the clothes he stood up in, he carried a change of underwear and a few personal items which he tucked into the leather satchel that had been sewn for him by Babka. The egg-shaped timepiece, he knew, was inherited on his father's side. Likewise, he thought, the broken gold necklace with the medallion – for it contained a picture of his father. He counted out for himself half of the gold coins wrapped in linen in his mother's secret drawer – he thought that, having reached the age of majority, this was his due. It was but a venial sin to take an advance. He wrote every detail on a card which he placed in the drawer.

He travelled over fields and forests, sometimes on foot, sometimes hunched on jolting carts. There were decent folk in the country at whose tables he would be offered food and drink; if asked about himself, he replied he was a wandering scholar, looking for his father. He had no particular goal; he just followed his nose along roads virgin to him. Along many byways, by twists and turns, he reached the countryside that he recognized from his visions, where the shoots of the vine curl upwards hungrily on the vine-stocks.

He had no need to seek the sharp bend in the stream – all of a sudden he was there at the edge of the water, his ears caressed by the soft murmur of the stream. Small fish flung themselves out of the water, plunging back with a little plop.

'Well, this looks like it,' sighed Szilárd.

He had no need to ask after the house of Richard Stern, his legs carried him there on their own. He stood for a while before the door, waiting for someone to come out or go in, but no one did. Then he wandered over to the other side of the street, to the building that housed the Stern & Stern Wine Emporium, which had had an attractive pavement laid in front of it since he could last have seen it, if that is indeed the right verb to express the way he had learned about this landscape.

Brand-new wine barrels were being loaded onto an oxcart by the labourers, under the direction of a grey-haired old lady whom Szilárd recognized as Yanna, his father's mother. He dared not say anything to her; he just watched, with the mournful eyes of a dog, his shoulders drooping, his lips curled downwards. The old woman soon noticed him and with furrowed brows repeatedly glanced up in his direction. In the end she went over to him and said somewhat aggressively: 'What would you be wanting then?'

Szilárd could not reply. Moved, he surveyed the family resemblances in the old woman's face. Yanna cleared her throat (recently she had secretly started to smoke a pipe) and could not herself understand why she said more gently: 'Would you like a spot of hot soup? There will be a flask of wine after.'

She led him through the ground floor of the house, where a dozen men were writing away at desks facing each other. At the far end of the three interconnected rooms they came to an elongated granary, used for storing the many different tools needed for viticulture. A substantial table, used in the grape assessment process, dominated the centre of the room, and there was a flat-fronted oven with a fire blazing in it. Yanna gave a little push to the pot with the lunch in it. There was plenty of food for the scribes; there would be enough for this spindly, clearly finicky eater. 'May I ask who you are?'

'Szilárd Berda, at your service. But truly . . . I don't dare.'

Yanna put her hand on her hips: 'What are you afraid of? I don't eat children. How many summers?'

'My sixteenth.'

'A grown man, then.'

At this Szilárd finally gave a smile, flashing tiny, pearly teeth.

The scribes did all in their power to make him feel unwelcome during the meal, pointedly looking right through him. Each had his own wooden plate and spoon. Yanna gave him a clean plate and a spoon so big that he could only use the edge of it and as a result kept dripping soup on his shirt. He knew this struggle must appear comical and could hardly wait for the meal to end.

When Yanna expressed, in a foreign tongue, the hope that they had enjoyed their meal, Szilárd said, half audibly, thank you in his mother tongue. The scribes returned to their writing desks. A servant girl rinsed the plates with sand.

'Well now, out with it!' said Yanna.

'Well, you see . . . I know it is something of a surprise . . . but . . . I . . . well, I also belong here . . . as I am a Stern . . . a Stern from the wrong side of the blanket.'

'What!'

He told her what he knew. Yanna did not believe a word. Since their star had risen high in the sky, any number of tricksters and conmen had striven in various ways to soften her heart so that she would open her purse for them. But Yanna was made of tougher stuff. She interrupted him midstream: 'If, and I said if, it turns out that this is all true, what do you want of us?'

'I have no demands. Perhaps I could make the acquaintance of Uncle Richard, may God preserve him . . .'

Yanna cut in: 'You should know that in our faith we are not allowed to utter His name!'

'I truly beg your pardon.'

'The pardon is in His hands,' said Yanna, jerking her thumb towards the sky.

That evening she introduced the newcomer to the family. They listened with suspicion. Could they really be seeing the offspring of Otto Stern? They all awaited the decision of Uncle Richard. Richard Stern was in his sixtysixth year, the tremor in his hands and neck meant that he could take liquids only through a straw. He observed the boy, taking his time to study the most minute details. He recalled the day that he had himself arrived here to seek out his long-unseen family and was astonished to detect in the boy's eyes the very mirror of his feelings at that time. He gave a mollified wheeze. 'Can you support your words with some concrete proof?' he asked in a creaky voice.

Szilárd showed him the pocket timepiece and the medallion he guarded with his life. Yanna gave a squeal of joy when the face of her firstborn stared back at her from the gold locket. Richard Stern's hook of a hand pulled Szilárd towards him and the old man's wet kisses fell upon the boy in a shower. This is how it is with us, thought Richard Stern, moved: We keep losing members of the family, only to get them back again in the course of time. He embraced his grandson, who could feel on his skin the old man's tremors. There followed the uncles in turn, whom Szilárd was able to name at once thanks to his voyages back into the past: Ferenc, Ignác, Mihály, József, János. No one was surprised.

'You have aged a lot since . . . since . . . you know . . .' Szilárd stammered. His voice was drowned by the clamour from the thirty-odd members of the clan. Questions rained upon him by the dozen. His mother? His stepfather? Where was he born? Whereabouts did he live? Why had he not made himself known to them before? How did he come to be called Berda?

Szilárd's answers were full of detail. Then he asked his grandfather to show him the completed Book of Fathers, which he kept under the floorboards. Richard Stern gladly took him into the library where he knelt down and conjured up the dust-covered folio. That evening and night Szilárd did not set foot in the guest room made up for him, but lay on his stomach in the library, burning candle after candle down to the stump. Greedily he devoured and enacted in his imagination everything that he had hitherto known about only from his visions. He spent ecstatic hours on the worn carpet pockmarked with cigar burns. He was particularly struck by the realization that some of his ancestors were vouchsafed not just the past but, to a lesser degree, also the future. He, to the best of his knowledge, knew nothing of what was to come. Although he could not elucidate certain images he had seen, these could just as easily be the harbingers of things still to come. We shall see, he thought.

The following day he was also able to hold in his hands the folio begun by Otto Stern, since he could inform the family of its exact location. This made him a true celebrity. However, he had to wait his turn to read it, as first of all Richard Stern, then Yanna, and then the five brothers of Otto Stern had priority in trying to decipher this much more challenging script.

'Would it be exceeding the bounds of decency if I asked, most humbly, whether I might be allowed to continue writing the story?'

Richard Stern was so moved that he found it difficult to reply. 'What your father began is, it goes without saying, yours!' and with a solemn gesture he handed it to Szilárd. 'The Book of Fathers. Volume the Second. Let it be yours – in view of the exceptional situation – now, before it is due. Guard it as you would the light of your eyes!'

By then it was very late. Szilárd thought it was an abuse of their hospitality to stay any longer. Richard Stern kept saying the opposite. 'Where are you hurrying to? For years we had no idea that you existed! We have so much to discuss!'

Szilárd Berda basked in the warmth of his grandfather's house for close on a month. It was a warmth that he had felt neither at Babka's nor at his mother's. Yet he was unfamiliar with the prayers, customs and everyday expressions of the people here; he did not even understand their language, yet he gladly put the borrowed yarmulke on top of his head when they held a service to their God and he received with rapture the phylacteries that his grandfather placed upon him. He knew that his decision was not unusual in this family, none the less he was surprised at the ovation that greeted his announcement at the high day table: 'If you have no objection, I should like as soon as possible to adopt the surname Stern.'

When I returned to my legal residence I managed to smuggle the gold coins I had taken back into their hiding place without being noticed. I informed my mother of my decision. There was a more heated response than I had expected: she threatened to disown me, which town clerk Béla Berda heartily endorsed, saying I was an ungrateful puppy. He repeatedly brought up his generosity and his kindness of heart towards me, and the bonds that arise from the fact that he gave me his name. Though I felt that there was some truth in what he said, I could do no other. They who have eyes to see, let them see. Though a citation from the Torah might perhaps be more appropriate, it will be a long time before I shall be in a position to orient myself in the ancient language of the Jews.

Soon a compromise was reached: I was to attend the Lyceum of Eger town, the costs being borne by my grandfather Richard Stern, who, alas, in the November of that year departed this life. I mourned him greatly then and my sorrow has not diminished since.

The upper school offers a varied curriculum to the young student, whom the locals here call student gentlemen. To my great joy, I was able to include among my subjects not only the study of the Hebrew language but also astronomy, as the science of stargazing is called. At the top of the Lyceum building is located the Specula, architecturally a fine match for the building. The Specula is an astronomical observatory famed throughout the land, reached by climbing 320 steps. There I was able to spend many nights exploring the glittering wonders of the heavens

*by means of the most up-to-date optical machines of English
manufacture, while by day I spent a deal of time on the rotating
cupola terrace with its camera obscura. In bright sunlight it
throws shadows of outside images onto a white surface: scenes of
Eger life, people walking, gardens, houses, birds in the air, and so
forth. Professor Varágh, the distinguished astronomer, allowed me
to make good use of my free evenings by cleaning and polishing
the precious instruments.*

In the Lyceum, Szilárd registered as Berda-Stern on the
various lists. From his mother and stepfather he had a
monthly hamper, with the finest from the kitchen and the
garden in it. From the Stern house there came with similar
regularity a letter, which was always begun by Yanna, after
whom the goose-quill passed to the other relatives in turn.
Sometimes there were visitors from either or both quarters,
though most often it was Yanna who undertook the journey
to Eger, accompanied by one of her grandchildren. She listened proudly to the boy's account of the progress of his
studies. Szilárd Berda-Stern once tried to address his
grandmother in Hebrew, but it soon transpired that Yanna's
Yiddish had precious little in common with the language of
the Torah scrolls, which they were translating with the help
of Professor Xavér Fuchs, scholar of the classical and pre-
classical tongues.

Apart from the stars, it was the dramatic society of the
upper school that gained his devotion. The ceremonial hall
next to the oratory was used for the students' performances, with its large auditorium and a substantial, raised
wooden stage. Szilárd Berda-Stern could not overcome his
shyness, so he never volunteered for an actual role, but as
the jack-of-all-trades for the company found a great sense
of fulfilment in the role of prompter. He showed great flair
for prompting players who faltered on the open stage, offering a carefully chosen key word from the next line, which

209

immediately reminded them how to continue. Béla Berda took great exception to his squandering his time on such frivolous nonsense, but dared not forbid him, for it had to be granted that the boy had inherited a certain bent for the poetic qualities of the stage. It was curious that his mother also disapproved of this way of spending his time: 'I had hopes that you were fuelled by more serious passions than this!'

'And I have to hear this from you, of all people?'

'I am your mother and I want you to make more of your life than I have done of mine.'

In fact, Szilárd Berda-Stern did not consider that being the dogsbody for a theatrical troupe was a career for life. What he considered as a possible calling was the investigation of the secrets of the stars. To this subject he devoted many more hours than the timetable prescribed, and he would stay in the observatory until the cleaners ordered him to leave. He crouched under the telescope with one eye closed, using his right hand to focus and his left to make notes – being left-handed was, in this case, a distinct advantage. (The teachers' beatings in the lower school had forced him to use his right hand for writing, and in the presence of others he dared not do otherwise, lest they mocked him as 'Left Behind'.)

On the far side of the Lyceum there stood perhaps Magyarland's finest church, the object of admiration, both inside and out, for visitors from near and far. Szilárd Berda-Stern, too, brought all his visitors to the church, showing them also the bishop's palace which housed the priceless treasure of the nation, the Gallery of Choice Pictures. Whenever he could he would spend his time in the square, among the trees of the bishop's garden. The view, which cried out for a painter's brush, was somewhat spoilt during the day by a dozen or so beggars, and after dark by a similar number of gillyflowers, which latter the Lyceum's strict regulations forbade him from spying on, though from the Specula he could see them simpering in their revealing clothes at the men who passed by. On seeing them he always felt two searing stabs of pain, one because of his mother and another because of his swelling male desire.

One dull afternoon he met in the Lyceum square the dramatic company of Kálmán Jávorffy. This troupe of players planned to put on two performances in Eger, and wanted to hold them in the ceremonial hall of the Lyceum. They intended to put on the noted comedy *Matilde*. But his grace the bishop decided at the last minute to withdraw his permission for the use of the venue. The company was thus obliged to seek an alternative stage and eventually found itself performing at the Restaurant Spitz. On these nights the auditorium was less than half full. Szilárd Berda-Stern sat in the front row on both occasions. The box-office took no more than 51 florins, as Kálmán Jávorffy complained to the correspondent of *Hungarian Life Magazine*, who happened to be in town. The reporter concluded his review: 'Woe unto you, poor players! From here, too, you will have to leave one by one without farewell, or fight starvation while performing gratis.'

He decided to adopt this as his motto in his new life and copied it into the Book of Fathers on his last night in Eger. Mariska Zalay, the troupe's soubrette with the unfading smile, had captured his heart. Kálmán Jávorffy, learning of his skills as prompter, offered him casual work and Szilárd Berda-Stern knew he had to accept; he had no other choice. He bundled up his earthly goods and early in the morning loaded them onto the covered wagon. He found Mariska Zalay even more attractive when he was sleepy-eyed than at any other time and held her hand tight when they settled into their seats in the second cart.

They bade farewell to the town in a biting, hair-ruffling wind. They headed for the Hatvani Gate, and constantly had to pull aside to avoid the laden peasant carts rattling along the uneven cobblestones as they headed for the weekly market. The southern gate's open doors were hung with motionless chains; above them, darkly, loomed the fortifications.

Eger had almost disappeared from view when they caught sight of the scaffolds, from which swung the now-black bodies of seven convicted thieves. The women of the troupe began to shriek. The heavy smell of decay hung about the clearing; Mariska Zalay snatched up her pocket kerchief doused liberally with eau-de-cologne and thrust herself in some agitation into the arms of Szilárd Berda-Stern. He tried to play the tough man, though he knew that in his dreams these seven unfortunates would loom large for some time.

From the second stop on the tour he managed to send word to his mother as well as to the Sterns, asking for their blessing and approval of his decision. Instead of his mother, it was Béla Berda who replied with an icy, threatening letter, full of *unless*es and *without ado*s, and eight occurrences in all of the words 'disown' and 'disinherit'. Yanna was briefer: *How you make your way in the world is up to you. I want you to find a space where you can make the most of your talents.* Into the couverture there had been slipped a high-denomination banknote. Szilárd Berda-Stern pasted both letters into the Book of Fathers with starch gum.

His duties were described by Kálmán Jávorffy as follows: 'My boy, you are going to be the maid of all work. So if someone asks for boiling water, you jump to it and boil her some water, and if she demands cold water, you blow on it until it cools . . . do you get my drift?'

He nodded his assent. He had no wish to alert the company manager to the fact that he well knew what the ladies of the stage were like, from somewhere very close to home. What he really loved in his job was the prompting, when he felt as if the success of the whole performance depended on

212

the sharpness of his wits. It filled him with an almost las-
civious thrill that the audience knew nothing of this. It was
like the work of the anonymous authors of codices: we discover many things in their codices but almost nothing about
these humble faceless servants of the spirit.

When he asked Mariska Zalay whether she would consent to be his partner for life once he came of age, the
wonderment on her face masked two different kinds of
emotion: 'Szilárd, my darling boy, how can I know that? You
are still only in your seventeenth year, are you not? And in
any event, do not forget I am eight years your senior. By the
time you might marry me I would be on the verge of old
maidenhood.'

Szilárd Berda-Stern protested and when Mariska Zalay
still refused to utter 'yes' to his proposal of marriage, he
moodily withdrew into himself. He felt he had been
betrayed. He had quit the Lyceum in the belief that he had
now found his better half. How long was he to live in such
uncertainty? He thought with increasing sorrow of the
Lyceum. Of his daily life there what he missed most was the
time spent among the stars, and he decided that as soon as
he had the time and the wherewithal he would make himself a telescope, so that he could continue his wandering
among the night sky's wonders. When he stared into the
light of distant stars he had the same feelings as when he
was able to look into times gone by.

Marika Zalay insisted that wherever they lodged in a
new town, she was accommodated in a room of her own,
claiming that if she had to share with another she would be
unable to prepare for her performance. Szilárd Berda-Stern
was always obliged to share with one of the coachmen,
though he was nauseated by the latter's powerful smell of
sweat. Some nights he would slip into Mariska Zalay's
room: they had agreed that if a candle or lamp was lit in
the window, he could come; otherwise he was to keep out.

As time went by, there was a gradual diminution in the number of nights that the flickering light appeared on a range of window-ledges. Szilárd Berda-Stern suffered in silence. His agony was noticed only by Kálmán Jávorffy, and on one occasion he offered the lad what was intended to be a consolatory lecture on the inconstancy of women who worked on the stage. 'You can better trust a viper than one of them!'

Szilárd Berda-Stern strove not to show how shattered he was by what he had heard. But the more he thought about it, the clearer it became to him that the manager was right. After all, he should have known from his mother what sort of a woman she was before she married. None the less it took him the better part of a year to build up the courage to break with Mariska Zalay; moreover, he had to quit Kálmán Jávorffy's troupe to do it. He joined the Hungarian Theatre of Pozsony, in a role similar to his position hitherto, though the recompense was half as much again.

In this town, where there is a permanent Hungarian theatrical company, I found what I was seeking. Beside my theatrical work, I secured some income from teaching the Latin language by the hour. In a curious twist of fate I met a lady, Margit Galántay, a fanatical devotee of the theatre, and when I had made clear the seriousness of my intentions, she told me that her father Márton Galántay was the town's clerk. Appealing to this chance congruity, I sought the consent of my mother and step-father to my marriage, which subsequently I did indeed obtain.

His wife presented him with a boy and a girl. Their names Mendel and Hannah were taken by their parents from the heroes of plays fashionable at the time, but this was not something they made a deal of fuss about.

214

The Berda-Sterns' doors were open to all, and many of the town's most distinguished citizens passed through their gate. On Thursday afternoons they organized five o'clock tea, where gifted amateurs read from their poetry. Particular success was enjoyed by Bendegúz Tolnai, the teacher of Hungarian language and literature at the gymnasium, whose work the *The Silence before the Storm* saw print in the *Anthology*. The Berda-Sterns subscribed to numerous literary and scientific periodicals, which Szilárd felt could not be missing from the educated person's bookshelves. He gladly spent money on these. Though, it must be said, not at all gladly on other things. Their family bliss was frequently punctuated by rows which were invariably to do with financial matters. Margit often accused her husband of being a tight-fisted Harpagon. Szilárd Berda-Stern countered by accusing his wife of profligacy and even wanton squandering of their money.

Disturbing news came from Pest-Buda, where the young writers were constantly at odds with the censor's office. In the salon of the Berda-Sterns the names of the novelist Jókai and the poet Petőfi were mentioned in awed tones. The evening after the latest *Pictures of Life* arrived bearing the headline 'The Press Is Free!' they held an extraordinary meeting at the home of Bendegúz Tolnai. The poet, trembling with an intensity of emotion that appeared truly life-threatening, wanted to read out the journal in its entirety to the gathering, but as he could nowhere find his eyeglasses, he devolved this honour onto Szilárd Berda-Stern. The editorial opened thus: *The revolution has begun. Magyarland begins to live its days of glory. Our correspondents in the regions will know what they must henceforth write about.* These words were received with joy unconfined. The company did not disperse until midnight or perhaps later, the March Youth were repeatedly toasted, along with the revolution and the breaking of the new Hungarian dawn.

The public reading of Szilárd Berda-Stern was to have the strangest consequences. When the Emperor's troops occupied the town, the first task of Géza Ráth, county commissioner plenipotentiary, was to have the leading rebels rounded up. On this list next to the name Szilárd Berda-Stern was written the word: *conspirator*.

It surpasses my comprehension still that I should be in prison, writing my farewell letter. What offence have I committed against the emperor? It must be such a small thing that he can hardly have felt it. But the commissioner wants to make an example of me at any cost. Now it has at last dawned on me that I did indeed see the future, for I stared many times down gunbarrels aimed at my chest, only I, misguided fellow that I am, believed I was reliving the last moments of Grandpa Czuczor.

He wrote separately to his son, daughter, wife, mother and the Sterns, though what he had to say was by and large the same.

At first light, the duty guard looked in and gave a salute. 'Last requests?'

'See that these are delivered to the addressees.'

'It will be done.'

'My last wish is that my gravestone should bear no word but Star.'

'Star? What for?'

'It was the fine Hungarian name of my earliest forebears.'

The guard nodded. Misguided fellow, he thought, imagining that the executed get some sort of tombstone rather than ending up in a ditch at the end of the cemetery. 'You have an hour remaining!' he said with a click of his heels, and left Szilárd Berda-Stern to his thoughts.

The life of Szilárd Berda-Stern was extinguished on 18

January 1849 at six of the clock in the morning by a firing squad of four. Two aimed at his heart, two at his head. One bullet landed in an eye and drenched in red the kerchief with which his executioners had sought to save his sight. His body was rolled up in canvas and tossed into the ditch at the far end of the cemetery, bearing only a few spadefuls of earth and disinfecting lime.

Unfathomably, some hundred years later in the damp heart of the ditch a dozen or more potato plants began to sprout. Their tubers were caressed by the winds of the west. This, too, Szilárd Berda-Stern had sensed somehow. By no means rare in his visions were the pale sad flowers of the potato plant.

VII

COOLING STREAMS OF AIR COME TO CLEAR THE LAND.
The smell of burnt leaf mould mingles with the more
oppressive fumes from the fumigation of the wine casks and
the raffish smell of mulled wine. The fermenting juice of
the grape is quaffed all around, keenly watched for its head,
an index of its quality. In the cellars the water in the glass
piping on the back of the barrels bubbles up as the gases
promoting the ferment gurgle their way through the slender
tubes. Those who have finished the wine harvest can
already hammer into this year's vintage barrels the taps with
their maize-husk seals. The landscape grows more barren
by the day. The autumn paints pale, dull colours, steadily
emptying the nests.

From his earliest childhood when he woke from a deep,
restful sleep he could taste freshly picked, dew-dappled
raspberries in his mouth and his tongue retained the imprint
of the cool fruit until morning coffee, which it had been his
habit since he had grown to manhood to ask to be brought
to his bedside. There was nothing he desired more than
strong Turkish coffee, with plenty of sugar and that soft top
of the milk which, like his mother, he called butterfroth. His

servants and chambermaids, none of whom found his service congenial – they followed on one another's heels almost monthly – brought the coffee into the bedroom at a fair gallop, as their master liked it boiling hot. But far worse than a cool cup was the spilling of its contents onto the silver salver, which was not an infrequent occurrence amid such haste; if this happened he sent it back with righteous indignation. He also noticed without fail if the amount of coffee used was incorrect and insisted that it be portioned out using the little copper kitchen scales: precisely one-tenth of a Viennese *Pfund* per cup. It often took three attempts to provide his morning beverage exactly as he desired. His servants got goosepimples down their backs from his monosyllabic interrogatives: 'Napkin? Clean? Boiled? Fwoth? Stwong?' – he had trouble with his *r*s.

There was only one person from whom Mendel Berda-Stern was prepared to accept his coffee irrespective of how it turned out: this was his younger sister Hanna, whom he addressed as Hami after a very early childhood attempt to say her name. After the death of their mother, Hami became the most important person in his life, the Ace of Trumps in his parlance.

His thirst for cards became evident while he was still a toddler. In his parents' house they regularly leafed through the Devil's Bible, the gentlemen playing Klaberjass or Mariage, the ladies gin rummy, though never for money. He was not yet four when – shortly before his father's imprisonment – he made himself his own deck of cards, cutting out the 24 cards from a cardboard box; half had figures on them, the drawings having some resemblance to the members of the family.

'And what's this?' his father asked kneeling on the floor beside him.

'Cawds! Show you how I play cawds!'

The little Mendel Berda-Stern shuffled the cards with

some expertise and cut them, explaining the while, his father listening with his mouth open. The child had invented a brand-new game, distantly resembling Hungarian Tarokk, in which the rules were based on pure logic. The top trump was Mother, a kind of all-conquering Joker.

Mendel Berda-Stern drew his mother wearing a hat that looked like a fruit-basket, with the house and larder keys hanging from her neck. Among the cards with figures there also appeared his sister and the dog Morzsa, and the Sterns from Hegyhát, József and János, both with beards down to the ground. His father was assigned a value somewhat higher than the guard-dog: he was recognizable only by the shape of his legs, just a little more X-shaped than in real life. At all events, his son's deck of cards made him reflect whether he had been right to let his wife wear the trousers quite so much in the house. He had, however, little opportunity to reconsider this policy, as within a few weeks he had been arrested.

At first his mother insisted that the Daddy had gone away. Mendel Berda-Stern realized later, having discovered the truth and read the farewell letter intended in part also for him, that at about the time that Szilárd Berda-Stern was staring down the barrels of the guns, he had had a very strange dream. A well-built, rather rotund man, in the shadows of a tent, with a brown-skinned woman whispering in his ear. On the table, cards and a mysterious, crystalline ball. Mendel Berda-Stern could clearly make out the words of the woman: 'Snow-white birds plunge into the fire and burn to death.'

The same man, in the company of other men, colourful cards in hand, crumpled banknotes before him in a huge pile.

A more substantial man, rolling around on the grass under God's heaven, singing for all he was worth, his resonant voice echoing far and wide.

A child-sized man, on horseback, in a uniform of black and white, galloping alongside other gentlemen riders. The finishing-line marked by a line of white dust, he is the first to cross, the clatter of hoofs becomes hurrahs from the spectators.

Mendel Berda-Stern woke with aching limbs, as if he had been riding the horse. For years these dreams, which made no sense, kept haunting him.

That autumn, when his voice began to break, they moved to Homonna, because his mother was taking over the direction of the lace-making factory hitherto managed by her much older and long sickly sister. She had distinguished herself at fillet-work while preparing her bottom drawer, having picked up the skills from her grandmother, who had died relatively young. The factory made light lace, suitable for collars and trimmings, and heavier lace for the table or for furniture, both using designs from abroad. Mendel Berda-Stern revelled in the permanently damp atmosphere of the workshop and the rich variety of spider's webs produced by the white strands of lace on the wooden frames. He liked especially to spend time playing with the giant set of scales used to weigh the yarns.

In school there was a card-players' circle for both students and staff. Mendel Berda-Stern could beat his fellows with his eyes closed. On the day of the school's patron saint, St Anthony, students and staff competed in mixed teams pitting their wits against each other. Whomever Mendel Berda-Stern had as partner would come out on top at the end of the game. His success was based on three factors. The first was his memory, which unerringly remembered which cards had gone, and so he knew exactly which ones were left in the players' hands. The second was his psychological insight. Not the slightest tremor of an eyelid, nor a barely perceptible touch of fingers, escaped his attention. The third was his sense of smell. The cilia of his nose had

221

learnt to detect the unmistakeable odour of excitement, fear or risk. He could even identify their synaesthetic colours: he sensed fear as deep green, risk was blood-red, excitement a golden yellow. These skills made it possible for him to tell at once if someone was lying or wanted to cheat him.

His mother had hoped that Mendel would help with the lace factory, but he showed neither the inclination nor the ability to follow her into the business. For a while it seemed that he might succeed in his father's footsteps, when he managed to assemble Szilárd Berda-Stern's telescope and other equipment with which to spy out the secrets of the heavens. On starlit nights he would climb up to the house's loft, pull aside a couple of tiles from the roof, and stick the telescope out. For hours he would but stare, listening to the delicate sound of silence and the occasional mouse. At such times, with the endless expanse of black sky before his eyes, the gates of the past would open in his mind. But the further back into the past he delved, the more he longed to espy the events to come, as some of his ancestors had.

By the age of seventeen he considered himself a professional gambler, though the life-and-death battles with fortune had to wait until he reached the age of majority. Then he decided to see the world. He travelled wherever he was able to do battle, all night long, for money at tables both square and round. He travelled the length of the French resorts, where English aristocrats and Russian magnates would lose everything with heads held high. He visited Swiss gambling-halls, whose croupiers maintained stricter order than their colleagues in other countries. But mostly he preferred to spend his time in the casinos of the towns along the Rhine, haunted by money-hungry gamblers from all over Europe. He met miserable pointeurs who carefully portioned out their money so that they could earn risk-free the cost of their room and one hot meal a day. But at least as intimate were his connections with the select few who had access to limitless funds. One of his closest friends was Prince Rochemouille, the uninhibited noble who in a good mood might fling louis d'or to the poor in the street, or Ali Ibrahim Pasha, heir of an Eastern potentate rich beyond imagination.

Now that the Book of Fathers begun by Otto Stern has come into my possession on my most important birthday, it seems to me appropriate to record here the lessons of my life, continuing the tradition of my ancestors and for the edification of my descendants.

Its contents are terrifying, said my mother as she handed it to me. I know not what she meant; for my part I received what I expected. My father and grandfather wrote relatively little in this book. The only innovation for me was my father's farewell letter which he sent to my mother and inserted in here, for it was word-for-word the same as the one he sent me. It is noteworthy that he wanted all of us to know exactly the same thing. That he loves us, that he is proud of us, that we should be sensible and careful, that we should look after ourselves, and each other.

I am not ashamed to admit that I have dedicated my life to the service of Fortuna. My better days are those when it is not I serving her, but she serving me. But this does not happen often enough. I have still much to learn, to reflect on, and to experience.

For me the espying of the future is necessary not out of passion, but rather to make me more assured in my craft. At the roulette and card tables it is inevitable that one will lose unless one has some inkling of what will happen in the next blink of the eye. This is why I am so intensively concerned with every aspect of telling the future.

In the Book of Fathers, too, he kept a tally of his losses and gains. These were to prove useful chiefly later for his wife, whose trustees were able to collect sizeable sums from the money-changers and money-lenders in various towns where Mendel Berda-Stern had deposited amounts of differing size, following the accepted practice of gamblers, in case he found himself in financial straits. Tight-fisted as he was with his wife until then, his generosity after his disappearance was all the more surprising. But before that happened, much water had to flow under the bridges of the Rhine, the Seine and the other great rivers that Mendel Berda-Stern was so fond of being able to view from his hotel window upon waking around noon with the taste of dew-dappled raspberries in his mouth. He would ring for his servant and demand his coffee, boiling, with butterfroth. However expensive the hotel, he insisted on bringing his own servants.

After coffee he rose, taking a hot and a cold bath, and over his underwear donned a peasant shirt and the wide, pleated culottes favoured by the market traders in Homonna, who called them *muszuj*. The next few hours were spent in meditation upon his reading and writing, and only then would he summon the barber to shave him and deal with his hair. His best ideas came to him when he was relaxed in the armchair, eyes closed, under the white napkin of the barber with the razor criss-crossing his face.

The lunch brought to his room was substantial. For choice he would eat the fat-marbled flesh of wild animals. He also enjoyed it if, as in the town where he was born, each course concluded with a spicy black soup based on blood and flavoured with prunes. In consequence, he was beginning to acquire something of a paunch which, however, was disguised by the expertly tailored cut of his clothes. Not a few serving wenches lingered on his chestnut-brown eyes.

He married young: his bride was Hami's best friend, Eleonora Pohl. He was immediately drawn to this slim girl, partly because she set as much store by silence as he, and partly because her father Leopold Pohl had also been arrested in 1849 as instrumental in establishing the town's Free National Guard. Leopold Pohl thought that it was his Jewish origins that had determined his fate at the court-martial: he was sentenced to eight years in prison, though set free after six. His assets were confiscated. Withdrawing to his wife's estate, apart from helping to run it he did nothing useful. His son-in-law was the first person in a long time that he conversed with at any length. They found a topic of which neither of them ever became bored: Leopold Pohl was also trying to peer into the future from the garden lodge which he had originally built as a toy house for Eleonora.

It was during the endless enforced idleness of imprisonment that Leopold Pohl realized he would have been able to predict some of the stations of his life had he devoted the attention necessary to those minute signs which fate had granted him. His childhood fear of water should have warned him to prevent his parents travelling on water; then they would not have suffered their unconscionably early death in a tragicomic accident on the River Bodrog in full spate. Whenever he touched a metal object – especially iron and lead – his skin would erupt in ugly welts: this should have warned him that for calling the youth of the town to arms he would be severely punished.

'The secret of the future,' he explained to his son-in-law, 'is hidden in the difference between human and divine knowledge. This was already known in the ancient world. Have you heard of the Oracle of Delphi?'

'Yes,' replied Mendel Berda-Stern. 'It lies in Apollo's sacred grove, where Zeus killed the dragon. Yes. The problem is, often the prophecy is in vain, because its gist can only be understood retrospectively. Pythia, the priestess of Delphi, told Philip II, King of Macedon and father of Alexander the Great: "Beware of the chariot!" When he was

225

stabbed to death, the sword of Pausanias bore an engraving of a chariot.'

'I see you are a man of great sophistication, Berda.'

'Mendel. Or Berda-Stern. But I am not in the least sophisticated. What I know, I know from my fathers.'

Leopold Pohl took this explanation as a form of modesty. He drank the pertu with his son-in-law, so that henceforth they were on first-name terms.

'The only question is, is it right for man to crave divine knowledge?' asked Mendel Berda-Stern.

'If He did not wish it, He would surely not permit it.'

Mendel Berda-Stern told his father-in-law that whenever he heard of a clairvoyant, he would certainly visit her. He had had his fortune told from cards, from lead, coffee grounds, crystal balls, but of course most often from his palm. He also admitted that on his unexpected trips he was not trading in property – as he let it be known – but visiting secret citadels of gambling, which were the source of his regular income. His father had left him only debts, and the exiguous annuity provided by the Stern family allowed for only a modest existence.

'Everyone to his own, according to his gifts,' said Leopold Pohl. After a few glasses of vintage wine he solemnly brought out his most treasured possession, *Les Vrayes Centuries et Prophéties*, the prophecies of Maistre Nostradamus.

'King of the prophets,' said Mendel Berda-Stern in an awed whisper.

The volume was published in the city of Lyon. Leopold Pohl had had it bound in mauve leather in Homonna.

'Do you know French?' he asked.

'Yes. My great-grandfather Richard Stern was a professor of French. I inherited my French from him.' He took the opportunity to explain somewhat diffidently that his knowledge simply arose in him, through force of memory, without any kind of study.

226

Leopold Pohl was unsure whether to believe him or not. 'Let us join forces in trying to interpret the quatrains and the presages.'

They spent many a quiet afternoon among the quatrains of Nostradamus, that is, Master Michel de Notredame, the majority of which Mendel Berda-Stern copied down himself. From one of these he suspected that Master Nostradamus was also of the view that he had received most of his knowledge from his forefathers. He lost his children and his first wife to the plague, on which he became an authority . . . a wretched and melancholy fate.

The famous Jewish doctor's *Mischsprache* led to much scratching of heads. He used Italian, Greek, Latin and even Provençal expressions and distorted words. With Provençal Mendel Berda-Stern was able to make some headway (his great-grandfather had studied this dialect), but in Greek he had to depend rather on Leopold Pohl. His imagination was much exercised by those of the prophecies of the king of prophets that had come true. For example, the foretelling of the death of Henri II, in a quatrain that Mendel Stern rendered thus:

A young lion comes to best the old,
A battle royal this pair will hold:
An eye is stabbed through a cage of gold,
Two wounds but one, a death foretold.

And this is exactly how it turned out: the king took part in a chivalric tournament in a golden helmet. He had overcome two of his opponents when the lance of the next, Count Montgomery, broke in two at the third assay, one end penetrating the golden visor to stab the king in the eye. The first wound was in the eye, the second in his brain.

Of the 1,200 quatrains they found one that concerned Hungary. After heated exchanges they joined forces to produce a faithful translation. They took it to refer to the years of the Hungarian War of Independence of 1848–49.

The Magyars' life doth change to death,
Than slavery worse the new order's breath.
Their city vast cries woe unto Heaven,
Twixt Castor and Pollux great battle doth beckon.

They debated whether it was Pest-Buda crying unto heaven or rather one of the major Transylvanian towns that had been captured. Perhaps Arad, where the thirteen Hungarian martyrs of the Revolution were hanged?

They ordered further books dealing with Nostradamus and the study of astrology. In respect of the latter, Mendel Berda-Stern also found relevant material in his father's bequest. In the Lyceum of Eger, Szilárd Berda-Stern had read his way through Kepler's three-volume *De Harmonice Mundi*, written in heavy Baroque Latin, which he found in the collections there. He noted how to cast a personal horoscope on the basis of computations based on the exact moment of birth.

Travelling in the city of Nice, Mendel Berda-Stern spared neither money nor effort in attempting to secure Jean-Baptiste Morin de Villefranche's 26-volume *Astrologia Gallica*. He managed to obtain only a French-language conspectus of the vast work. Four days and four nights he did not leave his room. He understood that the significance of the planets in the horoscope depends on which house they are lodged in. The calculations made about his own fate were in many respects modified by the arguments of Morin de Villefranche. He inserted what he read into the structure which he developed following Kepler. He experimented with complex calculations, to lift the veil covering the years, months and days to come. He came to Nice to gamble, but on this occasion he did not darken the doors of the casino.

228

On the morning of the fifth day he hurried to the street of the goldsmiths and bought an expensive gold ring with a mounted sapphire, paid his hotel bill, and went home by the shortest possible route. He had a difficult journey: January was saying its farewells with hard frosts and storms of snow. It was around noon that he reached the apple trees of his Homonna garden and ran to the back wing of the house, where they had moved when they were first married. He pulled off his boots, fur hat and coat, kissed Eleonora three times, and then said to her: 'My dear, I am so happy! At the end of this year, on the fourteenth day of November, we shall have a son, to whom we shall give the name Sigmund, though he will prefer to be called Sándor.'

'Oh come now, Mendi my dear, where on earth did you get that from?' asked Eleonora, bridling.

'Not really earth. I worked it out. But for some reason the boy will be born in Nagyvárad in Transylvania.'

'Nagyvárad? But I have never been to Nagyvárad.'

'Nor have I.'

On his next trip he won 90,000 francs. All evening he stubbornly put his money, all smallish bets, on 7; he lost again and again, but he waited for his turn and on the 77th spin he put all his money on the number 7. As the ball popped about, it looked as though it would settle into the adjacent slot, but then after all, it decided to jump right into the 7. Mendel Berda-Stern was in a daze as the congratulations showered upon him. His winnings were carried in a wooden casket after him by his manservant. The next day he moved on, because his calculations suggested that he was about to enter an uncertain period when it was not worth taking risks.

After this adventure he also visited Marseille. In the market of the old port he visited all its three fortune-tellers in turn. From the last woman, who read his fortune from the tarot, he could hear: 'You have already taken the path of

229

success. Advantageous journeys await, good plans are taking shape in your head.'

Mendel Berda-Stern nodded. After paying he asked: 'How much for the cards?'

'Pardon?'

'I'd buy your cards. The whole pack.'

'What are you thinking of?'

'A hundred.'

'Monseigneur, they would not work for you anyway.'

'A hundred and fifty.'

'I tell you, no . . .'

'Two hundred.'

'Please!'

He paid three hundred for the much-worn pack. He had already learnt how to put out a Celtic cross, but in the dark tents he had few opportunities to study properly the cards of the various colours. In the first alehouse on the way he ordered himself a jug of Champagne wine and studied the coloured pictures of the tarot pack. It consisted of 22 cards, of which one was unnumbered: LE MAT – the Fool. Number XIII, on the other hand, bore no name; it showed a skeleton reaping heads, hands, feet in a field of blue flowers.

He studied the cards again and again. He paused at VII: LE CHARIOT. A crowned man with golden hair stands on a cart resembling a pulpit, drawn by two horses, one blue, the other red. On the chariot a coat-of-arms, bearing two letters: M.S. Mendel Stern? The Berda is missing.

Leopold Pohl enlightened him later that the M stood for Mercurius or Mercury, the S for Sulfur. These two elements are of utmost importance in alchemy. 'If we ever try to make gold, we shall have need of them.'

Mendel Berda-Stern gave a little 'Hmm.' He already had a way of making gold. Though he did not actually say so, in the features of the charioteering king of card VII he detected himself, especially because of the wide, almond-shaped eyes and small but uneven lips. Not surprising if I win on number 7, then. The tarot and the computations of astrology confirm each other. He was troubled only a little: that the fortune-tellers generally regarded number 7 as the picture of the Reaper. (Of course, not in tarot and not Roman seven: VII.)

Eleonora did in fact fall pregnant and her belly began to swell nicely; her husband considered the increase between his two trips to be spectacular. Above them hung the unspoken question: how do they get to Nagyvárad? Apart from his wife, Mendel Berda-Stern discussed the matter with two others. Leopold Pohl was of the opinion that the solution to this problem had to be left to fate; if it had been decided that the child would come into the world in Nagyvárad, then fate would see to it that his parents got there in time. His sister Hami persuaded him of the opposite: 'What is the problem in travelling to Nagyvárad? Surely it cannot do any harm. While if you stayed at home and there was some complication . . . you would never forgive yourselves.'

They had a letter from the Sterns. Mendel Berda-Stern was nowadays even more reluctant to accept money and presents from them since they no longer actually needed it. But he knew if he refused, they would be mortally offended, and that was not a good thing either. He hardly knew the members of the large Stern clan; apart from a few courtesy visits he had almost no contact with them. The last time he visited them it was to introduce them to Eleonora.

They had moved from Hegyhát to Tokay. The Stern & Stern Wine Emporium, as well as the locally resident members of the family, had moved into Tokay after the serious conflagration of this year, 1866, as they had suffered severe damage to their houses and property. Hearing of this, Mendel Berda-Stern wrote them a concerned letter.

A sealed canvas satchel accompanied the reply, brought

by a young farm labourer. The lengthy letter was written by Móricz Stern. From his adventures into the past Mendel Berda-Stern knew that Móricz was Rebecca's eldest. Rebecca's father, Benjamin, had died early from tuberculosis. His mother, Eszter, was the sister of Éva, the wife of István Stern. Mendel Berda-Stern had seen the Lemberg tragedy any number of times: death by the sword of five-year-old Robert and three-year-old Rudolf. He would gladly have been spared further viewings. But he to whom is given the gift of seeing into the past does not choose what he sees.

Our dear Mendel,
You would not believe how often you are in our thoughts, especially since we moved to Tokay. Many of our beloved things fell victim to the fire, above all in this list stand the copper mortar that melted into an unrecognizable ball, found by Bálint Sternovszky in the clearing where he built his turret – as you will know, since you are of our clan, the first-born son of your honourable father. Those whom He gave the gift of seeing into the past can feel if disaster threatens. It is certain that grave events are about to befall us. For this reason I am sending you, and ask you to look after and protect, a few family relics, above all and especially the first Book of Fathers. Its continuation you already have in your possession. It is possible that I shall be obliged to come forward with further requests in the near future, in the hope that your feelings towards us owe more to the strength of blood ties than to the debilitating power of distance.

The mere sight of the soiled cover of the Book of Fathers so upset Mendel Berda-Stern that he put off opening it until the next day, though he would gladly have rushed off with it to Leopold Pohl, so that the two of them might browse the history of the Sterns, Sternovszkys and Csillags. But all this is only his business. He spent many a long and lonely night turning the parchment pages. He wrote comments in the margins. He found it difficult to imagine that he could ever return the treasure entrusted to him for safekeeping. When he gave up reading and reverie at dawn, he would extinguish the sooty candle, and in the dazzling darkness he would embrace the thick volume as a mother does her baby.

Summer was over and the branches of the apple trees and quinces were bare in the wind when a messenger boy brought a message from Móricz Stern: 'Mr Stern asks you to come and see him without delay in Tokay. He awaits an answer.'

'I shall be there tomorrow sundown.'

Mendel Berda-Stern packed. Eleonora's face clouded over when she saw him making preparations. 'Mendi, where are you off to this time?'

'They want me in Tokay, urgently.'

'Could I not keep you company?'

'If your condition permits, why not?'

It was still a month and a half till the child was due. Mendel Berda-Stern persuaded Hami to join them. Not counting the coachman they set off in the bigger carriage with a manservant and a chamber maid. They took little in the way of luggage, the heaviest item being the wooden chest which they had piled high with gifts, so that they did not arrive empty-handed. It had in it two complete Kassa hams, three truckles of Homonna cheese the size of small millstones, several bottles of cider made according to a local recipe, and four heavy Pozsony homespuns, ideal for hanging on the wall or as bedspreads.

The Stern family occupied virtually a whole street in the Tokay valley. The seat of the wine emporium loomed tall but unfinished. A little tower resting on Corinthian pillars had been imagined for its top by the Italian architect, which

233

was at present represented by a cylindrical skeleton. An unusual disarray ruled the ground; it seemed that the building works had been abandoned rather than left half-complete. The wooden planks of the foreman builder's lime pit were turned out of the ground and the white mass had spilled along the area in front of the house. The ladders and climbing frames appeared to have been lashed by storms. Above, the bare girders loomed black as if the roof had already burnt down. What had happened here?

Móricz Stern received his visitors in the first-floor salon, with tea and kosher plum brandy. 'Thank you for coming, my blood,' he kept repeating, with childish inanity (at least that was what Mendel Berda-Stern thought). Móricz Stern was no more than nine years his senior, yet he looked like an old man, because of his thinness and his unkempt, salt-and-pepper beard.

The afternoon tea seemed never to end: unnoticed it turned into the evening meal, for which the relatives began to arrive at around six o'clock. They came before them one by one and in their introductory smiles Mendel Berda-Stern seemed to detect the same childish inanity. He was waiting to be informed why he had been told to come. He had brought the two volumes of the Book of Fathers with him, but decided that if they were to ask for the first volume back, he would say he did not have it.

The Sterns pretended that they had gathered purely for a pleasant family meal – the usual jokes were heard, the usual toasts and good wishes. They tasted the firm's finest wines, the cheeks of the men quickly turned rosy pink, white collars were unbuttoned. The fire in the hearth increased the perspiration whose penetrating odour could not be blotted out by that of the food, even as the number of courses inexorably increased to eight. When they had drunk the sorbet, the men moved over to the library to smoke cigars. In the room there was no trace of either books

234

or of shelves; the carpenters had still a great deal to do here. The cigars and pipe-lighters had been prepared on the green baize card-table, in front of the seven-branched gold candle stick. For a while only satisfied noises of puffing and gentle wheezing could be heard.

Then Móricz Stern rose to speak. 'Now that we are all of us here, every mature and responsible male in the Stern clan, let us consider how we can maintain ourselves and our families intact during the coming disaster.'

'What kind of disaster?' asked Mendel Berda-Stern.

Indulgent smiles all around by way of reply.

Móricz Stern placed his palm on his neck; Mendel Berda-Stern could feel the serious tremor in his fingers. 'You cannot yet know. Perhaps up your way, in the north, there is still peace. But here the dam of mindless passions has been breached, since they voted into law our equality of rights.'

'Who voted?'

'Parliament! Where have you been living, young man? Since December 17th last, the inhabitants of Hungary of the Israelite faith have been declared entitled to exercise the same civic and political rights as the Christians. But this has not pleased all.'

Mendel Berda-Stern seemed to recall having heard something about this, but had immediately forgotten whatever it was. His life was spent in casinos, by card-tables: the intervening days were to him as other people's night-time rest. Suddenly he was seized by the same excitement as the others. Intimations of a negative kind had troubled him sometimes, but as he could not understand why, he took them to refer to himself and his betting. Now he learnt how individual members of the Stern family had been attacked by riff-raff in various towns. Again and again the frightening word from the past came to people's lips: 'pogrom'. The image of smashed-up shops was painted in bright colours. The emporium in Tokay, too, had suffered such an attack a week earlier. Fortunately neither here nor elsewhere had the members of the family suffered physically. 'For the time being!' said Móricz Stern with a meaningful intonation.

The council of the heads of families decided that something must be done in the interests of their safety. This is what they wanted to think through today, this is why he, too, had been invited. 'You, my dear boy, are undoubtedly one of us!' Móricz Stern added.

Mendel Berda-Stern was sweating profusely. He did not have the courage to say that he was a gambler, not a Jew. The Pohl family did not adhere to the traditions of the Israelites, as the practising Jews were now called, and he did not live with Eleonora in a Jewish manner. None the less he felt at home in this unpretentious room, where everything was reassuringly familiar, from the clouds of smoke to the hoarseness of the voices.

'It is a privilege of our first-born to know our history, looking back into the past, and sometimes into the future,' Móricz Stern continued. 'We are members of one family. Let us join together into a common asset, without keeping anything back, what we each of us own separately!' and he looked at Mendel Berda-Stern.

There was silence, only the crackling of the burning logs of wood could be heard in the fireplace of uncarved stone, and the sound of breathing, and the little sucking noises on the cigars. Minutes passed before Mendel Berda-Stern realized that all eyes were on him. That was why he had been invited, to make public what he knew. He cleared his throat: 'With your permission, it is difficult . . .' and he fell silent. He would have to review what he had seen or thought he had seen, and what conclusion was to be drawn from the various images. He remembered his computations based on the position of the stars and the signs obtained from the reading of the tarot, and the prophecies of the king of the prophets.

'Speak, even if what you have to say is of the most terrifying kind,' said Móricz Stern.

Mendel Berda-Stern blew his nose. 'This is too great a burden for me. But I know, for example, that on the fourteenth day of November a boy will be born to us, to whom we shall give the name Sigmund, though he will prefer to call himself Sándor. This young child will, moreover, be born in Nagyvárad, though we have never been there and have no other business there . . .'

Móricz Stern was seized by visible excitement when he heard these words. 'Nagyvárad?' he repeated with emphasis.

It became clear that Móricz Stern was contemplating whether it would be sensible for the family to collect all its valuables and emigrate, to a region where the Jews would be undisturbed. It was unclear though where such a region might be. Opposed to his view was that of the highly respected Lipót Stern. Lipót Stern, son of Mihály Stern, had become a famous Rabbi. Over on the far side of the country at Beremend he had been appointed deputy Rabbi and preacher of the community which, in view of his youthful age and limited experience, was regarded as a great honour. His first act had been to propose the building of a new school, whose syllabus he had himself devised, which was later accepted as a model by the Jewish communities of many nearby areas.

Lipót Stern's view was that it was no use fleeing. The problem was that one section of the Jews of Hungary was alienated from its traditions, another part shrouded itself in them. These extreme modes of behaviour give rise to justified negative feelings. 'Let us rather approach with a pure heart the spirit of the homeland, and accept the threefold tendency: we are human beings, Hungarians and Jews all in one. I quote the words of Rabbi Lőw: "Emancipation and reform are intimately linked, those who want the first

237

cannot reject the second." We must accept as our own the national ideals. Let us speak Hungarian in the synagogue, so that everyone can understand our words. If they can see what our intentions are, tempers will no longer flare.'

'Only by that time our houses and shops will have been destroyed, and it is by no means certain we shall survive the assaults of the people on the street!' countered Móricz Stern.

'We can in no way avoid our fate.'

'And if something happens to us, who will bring up our children?'

'Who will bring up the lilies of the field and the trees of the forests?'

The debate became more and more heated, and to Lipót Stern's Talmudic arguments Móricz Stern gave practical answers, which made the Rabbi increasingly angry. His voice sharpened into shrillness, his elongated skull began to tremble violently. Foam came to his lips, his words halted, and he fell in a fit on the floor. Dr Márton Stern, the surgeon, threw himself onto his body, forced his jaw open with the blade of a knife, pulled out his tongue and through the space between the teeth poured in some medication from a flat little flask. This scared only Mendel Berda-Stern; the family had often witnessed such a scene. In a few minutes the Rabbi was back to his old self, his eyes clear, the lines on his face smoothed out, and the fit had no after-effects of any kind. 'Where was I?' he asked calmly.

'The parable of wine and honey,' said Dr Márton Stern.

'Ah, yes. So you are all thoroughly conversant with my view. The Jews of Hungary must join together, whether they be of the orthodox or the neologue persuasion. We must go to the conference in Nagyvárad, where the formation of a national organization of Israelites must be the main item on the agenda.'

There was silence again, and Mendel Berda-Stern was

once again the object of every pair of eyes. He blew his nose again – he must have caught a chill on his way here – and then said very quietly: 'I shall say something which I have been pondering for a long time, in the hope that perhaps your intellects can divine its essence, which has remained a mystery to me. The great Nostradamus, the king of prophets, wrote a prophecy that will not let me rest. This is how it goes:

Whence we await starvation,
Thence welcome we repletion:
The sea with the greedy dog's eyes
With oil and corn shall us surprise.'

'Once more, if you don't mind,' said Lipót Stern.

He repeated the doggerel.

There was a lengthy pause in the conversation. Leopold Stern removed his pince-nez and wiped it on the edge of his smoking jacket. 'This is a tough nut for me to crack,' he muttered.

For me too, thought Mendel Berda-Stern. We are not living in a barbarous age when people put others to the sword for no reason and raze people's property to the ground. Now a lawful order reigns in society and if a bandit should upset it, the authorities will take the necessary steps.

The Rabbi went over to the window, his hands folded behind his back, and stared out for a while, then solemnly declared: 'Within minutes it will be Shabbos. We must postpone our deliberations for 24 hours.'

The candles were left to burn all night in every house, since extinguishing them counted as work, as was their lighting. Food was brought in by Slovak servant girls. For the duration of Shabbos Móricz Stern thought it best not even to emerge from his bedroom, thinking it was most appropriate if the day He designated for rest was spent by man in sleep. No wonder that his belly had swollen into a watermelon and was testing his trouser belt to its limits.

Mendel Berda-Stern, Eleonora and Hami were allocated two rooms on the ground floor of Móricz Stern's residence. Their staff were lodged in the servants' quarters. Mendel Berda-Stern gave an account of the discussion only to Hami, desiring to spare his expectant wife such unnecessary excitements. Hami did not understand: 'Mendi my dear, does that mean we should now be afraid?'

'Ach, stuff and nonsense. Every county has its handful of youngsters who have a drop or two too many and go on the rampage a bit. There's no point in getting too worked up about that. Don't you worry at all, my sweet.'

He himself, however, was not at all convinced that the fears of the Stern family were entirely without foundation. That night he set about completing his own computations on the basis of Morin de Villefranche's methods, focused on a given geographical location and a specified period of time, on the basis of the ephemerides. When taken together with his own horoscope, the results had in the past often helped him to considerable winnings in the casinos. He knew that in this wise he could glean some indication of the direction of the future, only he was never certain whether it referred to the week, month or year to come. Whether this way or that, the position of the stars boded no good. In the twelve houses the eight astrological bodies were rather unpropitiously arrayed, the Moon, the Sun, Mercury, Venus, Mars, Jupiter, Saturn and Uranus. Especially Saturn, which formed a horrific quincunx with Mars, and all this in the twelfth house ... O woe! If he were now on one of his money-raising trips, he would give the gambling dens a wide berth.

The candles gave off sooty eddies in the direction of the wooden inlaid ceilings. It was first light outside. Mendel Berda-Stern felt totally exhausted, but suspected he wouldn't be able to fall asleep. He took out the thicker of the two Books of Fathers, and read a page or two here and there, though to be honest he knew most of the text by heart.

He had a sudden hunch, which further multiplications and divisions seemed to support. He realized of a sudden that it could not be an accident that the ability to read the stars had fallen to him. He knew that his astrological sign was Libra, and his father's, Szilárd Berda-Stern's, was Virgo. Regarding the determination of the point where the ecliptic intersects the eastern horizon, that is to say, in determining the ascendant, he was also well versed. His was Scorpio, his father's Libra.

It began to dawn on him that his ancestors' zodiacal signs followed the pattern of the Ptolemaic duodecimal system: Otto Stern was Leo, Richard Stern was Cancer, and so forth. But while he was able to calculate the ascendants, these too followed in the ancient order of astrology, always one sign further on from the birth sign. That is why his ascendant had been Scorpio, and his father's Libra. Following this rhythm his grandfather's must have been Virgo. If that is so, that of any of the ancestors could be worked out mechanically, following the sequence of the zodiacal signs. So for example Kornél Csillag's star sign could be only Aries, and his ascendant Taurus. It was not possible to support this by casting a horoscope, since only his father's and grandfather's exact moment of birth was known to him.

In the light of this, it is striking that his vision of the future is exactly right: his child, Sigmund Berda-Stern, will arrive on 11 November not by chance but in compliance with this mysterious rule, for the sign of Scorpio was the next one, which the astrologers of olden times still called Eagle. A Scorpio is a man of extremes, either very good or very bad, but at all events passionate, unreflecting, at war with his instincts – we shall have our hands full with him. At the same time, accepting the above, it is beyond question that his ascendant is Sagittarius, which can exercise a great deal of moderation on the qualities of a Scorpio.

He could scarcely wait to bring all this to the attention of the assembled males. His convoluted explanation of the unpropitious angles of light was not received as he had expected. He did not get even as far as the horoscope of the ancestors. Dumbfounded faces verging on the hostile stared back at him. Lipót Stern was the least impressed: 'Are you seriously suggesting that instead of our ancient faith we should believe in the patterns that the stars form into in the sky?'

'It is not my suggestion, but astrology has for millennia looked on matters this way.'

'Do you not think that the matters of the sky are also moved by the Everlasting, and His will is not so easily divined?'

Mendel Berda-Stern had no answer to this.

'Our topic is different just now,' said Móricz Stern in a conciliatory tone. 'Let us discuss what we should do!'

Mendel Berda-Stern was not prepared to say another word, so offended was he. I told them the truth and they have sealed up my lips with mud, he thought. When the Rabbi again brought up the issue of family participation in the conference, he volunteered to join him. He had firmly decided that independently of the gathering of Hungary's reform Jewry, he would certainly pack his bags and take the cart to Nagyvárad with his wife. No harm can come of that. He thought it natural that Hami would go with them. It was the end of October when they finally departed for Nagyvárad.

In Nagyvárad it was rain and shine together. The languid rays of the sun were bathed in heavy sleet.

Despite strenuous efforts by Lipót Stern, the conference came to no significant conclusion. The majority of the representatives of the Jewish communities feared that whatever organization they established, they would bring down upon themselves the wrath of the authorities and of the monarch. Better to keep quiet and lie low.

'Shall we just resign ourselves,' said Lipót Stern, 'to the fact that from time to time we shall be struck by those who hate us? To the fact that despite the clear import of the letter of the law we shall never feel we have equal status in our homeland? To the fact that we shall have to be afraid for ever because of our origins?'

'Better reined in than rained on!' shouted Simon Schwab, the Rabbi of the Jews of Pécs, who had long had it in for Lipót Stern. He suspected that for Stern his position at Beremend was merely a stepping stone to his own, much better-paid post.

Mendel Berda-Stern sat through the conference patiently. He had time; they were still four days short of the 11th of November. He had ordered for that day to their corner suite in the Three Roses Hotel not just the town's most highly reputed midwife, but also a professor of medicine. Hami was also present at the birth – it was she who swaddled the baby and held it up to the mother, with bloodshot eyes, swimming in sweat.

My son Sigmund Berda-Stern was born after three and a half hours of labour and left the womb in a caul, which I took to be a more propitious sign than any of the astrological ones, though the professor of medicine and the midwife, perhaps getting in each other's way, had difficulty in divesting the child of it. I beg all the higher powers, honoured by all religions, and even those not nameable, who are the rulers of the Universe, who have created heaven and earth, to bless and protect my son, give him and all of us health, plenty and peace.

Nagyvárad, which means approximately 'Great Castle', proved worthy of its name; Homonna by comparison was a dusty little one-horse town. Mendel Berda-Stern greatly enjoyed strolling in the main square, drinking beer and coffee in the cafés, imagining how pleasant might be the spring and the summer here, when the round tables are moved out onto the pavements and gardens, and striped awnings are unrolled above the public's head, shielding them from the strength of the sun's rays. It took him no great effort to find the secret card-playing halls, of which he at once became a regular. Thanks to the stars and his own skill, he lightened substantially the pockets of those who tried their luck with him over the green baize tables.

He felt little inclination to return home, sending evasive replies to the letters of Leopold Pohl urging him to return. His father-in-law, however, grew tired of writing and turned up in town. He reproached them before he greeted them: 'Why are you wasting time and money here instead of packing? What are you waiting for?'

'Calm down. Obviously you have been raring for a fight!' Mendel Berda-Stern kept pouring the kosher plum brandy.

Leopold Pohl downed the drink. 'Has something happened?'

'Everything is absolutely fine. Little Sigmund is hale and hearty, just like his mother. The only thing is . . . we feel so good in this town.'

These words did nothing to dispel the suspicions of Leopold Pohl. Like a bloodhound on the trail he sniffed around, interrogating his daughter, the servants, examining his grandson, and searching every nook and cranny in the three interconnecting rooms that they occupied. 'Will you please tell me how long you intend to stay here?'

'Until little Sigmund builds up his strength!' said Eleonora.

That afternoon Mendel Berda-Stern revealed to his

father-in-law all that he had come to understand in connection with his ancestors' horoscopes. Leopold Pohl became feverishly excited: 'Perhaps it is like this in every family. That is, if I am Aquarius, my daughter . . . no, no, it doesn't work, Eleonora's sign is Gemini . . . and as far as the ascendant is concerned . . . it progressed in this double series only in your family . . .'

Why fate determined that we should come to Nagyvárad I have never understood to this day. In that town I played with a lucky hand and won a large amount of money. I don't know how I might take it away with me safely: the forests are crawling with thieves who regularly pounce on carriages and caravans of carts. I have sworn that if I am attacked I shall resist to the last drop of my blood. I have carefully obtained the revolvers and the ammunition I need for this purpose. In one of the clearings in the Old Forest I have trained suitably both of my manservants in the arts of warfare and tactics. While the stars foretell no danger to us in the present period, there is never harm in being careful.

Leopold Pohl soon travelled back to Homonna, together with Hami. Mendel Berda-Stern and his wife stayed in Nagyvárad. Eleonora found herself once more expecting a child.

Soon came news from Tokay, that the Stern family's properties had been ravaged by hooligans and part of their vineyards also burnt down, as a result of arson. Móricz Stern's weak heart found the stress too much and gave out.

Mendel Berda-Stern set off for the funeral in a fringed surrey accompanied by a manservant. The first ravages of the bleak winter swept floes of ice down the River Tisza; the ferrymen would not cross the troubled river that day and like it or not Mendel Berda-Stern was obliged to send the surrey back to Nagyvárad. In the company of a few

lambskin-coated merchants he tried to pay five suitably ine-
briated lads to take them over on the big boat which in
suitable weather plied to and fro between the banks as an
auxiliary means of transport. They were Swabians from the
Slovak Highlands and spoke poor Hungarian.

'Out of the question, just look at the water and the floes!'
said one boatman.

'We can wait till it calms down and then cross quickly!'
said Mendel Berda-Stern. He switched to German: 'I really
must cross.'

'What did he say, what did he say?' the merchants asked.

'*Wartnbisschen!*' Mendel Berda-Stern turned to the boatman he thought keenest on the money. He offered the
sum as he was accustomed to doing at the green baize
table, on behalf of the merchants too. The sum on offer
eventually grew so that three of the Swabians were now
willing to make the trip. The travellers had difficulty
stepping from the wooden planks of the shore onto the
creaking and groaning wave-tossed boat. Two lads tried as
best they could to keep it level somehow and the third
grabbed and pulled them on. 'Lie on your back if you
value your lives!'

Pressed to the footboard, the backs of their necks kept
bumping against planking wet with spray. As soon as the
lads cast off and the boat was left at the mercy of the waves,
it stood up almost vertical. They all rolled to one end.
Mendel Berda-Stern ended up at the bottom of the heap, in
a close intimacy with his manservant that he wittingly permitted only to his wife. He was now regretting that he had
undertaken the crossing, though he was the only one who
suspected that it was bound to succeed, as quite a long
period of life awaited him – at least, that is how he saw his
own prospects. But at that moment he found it difficult to
believe: he was soaked to his bones in the freezing water,
the cold wind stabbing him in the eye.

The Swabian boatmen wrestled with the stormy river and the ice floes which arrived pell-mell. At this point the Tisza took a wide turn, and the locals knew that the most treacherous eddies were on this side of the water; once the craft survived the halfway mark, it was virtually certain that the far bank could be safely managed. This time, too, the waters were stilled as if by command, once they had got to the imaginary halfway line. At the same time, the ice floes appeared to come thicker and faster; one of the boatmen was no longer rowing but spent his time fending them off with his oar. The roar of the river grew more and more painful to the ear, and despite every effort some of the blocks of ice thumped into the sides of the boat. The lads shouted warnings at each other to try to avoid disaster, but so many floes were adrift in the stormy waves that the boat could scarcely get through them unscathed. One rather weighty triangular slab of ice hit the boat so loudly that pea-sized particles of the caulking strayed onto the footboard. Two of the merchants gabbled prayers in their mother tongue, from which Mendel Berda-Stern realized that these were not Magyars after all, but Ruthenians.

By then the boat lay in the tight embrace of the ice floes, and in vain did the lads try to prise them loose with oars and boathooks: they would not move an inch. The mournful creaking of the timbers rose higher, as did the Swabian cries of the boatmen – the entire wooden structure could be snapped in two by the power of the floes.

'*Lullei, Lullei! Nochinmal! Lullei!*' cried the Swabians.

Mendel Berda-Stern did not understand what they wanted, but the merchants did, and linking arms, in the rhythm of the Lullei! swung their hips to the left and then to the right, thus making the boat rock from side to side and thus – to the great surprise of them all – the boat slid out from the ice floes' murderous grip.

Whereupon the Swabian lads managed to use their oars

to get them to the shore. Despite the stinging cold they were all bathed in sweat. Mendel Berda-Stern at once headed for the post station, but at this late hour could secure neither a horse nor a carriage. He spent the night in the lodge opposite the post station. The following morning he woke to find the countryside knee-deep in snow and it was neither advisable nor possible to set off. He was quite certain that by no stretch of the imagination could he be in time for the funeral. From the lumpy sack of straw he rose only to attend to the call of nature; otherwise he lay staring at the ceiling, ordering boiling hot coffee with butterfroth. He even ate his meals in bed. His window looked out on the swollen Tisza, its caravan of ice-floes relentlessly drift-ing south.

'My dear good sir, should we not be going back?' asked his manservant.

Mendel Berda-Stern did not bat an eyelid. His murder-ous glance froze the words on his servant's lips. On the third day he sent the boy for paper, pen and inkhorn. He doodled and did calculations, sighing ever more loudly. Later he recalled this thus in the Book of Fathers.

For six days and six nights I was slumped in the rundown lodge, where they did not hesitate, because of the vileness of the weather, to put strangers together in the same room. It cost me a tidy sum to be given my own room. In the hours of doing nothing, which felt as if they would never end, I had an opportunity to think everything through. In the course of my life hitherto, I do not detect any mistakes: my lucky star has protected me faithfully, and never left me in the lurch. I have secured sufficient funds at the card and roulette tables to ensure that neither I nor my descendants will suffer want of anything. But true wealth does not manifest itself in financial terms.

Woe is me! According to my astrological calculations and even more the future according to the tarot, my cloudless sky will soon cloud over. I received the prognostication of the stars with dread: I shall have two more sons, Bendegúz and József, but both will be stillborn. Even more horrendous: József's death will entail that of his mother. All this will happen within the next two years. If only I could doubt! If only I could make our fate do otherwise! If only the heavenly bodies could err just this once!

Somehow or other liberated from the prison of the weather, as soon as he could he reached Nagyvárad. There he checked his diagrams and calculations again, with great care. The result remained the same. He wondered how he was to bear the burden of this dreadful secret. 'My dear! We are off on a journey!' he said to his wife.

'When? Where to?'

'Now, straight away, home to Homonna.'

'Is there something wrong?'

He opened his mouth to speak, but did not have the strength to utter the heavy words. He mumbled something about business.

At home, he thought, it must be easier to take every imaginable step to safeguard ourselves. Perhaps we can somehow wrest ourselves from the clutches of fate. But how? It is difficult to win a battle against the dispensation of providence.

Leopold Pohl and Hami received them with tears of joy. Mendel Berda-Stern feared that he should open up before them the bundle of the future; perhaps more of them would see more. He worked himself up to it a hundred times, but he was unable to go on.

'What woes of care afflict my husband?' asked Eleonora.

'I am just thinking about things,' replied Mendel Berda-Stern, forcing a smile upon his lips.

'Why have you been sitting around on my skirt hems lately? Have you given up chasing fortune?'

249

'I haven't given up, I'm just pausing . . . so I can spend more time with my loved ones.'

His wife knew that this was not the whole truth, but also knew that wild horses would not drag the latter out of him. As the days and the weeks passed, Mendel Berda-Stern watched Eleonora's swelling belly with increasing concern. Despite the woman's protests he had learned medical professors from Pécs and Karslbad examine her. He personally supervised the diet they prescribed, the herbal teas he portioned out himself on the apothecary's balance he had bought for this purpose, and infused the herbal mixtures himself. Eleonora found this overzealous protectiveness distressing, but her husband proved the more determined.

Despite every precaution little Bendegúz was born bluish-red, with the umbilical cord fatally twisted around his tiny neck. Eleonora is keeping her spirits up, but my father-in-law is inconsolable; he has aged ten years. I would do anything to prevent the next tragedy from occurring.

Once his wife's health had recovered somewhat, Mendel Berda-Stern went off to Pest-Buda with great suddenness, taking a room in the Queen of England Hotel. That evening in the restaurant he recognized, from lithographs in the newspapers, at the next table, the statesman Ferenc Deák. He was smoking his usual Cubanos. He conversed with him briefly.

'In Pest, March is the most dangerous month, November the saddest,' said the sage of the homeland. It was the beginning of April.

On his suggestion Mendel Berda-Stern ordered roast lamb and was not disappointed. He thought he would go out on the razzle, seeking out the card dens of the city, and concentrate on the number 7. But he did not in the least feel like it. He no longer needed any money, so why should he squander his life on further battles on the green baize, where winning was not guaranteed?

He sought and gained entrance to the salons of distant acquaintances. His name cards, though curled up at the edges, opened doors carved in the urban style. Amongst others he met the industrialist Mór Wahrmann, to whom he was very distantly related through the Sterns. Mór Wahrmann was pleased to meet him and immediately launched into a disquisition on the unavoidable necessity of uniting Pest and Buda. Mendel Berda-Stern adopted these views. The enthusiastic relative filled his head with so much information that he ended up donating 500 crowns to the city's poor.

'Which city's poor?' asked Mór Wahrmann.

Mendel Berda-Stern opted for Pest.

Eleonora sent fresh messages urging him to return home, where he was sorely missed. The letters were also signed by Hami. Then a purple wax-sealed envelope arrived from Leopold Pohl, asking him kindly to return home to Homonna.

> I miss dearly our substantial afternoon discussions about the future, the fate of the world, about Nostradamus, and the rest. Why are you dallying by the Danube?

Mendel Berda-Stern replied curtly declaring that urgent matters kept him in Pest-Buda. But Leopold Pohl was made of sterner stuff and would not be satisfied with this response. Mendel Berda-Stern was bombarded with letters every third day, each more formal than the previous one.

> My dear son-in-law,
> Your whimsical change of residence has visited upon all of us suffering and uncertainty. It is time you heeded your husbandly duties before it is too late!

He received this threat apathetically. Nostradamus, the king of prophets, taught the ruler to follow the path of least resistance.

Summer in Pest was hotter than in Homonna or Vienna, as the newspapers kept reiterating. Mendel Berda-Stern had just dismissed his current manservant, because he was unable to serve him his coffee as prescribed. Mendel Berda-Stern suffered more from boredom than from the heat. He could never have imagined that it was possible to lose interest in one's fellow human beings. Perhaps it was Hami that he missed most, when he was having his lonely evening meal.

He spent most of his time reading. He immersed himself in the study of the stars. He made a primitive telescope, which he kept tinkering away at. He worked his way through every book on the subject that he could get hold of. He would regularly visit the observatory on top of the Hármashatárhegy, at first for conversation, later to pursue scholarly work.

One evening in the foyer of the hotel he was met by Hami, who flew into his arms. Mendel Berda-Stern became livelier. He introduced her to everyone and made a thousand plans as to where to take his beloved sister. He wanted to show her every one of the city's sights and would have dragged her along to all the salons he knew. In the hotel the rumour spread that she was not his sister but his lover – they were often to be seen holding hands.

On the very first evening he admitted to Hami what was keeping him away from home. The girl was open-mouthed. 'How on earth can you believe in that stuff?' Mendel Berda-Stern listed his most serious evidence, from the birth of Sigmund in Nagyvárad to the death of Bendegúz. Then he told her of the fabulous amounts of money he had won at roulette and baccarat and on other fortune-hunting expeditions, which he more or less calculated in advance. May

God take it not as a sin, but he could not be wrong this time.

Hami broke down in tears. 'So we shall never see you at home again?'

'Of course you will. Just this dangerous year I have to spend away from Eleonora because . . . you understand.'

'So why do you not explain this to her?'

'Do you think she would believe me? I'm sure you don't.'

His sister left, mission unaccomplished.

The letters from Homonna dried up. Mendel Berda-Stern was not troubled by this, though he would gladly have read of the physical and mental development of his little Sigmund. He continued his uneventful inactivity in the capital. *Peragit tranquilla potestas, quae violentia nequit.* Quiet strength achieves what violence cannot.

He had less time ahead of him than behind him when he had news from his father-in-law. Leopold Pohl informed him as delicately as possible that Eleonora was once again pregnant. Do not ask who the father is – she is not prepared to tell me. You have no one to blame but yourself!

Mendel Berda-Stern knew he was right. He spent a few days sorting out his financial affairs, then travelled to a little village in the back of beyond where he sought admission to the Piarist Order. The good will shown towards him by the order he repaid with a substantial gift of money. His whereabouts were revealed only to Hami, whom he asked to keep it a secret. His sister bowed to his wishes. Once in a blue moon she visited him. It was she who brought the news that Eleonora had had a second stillborn child, József, and had died giving birth.

'Never come here again. I have finished with the outside world!'

As his sister sped away in tears, the person who was once called Mendel Berda-Stern hanged himself on the window

253

catch. He used the rope that served as the belt of his habit. The catch being a little low, he was successful only at the second attempt. In his death throes his last words cursed the stars.

VIII

BY DAWN THE BARE BRANCHES ARE WREATHED IN HOAR frost. The surface of the puddles thickens as the frost bites deep into the soil. Even the watchdogs would fain curl up with the cattle or the horses for the night, seeking the warmth of their larger bodies' exudations. Breath steams from mouths like pipe smoke. The birds wintering here at home are already ashiver, as are the four-legged beasts sleeping through the freezing months. Out in the country life almost comes to a halt. In town, too, there is less activity, people shut themselves in. The city sentries, known popularly as *bakters,* patrol the city's better streets with urgent steps at night, their lanterns repeatedly extinguished by the beard-tousling wind.

Sándor Csillag awaited the end of the 1800s with excitement verging on hysteria. He had lived to see as many years as he had white teeth, and all of them were intact. Only from his mother could he have inherited such a magnificent array of ivory teeth, for his father had had many problems with his teeth, especially in his later years. Of such matters Sándor Csillag had no direct knowledge; only from Hami had he heard stories of his parents, who had both died relatively young. In his wakeful dreams he saw their faces and figures with as much clarity as if he were looking at life-like paintings in oils. Why had Father not had any pictures painted of themselves?

Hami was of the view that the boy she had been left to bring up required the strictest possible education, for he exhibited from his earliest years a wild and untrammelled nature. He was still in nappies when he set fire to the kennel of the dog Berta, by means of a lantern he managed to carry there. The shed and the woodpile also went up in flames. The dog, chained up, was saved from being burnt alive only thanks to the neighbours. Hami never worked out how little Sigmund had managed to climb from the chair onto the table, whence he could reach and unhook the lantern. Aged six, he could not be left alone with girls of his age, since their undergarments were of intense interest to him.

Lower school he completed in three years; that was because in Homonna and the districts surrounding it, that was the number of years of primary school available. And Hami did not have the heart to send such a little lad away to board. She planned to do that in later years. But Sigmund again put a spoke in Hami's wheel. Before she could be told of his very poor third-year results – which barred progression to the upper school – he left home in his school uniform. His foster mother had no news of him for two weeks, during which her hair fell out in clumps.

A postcard covered in laboriously articulated letters arrived some weeks later, in a red envelope, from the city of Miskolc. Sent by one Tihamér Vastagh, tapster and coffee merchant, it respectfully informed Madame Hanna Berda-Stern that the young man Sándor Csillag had sought and entered his employ as an assistant in his trade. He had claimed that he was an orphan, who had been cared for hitherto by the addressee.

'Who is this Sándor Csillag?' asked Hami out loud,

though she suspected the answer. She at once had herself conveyed to Miskolc by cart.

Tihamér Vastagh's hostelry lay at the far end of town, in a street of dubious repute. Among the circle frequenting his premises there were just as many ladies of the night as poor and dissolute artisans or nobodies begging for credit. Hami had never set foot in such an establishment. Now she hardened her heart and lifted up with both hands her black lace skirt that swept the ground, so that not even its hem should touch the oily floor, and pushed her way towards the bar. 'Good day, my good man. I am looking for Mr Tihamér Vastagh.'

'That would be myself,' said the sharp fellow, whose Adam's apple was the size of a medium-sized apricot.

'I have come about the boy.'

'Little Sanyi is asleep: he is on nights.'

'Little Sanyi? Hm! I want him at once.'

'I tell you, he is asleep.'

'And I tell you I don't care!' She brought the metal-shod heel of her travelling knee-boots down on the wooden floor so hard that it retained the imprint. The boy who staggered out from the back half-asleep she brought round with two sharp slaps across the face. The boy slapped her back. Hami was speechless. The eyes of Sigmund/Sándor radiated the rawest hatred, like some wild animal. Hami was shaken to her bones.

Their conversation was bleak and to the point. The boy declared that under no circumstances would he return. Hami had never loved him and if that was how things stood, it would be best if their ways parted now. If his foster mother did not give her blessing to his life here, he would drown himself in the nearby River Bodva. 'Don't think for a moment that I am less determined than my father!'

Hami sighed. It was hopeless. She had never told the boy how Mendel Berda-Stern had ended his life by his own

257

hand, but in this family the first-born sons did not have to rely on second-hand accounts. 'But you have no need to rely on charity!'

'This is not charity! I do a decent job of work for my living!'

'But when you come of age you will inherit a great deal of money, you idiot! It is all yours by right, all that your poor father put away and which I have looked after for you!'

The boy shrugged: 'I know. You can send it in due course.'

Hami wept openly, laying her head on the hostelry table. She thought this was the last time she would see her adopted son, the adored child of her brother. And so she would be left on her own in her old age. Since her father's death, this boy was her only relative. Eventually she pulled out a handker-chief, blew her nose trumpet-like, and asked: 'And how did you come to change Sigmund Berda-Stern to Sándor Csillag? Why have you thrown away your honest name?'

'Why did my ancestors throw away their ancient name?'

To this question Hami did not know the answer. The fire blazing in the boy's eyes seared holes in her heart. She felt that the person she had sat down to talk to was a wayward relation, Sigmund Berda-Stern, while the person she left at the table, Sándor Csillag, was a stranger over whom she had no influence. She returned to Homonna without achieving her goal, or rather, having given up her goal.

In three years Sándor Csillag progressed down the country crescent-wise. From Miskolc he went to Büds-zentmihály, from there to Nyíregyháza, and then on to Debrecen. He earned his living in a variety of hostelries. His feel for numbers and his hard-working nature and brains everywhere assured him of rapid advancement. Then he came to Nagyvárad, the town of his birth in Transylvania, where he worked as an assistant in a men's outfitters. He thought he might spend the rest of his life in this attractive town, but the owner of the outfitters did not like the way he

258

was drawn to his daughter, an attraction which she seemed to reciprocate. Sándor Csillag again had to pack his worldly goods, going to Arad via Gyula and from Arad to Makó, where he now found himself a job in women's apparel. There followed Szeged, Baja and Pécs. In every town the dashing young man who claimed that there were few more keenly aware of the latest fashions of the capital, the materials of choice, and the comme-il-faut was gladly offered employment. He did not admit that he had never been to Pest-Buda, that is, to Budapest, as it was now called.

In Pécs he found employment in the Straub shoe shop in Király Street, where leather and boot-making equipment was also sold wholesale to the shoe- and boot-makers of the town. He rented a monthly room in Apácza Street from an elderly couple, whither his sixth sense led him. In front of the window of that house blossomed delicate lilacs, visible from far away. Sándor Csillag was seized by the desire to wake up every morning in a room like this, with lilacs at the window, which as he rose and opened the window wide would fill with their deep scent. He had already shaken on it with the old folks when it dawned on him that the lilac dons its wonderful robes only for a few weeks every year and at other times it is but a sadly stunted dry bush. Still, he had no reason to regret his decision. It was delightful to stroll along Apácza Street, whither the crackling smell of the nearby coffee-roasters and cafés was invariably borne by the wind. Above him the sun traced a diagonal path, soaking in timeless filtered colours the walls painted a daisy yellow.

The Straub shoe store was the town's most recent to be established, but it was already giving the competition headaches. Old Miksa Straub was given preferential treatment not just by the tradesmen but especially the shopping public, because he gave sensible advice to those he thought fit, and also offered his wares on credit. To parents seeking footwear for their offspring he honestly explained which

259

shoes were the most hard-wearing, even if they might be a little less comfortable than some others. To older women he was able to point out unerringly if a pair of shoes was likely to give rise to corns on their feet. Any shoes which failed to please he was glad to exchange even months after purchase, declaring: 'Here the buyer is God!' then he would clap his palm over his mouth and look up apologetically towards the ceiling. Though born a Jew, after his marriage to Elsa Ráchel Rommwalter the two of them converted to Christianity. He summed up his reasons thus: 'When in Rome, speak Italian!'

Everyone loved Old Miksa Straub: his tall, balding head and white whiskers were recognizable even in thick fog and were honoured with a doffed hat. When Sándor Csillag first entered the shoe shop, making the bell above the door's glass window jingle, Old Miksa Straub was just looking through the local paper. Hearing the bell, he put it down at once and clicked his heels unassumingly. 'Top of the morning to you, young man. What service can I be to you?'

'I am looking for work.'

'Well now. And where were you sprung from?'

'I have come from Baja, where I worked for Spolarich and Lindner, ladies' gowns, frocks and mantles. Before that I worked in other clothing businesses, but I have had my fill of the rag trade and I would rather like to sell shoes.'

'How right you are! She might be wearing a dirty raincoat, but if the shoes on her feet light up the lady, that makes her elegant at once.'

'And I love their smell,' Sándor Csillag added.

'Well then, off you go round the back, you can sniff around to your heart's content. My Elsa will tell you what's where.'

Sándor Csillag's enthusiasm for stacking the firm's grey boxes on the shelves was, according to Aunt Elsa's instructions, unflagging. Once Aunt Elsa had been a shrunken little female, but since the shoe shop was doing well she had swelled up into something like a small commode, and on the dressing-gown she wore as an overall the decorations reminded one of porcelain drawer-knobs. She took Sándor under her wing the moment she saw him. 'That lad's a hard worker!' she reported to her husband that night in bed. Old Miksa Straub gave a little hmm. 'To me he said he'd buy us out in time.'

'Lad's got ambition and no mistake.'

They laughed.

Sándor Csillag was serious. When he came of age, he gained access to all the riches that Hami had preserved for him. He travelled up to Homonna to have a word with the executor. Taking all of his inheritance into account, he came to the conclusion that he had enough assets to give up work for ever. He ordered the house to be sold, giving the furniture to Hami as a present. Both Books of Fathers he took in his hand luggage and read on the way. There was no space left even in the second volume: Mendel Berda-Stern's astrological diagrams, calculations and notes had filled up the pages and left no margin.

As soon as the opportunity presented itself, he seriously inquired of his employer: 'Uncle Miksa, how much would you sell your shoe shop for, all in?'

'In cash?'

'Not beans, that's for sure!'

Uncle Miksa Straub smoked half a pipe of tobacco before replying. He gave a figure which he did not dream of getting.

'Done! Let's shake on it!'

'You are having me on, sonny Jim! Where would you get your hands on that sort of money?'

'Leave that to me! Well? Shake on it?' And as the old man stared at him blankly, he added: 'Hurry up with your answer or I'll think better of it and open up a rival shop diagonally across Király Street!'

'Elsa, you hear this? Wonders will never cease!'

The deal was completed that summer. Sándor Csillag had the whole shop renovated. He had gas lamps fitted to the two wrought-iron chandeliers at the entrance; they were the wonder of the street for the evening strollers.

'Not such a big deal,' said Sándor Csillag. 'In Budapest the best streets have had electric light since 1873. You have to keep up with the times.'

On the new shop sign it said: Straub & Csillag, since he thought dropping the well-established name would have damaged the firm's reputation. He offered the Straubs the chance to continue to manage the shop for a fee that was so high they could not refuse. Soon the attention of mothers with marriageable girls was also attracted to the ambitious young man, who was regarded as a good match. He, however, spent little time in Pécs, despite having also purchased the house in Apácza Street. The rumour was that he was busy wooing some aristocratic lady in his home town, which they took to be Homonna; some spoke of a baroness, others of the daughter of a count.

Sándor Csillag took every opportunity to visit the capital. He maintained a permanent suite at the Queen of England Hotel. Nightfall generally found him in houses with red lights. His generosity was suspended in the case of the ladies of the night, whom he paid only as much as he absolutely had to. He was rough with them.

'This one scratches and pinches, like a scorpion,' one of them complained to the madam.

'You would die if that were true,' she replied. A romance set in South America was doing the rounds in that house.

In the mornings Sándor Csillag would sit in the Hotel Bristol, staring at the Danube and the bridge arching over the grey waters, over which carts trundled on their way to Buda. It was the month of November; snow fell in a soft drizzle. He ordered yet another Viennese coffee. He shook his head when the blue-uniformed young waiter brought the plate in his left hand, grasping the handle of the jug in his right. 'Just one hand,' he ticked him off strictly.

He was reading the Books of Fathers for the umpteenth time. It was time to start writing his own section. From Gorove and Partner's stationery shop he ordered an album in a large format, which even came with a tiny little lock. As soon as he bought it, he carried it with him, for a while wherever he went. He kept the key in the watch fob of his waistcoat. He spent days caressing the pristine white pages with deep satisfaction. There is something sublime in the fact that they are all blank, he thought. He kept putting off the day when he would disturb their blankness and was himself surprised when he asked for pen and ink at the Bristol.

Let the third one begin. I wish Sándor Csillag and his descendants that only joyful matters should grace these pages.

PRAYER

If only I had enough strength not to squander my abilities on lowly enjoyments. These shake my whole being, yet the greater the ecstasy, the emptier I become. I must conquer my mortal passions, otherwise they will conquer me. My task: to kill the miserable, inferior being within me, so that, being purified, my spirit might guide me to the world of rationality.

My clan possesses the exceptional gift of memory, a privilege that belongs to the first-born; sometimes even the gates of the future open before us. But whither have we got by means of this? Our fate has been no easier, our life has not been better; we have not managed to spare either ourselves or our loved ones from an evil fate. It is wiser to concentrate all our strength on today, for yesterday has gone and perhaps even the future is foreordained. As Horace says: carpe diem.

As long as the Straubs were spared the assaults of gout, the travels of Sándor Csillag had little effect on the trade of the Straub & Csillag shoe shop. But later they had little strength to spare for the supervision of the newly recruited employees. These were not as loyal to their masters as the former owners, their sticky palms and nonchalance had a cumulatively damaging influence. Sándor Csillag could observe this whenever he ran his eye over the books, yet he showed little concern. The cost of my way of life is amply covered by the shop. Why should others be denied their share? he thought.

In the life of the nation Gyula Szapáry had now been replaced by Sándor Wekerle as prime minister and it was preparing to celebrate the millennium, a thousand years since the first Magyars arrived in their homeland. The face of Budapest was being made up like those of girls at their coming-out ball. There was a lively debate in the newspapers about the construction of a viaduct for the tram to run on the Pest side of the Danube. The majority thought that such a long viaduct would disfigure the corso, the prime venue for the citizens' strolls. Yet without a viaduct, the tracks would have to be laid along the quayside, which was liable to annual flooding. Sándor Csillag backed the viaduct. 'One must keep up with the times!' He adored every form of transport.

New Year's Day 1896 found him staying the night in Pest, the carillon of bells that rang out in honour of the millennium long reverberating in his head. A few days later he travelled to Venice. He took the tram to the Western Station and boarded the fast train to Trieste; this left at eight in the evening and arrived in Venice at two-thirty in the morning. At night, after the bed had been made up for him, he stood for a long time in the corridor, smoking a cigar and staring out at the landscape shrouded in darkness. He had a flash-forward of a sudden: in a hundred years' time, folk would travel on this train just as today, though – oddly – the journey would take only an hour less than it does today, even though it will be powered by an electric engine that belches neither smoke nor soot. Is that credible? An electric engine? Where from? How? Ach . . . stuff and nonsense.

Despite his best efforts and resolutions, in Venice, too, the hectic in his blood drove him to women of easy virtue. Not only to the downmarket type hovering around the Rialto, but to the courtesans, who here held court on a small island, whither the gondoliers would carry you for a hefty extra fee. Sándor Csillag penned ever-new pledges and oaths and vows in the Book of Fathers about self-restraint, a pure and spiritual life, and a sedulous life. And when he failed to honour these, he added remorseful, repentant lines to his text.

He had a sudden craving for complete peace and solitariness: from the albergo near the Accademia he moved to the Lido. This summer resort was almost entirely deserted in January; only one hotel was open and even that had only half-a-dozen occupied rooms. As he found out in the dining room, most of the guests had come for a salt cure, recommended for weak lungs by some doctors.

Sándor Csillag forgot that he had come here in order to be alone the moment he heard the sound of Hungarian being spoken in the room. Bowing as he clicked his heels – something he had learnt from old Miksa Straub – he presented himself at the table of his compatriots. The Goldbaum family, father, mother and two young girls, burst out in vibrant laughter in four different pitches when they learnt that the person bowing before them was none other than the second element of the Pécs firm of Straub & Csillag.

'We have been buying our footwear from you for years,' said Helene Goldbaum, the mother.

'Come over and join us!' urged Manfred Goldbaum, the head of the family. 'How long have you been in these parts?'

As they partook enthusiastically of coffee à l'italienne, in the course of the rambling conversation it transpired that the Goldbaum family lived in Beremend, half an hour's ride from Pécs. Manfred Goldbaum had begun as a trouser cutter and taken over as owner of a clothing firm employing fourteen qualified tailor and cutters, working for him on foot-treadle sewing machines imported from Germany. The daughters, Antonia and Ilona, were of marriageable age with – and at these words Manfred Goldbaum gave a knowing wink – substantial dowries. Sándor Csillag's mouth drew itself into a smile.

Perhaps it was divine inspiration that these two beauties should cross my path. We spend much of our time as a threesome. I would happily marry either of these girls, but preferably both of them ... what an impossible notion! Our trio grows daily more carefree and melds more and more into one. But the tension keeps growing. I wonder if I can be honest with them both? I fear that if I reveal my true feelings it would spoil everything. Therefore I must somehow cut the Gordian knot myself. For this decision there remain but three days, until their departure.

Antonia was 21, muscular in the manner of a young dog, black as coal, introspective, wilful. Ilona was 20, gentle like the chestnut trees, brown as a fawn and as easily startled. It would be difficult to imagine two sisters less like each other. Ilona was like her mother. And a little like her father. Antonia most resembled, perhaps, Hami. This made the choice both easier and harder.

On the afternoon of their last day, Sándor Csillag asked for the hand of Ilona Goldbaum in marriage. The couple heard him out with faces impassive. Then Manfred Goldbaum said: 'You may certainly have Ilona's hand. But first we must marry off Antonia. As soon as there is a ring on her finger, you may have our little Ilona!'

Sándor Csillag resigned himself with some sadness to the uncertain duration of his engagement. He had not counted on Antonia Goldbaum presenting her fiancé to her parents that very month, in the person of Imre Holatschek, only son of the apothecary at Beremend.

My ship has sailed into port. With this respectable marriage I hereby renounce the days of my feckless youth. My young bride is the first woman I have encountered whose company brings me joy at any time of the day or night. In her parents I have found a true father and mother. My egg-shaped fob-watch, my father's sole bequest to me, I presented to my father-in-law on the night of my stag party, in a sudden access of generosity. Though I was highly intoxicated, I don't regret it for one moment. I know that this timepiece dates from the age of my ancestor Kornél Csillag, who chose later to be known as Sternovszky. To the best of my knowledge, it was found in the mud by a bandit called Jóska Telegdi. At the time it was broken, showing 9 October 1683, that is, it stopped on the day of the battle of Párkány. What an amazing coincidence! It was on that battlefield that the father of that bandit died! Telegdi, who was killed at the scene, left there all his possessions, and that is how the timepiece came into my ancestor's hands and has ever since, having undergone many repairs, always been passed on to the first-born. The chain of ownership was not broken by Fatimeh's thievery; on the contrary, it was she who righted matters when they were out of kilter as a result of Otto's murder. It is no bad thing that this valuable relic leaves my possession. I never wore it myself. It fits Manfred Goldbaum's waistcoat pocket far better; may it therefore bring him good fortune always.

The Goldbaums did not observe the religious customs or the dietary regime of the Israelites, nor did they go to synagogue; rather, they saw themselves as Hungarians, considering their ties to their homeland more important than their ancestry. Manfred Goldbaum went so far as to contemplate changing his surname, and if only he could have come to an agreement with Helene over their new name, they would now long have been called something resoundingly Hungarian like Garay, or Gárdonyi, or Garas. In the end the double wedding was held in the Pécs synagogue, the two couples married by Chief Rabbi Lipót Stern, who turned out to be distantly related to Sándor Csillag and invited him round for tea. Sándor Csillag gladly accepted, but never kept his promise.

After the wedding both couples moved into Sándor Csillag's house in Apáczai Street, though Antonia and Imre did so only temporarily. Imre Holatschek wanted to make a career in Harkány, where he thought the warm spa waters offered sure-fire business opportunities in the curative and recuperative sphere. He used his dowry to make an offer for the local apothecary's shop, and when this was declined he opened his own chemist's in the building of a public house that had closed down long before. At the same time he set about building a house of his own.

Ilona regretted that the foursome would not stay together in the longer term – it would have been most agreeable to share with her sister the mysteries of married life, of keeping servants, and of discovering the world of cookery. The two Goldbaum girls continued to behave like sassy girls, their peals of unrestrained laughter rose high in one room or another, in the postage-stamp of a garden, ringing out through the windows and along Apáczai Street, even reaching the neighbours. 'The laughing ladies' they were called in the area. His wife's joy-filled peals of laughter, an octave higher than Antonia's, were music to Sándor Csillag's ears. He would not have minded his brother- and sister-in-law staying with them for ever. This would be one way of achieving his ideal of living with both the Goldbaum girls at the same time.

Antonia never gave any indication that she resented Sándor Csillag for choosing her younger sister. 'I love you both!' was her eternal refrain, accompanied by a gentle, dreamy smile.

Not long after the wedding Sándor Csillag had a burning desire to see Budapest again. He knew it was no longer acceptable for him to set out on his own, though that, above all, is what he truly desired. So he tricked out this trip as a birthday present for Ilona. Ilona clapped her hands in joy. 'Can we go to the Opera? Can we take the viaduct tram? Can we ride on the underground railway?'

Sándor Csillag had told her many tales of the capital's wonders: the underground train that had opened last spring, and the recently completed Comedy Theatre. But there were things about which he told no tales. Ilona jumped up around her husband's neck landing kisses wherever she could. Then she grew sad: 'And . . .'

Sándor Csillag knew precisely what she meant. He gave her a gentle caress. 'We'll take them, too. Why not?'

The two couples took rooms in the Queen of England Hotel, their two suites opening onto a single reception room. The very first night they clapped their palms raw at the Opera, where the contemporary Italian composer Giuseppe Verdi's *Aida* was performed with the chief roles sung by György Anthes, Mesdames Gizella Flatt and Itália Vasquez, and Rikárd Erdős, to whom the audience gave a particularly warm welcome, those in standing room pounding the floor with their feet as well, a thunderous noise that frightened Ilona and Antonia. The orchestra was under the baton of Henrik Benkő. The cast list and the tickets were retained as a permanent souvenir of the event in the ladies' embroidered evening bags. The box seats cost 10 crowns each. In the intervals they consumed champagne and caviar, served in the boxes by the staff. Imre Holatschek repeatedly offered to contribute to the costs of the evening but Sándor Csillag would not hear of it. 'This is my pleasure.'

Other visitors to the capital at this time included Kaiser Wilhelm II, accompanied by Apostolic King Franz Joseph. All the papers were abuzz with this news. The Emperor found the city on the Danube most pleasing, but desired to know why there were so few *Denkmaler* in Budapest, that is, statues and other memorials. Sándor Csillag agreed. It occurred to him to launch a collection for the edification of the city. Though perhaps he should have urged the embellishment of the streets and squares of Pécs, which he saw more often, and where, too, there was no plethora of *Denkmaler*. They had returned to their house in Apáczai Street when he read in the newspaper that the Apostolic King Franz Joseph had donated 400,000 crowns of his private funds to erect ten historical statues in Budapest. A very noble gesture, thought Sándor Csillag.

Though he devoted little time to the affairs of the footwear shop of Straub & Csillag, this was more than made up for by Ilona's contribution to the family business. At first she would go in only to pass the time of day with the Straubs, but gradually she took over the reins and in due course held them very tight. This proved increasingly a test for Miksa Straub's character. He was used to having to answer to no one but himself, but Ilona's doe-like gentleness proved to be allied to a steely business will. When the old couple had finally had enough and threatened to leave, Ilona did not stand in their way and took over the running of the office, whose drab furniture it was her first task to exchange for something bright and new. 'Well, how do you like it?' she asked her husband as she showed him round.

'Hm,' said Sándor Csillag, uncertain.

'Go ahead, tell me!'

'It's like a . . . boudoir.'

'That's right!' said Ilona, squirting a diluted fragrance into the air. 'At least the gentlemen I have to haggle with feel relaxed and uninhibited.'

Sándor Csillag was not sorry. Let Ilona play with the shop. Without noticing it, they had exchanged roles. After breakfast it was not the man of the house who went off to work but its lady. Sándor Csillag's goodbye kiss was every day accompanied by the words 'I'll drop in!' but he avoided honouring his promise whenever he could. He was much happier dealing with the running of the house. He found less joy in browsing the business ledgers than in planning the menu for lunch and dinner. This capacity of his the two women and Imre Holatschek never tired of praising, and in only one respect was he sometimes criticized: he allowed the cook too free a hand in the matter of red onions.

His taste in decorating the rooms was exquisite: he readily lavished money on Japanese vases, Brussels lace, exquisite clocks and antique weapons. He also devoted his attention to the minuscule garden, demarcating with his own hand the place of the flowerbeds and bedding down blood-red geraniums, while along the stone wall he planted four box trees which, once they were established, the gardener trimmed into amusing shapes on his directions. The topiary took the form of a dog kennel, a helmeted German soldier, an Egyptian obelisk and a fat python.

Thus from the house in Apáczai Street there would be two people departing of a morning: Mrs Sándor Csillag and Imre Holatschek. The latter was awaited by a trap and pair which trundled him to Harkány or Beremend. Ilona waved after him, then walked slowly along Apáczai Street and crossed the main square: and as her high heels were heard on the cobbles of Király Street, men ran out of the shops to greet her in suitable fashion. The pointed comments – that at the Csillags' the woman wore the breeches – were made only behind her back.

271

Ilona fell pregnant almost on her wedding night. My son Nándor was born on 7 December, six weeks early. For a long time his skin had the colour of the yolk of a duck's egg which it was impossible to wash off. Once he was bathed and wrapped in his swaddling clouts he was handed to me and I was overcome by that fever of joy, unlike any other, that is the essence of fatherhood, and which made both body and soul tremble as never before. I remembered that this was something that all my ancestors lived through, when they took their newborn child into their hands. This breast-swelling joy must be the driving force that commands us, mortal creatures, to take on the yoke of family life, this is why it is worth struggling and living.

The care of the infant became the focus of the everyday activities of Sándor Csillag. He brooked no interference in the boy's upbringing, even from Ilonka (his term for her from the day after the birth). Imre Holatschek made more and more allusions over the evening meal to the fact that it was high time Antonia also came into a blessed state. Antonia was distressed even at the mention of the topic and her blushes reached down to her neck.

They all four knew that this was a sensitive issue for the young apothecary. The situation was exacerbated by the fact that Imre Holatschek's efforts in Harkány were not crowned with success – the chemist's did not become truly popular. People stayed loyal to the Pachmann family's reliable chemist's, and the public house of ill repute that Holatschek's Medicaments and Medicines shop had replaced very much lived on in folk memory. The building of the house was also proving problematic, with Holatschek continually at odds with the builders, and when he ran out of funds well before completion, he high-handedly rejected Sándor Csillag's offers of a loan. Antonia and Sándor Csillag often discussed ways of trying to get the tense and over-stressed man back onto the rails, but they found no solution.

'You should have a child!' said Sándor Csillag.

'It's no fault of mine that there isn't one . . .' said Antonia, running out of the room.

Sándor Csillag found her in the garden. He put his arm around her shoulder. 'Don't be ashamed in front of me, sister-in-law. Tell me what the problem is.'

From her halting account it became clear that Imre Holatschek's organ was not functioning the way it should. Hardly does it make an effort in the right direction, it springs into action well before it should.

Antonia's face was crimson. Sándor Csillag gave a sigh. 'This is not so rare. Ejaculatio praecox.' He regaled her with an exhaustive account of the meaning of the medical term.

'How do you know about this?'

Sándor Csillag shrugged. He did not feel obliged to tell his sister-in-law that his source of information on such matters walked the streets. They were very close, by the fence, their shoulders touching. Antonia was hot and panting. Now it was the man who turned red. There could be no question of this, under no circumstances! In those months he filled pages of the Book of Fathers with vows and pledges, writing down again and again that we must resist temptation, for what makes man different from beast is that he can command his base feelings by the use of reason, feelings to which in his youth he had been in thrall like a slave.

It poured oil on the fire when Ilona soon began to swell up again and, hardly a year after Nándor, gave birth to Károly. By then the Holatschek household was almost permanently at war, their bickering echoing the length of Apáczai Street. Sándor Csillag and his wife reached the stage where they could hardly wait for their move to Harkány, their temporary stay having become rather protracted. But they could not bring themselves to mention this to the Holatscheks.

On Antonia's face a bitter crease of shamefulness, for disrupting the lives of her sister and her husband, assumed an unsightly permanence. Ilona was once again pregnant, welcoming the congratulations with a beatific smile. Throughout her pregnancies, apart from the final days, she always carried out her work at the shoe shop without fail. She had lunch brought from the Elephant hostelry, and afternoon tea from the Nádor café. Laky, the lacquered head waiter at the Nádor, personally brought Ilonka her soft-boiled egg on a silver salver, with two toasted rolls and a frothy cappuccino. Halfway through the second pregnancy, Laky made so bold as to ask: 'My dear lady, how can you keep up this pace in your condition?'

'Well, I have to push the chair a little further away from the writing desk.'

This bon mot was often repeated in aristocratic circles around the town.

One autumn day, as the wind churned the dust into funnel shapes, Imre Holatschek failed to come home. Instead, he had a letter delivered by his coachman. Antonia read it and then tore it to shreds and cried her eyes out. Wild horses could not drag out of her what her husband had said, but they had their suspicions. Days later Antonia told Sándor Csillag: 'He has grown exhausted by his daily struggles here, so he is going away for a time; I should not look for him nor expect him; he will let me know when he is ready to return.'

Sándor Csillag was lost in thought. Something pressed against his chest from inside. He was unable to put into words the confused feelings he felt. He could hardly believe that he . . . well, that he envied his brother-in-law. He had not been alone for years. His nights out, especially those in Budapest, now came back into his thoughts more and more.

Wasn't it high time to see if the ten historical statues paid for by the Apostolic King were up yet?

'Do you remember the piece we saw at the Opera?' he asked Antonia.

'Of course I do. Those were the happiest days of my life.'

'Really? Why is that?'

'We were together day and night . . .' and she lowered her eyes to the ground.

But their eyes soon met. They were talking in the salon, on the couch with the floral pattern. Sándor Csillag was drawn to Antonia by a force a thousand times more powerful than electricity. There was no stopping, no reasoning.

When they came to, Antonia's tears were in full flow, streaming down her cheeks and shoulder and gathering in a darkish pool on the covering of the couch. Sándor Csillag tugged at his bits of clothing and urged Antonia to do the same – a servant could come in at any time. They had been trained to knock before entering, but they often forgot. A few minutes later they were both sitting, clothes properly adjusted, on the floral-pattern couch, one at each end.

'Oh my God, what have we done? What will become of us?'

Sándor Csillag was incapable of consoling her or calming her; his desperation was deeper than the woman's. 'What if my Ilonka finds out?'

'She must not find out. Ever. Let's swear on it!'

It proved harder than they thought to keep their oath. They had not reckoned with Antonia's blushes, which she found difficult to give reasons for in the presence of her sister. They could not have been prepared for how difficult they found it to keep their looks and gestures under control. Left alone in the house they would have fallen upon each other at once, but fortunately Antonia kept her head and loudly ordered the coachman to bring the carriage round at once: 'A constitutional, along the bank of the Tettye!'

Arm in arm, enforcing stillness upon their limbs, they walked toward the thick of the forest. They ascertained that the coachman could no longer see them and then they tore off their clothes. In the course of an hour or so they managed to make each other reach the highest peaks many times. Sándor Csillag clutched Antonia's neck in ecstasy, at which she by no means protested but uttered a thin, high-pitched squeal which sent the man into seventh heaven. For these honey-sweet little sounds he would have walked barefoot to Trieste or even Rome. They would scratch each other too, violently, until blood came.

They knew they were playing with fire. Sándor Csillag repeatedly hardened his heart and tried to avoid his sister-in-law. To achieve this, he spent more and more time in the shoe shop. Ilona was delighted. She told anyone who would listen: 'It looks like Sándor's drying up behind the ears at long last.'

Antonia understood and was resigned to her fate. She dared not hope that their relationship would flare up again and was always surprised when it did. She was long resigned to Imre Holatschek never returning to her. She strove to prepare her soul for the loneliness that she thought she would have to endure for the rest of her life, which was only assuaged for some moments by her brother-in-law. She tried to make herself useful around the house, especially with the children, and the nurse was quickly dispatched because Antonia was very pleased and happy to carry out her work. In her, little Nándor and Károly gained and adored a second mother. They called her Tonchi, which became the most frequent word they uttered. Ilona and her husband too started to call Antonia Tonchi.

This was the last year of the nineteenth century, with the next approaching apace. Sándor Csillag was enormously excited at this prospect, as if the turn of the millennium offered some hope of regeneration or rebirth. He decided they would spend this special New Year's Eve in Budapest, in the Queen of England. His wife was not thrilled at the idea. 'I'll be seven months gone.'

'Don't worry, my dear. We shall take Professor Huszárik with us.'

'And Tonchi?'

'Tonchi too. And your parents. I have booked an entire floor.'

The shoe shop of Straub & Csillag was doing so well that money was truly no object. They had opened two branches, one in Jókai Street and another in Nepomuk Street. Sándor Csillag missed no opportunity to shower his beloved Ilonka with expensive gifts. At the Armenian jeweller in the lower town he opened a current account, so he could expect to be the first to be shown the latest *nouveautés*. He had the most fabulous clothes brought over from Paris, from the highly regarded house of Worth. He ordered Caron perfume by the bottle, and red Russian caviar, which his Ilonka could never resist, imported by the crate, and they drank with it the most exclusive champagnes of Moët et Chandon.

The millennial trip was scheduled to begin on 28 December. But the day before this Ilona fell ill with dreadful spasms, and she reported to her husband with a deathly pale face that she was bleeding a little. Dr Huszárik came post-haste and ordered her to bed and to be rubbed with a special unguent he brought. 'Obviously, travel is out of the question!'

'We are not going,' said Sándor Csillag.

'Don't . . .' said Ilona. 'Don't worry about me; you go.'

'How could you imagine such a thing!'

'I'm absolutely sure you should go. There's no need for so many people to suffer because of me. Everything will be fine; the professor will take care of me.'

'Always at your service, Madame,' said Dr Huszárik.

277

Sándor Csillag resisted until almost the moment of departure, but his wife was adamant. An entire little caravan of carriages swung onto the winding road, with Manfred and Helene Goldbaum in the first, Sándor Csillag and Tonchi in the second, and the servants in the third. Little Nándor and Károly stayed at home, looked after by a nun hurriedly recruited from the Sisters of Mercy. Before stepping into the carriage, Sándor Csillag looked back once more and saw Ilona through the window. She sat up in bed and waved with a tired smile.

Budapest received its visitors with quiet, cloudy weather. The Queen of England was covered in flags and its windows were decorated with pine branches, ready for the celebrations. Sándor Csillag took over the suite which on his own he found rather too big. The children's canopied beds and the double bed reminded him of the loved ones he had been obliged to leave in Pécs. As he was constantly cold, his manservant kept the fire in the stove red-hot. Whenever possible he would sit on Antonia's skirt, though at a suitable distance, as here they were even less secure from the eyes and ears of the hotel staff. In the depths of night, however, she always stole over to his bed and they gave each other a few hours bathed in gold. Their only care was that their cries of joy were muffled by the pillows.

The sound of church bells, ringing out seemingly interminably the arrival of the year 1900, found them in bed. They had no appetite for the monumental pork cuts, the sturgeon, the house speciality of cabbage broth with lemon; they managed to keep each other fed on fruit, everything that was forbidden fruit to them. Sándor Csillag lay back on the sheets and kept his thoughts to himself. Why hurt Antonia's heart? Sentences that begin 'If only . . .' are harmful. Only one such was heard, and that from her mouth. At four in the morning, as she slipped out of the room, she whispered: 'This was the most wonderful night of my life. Will every *fin de siècle* be like this?'

Twentieth century, what do you hold in store for me? Is there something of which I know not that is still to come for me? My life has settled into a trough and will surely dribble down into the ocean that disappears into the dark fog generally called death. I shan't ask it to happen, though! – it will come of its own accord.

On 2 January 1900 – how difficult it is to write this date – my third son was unexpectedly born and received the name Andor. I could not be at the birth, as I was on my way home from Budapest. This little creature, like the other two, asked to be admitted into this world much earlier than planned, so it appeared somewhat scrawny and little viable. This however no longer startles us. Indeed, little Andor caught up in a matter of weeks.

May the heavens give me the peace to resign myself to what cannot be changed and the strength to carry out that which depends on me.

His new resolution he was able to keep for nine months. He could not overcome his desire for Antonia for a moment longer than this. His sister-in-law received him with unaltered joy, never reproached him for the time in between; she understood perfectly and herself prayed for this agonizing attraction to turn to ashes.

Sándor Csillag devoted ever more time to the shoe shop and as much to the careful care of the three boys. He loved to see them growing up: he imagined Andor as a judge, Károly as a doctor, while the eldest, Nándor, would take over the family business. They were good brothers to each other, always helpful, forming a close-knit sixsome with their wives and in due course presenting him with nine healthy grandchildren.

279

These fine plans seemed already vain hopes when the lads went to primary school. All three proved to be rascals of the first order, taking leading roles in all the pranks, and no roles at all in their studies. They were always the ones kept in after school; it was always their blotchy, dog-eared exercise books that were displayed on the notice 'shame' boards by way of warning; they were the ones constantly berated loudly and threatened with expulsion. Nothing helped: neither the cane nor being forced to kneel on maize cobs, though both were plentifully employed by their father and the schoolteacher. They avoided having to repeat the year always and only thanks to bespoke packages for the head teacher and his staff being supplied from the quality stock of Straub & Csillag.

'All the teachers are walking on our soles!' – Sándor Csillag's despondent declaration went the rounds in the *Wild Man*, the intellectuals' watering hole. The quality of its cuisine and wine often brought it Sándor Csillag's custom, and on occasion this was the scene of trysts with Antonia, too, and although they behaved with decorum here, their rendezvous were not something they burdened Ilona's business-oriented brain with. The windows of the *Wild Man* were set so low that one could go in and out of the building through them. On one occasion, Antonia's parents turned up. As soon as Manfred and Helene Goldbaum hove into sight Sándor Csillag unchivalrously abandoned Antonia, fleeing through the windows. A flushed Antonia welcomed her parents, who could not imagine what their daughter was doing in a public place unaccompanied. Antonia managed to stutter something embarrassedly about a music teacher she was to take lessons from, whom she was supposed to meet here and discuss the matter with.

'Well, where is the teacher then?' Manfred Goldbaum inquired, his eyebrows arching to ever more interrogative heights.

'Well . . . he's late.'

In the autumn of 1908 there was again a long period of self-restraint mutually imposed on and by Sándor Csillag and Antonia. For weeks on end they barely exchanged a word. The family was preparing for Sándor Csillag's fortieth birthday. In the forenoon the children were – hopefully – at school, and the staff were putting the final touches to their spring cleaning. Sándor Csillag and Antonia were watering and arranging the indoor plants. They enjoyed the harmony of their movements. The house was filled with pure winter sunshine and in the contented silence only the two Hungarian vizsla dogs' claws made little noises as they scratched the veranda door; they would gladly have come indoors, but Ilona forbade this, though in her absence Sándor Csillag and Antonia would sometimes allow them in none the less.

They had been standing on two sides of the palm for several long minutes; the round wooden pot had been painted dark brown by Sándor Csillag himself. They wiped the leaves down with a soft cloth and sprayed them with water, refreshing the soil with little wedges of compost. They found nothing more to do. Time passed, Antonia's breath felt hot on Sándor Csillag's neck. They chanced to glance at the Venetian wall mirror at the same time. Time had ploughed streaks of grey in his hair; the keen cheekbones seemed less able to tolerate flesh upon them. The difference of eight years between them had never before seemed to matter; now it showed clearly, and they both saw this and thought this and with the identical movements of the head acknowledged it.

It was then they realized that Ilona was watching them from the veranda, as she stroked the two dogs. They both thought she had long ago left for the shoe shop and looked at themselves and at each other in some embarrassment. But we have only been standing here. She could not have

281

seen anything, they thought. Antonia blushed, Sándor Csillag too.

Ilona was gone. They were not even certain that they had seen her and that it was not their guilt that had played a trick on them. Antonia hurried into the kitchen, while Sándor Csillag set off for the shoe shop. He found Ilona bent over bills. She asked him, as usual: 'Have you come to work?'

Whereupon he clicked his heels and replied: 'Reporting for service, ma'am!'

This little routine they performed nearly every day.

For his birthday, he received a short, perfumed letter, with two seals upon it. He found it on the rococo table in the room they somewhat grandly called the music room, since it was host to a white upright piano.

Dear Sándor,

On the occasion of your fortieth birthday I urge you bravely to cast out from the boat of your life all falseness and pretence. Believe me, it is a waste to squander your energies. Do not be concerned about following the path whither your instincts direct you. Life is short. You can always count on me, as long as I feel the need I will absolve you of your sins and forgive everything that you have done in the past, that you are doing now, and that you will do in the future. Accept this as my birthday gift to you.

With the embrace of your partner, your travelling-partner, your work partner and your parent-partner,

Ilona.

He rubbed his eyes. Does this mean that . . . ? Surely not . . . He read it over and over again. A heavy weight began to press on his chest. What a piece of dross I am . . . and of what noble clay my wife was cast!

282

Shackled by lethargy, he found it hard to rise and go over to the salon, where the table was already being laid for twelve in honour of his birthday.

'Sándor!' His wife's head popped round the door. 'Time to put on evening dress.'

'Ilona—'

'Later,' and she was gone.

There proved to be no later in which to discuss the painful topic. Sándor Csillag kept putting it off, and Ilona acted as if she had not a care in the world. He showed the letter to Antonia, who was also smitten by the heavy burden of her sins and wanted to pack her bags at once so that she would not for a moment longer pollute the atmosphere of her younger sister's house. But before she could fill even one suitcase, Ilona told her in no uncertain terms to pick up Nándor from school. Nor did she later have an opportunity to clear the air with her sister. When she finally plucked up the courage, Ilona cut her short: 'No need.'

So Antonia stayed. She and Sándor Csillag avoided each other in the house and even tried to avoid exchanging glances. Sándor Csillag spent less and less time in the house in Apáczai Street. He joined the Townsmen's Bowling Club and then the Pécs Male Voice Choir, enjoying in both a measure of success. In the Male Voice Choir he was on occasion assigned a solo, and his burnished baritone would cleave the air.

Years later he realized (saw in the time that had become the past) that one night Ilona had lifted from his waistcoat pocket the key to the third volume of the Book of Fathers and had carefully read everything in it. So that was how she knew. But not even the pain of this realization could rouse him to anger with his wife. He knew it was a case of motes and beams. Rather, what drove him to fury was the Book of Fathers and the accursed ability of the Csillags to remember.

283

Happy are they who do not know that of which they have no need.

Of an evening the couple would try to heal their wounds by performing private spiritual exercises. Ilona was gnawed by jealousy but knew she could truly not afford to let it show. She consoled herself with the thought that there was no such thing as a good marriage, only a bad one and even worse one – in this light she could lay claim to a reasonably successful marriage. What has happened, has happened; at least it was all within the family. Do not be petty, she kept telling herself silently a thousand, a hundred thousand times; do not be jealous of such a petty thing; one is your husband, the other your sister.

Sándor Csillag made only two further entries in the Book of Fathers.

I give thanks to Heaven that
1. *I have Ilona's understanding.*
2. *My children are growing up fine.*
3. *Every member of the family is hale and healthy.*
4. *Our material advancement gives no cause for concern.*
5. *Heaven has not smitten me for my faults and the error of my ways.*
Can a man reasonably hope for any more than this?

That very week he was able to read in the newspaper that war had broken out, though Pécs felt few consequences of this for a long time. Those who had been called up were bidden farewell by the brass band of the Town Fire Brigade and ladies who threw bouquets of flowers. Sándor Csillag knew that he was himself too old, and his sons too young, to be called up for the army.

'You'll see, the war will drag on for years!' he would repeat in the *Wild Man*. More quietly, he would add: 'And we shall lose it.'

284

His assertion was received with much mocking laughter. It was then that they began to whisper behind his back that he was no longer entirely compos mentis.

Visions of horror assail me. I sense that the thread of my life will not soon be rent. I think there will be another world conflagration, well after the first. Most horrifying of all: I foresee that I shall die of hunger. How can this be? Will some business disaster force me into bankruptcy? I strive to avoid every risky step, my prudence – my cowardliness? – is almost rabbitlike.

This was to be Sándor Csillag's last contribution to the Book of Fathers for, following tradition, he passed the Book to his first-born. With a heavy heart. He was deeply concerned. It was possible that this family heirloom did not bring with it good fortune.

The years passed. The 70,000th inhabitant of Pécs came into the world, in the person of one of the grandchildren of old Straub. The mayor of Pécs presented the parents with a memorial plaque and diploma; among those invited to the event were Sándor Csillag and his wife.

Alas, Sándor Csillag did not foresee the coming of the Jewish Laws. When he was rounded up, with the rest of them, at the railway station, to be pushed onto the cattle-truck at bayonet-point, together with Ilona and Antonia and his two sons, who had been hiding out at home, his diabetes was already well advanced. He was 76 years old, grown very old indeed, and withdrawn deep into himself. On the second day of the journey his body was thrown off the moving train into the bushes. Stray dogs and foxes had their share of the corpse. His remains were identified only at the end of the war, and were buried together with those of the German and Russian victims of the tank battle that had been fought near by.

IX

NO ONE WHO NEED NOT WOULD BE OUT IN WEATHER like this. Those who are unfortunate enough to have no choice encounter the rage of winter: entrance doors blocked by snow and rarely any light penetrating the darkness of the clouds. The snow clots into lumps of ice, stiffening resistance to the work of the wooden shovels dedicated to scraping them off the pavements. The sky blinks in innocent incomprehension of how it could have emptied so much whiteness onto the world. Soon it grows dark, and the heavens' bottomless sacks of fresh snow open up again.

Before taking the stage he needed at least three hours to get himself into proper shape. He would begin with diaphragm exercises, placing his palm in the small of his back and pacing up and down, inhaling the life-giving element and sending it coursing into the deepest chambers of his lungs. At such times he could feel in his fingers the pressure which he always needed to ground his voice. Then, with a snake-like hiss he would let out the column of air, evenly, like an invisible length of string.

There followed meditation, in the course of which he

strove to think over the period from the previous performance to today. However powerful the discipline he applied to the workings of his brain, it always ended with his mind wandering away into the furthest recesses of the past. The week which he spent in Budapest with his father, his younger brothers and his aunt Tonchi quite often came to mind. These were the most wonderful days of his childhood, perhaps of his entire youth. It was 1913 and he was 16. His nose tingled with the spicy smells of the metropolis, his ears rang with ceaseless noise of carriages and cars and the wheels of the electric trams' unique squeal on the metal rails. Even snow was incapable of bringing to a halt this form of transport for more than a few hours or so, unlike the horse-drawn carriages of the Omnibus Company, which – to his infinite regret – suspended their services in both directions. They rode on the electric tram four times, sometimes in the direction of Lajos Kossuth Street, sometimes towards the Elizabeth Bridge. They also tried out the carriages of the underground railway. Nándor alighted and hopped back at each stop, with the conductor's encouraging comment: 'No extra charge!'

'You're grown up!' Aunt Tonchi kept repeating to him. He thought she was making fun of him; after all, when they lined up at school for PE he was always last but one. He knew that his looks and build were reminiscent of his ancestor Kornél Csillag. His fellow students dubbed him Pumpkin Seed, which he resented deeply, and fought the ascription tooth and nail.

Never had he seen his father as relaxed as on that trip to Budapest. Business matters had kept his mother in Pécs and it seemed as if the absence of Mama, who almost always wore black and for some reason radiated an atmosphere of permanent mourning, had an uplifting effect on Papa. He was like a child, wanting to see everything. Aunt Tonchi followed laughing in his wake, without for a moment releasing her hold on the shoulders of the two actual children. 'Károly,

Andor, you are both in Aunt Tonchi's care and mustn't take a single step without me, do I make myself clear?' – but her eyes twinkled with laughter, so that her exhortations were not taken entirely seriously. He, Nándor Csillag regarded himself as being one of the adults, though he romped around happily with his younger brothers.

Aunt Tonchi and his father took quite a number of steps without them. Though Nándor Csillag did not notice this at the time, now, as the heir to the family's visions, he knew.

The beginning of the trip in 1913 did not augur well; contrary to plans, they did not stay at the Queen of England, as his father took offence when he did not manage to secure the suites that he considered practically his own. They took rooms in the Hungária, on the bank of the Danube. Nándor Csillag spent hours just staring out of his window at the view of the castle in Buda, the snow-covered hills, and the ice floes sweeping downriver on the grey surface of the river. He especially liked to sit there in the hours of darkness and touch his cheeks against the cold of the plate glass. He breathed out steam. He counted the lights twinkling on the opposite side of the Danube several times, but by the time he reached the end, some had gone out while a few new ones had come on; he lost count generally somewhere between sixty and eighty.

They went out to the Zoological and Botanical Gardens, which the boys were even more enthusiastic about than he had hoped. His father informed them that their renovation had been completed the previous year, when the municipality had decided to rescue them from their miserable and run-down condition, and spent some five million crowns on their restoration. Papa could hardly recognize the place and lavished praise on it as if he were personally responsible for the transformation: 'What a wonderful stock of animals! What fine buildings built with devoted skill! The cliffs and mountains are so true to life that you would think they were real! And the promenades and paths furnished with comfortable places to rest! The facilities for summer and winter sports! The playgrounds and the free mobile library!'

Papa had a bit of a lisp, which meant that his speech was an endless source of amusement for the boys. Sándor Csillag was aged 45 by this time, but his youthful enthusiasm for all things progressive had not diminished one jot. He planned to encourage a similar zoological and botanical garden back home in Pécs (a plan of which, however, nothing came). He also thought it desirable to follow in Pécs the example of Budapest in establishing public conveniences, in the capital maintained by the Ferenc László Company. These were an object of his admiration even if he felt no need to make use of them.

They spent a memorable morning in the Rudas Spa Baths, where Papa explained that it owed its name to the 'flying' bridge across the Danube, that is to say, the ferry with its huge pine mast (in Hungarian *rúd*) berthed at the entrance to the baths. The municipality had rebuilt the old Turkish baths as a steam baths in 1883, creating a roof for the main pool and the four smaller pools around it, and opening two large public baths, one for each of the sexes. Papa showed them the effervescent tubs, the various baths lined with pottery, marble and stone, and the boys had to take a dip in every single one. They listened to the list of the many different ailments that could be successfully treated here in the medicinal baths, whose temperature – Papa knew even this by heart – was maintained at a steady 44 degrees centigrade, summer and winter. The visit continued in the newly opened sweating and slimming dry-air rooms, the tepidarium, the sudatorium and the calidarium.

Nándor Csillag was not as keen on the animals and the baths as were either his father or his younger brothers, but was more thrilled than any of them by the theatres screening motion pictures. They paid two visits to the

Metropolitan Mighty Movie House in 70 Rákóczi Street, where the company's advertising promised *a non-stop programme of outstanding films* for the discriminating moviegoer. The hotel porter ordered them tickets by telephone, itself an event so sensational at the time that he recalled the number to this day: 53-27. The screenings were accompanied by highly professional tunes from the piano of a round man with a Kossuth-style beard, who doffed his bowler whenever the audience showed its appreciation.

There were five or six short films per programme. It was in one of these that Nándor Csillag saw an opera singer for the first time. The face of the man, in a dark waistcoat, was quite frightening to behold; he sang his arias with a wide, gaping mouth and would stab at the sky with his right hand, at least when he did not do so with his left, too. He rolled his eyes the while, as if he were in his final death throes. Nándor Csillag had been taking piano and violin lessons for some years from Mr Ibrányi, who would come to their house in Apáca Street. Their father had intended that all three boys would take lessons, but neither Károly nor Andor had an ear for music. Nándor Csillag showed little ability at the piano, but was able to whistle or hum any melody he had heard just the once, at any time and with little effort.

'You take after old Bálint Sternovszky!' his father would say.

At his parents' urging the boy would entertain with this trick the social gatherings at their house, hesitantly at first, but quickly getting into his stride. The audience mostly asked for songs and folk tunes, and the ladies would reward him with banknotes tucked into his pockets, while the more intoxicated men would plaster them on his forehead, as if he were leader of a Gypsy band.

From the age of 12 he also sang in the choir of the Catholic church, which some looked at askance, considering that however Hungarian Sándor Csillag declared himself to be, he was after all Israelite, as were the family of his wife, the Goldbaums. The wedding of the two Goldbaum girls, too, was held in the synagogue and not the Catholic church. Sándor Csillag did not give the whisperers behind his back the time of day and was triumphantly installed below whenever his little Nándor sang a solo at the base of the organ. 'That's my Nándi!' he would inform those sitting in front, behind, or to the side, despite repeated hushing noises all around. Nándor Csillag found his father's singing of his praises deeply embarrassing and asked him many times to control himself. Sándor Csillag solemnly promised to do so, many times, but he could never keep his promise when he heard his son's gentle, mellow tones – the flush of pride carried him away. 'At this rate, he could be a second Caruso!'

He could not forbear to note that he, together with his wife and sister-in-law, had seen and, what is more, heard with their own eyes and ears the divine Caruso in Budapest, where he proved an ignominious flop. He only ever made one appearance in the Hungarian Royal Opera House, a benefit for the Prince József sanatorium. 'He was Radames and I was 50 crowns poorer for each ticket; even so I had trouble getting them, and I ordered by telegraph. The crowds were vast, people had gone mad, many bought shares in a single ticket, say a foursome, and passed it round to the next for the following act. The divine Caruso was not entirely well and only after the scene by the bank of the Nile did he manage to pull himself together somewhat. He was about forty, a well-built man . . . at that time. 12,000 crowns he got for that appearance, 12,000!'

Nándor Csillag was still in nappies when he first heard his father's Victor vinyl recordings, which he was never allowed to place on the deck himself. On the cardboard covers of the records he could soon make out: 'Enrico Caruso, the greatest tenor singer of all time, is under the exclusive contract of the Victor Company.' *La donna e mobile!* sang Caruso, to a piano accompaniment and with him little Nándor Csillag, in his piping little voice, to the great joy of his father. Soon he knew it inside out, just as he did the song of Nemorino, and above all the sobbing aria. *Ridi, Pagliaccio!* – he understood not a word of the Italian text, but still gleaned from the music what it was about.

His first teacher of singing was the Italian-born organist of the cathedral. He had some time ago abandoned a promising career in opera in Italy because of a false little Italian maiden. He had eloped to Trieste with her and thence came to Pécs alone. The man was brash, had a moustache and a goatee, and was universally known as Signor Supercilio, because he was a man of few words but many cigarettes and made friends with hardly a soul. They did not know that the reasons for his introspection were quite prosaic: in ten years of residence he had failed to master the Hungarian tongue, of which fact he was deeply ashamed and thus tried to conceal it. He taught Nándor Csillag with unremitting harshness, but rewarded good work at the end of the class with a piece of chocolate. On one occasion he let slip that he had himself been a student of Guglielmo Vergine, the Neapolitan maestro who had taught, among others, Missiano, the acclaimed baritone, and Caruso, the famed tenor. When Nándor Csillag passed this nugget on at home, the standing of his singing teacher rose vertiginously in the eyes of the parents.

Quite soon Signor Supercilio was urging his parents to let him take Nándor Csillag to audition for the Budapest Academy of Music. There he caused a considerable stir – he was proclaimed a Wunderkind. From then on they went up to the capital once a month to work with a répétiteur. The proud father doubled the monthly amount allotted for the musical training of his son.

Nándor Csillag was in fact having a singing lesson when

the heir to the throne was assassinated in Sarajevo. For days the name on everyone's lips was that of the Schiller grocery, the scene of the fatal shots, at the intersection of Franz Joseph Street and the quayside. A horrified Sándor Csillag was exercised chiefly by the latter detail: 'What a dagger in the heart it must have been for the Kaiser u. König that the heir to the throne should have been killed on the corner of a street that bore his name!'

Only a month later the sky turned completely dark and there was a hurricane such that even the oldest locals could not recall its like. There was no rain, but flashes of lightning sizzled to and fro. Even trees with massive trunks were uprooted and seemingly solid roofs went crashing onto the road. The papers reported seven seriously injured. In Budapest a whirlwind resembling an American tornado caused the deaths of several people, ripping the belfries off three churches, and also caused some structural damage to the Chain Bridge.

'Is appen soon, sumsinna bigue,' said Signor Supercilio.

The Monarchy severed diplomatic relations with Serbia. In Pécs there was no end of patriotic marching up and down the city streets. A military band played the rousing Rákóczi March and other popular recruitment songs, enthusiastic gentlemen of a certain age raised their walking canes gun-like to their shoulders and marched to and fro as the ladies and children waved lanterns and pennants.

'Where will all this end?' asked Ilona of her husband several times a day.

'Storm in a Serbian teacup,' he would reply.

At first Nándor Csillag sang at weddings and family celebrations. His fame spread far and wide. Soon he was being invited to perform at musical soirées, together with professional singers. The posters proclaimed: Nándor Csillag, the golden-throated boy wonder from Pécs. When he performed he was chaperoned by his father or Aunt Tonchi.

The front pages of the newspapers were plastered with military reports when the postman brought a rust-brown envelope. It was from Milan. Signor Supersilio translated it for them: 'You are asked performance, for charity, in Milano.'

It turned out that the concert was to raise money for Italian workers stranded in Germany: these unfortunates had already lost their jobs and were anxious to return home. Nándor Csillag's mother was opposed to the trip. 'Have you quite lost your senses? There's a war on!'

Convinced that Italy would remain neutral, Sándor Csillag took his son to Milan. From the evening papers in Italy he managed to deduce that the following day Caruso would also be performing for charity in Rome, so they took the train to see him perform. Many years later, that evening was to be recalled by Nándor Csillag in the Book of the Fathers.

On 19 October 1914 I had the good fortune to be among the select few to hear Caruso on the stage of the Teatro Costanzi. The audience gave an ecstatic welcome to all the performers. But nothing could compare with the whistling and torrential clapping that greeted the performance of Enrico Caruso. When Caruso sang the aria he made his own, Ridi, Pagliaccio!, his compatriots stood up to shout their endless Bravos and the display of joy seemed as though it would never end. The conductor, Maestro Toscanini, spent at least fifteen minutes tapping the rostrum, asking to be allowed to continue the programme and unwilling to permit an encore. The theatre manager hurried over to him and with much wringing of hands prevailed upon him to make an exception just this once. Caruso was then able to reprise the song, to the enormous satisfaction of all. This was for me the most important experience of my life. It is only since then that I have had some conception of how to perform in public.

There was no stage nor role in the course of his career that was not blighted by the oppressive presence of the great Caruso. His efforts hardly amounted to more than a striving to shake off the harrowing burden of the Italian tenor, and he was unable to resist imitating even the least remarkable aspects of his technique. Ede Karsay, his manager in Budapest, was blunt: 'Please to abandon this behaviour at once. Genius cannot be imitated; by trying to do so you merely make yourself look ridiculous. Better a mediocre Csillag than a first-class imitator of Caruso.'

It was easier said than done. A mind as receptive as his, having heard Caruso's painful tale as Canio, could free itself of the experience only the way a viper's poison can be removed from the flesh: with the blade of a sharp knife. Nándor Csillag was always having to put an imaginary blade to himself if he wanted to be able to perform on stage at all. To his eternal misfortune the roles he was most often asked to perform were those of Canio and Turiddu, in which Caruso was simply unsurpassable.

When he had set out on his singing career, Nándor Csillag tended to give himself airs and let it be known that he would be a bigger star in the firmament than Caruso. They smiled at his punning on his surname. But he was serious. He would have liked at least to have been known as the Hungarian Caruso. With his extravagant coiffure and dress, too, he copied his model. In time he gave up the wearing of jackets, cloaks, pelisses and headgear reminiscent of stage costumes, but even then in the opinion of his father he tended to the bohemian rather than to the middle-class in his attire. He adored expensive Parisian perfumes, the wilder shores of fashion, and even more the latest triumphs of technology. He acquired novelties of the hugely expensive type partly in the interests of promoting his health (waves of hypochondria would sweep over him in a rhythm now gentle, now more serious), and partly because of his temperament (constructing objects with his hands always had a soothing effect on him).

His orders to the importer Gyula László for an American ball-bearing-operated power drill, suitable for drilling to a depth of five millimetres in marble, stone, iron or wood, were more quickly delivered than those of any Pécs craftsman. He similarly secured the wonder hammer, which united 18 different tools in one, from adjustable S-wrench to saw, reamer to metal rule, all these nickel-plated, with a miniature anvil and vice, from the toolmakers V.M. Weissberger, by appointment, K. u. K. suppliers of tools.

He was certainly the only inhabitant of Pécs to order from Vienna a heatable bath with artificial waves. This piece of equipment, serving both one's physical and mental welfare, was crescent-shaped when seen from the side, but head-on it was like a giant cradle. Filled to its capacity of 40 litres of water, one could take a wonderful bath in it, waves being produced if one managed to use one's own weight to rock the construction to and fro. Nándor Csillag also purchased a steam generator sauna. The manufacturer Károly Becker guaranteed that his bath would resist spillage even in the case of the most powerful generation of waves. In this product Nándor Csillag was not disappointed. He ran a bath so often in the contraption – every other day – that his manservant called him Water Vole behind his back. He was, however, disappointed by the flat-foot corset, which was uniquely manufactured by Székely and Partner, orthopaedic shoemakers of Budapest, at 9, Museum Boulevard. The genuine Zagorian Mountains chest cordial lived up to the claims made for it: a glassful of this herbal decoction consumed every morning certainly prevented him from acquiring any kind of cough or wheeze.

Naturally he purchased a number of gramophones, in this sphere insisting on the products of Schwartz & Manotone as manufacturers. The record players of Schwartz &

Manotone, as the firm's slogan proclaimed, *Speak, laugh and sing, out in every tongue they ring*. In their record catalogue were the recordings of artists of the first order, which Nándor Csillag bought, virtually without exception. He dreamt of his voice being recorded at some point, like the arias of Caruso, but this never became a reality.

Several other things he had hoped for stubbornly and persistently also failed to materialize. Despite every effort he failed to secure contracts from either Covent Garden or La Scala, Milan. It was in these two opera houses that his unsurpassable ideal had heaped success upon success. By the time this would have been timely for Nándor Csillag, Enrico Caruso was arousing feverish excitement among opera-lovers overseas, chiefly in the diamond horseshoe seats in the Metropolitan Opera House. Nándor Csillag envied him from the bottom of the purest of hearts not just for the hundreds of thousands of dollars but the ten- or four-teenfold encores, lasting more than fifteen minutes, in which the New York Italians excelled, climbing onto the gallery for the Bravos! and stamping the floor. Nándor Csillag scored the greatest success of his career at the Vienna Opera, where he twice had to reprise the Glove Aria from *Rigoletto*, but for him the audience never rose to its feet. This was something he could never forgive them; sometimes he would call them ticket-buying riff-raff.

His most secret desire, to sing on the same stage as the maestro, seemed quite unattainable. Nándor Csillag appeared in many places in Europe in second-rank compa-nies and theatres, which secured him a comfortable way of life and a decent reputation, but neither happiness nor peace of mind. Only at the small workbench he had con-structed in his shed did he find, while he worked there, himself at peace, or perhaps at ceasefire.

Rare were the moments when the suspicion dawned that his gifts and his skills were perhaps not after all of the same order as those of the great Caruso, and between such flashes of insight long years would intervene, during which he attributed the imperfect arc traced by his career to ill-intentioned impresarios, illiterate audiences, corrupt managers, crass reviewers and scheming rivals. Sometimes he put it down to downright misfortune. From his pale face the unusually round, light brown eyes blazed out; around his lips a constant, tense dissatisfaction had etched curlicues of bitterness.

He several times toyed with the idea of settling abroad, especially when he had seasons in Amsterdam and Branstadt. Most seriously in the latter, as this was where he met his future wife. Ilse was the daughter of a priest who was fanatical about opera. Across the river that ran through the little town, south of the two stone bridges, there was also a mercantile bridge 980 Viennese paces in length. After a performance it was across this bridge that Nándor Csillag would stroll towards his lodgings in the moonlit night, in the company of some of the singers and members of the orchestra. They were often joined by some of the audience, their faces red from the cold. Sometimes the entire company would land up at the brasserie, which was open until midnight, for a stein of beer. Nándor Csillag never drank, but attracted attention with his elaborate toasts. The tall, strawblonde Ilse attracted attention because she was able to down a single Maas at one go. When Nándor Csillag expressed his astonishment, she replied: 'We Germans like a good beer. Try it!'

'Thank you, but no, I'd rather not. It harms the vocal cords.'

'It's medicinal! If anything harms anything, it's that watery Brause you are supping.'

Ilse told him her life story that evening. The Creator had called her mother unto Him all too early and her father had married again; she and her stepmother were constantly at loggerheads, both of them hoping that the girl would at last get married. Ilse let her corn-blue gaze rest on Nándor Csillag, as if waiting for an answer.

The answer came three weeks later: the Hungarian singer came to pay his respects to the parents and ask for the daughter's fair hand, with a bouquet of burgundy-red roses the size of a millstone. Ilse's father strove not to show how pleased he was, in case it encouraged exaggerated ideas about the dowry; but in fact he had begun to fear she might be left on the shelf. The wedding feast was the biggest ever seen in those parts, and was long remembered in the girl's village; even the dogs had their share of the roast venison with cranberries.

The Csillag side of the family were not in the least happy with Ilse, regarding her openness as vulgar and her frequent laughter as the neighing of a horse. They were certain Nándor Csillag would set up home on German territory, but after the expiry of his contract he turned up with his wife in Pécs. They set up home on the ground floor of the house in Apáca Street, but they soon moved to their own place: Nándor Csillag bought a run-down and disused grain barn. To general astonishment Ilse was using words of Hungarian within a fortnight, and forming sentences by the second month, and within twelve months only the characteristic articulation of her *r*s revealed her German origins. She also showed great skills in the organization of soirées and receptions; their cherrywood-panelled salon became a regular meeting place for the town's intellectual elite.

Nándor Csillag was, in his active days, little able to enjoy his house and home, living the bird-of-passage life of artists. He would have liked Ilse to become his permanent accompanist, a kind of maid-of-all-work ready to wait on him hand and foot. But Ilse hated travelling. This became a recurrent source of trouble. She accused him of wanting to haul her around with him out of sheer jealousy; but she was not prepared to pass her time being bored in a selection of hotel rooms in various parts of Europe. So Nándor Csillag joined an international company that was to spend three months touring South America with two Puccini operas. 'You are not coming with me even if it's Argentina?' he asked angrily.

'I can't,' Ilse said smiling coyly.

'Why not?'

'Because of the state I find myself in.'

Thus did Nándor Csillag learn that he was to become a father. He had little time to rejoice, as he had two distinct roles to learn in Italian.

Balázs Csillag came into this world after a labour that stretched away like strudel pastry, bearing out the truth of the old saying: all beginnings are difficult. Not for the first time did I realize that I had serious responsibilities to my family. I can no longer allow myself to be devoted only to the holy altar of art; I have to consider my decisions in the light of finances also. Following my father's advice, I split my income into three parts. One third I placed in the Post Office Savings Bank, for our everyday needs. One third I deposited in the Swiss Bank that he recommends. Out of the remaining third I shall maintain and expand our property.

I am resolute in resisting the urging of my fellow musician Bertalan Szalma, who claims that shares in a mill, which might be purchased with the assistance of his uncle, would yield profits three times the size of the investment. In size, maybe, but at a much greater risk. Whereas for a paterfamilias the primary consideration must be security. If only people did not forget this, many of the world's problems would be solved and instead of tensions that seethe towards an explosion, a reassuring order would prevail.

One afternoon his father visited them. He asked his son whether he often wrote in the Book of Fathers.

'Quite often,' said Nándor Csillag.

'You make me curious. Can I take a look?'

'By all means.'

When his father had read the above, he immediately wanted to know how he might contact Bertalan Szalma.

'I am told he has a contract at the Opera House in Monte Carlo,' said Nándor Csillag.

'And his uncle?'

'Him I don't know. What would you be wanting with him, Father?'

'I'd buy shares in mills.'

This made Nándor Csillag ponder. He discussed the matter with Ilse, but his wife preferred not to take a view on this matter. 'Do what you think is best, Nándor dear.'

By the time, after lengthy deliberations, he had decided to commit himself, those particular mill shares had long been sold. He did not have long to regret his failure, as a series of shady deals resulted in the mill company going bankrupt – the shares were soon not worth the paper they were printed on. Nándor Csillag blessed his own good sense and swore again never to take action without lengthy and substantial deliberation.

His father could not stop wringing his hands. 'What a fool I am! What a miserable fellow! Why did you not bind my hands? Lock me up? What a meshuggah I am, ay, ay, ay!'

Nándor Csillag had a sudden thought: 'Father, why did you not try to find out about the future? We are supposed to be able to do that, to some degree. Or aren't we?'

Sándor Csillag wiped the sweat from his receding brow. 'I'm out of practice . . . You think I haven't tried, time and again, for the lottery? Ach, we are in decline, we are getting old . . .'

Nándor Csillag nodded. As far as he was concerned, of the first-born's capacities only a fraction remained to him.

He didn't even practise the skill much, having little interest in the past and even less in the future. Yet, he thought: I should perhaps pay more heed, in both directions.

He devoted his siesta to leafing through the pages of the Book of Fathers, slowly, line by line, to garner the significance of every possible connection. Perhaps this was a suitable way of strengthening his powers of vision.

For the first time in his life he found his singing ambitions ebbing away. He was no longer unhappy if a tempting contract failed to materialize. He spent his free evenings tinkering in the shed. Increasingly prominent among his interests, alongside wood-carving, was the restoration of old clocks. He had two gramophones on his shelves, so he could play his records alternately, the period of silence between changes of record being thus reduced to the minimum. The sounds of Melba, Caruso, Galli-Curci soared in the light of the shimmering lamps, wondrously outdoing the ticking and striking of the clocks.

As if in the society of the time-measuring instruments he was more likely to sink into Time, it was on one such peaceful evening that he was vouchsafed a glimpse of the fate that awaited him. He was drowning, with many others, in semi-darkness. He could make neither head nor tail of it. He wondered if he should share the vision with his father. But Sándor Csillag had just gone to Balatonfüred, for major treatment on his weak heart.

Though in the years '26 and '27 I found peace of mind, I was much afflicted with troubles. It began with my Father's illness and continued with irregularities with my larynx. I had to cancel several performances, more than ever before in my career. However, our financial situation – thanks to my prudence and savings – did not become critical. Though I lost a great deal on the exchange rate when the pengı was brought in, I still managed to purchase a summer cottage on Lake

Balaton, at Szemes. I plan to spend there the winter of my
days. I have already started to set up a workshop in the out-
house.

My second son was christened Endre, and was born, by
comparison with the first, with amazing straightforwardness,
hale and hearty. It seems my Ilse has now got the hang of the
business. Maybe we shall not stop until we reach six, the family
record, held by my ancestor Richard Stern. The blessing of
a child is perhaps the greatest joy a man can experience, so I
have nothing to complain of. Perhaps only my 'daymare'
visions of misfortune make me restless, but I have determined
not to let them exercise me too much.

I wonder if anyone but my descendants will ever read these lines.
And if so, whether they will be able to deduce from them how
were passed our days on this earth.

He was at the peak of his career. As an unexpected gift
he was given a benefit performance by the strolling players with whom he frequently performed. At his request
this was *Cavalleria Rusticana* and *I Pagliacci*. They performed '*Cav* and *Pag*' for two months the length and
breadth of the country with the exception – to Nándor
Csillag's profound regret – of Pécs, which did not feature
in the schedule. They enjoyed modest success, never
being humiliated, but the jubilations for which it is worth
making so many sacrifices were this time, too, not in
evidence.

At the end of the series, Nándor Csillag was making his
way home, having to make several changes of train, and was
already wondering on the journey how to spend the autumn
of his life once he had given up singing. He calculated that
his resources, including the summer cottage in Balatonszemes, would be exhausted in eight to ten years if there

were no increase at all in the value of the property in the interim. He could hardly make the repairing of clocks a career. So what should he do?

He pondered the question for months. He undertook few appearances, none at all in opera, rather only in concert halls or on an ad hoc basis, singing showy Italian songs.

Ilse fell pregnant for the third time; as she put it: 'Proof of the pudding club that you are spending more time at home these days,' making her husband smile at her turn of phrase.

Nándor Csillag one morning surprised the household by entering the kitchen. The cook almost dropped her copper frying pan. 'Sir desires something?' she asked nervously, thinking there must be something wrong: Nándor Csillag was generally asleep at this time.

'What's for breakfast?'

This was even more surprising, as no one could recall the singer ever taking breakfast. Speechless, the cook pointed to the omelette and wafer-thin toast she was preparing for the lady of the house.

'Is this what my Ilse ordered?'

'No.'

'Well, how do you know that that's what she would like?'

'Forgive me sir . . . but my lady always has this for breakfast.'

'More's the pity,' he said and crashed on into the dining-room, where a rotund Ilse was adjusting the curtains and staring out into the sunlight. Nándor Csillag rested his hands on her shoulders and, instead of a Good Morning, said: 'What to the heart is love, appetite is to the stomach.'

Ilse took a step back. 'I beg your pardon?'

'The stomach is the conductor in command of the great orchestra of our passions.' After a pause, he added: 'These are the words of maestro Rossini. You know, *Barber of Seville*, *William Tell* and all that.'

304

'I am fully aware of the operas of Rossini. But what have they got to do with it?'

'Starting today, I am in charge of the daily menu.'

The diet of the Csillag household underwent a radical change. Specialities such as quail's eggs, truffles and snails surfaced on the menu. Nándor Csillag acquired a raft of Hungarian and foreign cookery books and wanted to bring their recipes to life. The cook was dispatched and her successors achieved a high turnover rate. Nándor Csillag was quite prepared to supervise the market shopping, to order the meat at the butcher's and on occasion took in hand the direction of the kitchen itself. Whenever Ilse or some other relative took exception to this, he declared with an expression of hauteur: 'If the Swan of Pesaro could do it, then so can I!'

Everybody knew that Gioacchino Antonio Rossini was the Swan of Pesaro.

'Nándor, Rossini was never your cup of tea. What is this with him now?' asked Ilse.

'Just because I did not sing him, I can still follow his philosophy, no?'

At the noontide of my life I sought my happiness – and no one was more surprised at this than myself – in Epicurean joys. In food, in drink, in reading, in the making of watercolours, in peaceful hours of meditation. I observed the sun setting on the Tettye, building a fire on the hillside, barbecuing food under the open sky, drinking fine red wines: thus did I at last find peace of mind. I awoke to the realization that there is no greater joy than when mind and body rest well replete.

I am toying with the idea that I should host a grand dinner for the gourmets and the gourmands of my town, using dishes from my own recipes in a restaurant for Feinschmecker. It will be a joy to revel in their joy. My plans are opposed as much by my father as by Ilse, perhaps by him more, since he is now at the

*stage where he opposes everything. But whom would I offend by
spending my spare time supplying food of the finest quality for
my guests? Why should this be more despised an occupation than
ownership of the famous Csillag shoe shop? From the name of
the firm, my father at the beginning of this year ousted that of old
Straub, on the grounds that it sounds too Jewish. What a hyp-
ocritical notion! If Papa looks in the mirror he will see
something that characterizes our origins more substantially than
a name like Straub.*

*But I must now take up arms against a more serious threat.
I dare not even write it down, so superstitious am I. May
heaven grant me a sufficiency of strength and patience.*

Nándor Csillag kept stubbornly to his original intention.
He found a house garlanded in ivy that now stood empty and
forlorn. Constructed more than a century earlier by the town's
Fire Brigade Union, it had not been used since they built a
new storage building in 1910. This was the building leased by
Nándor Csillag. He gave his restaurant the sonorous name
'Restaurant à la Rossini', but this never really caught on
and regulars would say 'Let's go to Nándi Csillag's!' Because
at Nándi's you could get French soups, Italian roasts and
Spanish desserts for the gentry like nowhere else. There were
just seven tables, and the inhabitants of Pécs had, willy-nilly,
to get used to the notion of booking tables, whether in
person, by telephone, or foot-messenger. At Nándi's Slovak
waitresses served the specialities decked out in tiny candle-
lights and in the evenings the gramophone would play arias
by Verdi, Rossini and Puccini.

Nándor Csillag had a rose window cut in the tiny space
which had been used by the duty officer of the fire brigade,
and so could keep a constant eye on his guests and staff. If
the diners were acquaintances – and virtually all the towns-
folk counted as such – he made sure he greeted them in
person. He put on weight rapidly, which made his delicate

306

frame appear rather humorous. Ilse pointed out that people might think they were both pregnant – she being now in her eighth month. Nándor Csillag had no regret about his corporation, and grew nineteenth-century mutton-chop whiskers to match. This hirsute growth turned white in the course of a week when the event foretold in the Book of Fathers in fact became reality.

Ilse's behaviour grew more and more strange. She gave birth to Tamás, but would not give him suck even once. Among ladies of standing it was accepted that this task was done in their stead by a wet nurse; but in the case of her first two sons, Ilse had insisted on breast-feeding them herself. She often voiced her conviction that the health of the infant was contingent on mother's milk and urged her friends to follow her example.

Her knowledge of Hungarian seemed to deteriorate rapidly, with errors in her grammar and difficulty finding the right word. 'Am I getting oldster?' she would ask, her face a map of fear. Her husband's remonstrations failed to reassure her. Her chambermaid would often find she had locked herself in her room and showed no inclination to answer the door or even to reply to her repeated pleas. Once she spent a day and a half in her room without food or drink, totally indifferent to the calls of her husband, father- and mother-in-law. Nándor Csillag could not understand what had got into her, and Ilse never gave an explanation.

When one afternoon she set fire to the brocade curtains, the house all but burnt to the ground. The staff, horrified, rang for the fire brigade. Once the flames had been extinguished the fireman in charge drew up an official report which gave rise to rumours about Ilse's mental state that spread like the wildfire she had created. The family doctor kept reassuring Nándor Csillag that these things happen, that the stresses and pains of giving birth often short-circuited the nervous system of the female body. 'The ordinary folk say: the milk goes to the brain. It would be better if the good lady were again to give suck to the infant!'

Ilse listened to the doctor with an expressionless face. In vain did her husband prompt her, gently at first, then with increasing urgency, but she had nothing to say. Hardly had the doctor left the house when Ilse threw herself on the ground and began to pound the wooden floorboards with her head, as if it were her intention to crack open her skull. Not even with the help of the chambermaid could Nándor Csillag make her stop.

These fits of self-destruction soon assumed a chronic character. Tonchi was the only person who was able to still Ilse's ravings, drawing her gently but firmly to her ample bosom. First the doctor, then other members of his family suggested that he should have his wife committed to an institution before she inflicted fatal damage on herself. This proposal would make him stamp his feet with rage: 'That will be the day! I won't have Ilse taken to the yellow house! Out of the question!'

But the situation deteriorated further. Soon even the safety of the children could no longer be guaranteed. Nándor Csillag took on two nuns trained in the treatment of such conditions, who tended Ilse day and night.

It is beyond imagining what sins we may have committed to deserve such punishment from fate. I had hoped to be able to live out my final days in peaceful isolation from the world, but an unending horror has blighted my everyday life: the illness that is taking her over is driving Ilse to commit appalling acts. I am pointed at wherever I go in town and my misfortune has become the gossip of the women of the town as well as of the men in the coffee-houses. Our tale is a tragedy worthy of an opera librettist. No greater calamity could befall us.

He continued to hold this view even after the Hungarian parliament passed Law XV of 1938. A printed copy circulated in the *Nándi* and in the *Wild Man*.

Paragraph I.
In the interests of achieving a more effective balance in the life of society the Hungarian Royal Ministry is hereby authorized to implement without further delay certain essential and important measures – including measures deemed necessary to eliminate unemployment among the intelligentsia – within three weeks of the promulgation of the present law, and in the spheres and according to principles delimited in the paragraphs below may implement such legal measures even if their implementation would otherwise require legislation.

Damned officialese!
The essence of the measures was explained to him by the lawyers among the regulars. Chambers would be established for lawyers, journalists, engineers, doctors, artists and virtually all those in the professions, but the percentage of Jews in each such chamber would not be allowed to exceed 20 per cent.

It soon became clear that he, Nándor Csillag, who in the recent past had performed in the leading opera houses of Europe, could not become a chamber member, because someone had decided he was to be counted as Jewish, since he had never formally converted to an 'accepted and recognized' faith. Though this hurt, in practice it did not matter; he had long regarded his career as an artist as over.

He still persisted in maintaining that no greater blow was imaginable than Ilse's illness even when Law IV of 1939 came into force, restricting the areas of public and economic life that could be occupied by Jews. A summary of its general principles – *Document No. 702 from the Lower House* –

appeared in the newspapers. This document was all too easy to understand.

> While before the passage of this law only this country's western neighbour, Germany, had taken resolute action to drive out the Jews, many other countries of Europe have since followed.

Mother of God, he thought, are we going to be driven out? He could not begin to imagine how this might be achieved.

> It is being increasingly recognized that the Jews are a distinctive ethnic group, sharply differentiated from all other peoples.

Nándor Csillag had a fit. He bellowed and howled so much that it took five people to hold him down. In the town it was rumoured that he had caught his wife's illness. He would stop people in the street, begging them to read a crumpled copy of the newssheet with the preamble to the law, while repeating incredulously and obsessively: 'Me, not a Hungarian! Me, whose Hungarian name brought glory to my homeland in the greatest opera houses of Europe? Who speaks Hungarian perfectly, and not a syllable of Hebrew? Who has ancestors who were executed in 1849 because they fought for Hungary's freedom? Has everyone here gone completely mad??'

He would read out long extracts from the despicable text and in vain would people try to flee; they had to listen to it all, for he would hold them by the sleeve. At the most agonizing paragraphs, he would have to gasp for breath.

For a while he kept the document among the family papers. Later he stuck it into the cover of the Book of Fathers, which had split at the spine and acquired a crack.

His son Balázs threw it out when the volumes ended up with him.

Jews have taken part, and continue to take part, in a proportion that far exceeds their number, in the commission of crimes for selfish financial reasons, especially those which are liable to undermine the economic foundations of the country. Those who commit abuses of financial instruments involving the exchange rate are almost exclusively Jews, and the state authority must take wideranging measures to ensure permanently that abuses in this area do not harm the country's economic prospects.

In terms of the law the words 'Jew' and 'Jewish' define the group in relation to which it desires to implement special regulations. By contrast, the term 'Israelite' applies to the definition of the faith group. Those that the law subsumes under the term 'Jew' are not necessarily to be identified with those belonging to the Israelite confession; the circle of Jews is a broader category.

The law restricts the role played by Jews in legislation, in bodies with legal authority and in local government and in the exercise of the ballot with reference to these;

participation in public office by Jews is in future entirely withdrawn;

the percentage of Jewish members in the chambers of law, engineering, medicine, journalism, theatre and film, is hereby limited to six per cent;

positions involving the intellectual and artistic direction of the press, theatre and film companies are forbidden to Jews;

licences held by permission of local authorities are no longer to be held by or issued to Jews;

in the sphere of public transportation and carriage the number of Jewish entrepreneurs will gradually be reduced to six per cent;

certificates to practise trades and industries are generally forbidden to Jews until the number of such
certificates and licences falls below six per cent of the
total;

in trade and other fee-earning occupations, of those
employed in white-collar work Jews shall generally not
exceed twelve per cent in number;

the ministry is hereby permitted to take steps to promote the emigration of Jews;

finally,

legal steps will be taken to ensure that any attempt to
flout the law will be dealt with severely.

'Well, perhaps now is the time to emigrate,' Ilona said
when the family met to put their heads together. 'If it's
really going to be implemented.'

'But this is our land, too!' said Nándor Csillag. 'Why don't
they emigrate!'

'Don't shout, my dear, my head is throbbing. You are not
on stage. We can hear you at normal pitch.'

Sándor Csillag travelled up to Budapest to try to secure
the necessary documents. His old contacts had been severed, however, and doors closed on him one after the other.

In the daily *Magyarság*, venomous articles berated the
Pécs authorities for their kid-glove treatment of the town's
Jews. Among the examples cited was Sándor Csillag, 'the
shoe-baron with the effrontery to charge sky-high prices for
his shoes, who thoroughly and disgracefully fleeces the
poor', and his son 'the illustrious representative of the
Jewish fat-cat oligarchy, the owner of the *Nándi*, who always
has room and food for his fellow Jews, who suck the blood of
our patriots'. In both cases the name (Stern) was given in
brackets.

Nándor Csillag bared his teeth, like a horse being shod.
'What impertinence! I have documentation by the cartload

312

that we are Csillags! And anyway, where did they dig that up?'

The family had difficulty persuading him not to sue the editors. It would just pour oil on the fire. The licences to run the restaurant and the shoe shop were under threat of withdrawal shortly.

'What next?' asked father from son and son from father. It would have been logical to save the businesses by transferring their ownership to the incontrovertibly German Ilse, but unfortunately by this time and on her husband's request, she had been declared incapable of managing her own affairs and no longer of sound mind.

'We need an *Aladár*!' said Sándor Csillag (Stern).

'An *Aladár*?' Nándor Csillag (Stern) was puzzled.

'Are you deaf? *Aladár*! A front man! Got it?'

Anti Kolozsvári became the family's *Aladár*. Anti Kolozsvári was a well-known freeloader and sponger in the coffee-houses of Pécs. Nándor Csillag regularly supplied him with small sums, which in his notebook he put under the heading 'Antimatter Tax'. Anti Kolozsvári had drunk himself out of a job in journalism and was not sober even as he officially and formally – for an increased fee – took over the ownership of the shoe shop and the restaurant. In the document that effected the transfer there were even two spelling mistakes in the signature of the beneficiary, but it bothered no one that in the document he recorded his name as Antall Kolosvári.

The Germans had overrun Poland when Nándor Csillag began to wonder whether what awaited them was in fact as serious as Ilse's disturbed mind. The possibility of emigrating did crop up, but the family could not agree on a destination. Nándor Csillag voted for Switzerland, Tonchi for the USA, while Sándor Csillag chose Australia, because of the kangaroos. Ilona and her parents preferred Canada, where two younger brothers of Manfred Goldbaum were already well established.

This was the only topic to which Ilse made a contribution. 'Germany! Deutschland!' she repeated.

'Come now . . . Hitler is the very reason that we have to emigrate!'

'Not Hitler! Germany!' responded Ilse, impatiently. She was one of the few in Europe who had yet to acknowledge the existence of the Führer.

They went on talking until most of the family had been deported, chiefly by train. As Ilse passed under the double iron gates surmounted by the slogan ARBEIT MACHT FREI she had a fit more severe and frightening than ever before. Her two young sons, painfully gripping her hands, were kicked away from her side. Ilse was about to throw herself after them like a lioness after her cubs. When she was trodden into the mud, she lashed out repeatedly, screaming something in German. The two guards bashed her brains out with the stocks of their rifles, oblivious of the fact that Ilse was reciting a Heine poem, studied in the fourth form of German primary schools, describing the glories of the autumn landscape. (While it is true that that particular textbook had been, together with Heine and many other poets, withdrawn by 1936, the two soldiers must certainly have attended school before that date.)

Nándor Csillag saw none of this, having been separated from his family earlier. He was fortunate. He ended up in Canada. The sorter brigade in the camp was called Canada, because the name, which originally referred to the untold riches they found as sorters, came to symbolise survival. Those who were in Canada sorted out the rags and scraps that remained of those who had been gassed to death: gold teeth, rings, eyeglasses and other valuables that could be rescued for the benefit of the Third Reich from rubbish that was otherwise destroyed. Their primary acts of quiet sabotage involved secretly smuggling out anything that looked remotely valuable and flushing it down the toilets.

The Canadians watched with profound sympathy as the work brigades came and went. They were ghosts supporting each other as they struggled down the middle of the road, their little food bowls dangling from their string belts. The work brigades were frisked every day, any remaining bits and pieces reaching the depot or the litter-burner via the Canadians.

Some time after Nándor Csillag there came to Canada a quiet man with a large Adam's apple. From the time he was assigned to a place next to Nándor Csillag he delivered himself of only one sentence: 'Tivadar Fleisch, tradesman of Kiskunhalas, at your service.'

They had several weeks to wait for his next utterance. This consisted of the word 'Look!'

He had come across an egg-shaped fob-watch in one of the jackets matted into filth. It showed the day, the month, and even the year. It was accurate, with a firm tick that harked back to the good old days before the war.

'Gold?' asked someone.

Without a word Nándor Csillag took it from Tivadar Fleisch's hand. He looked at it for a long time, raising it to his eyes; his vision had worsened a lot in recent times.

'Recognize it?' asked Tivadar Fleisch.

Nándor Csillag nodded. Seeing his tears, they asked no further questions; the Canadians understood everything. Nándor Csillag clutched the timepiece, the back with its carved curlicues conjuring up the past. The indentations must have been felt in this way by his father, grandfather, great-great-grandfather, and all the way back to Kornél Csillag/Sternovszky. He knew that the pocket watch had been presented to his future father-in-law on the night of his stag party. So poor Uncle Manfred, the Beremend trouser king, had . . .

May his dear soul rest in peace. Him the *Arbeit* had indeed made *frei*.

Nándor Csillag hesitated only for a few minutes, then, burying the watch in his pocket respectfully, asked to be excused. He mumbled a few Hungarian prayers, and the only one he knew in Hebrew, then consigned the watch to the latrine. *Baruch ata Adonai*.

At Christmas the prisoners' theatre organized a lively evening. Nándor Csillag was asked to perform something that gave him pleasure. He demurred, pleading that he could no longer sing.

'Does it matter whether you can or not?' said the organizer. 'I'm going to dance, after all . . .' and he made a dismissive gesture with his hand. He was called Béla Lajtai and had been the ballet master at the Prague Opera. He was now the most skeletal person in the entire barracks. By comparison Nándor Csillag seemed almost fat, even though he had lost half his body weight.

Well then, let's set about rehearsing!

In the evenings, bent double, he tensed himself against the barrack walls in the brace position, which he had not employed for so long. His diaphragm exercises involved little disturbance of others, but to do his scales he went out into the yard, thinking his fellows would not tolerate the noise. But no sooner had he begun than his fellow prisoners crowded round, hungry for the sound of music. He never could resist an audience: he did not need asking twice, and he sang for them from his former repertoire. His sob-filled tenor voice soared high above the darkness shrouding the camp, vibrating along the barracks, so that many of the thousands locked up were able to hear it. Here and there came sounds of clapping.

I'm a success, at last, he thought. If the great Caruso heard me now, perhaps he would offer a few words of praise.

For the show he made himself a makeshift clown's outfit from a torn bedsheet, drawing the big buttons on it with a branch he had burnt at the end. 'Laugh, clown, laugh!' he sang for the audience of twelve nationalities in Hungarian, and at the end of the aria, sank to his knees, weeping. The thunderous applause would not stop but he could not acknowledge it. He had a sudden bout of fever and slipped out of consciousness. In the morning he could not rise from his bunk, even after repeated kicks from the Schenführer. He was shivering, his eyes had turned heavenwards, his skin came out in blotches.

Tivadar Fleisch helped him out to the Appel Platz. They were both ordered to go over to the line by the fence inching its way to the side building. They reached the anteroom of the showers. Tivadar Fleisch helped Nándor Csillag off with his clothes, lined up his shabby shoes neatly by the wall. When they were fighting for their lives under the roses of the showers, Tivadar Fleisch spoke again. 'Mother, my dear mother!' He can speak when he wants to, thought Nándor Csillag. His own mother he remembered, then his children. Of Balázs he knew that he was in labour service somewhere in Russia. Ilse perhaps in the women's camp. Endre and Tamás though . . .

As his throat constricted he could taste blackberries and cranberries. The final image on the screen of his mind was of a fleeing flock of deer, running up the hill, reddish-purple dust swirling round their hoofs, their antlers scraping and scratching the sky that covered the ground.

X

AROUND NEW YEAR THE AIR BECOMES GRADUALLY
clearer. Infinity dangles in the searing cold; end-of-year
longings, resolutions and hopes drift heavenward. The
foggy rim of the moon bespeaks better weather. The pines
jaggedly stab the air in all directions; in their cones the
seeds of trees to come prepare for the journey of life. Many
folk interrogate the skies from their homes or far away from
them. Those already – or still – awake at daybreak can see
that the Virgin Mary's grey clouds swallow up the moon and
then the stars. At the end of nights like these it is common
for the plumped-up cushions of the sky to burst and spill
their filling: not snow, nor rain, but a variety of ice-clad hail,
which augurs ill as it batters eaves, ledges and roofs.

There were no lights on in the office, petroleum lamps had
been dusted down and lit. Three old women were leafing
through the large, brick-sized business books, their faded
blue lab coats reeking of chemicals. The shades of death
hovered about in the gloom of ancient smells, as every
client's inquiry or scrap of information involved them. Their
fingers swollen with all the writing, the three old women's
hands trembled their way along the wide pages of the black-

bound tomes. If they found the name they were looking for, they tapped the surface of the page with the same curl of their claws.

Balázs Csillag joined the end of the queue, guessing that it might take three-quarters of an hour to reach one of the shabby desks. His stomach gave a rumble. From the bakery in Jókai Street the wind brought the smell of fresh-baked loaves, which managed to penetrate the poorly insulated windows but was immediately overlaid by the doom-laden odour that suffused the huge room. Balázs Csillag suddenly remembered the *Brotzettel*. In the days when the family was still together he would fight to the bitter end with his brothers for the slice of bread with the baker's tiny label on the crust, bearing his name and the time and place where the loaf was baked. Mother strictly forbade the eating of the *Brotzettel* – printing ink is pure poison! – but they ate it anyway. They took it into their heads that the tastiest morsel of the whole loaf was where the paper has fused with the crust of the bread and they have together hardened into a special delicacy. They loved that little bit of crust more than any of the masterpieces of the baker's art conjured up by the cook, which the guests of the Csillags never tired of praising.

It would be difficult to say what they loved about that tiny flour-stained little label. Balázs Csillag clung grimly to this memory, and when he returned to Pécs his first port of call was the bakery of the Császárs. The young woman there, whom he had known since childhood, burst into tears when she saw him and would not accept payment for the kilo loaf. Balázs Csillag sat down on the edge of the pavement in Széchenyi Square and ate the whole loaf in one go. First he took out the soft innards a handful at a time and only then did he attend to the crust, which he tore into strips. He left the *Brotzettel* to the very end. But it did not taste as good as when they had fought over it, he and

319

Endrus and little Tomi. From now on, he knew, even the *Brotzettel* won't be the same as in the old days.

The others in the queue were all women. He was trying to work out which of the three old women he would get to. There were clients at all three desks and at this moment all three were in tears. Balázs Csillag listened to the sounds, which were like nothing else on this earth, and kept thinking that whatever happens in this world, it all ends in the crying of women. But if one is at least surrounded by crying women, that cannot be as bad as . . . They are, at least, alive.

He had been told that the procedure that takes longest is formally declaring that someone has disappeared, and he hoped that the others had come for other reasons. When two of the old women apologetically disappeared into the cellars that they called the archive store to look for old documents, he was overcome by despondency. And yet: what is the rush? You have nothing to do.

Two months earlier he was still in Lager 7149/2, with fifteen thousand others. Mainly Germans, Italians and Romanians. The Hungarian contingent came to about fifteen hundred. There were constant rumours that liberation was imminent.

'We're going to be exchanged!' was the mantra of one chap, a stockbreeder from Szilvásvárad who had had a gangrenous leg amputated in the prisoners' hospital. He never gave up hope, not for a single moment of the day; even in his sleep he kept mumbling something of the sort. There was a widespread belief that the end of the war was in sight, and everyone would be able to go home in peace.

Of the more impatient folk there were always a few with plans to escape, and those brave enough sometimes actually gave it a try. The oldest group of prisoners recalled that a small group of Romanians had succeeded, allegedly. But hardly a week would pass without would-be escapees being brought in, bound and gagged by the guards; they would

320

then be taken to the basement of the command post and beaten to within an inch of their lives. Balázs Csillag had been in on three planned attempts to escape, none of which had come to fruition.

He had been taken prisoner with two of his labour service friends, Zoli Nagy and Dr Pista Kádas, both of whom he had known back in Pécs. They had been surrounded at the bridge of Verete by a unit on skis in white snowsuits. By then not only the labour service battalion but the entire Hungarian Second Army had disbanded, and in the general chaos everyone fled wherever they could. The three of them wanted to drink from the river that had frozen over and were just trying to break the ice with a stick when they heard mellifluous Russian words of command behind them. There were 150 soldiers on the bridge, 150 snow-white ghosts.

Balázs Csillag began to run towards them, the warm flush of relief beginning to course in his veins. '*Dobry den! Ne strelayesh! Mi vengerski!*' he shouted. They all knew this much; in the camp it was passed on by word of mouth that this is what you must say. But instead of welcoming arms, he was received with pistol-butts and hit so hard in the chest that he fell back under the bridge, only just caught by his mates. Dr Pista Kádas knew a little French and started to explain in the language of Rousseau that they were Hungarian Jews, who had been forced onto the minefields because of their origins. The Russian officer must have got hold of the wrong end of the stick, because at the word for 'minefield' he gave a snort. '*Shomp de mean?*' he repeated in a threatening tone, then hit him. Balázs Csillag and Zoli Nagy would have knelt down to the motionless body of Dr Pista Kádas, had they not been led away at gunpoint.

It was in the Lager that they met again. They didn't know why they ended up here, together with members of the Wehrmacht and other regular army units, but there was no one to ask. Zoli Nagy had been born in Beremend and knew the Goldbaum family well, and the Holatscheks, too. They had not yet heard that all the members of these families had been deported and not one of them was left to tell the tale. Zoli Nagy had been studying law at the Royal Elizabeth University of Pécs, until he was excluded by the second Jewish law. Because of the same law, Balázs Csillag could not even apply. Dr Pista Kádas was a lawyer; he was excluded from the chamber by Law IV of 1939, after which he tried to maintain himself by writing and publishing under a nom de plume.

The three of them had been called up for labour service on the same day. Balázs Csillag was not unduly upset. This was the fourth time he had been called up, and three times his father had managed to sort the matter out and got him off the call-up list. He thought his father would be able to do the same this time.

The call-up papers marked UHI – Urgent, Hurry, Immediate – said they were to present themselves at Nagykáta. From the train he alighted in the company of Zoli Nagy and Dr Pista Kádas as if they were young men on some study trip without a care in the world; in the yard of the company HQ they were transformed at a stroke into cannon fodder. The officer who bellowed at them inarticulately gave them to understand: if they had hitherto been suffering under the delusion that they were human beings, they were to forget at once this grave misconception, because they were nothing but filthy Jews. They could not speak to members of the guard staff; they were to reply only if they were asked a question and even then they had to stand at a distance of three paces. Their civil possessions were to be placed on the table and they should bid them a fond farewell. Their wallets likewise: they are to retain a maximum of fifty pengő. Parcels from home are not permitted. Their letters will be subject to censorship. They may receive visitors once a month, exclusively from their nearest and dearest. They may not smoke, since the regulations do not entitle them to tobacco rations. They are obliged to wear the yellow armband day and night. Christians of Jewish origin receive a white armband, communists and other criminals a yellow armband with black polka dots. They are obliged to look after their regular uniform; they are liable to pay for any damage to it. Rosettes may not be worn in their camp caps.

Balázs Csillag could not help but guffaw. He found it amusing that any filthy Jew should obtain a rosette for his army cap, from which it had been carefully removed on arrival. His sense of humour was rewarded by being lashed to a tree by the full-throated officer, who they were soon to discover was Lieutenant-Colonel Lipót Muray, known among the labour battalion workers as the Hangman of Nagykáta. His arms, which had been forced back, and his shoulders, which were all but dislocated, were within three minutes of being tied to the tree, engulfed by agonizing pain; within five minutes this had spread to all of his body; and by the eighth minute he had lost consciousness. On the orders of Lieutenant-Colonel Muray a bucket of cold water restored him to the land of the living. The Hangman of Nagykáta was not keen on his victims fainting; let the filthy Jews experience every single moment of their punishment.

He had no choice but to realize that he no longer enjoyed any kind of protection. There followed some weeks of 'training', of which the daily high point was five o'clock tea, as Lieutenant-Colonel Muray designated his very own invention: precisely at five in the afternoon – seventeen zero-zero, as they called it – the Jews selected for this purpose would be herded into the cellars of the HQ and there the supervisory staff of the forced labour unit would beat them as long as they detected a single movement in any of the bodies. The blood-curdling screams for help were perhaps audible even in the surrounding villages. Balázs Csillag was never chosen; Zoli Nagy was, twice: the first time he returned with a broken arm, the second time with a shattered shinbone. He was still limping when they were wagoned up and taken to the front, as part of the 14th Light Infantry. The journey took several days by train, to Rechitsa, whence they continued on foot towards the east.

By the time they reached the Don, their numbers had halved. The staff became increasingly hysterical, but the cause of the majority of deaths was frostbite and hypothermia. Many remained by the roadside, turning with blank faces into the snow, thinking that they would stagger up again after forty winks. The soldiers knew there was no point wasting a bullet on them.

The work of the labour servicemen was to build minebarrages and barbed-wire barriers and to repair railway lines repeatedly blown up by the Russian partisans. This Sisyphean task seemed increasingly pointless; sometimes the engines were able to move only for half a day. There were sections – Balázs Csillag counted them – where in the course of two weeks they changed the rails, bent and blasted by the explosions, no fewer than nine times, and the sleepers burnt to charcoal.

In the freezing cold of January they received orders to clear the ground for the regular army; that is, to pick up the mines in a clearing, on the far side of which some tall pines were bending and bowing in the fierce wind. In the labour battalion the rumour went around that that forest already sheltered advance units of the Russian army. Balázs Csillag did not believe this. Those pine needles reminded him of Balatonszemes, Papa's holiday cottage. What if they were there? When one has to lie on one's stomach to dig antipersonnel mines out of the frozen soil with a trench spade and any one of them can explode at any time, *shetsko jedno* whether there are Russian soldiers in the woods.

324

There was movement in the shadow of the trees. They hissed at each other to lie low. A smallish goat emerged and gently trotted over to the minefield, starting to graze on the tasty green scrub. The labourers held their breath to see when it would be blown sky-high, but the goat, it seems, was too light to trigger an explosion, the mines having been set to respond to a human's weight. Balázs Csillag watched the oddly graceful creature with great pleasure. The Russian goat is rather similar to the Hungarian goat, except that it is slimmer. Much, much slimmer.

About this time, some eight versts away, the Russians launched an offensive. They broke through the middle of the front, driving a wedge between the German, Italian and Hungarian forces. Balázs Csillag's labour battalion was almost entirely wiped out. The three of them, however, by some miracle, managed to survive.

Zoli Nagy, Dr Pista Kádas and Balázs Csillag were always together, because of shared sympathies and identical fields of interest. 'The legal eagles' the others called them. They formed an alliance, promising each other that they would use their joint strength to survive the war. This promise was not kept by Zoli Nagy, who suddenly, while loading wooden logs, felt dizzy and was torn to unrecognizable shreds by the sleepers and logs that collapsed upon him. His few possessions were shared out equally. Balázs Csillag ended up with a book and a photograph. A curly-haired brunette smiled back from the photograph, with unquenchable optimism, in a bathing suit of some soft fabric, on some kind of a beach, leaning against a blindingly white wall. On the back of the picture, in Zoli Nagy's careful script: 'Yoli, the very first time. 21 Aug. 1943.' Balázs Csillag wondered any number of times what and how it was that very first time on 21 Aug. 1943.

The book was a Household Companion from the turn of the century. Balázs Csillag tried to guess why Zoli Nagy had chosen to go to war with a specialized volume of this kind, but from the ex libris which said 'The property of Helga Kondraschek – Not on loan, even to you!', he guessed that Zoli, too, had found it, or inherited it as he had done.

In his most difficult moments he always found refuge in this volume. If he was very hungry he read all the clever household tips and the five- or six-course meals that husbands returning exhausted from work could be dazzled by. If he was cold, he studied the knitting patterns. If he was plagued by fleas, he read up on the techniques of washing and ironing. He knew every paragraph of the 365 pages of the work. He could not get enough of it.

No sensible gentleman gives serious thought to marriage until he is assured of an income of at least 3,000 crowns per annum. 1,000 crowns is adequate to live on only if one draws the reins in tight and lives a singular life. A married couple require at least twice, but preferably three times, as much.

A young couple of the middle classes can settle quite comfortably in a three-room flat. One bedroom, one lounge and one dining room will be adequate for the official, civil servant, or young tradesman of limited means. Today it is no longer sensible to rent a flat without a bathroom; to have one built is not the modern way. The old-fashioned faïence room basins or lavoirs no longer meet modern standards of cleanliness.

A separate reception room, or as it is fashionable to call it nowadays in Hungarian, a salon, must be accounted a luxury, since it is always possible to furnish the living room so that it functions as a reception room.

A reception room amongst the middle classes plays a role of unusual importance. This is the centrepiece of the home, the pride of the lady of the house; here are the most expensive pieces of furniture and the most eye-catching décor. A crushed velvet or patterned silk couch in the centre along the wall, with armchairs on either side and cushioned chairs in a semicircle. On the table a visiting-card holder and books in fine bindings. Richly pleated heavy curtains for the windows; on the walls and on the furniture, paintings and pictures of various sizes and ornamental plates, Makartstil bouquets and porcelain figurines. This is where we can receive more distant relatives, acquaintances, business contacts; and here the family's celebrations can be held.

When he reached this point Balázs Csillag's eyes filled with tears. He remembered his grandfather's house in Apáca Street, then the one in Nepomuk Street, at Sunday lunch. When the grandfather clock struck twelve and Papa poured himself a thimbleful of bitters and tossed it down. The maid laid the big table. Half an hour later the cook sent the message, via her, that the family might take their places at the table. Papa insisted that they dress for the occasion and the three boys had in turn to go to Ilse, with her clockwork smile and drugged eyes, and give her hands a ritual kiss. He himself did so after them.

'*Dankschön!*' intoned Ilse four times, identically, like a recording.

In Lager 7149/2 time had ground almost to a standstill. From here he could no longer write home on the Russian and Hungarian form-postcards of the Red Cross which were pre-printed SENDER PRISONER OF WAR. There was room for only a few lines on the card, but Balázs Csillag did not need even those. I am fine. How are you all? Write back soon! Answer he received none. He often tried to imagine what it would be like to see his loved ones and his home town again; sometimes he even dreamt of this. Usually he was a child walking through the vaulted gate of the house in Nepomuk Street; it would be late at night, his mother and father would be sitting by the fire (though only the house in Apácai Street had a fireplace), by the light of candles; they would acknowledge him as he entered and then his mother would say in her German-accented Hungarian: 'Go up to bed, quickly!' and he obeyed.

He was the mainstay of Dr Pista Kádas, who was inclined to depression. 'You'll see, we'll get out of here and get home sooner than you might think!'

In the evenings he would make him tell stories. The stories of Dr Pista Kádas always ended up with his years as a lawyer, and his manner of speech also veered towards that of the courtroom, with its circumlocutory turns of phrase, liberally seasoned with 'well, now's and 'be it noted's. He revealed to Balázs Csillag a world into which he sought admission in vain, though everyone in the family assumed he was destined for the Bar. He was still at primary school when he made speeches for both the prosecution and the defence at the dining table.

'Bravo, bravissimo, my dear counsellor!' said his father.

At school Balázs Csillag's most distinguished achievements were in Greek and Latin. He could recite poems by Homer, Virgil and Ovid after just a few readings. Latin, too, seemed to be a milestone on the road to a legal career.

'I know I shall be a lawyer when I grow up!'

'How do you know?' asked Dr Pista Kádas.

'In our family the first-born know a lot of things. I am not sure why this should be so.'

Dr Pista Kádas continued to press the matter until willy-nilly he explained how these things were in the Csillag family. Dr Pista Kádas heard the account with mounting disquiet. It was not the first time in the Lager that someone hitherto completely sane appeared to lose his mind overnight. He did not dare challenge the story; rather, he probed further, hoping that his friend would suddenly burst out laughing, like someone playing a joke. Balázs Csillag, however, stuck to his guns and insisted that for some mysterious reason he was able to see the past and the future.

'So you knew that we would end up here, too?'

'No, all I knew was that there was going to be trouble, big trouble. The way it happens is that the pictures, the images are often very fuzzy.'

'But then if your Papa also knew . . . what would happen, why did you not emigrate while you could?'

'That's something that has been bothering me, too. Perhaps it's one thing to see, and another to believe what you see.'

'Hm . . . You wouldn't by any chance be able to see whether we will ever get out of here?'

'I told you: we are going home, sooner than you might think! And . . . our liberation is in some way connected with milk . . . Don't look at me like that. Really, I am not mad!'

'Milk . . .' Dr Pista Kádas gave a sigh. There was no more incongruous word that Balázs Csillag could have uttered. The prisoners of Lager 7149/2 never saw any milk; at most they might have caught sight of that sticky, white condensed stuff which made you nauseous even when stirred into ersatz coffee. It came in metal tins of the kind that the Csillag shoe shop sold as Csillag shoe polish.

In logging Balázs Csillag proved to have two left hands, but he was very good when it came to estimating the size of the tree trunks and calculating their volume, and the Russian guards soon made him responsible for producing the lists and the final figures on the dispatch notes. Balázs Csillag learnt to speak Russian quite quickly and was therefore also used occasionally as an interpreter. He did all in his power to ensure that Dr Pista Kádas was always by his side, but this did not always work out: the sickly, aquiline-nosed Kádas was for some reason found unsympathetic by the Russian soldiers. Balázs Csillag was certainly more like them physically, with his small, sharp grey eyes, quite long

329

but somewhat bandy legs, and the black moustache which he grew in the Lager. This impression was reinforced when winter came round again and he wore the quilted jacket and ushanka that the Russian guards had cast off.

It was deemed a special favour if someone was ordered to take goods into town. They left the Lager riding on two double-wheeled trucks through the iron gates; this was the most spine-tingling moment, when you left the barbed wire behind. Each driver had a Russian soldier in the cab, while the prisoners stood in the back, shaken and tossed about. On the way back they could lie on the goods they brought, hanging on for dear life with their hands and feet. Sometimes one of them might fall out of the truck. The truck would then brake and reverse, two men carried out the order to throw the lifeless body back, and it would be held all the way to make sure it did not fall off again. Alive or dead, the Russians didn't care, but a body was an item in the inventory and had to be accounted for.

Balázs Csillag was frequently chosen as transporter; Dr Pista Kádas more rarely. There was one occasion when the trucks set off for the far end of town. They were rarely informed where they were headed; it was thought enough to tell the prisoners their duties when they got there. This time they drove into a yard, surrounded by a tarred wooden fence, where they saw a wooden structure resembling a barn. The prisoners jumped off and immediately lit up; the guards permitted this on arrival. One of them went into the office, the other joked with a fat woman who seemed to be the caretaker and was smoking a stubby cigar just like the soldier's. His companion soon returned and motioned Balázs Csillag to come closer: 'You go in, bring out the churns, up into the truck, one row stands, one lies on top of them, got that?'

The building was the milk-collecting station of the kolkhoz. Well-built women were in charge of the large milk tap hanging from the ceiling, and drew the heavy-duty churns underneath it one at a time; these would clatter loudly on the hardwood floor. The prisoners longingly eyed the thick stream of milk flowing from the tap. The women offered them some. Almost all of them drank their fill and more from the carved wooden bowls, an overindulgence that resulted for many in a bout of severe diarrhoea.

As the company began to carry the churnss outside, Balázs Csillag stood to one side to relieve himself. Dr Pista Kádas followed suit.

'There's no fence at the back,' said Balázs Csillag. 'Count to ten and then . . . !'

Dr Pista Kádas looked shocked. But as Balázs Csillag strode off determinedly in the direction of the wooden building, he followed like his shadow. They expected any moment to hear Russian words of command snarled out, and the metallic click that indicated the safety catches of guns being undone. But nothing happened. When they got beyond the missing part of the fence, they broke into a run, jumping over the stream that wound its way here (which Balázs Csillag thought looked familiar), to reach the reedbeds as soon as possible; here they would stand more of a chance against any bullets fired at them. But there were no bullets. They ran as fast as their legs would carry them, knee-deep in the boggy soil, hampered by the reedgrass that clung to their limbs. They ran for three-quarters of an hour, deep into the reedbeds, stepping on each other's heels. The first to collapse into the bog was Dr Pista Kádas; Balázs Csillag stopped above him, wheezing as he kept glancing back. Apart from their uneven breathing there was silence; only the drops of their sweat could be heard as they dripped into the stagnant water. We've had the milk, then, thought Balázs Csillag; but what now?

Two weeping willows marked the line where the bed of the stream must have run before the floodwaters at the end of winter altered the lie of the land. They climbed up the bigger one to dry out. Undressed, they shivered in the cold. Hissing in the freezing air, they slapped themselves and each other with their clothes.

'Let's go on, before they catch up!' said Dr Pista Kádas.

'Take it easy. In wet clothes we're certain to fall ill, and a long journey lies ahead of us . . . if we're lucky.'

'Yes, if . . . !'

As soon as their stuff dried out a little, they continued on their way. Balázs Csillag clung obstinately to the line of the stream, thinking that this was the best way of ensuring the dogs lost their trail. He had read something of this sort in his childhood in the Karl May stories about Red Indians. He battled on ahead, his boots raising spurts of liquid mud. Behind him, more slowly, came Dr Pista Kádas. He could not imagine how they could ever, on foot, reach anything worth reaching. He was getting colder and colder, as hunger froze into an icy sponge in his stomach. He begged Balázs Csillag to stop and catch their breath.

'Impossible. If we survive the first day we have a chance. Come on!' He took him by the arm and pulled him along.

This forced march lasted until night fell. Then Balázs Csillag again sought out a suitable willow, whose trunk divided into four main limbs; they climbed up and perched on the thickest limb, propping each other up back to back.

'So far, so good,' said Balázs Csillag.

'We shall die of hunger by morning.'

'Nonsense!'

'Or freeze to death.'

'Nonsense!'

'And we'll have no cares.'

'How many times do I have to tell you: we're going to get home!'

Dr Pista Kádas was no longer able to reply; his teeth were chattering so loud, it was painful to hear. This noise irritated

Balázs Csillag, who put his arms around Dr Pista Kádas and rocked him like a child. The clan's ancestor, Kornél Csillag/Sternovszky, had survived for a long time living like the smaller creatures of the forest in an isolated clearing, even though he was but a child and lacked the use of his injured legs. Even so he managed to learn how to catch fish in the stream.

When dawn broke Balázs Csillag carefully disentangled himself from his still-sleeping companion, adjusted his position on the branch, and then climbed down. There is a stream here, too, wider than the other; surely it will see us through. He could test if the technique still worked some two and a half centuries later. Does man function the same way in the middle of the twentieth century, and do the fish also function likewise, the Russian fish, here in the boggy forest in the back of beyond? He lay flat on his stomach on the bank of the stream, dangled his arm in the ice-cold water, and waited for food to swim by.

He nodded off a little. He awoke to a hissing in the water. Less than a span under his fingers, frozen to insensibility, there fluttered a plump little fish with an opalescent back. Balázs Csillag thought he could see the foolish expression in its eyes: 'What are these five red sticks? I have never seen the like!' as it warily approached. Balázs Csillag employed the technique of his ancient kinsman, waiting until the fish touched his skin and then closing his fingers around it with a slowness that was almost imperceptible. Provided he pays enough attention to this manipulation in time, suddenly it will be as if he has the fish in the palm of his hand and there will be nothing left to do but suddenly fling it onto the bank.

He counted silently to three and pounced: but the fish clung to his hand, producing a stabbing pain. Ouch, it's bitten me! – he shook his lower arm but no way could he free himself of its grip. The little dancing–dangling creature – it couldn't have been more than three spans long, it had looked bigger in the water – would not let go until he picked up a stone with his left hand and beat it into shreds. His index finger was left a bloody mass of flesh. He bound it up with a rag and watched in growing disbelief as the throbbing increased. Even the fish are thirsty for blood these days, he thought.

After this injury his index finger was never again to be straight and would always be awkward to use. But this did not bother him at the time. He experimented further, hunting for other types of fish. He came back to Dr Pista Kádas clutching a dozen or so. They crunched them, raw, competing at spitting out the bones.

They spent two days hiding in the bog, moving west as they had intended. On several occasions, however, Dr Pista Kádas became convinced that they were going round in circles. 'We've been here before!'

'Impossible.'

'But I remember this rotting tree!'

Balázs Csillag became uncertain. He tried to orient himself by the rising and the setting of the sun, and the mossy side of the tree-trunks – at school they were told that north was that way. But still . . . they needed a map. Sooner or later they had to leave this boggy forest. Without the help of the locals, they stood no chance of survival. He tried to work out how far away they were from Pécs. He knew how many versts the Russian part of the distance was, and on this scale those 67 metres extra per kilometre could be ignored. Even just saying it was appalling: some 1,400 (that is: ONE THOUSAND FOUR HUNDRED) kilometres separated them from their birthplace.

Before he was called up, he and a couple of friends had walked to Budapest for a bet: it took six days; at night they asked if they could stay in barns and stables. On this basis, their tramp home would take about a month and a half, always assuming they did not have to break the journey and further assuming that they were not caught by the Russians. Or the Germans. Or the Hungarian Military Police. Sooner or later they would have to cross the front line.

They were fighting their way through scrubland, the thorny branches tore at their skin. They lost track of the stream. They reached the trail that crossed the scrubland bleeding from a number of wounds. Fresh wheel tracks in the mud indicated that carts plied their way through here, and that meant there must be a settlement hidden somewhere near by in the hills. Dr Pista Kádas had a lucky coin which they tossed to decide which way to go. The track took whimsical turns to the left and right. Soon they reached a wooden hut with black smoke rising from its chimney towards the steel-grey sky. A chained wolfhound noticed them and began to bark loudly. They flattened themselves on the ground, just watching for a considerable while.

From behind the house there emerged a squat shape they at first took to be a man, but which turned out to be an old woman in a fur hat. She told the dog to stop that row, but the dog continued to bark away. The old woman threw him something and the dog jumped up and clamped the item in its jaws, gnawing and then swallowing it with much growling and snarling. It made Balázs Csillag and Dr Pista Kádas salivate. They began to inch their way towards the house, slithering along the ground with great care. But the beast kept barking at them, though he could not even have seen them. The old woman again gave it a piece of her mind and a piece of something more solid, and when they heard the jawbone crack hard, a shiver ran down Dr Pista Kádas's back.

'Steady,' whispered Balázs Csillag.

And that was when the old woman noticed them. She stared in their direction and then went back indoors.

'Let's get out of here!' said Balázs Csillag. Dr Pista Kádas shook his head in resignation; he felt he could not stand up.

By then the old woman had popped up again. She brought steaming hot food in a wooden bowl and left it on the snow-covered grass. The dog detected the smell, but his chain did not stretch that far and his eyes swam in blood as he threw himself around and whined. Balázs Csillag straightened up and ran for the food. He wanted to thank the old woman, but she had gone indoors again. The bowl contained potato soup, with two dark-brown Russian rolls on the side. Not having a spoon, they used the crust of the rolls to measure the food into their mouths. It was, they thought, a feast fit for a prince. After so long on almost empty stomachs, they were a little unwell after they had had their fill.

In the course of their seemingly endless wanderings they received food any number of times in this manner. It was as if the old women of Russia were hoping that this would ensure that their sons and grandsons, ordered to fight so far from home, would also be fed like this in other lands. Balázs Csillag reminded himself a thousand times, and Dr Pista Kádas a hundred thousand times, that such experiences should not make them lower their guard. They were in an enemy empire, where they were prey to at least four sets of uniforms. To make real progress they continued to consider the dark of night safer. Since they had no map, they walked for a long time northwards instead of west, almost as far as Kursk. They had difficulty crossing the rivers Sosna and Tuskar; at the former they built a simple raft, while the latter, where they were disturbed as they were slipping the mooring rope of a boat, they decided to swim across.

From the shoulder bag of a dead German they liberated a map, a compass, binoculars and a quantity of marks and roubles, so they were now able to buy themselves bread and salt fish on the way. Using the map they could plan their route more accurately: Glukhov, Konotop, Nyezhin. They were on the Ukrainian slopes. They had to cross two more wide rivers before reaching the vicinity of Kiev. Here they spent a few days in an abandoned granary, where the former owner had left two dogs on chains; both had starved to death.

Then they set off towards the south-west. For days they were battered by icy sleet. One night Dr Pista Kádas felt unwell and voided all of his contents through every orifice. Balázs Csillag suspected that his friend was beyond saving; here exanthematic typhoid was untreatable.

They hitched a ride on a cart. Balázs Csillag feared that the peasant with the deeply lined face would realize what state his friend was in, whip up his horse in terror, and leave them standing. The elderly Ukrainian was, however, made of sterner stuff. He helped to lay Dr Pista Kádas, who was now delirious and babbling continuously, on an improvised stretcher. He was imploring his mother not to beat him on account of the Chinese vase.

Balázs Csillag sat up on the driver's seat. The Ukrainian peasant could manage a little Russian and complained that times were hard and that everything had been destroyed by the Nemetska. Balázs Csillag thought this was the local term for the Germans but it turned out to be the name of the river. 'All three villages,' the Ukrainian explained, 'are waist-deep in water, the foundations of the houses are being washed away; they will slide down the hill and we shall all be made homeless.' Then he asked where the two of them were from. Balázs Csillag explained as best he could with the vocabulary at his disposal. Every time he mentioned their word for 'Jew', 'Yevrei' a flash of fear lit up the peasant's eyes. Balázs Csillag did not take any notice; he thought the man would say if their company was proving burdensome. At the end of his story, they were silent for a while, then the Ukrainian mumbled: '*Nye kharasho.*'

'*Da,*' nodded Balázs Csillag in agreement.

The peasant offered him some mahorka. He had five sons, he said, three at the front, one already in the ground, having fallen at Volokalamsk, and one buried by the chimneystack – he had been born limbless.

'A blessing not to die here,' said Balázs Csillag.

'*Da*,' agreed the Ukrainian.

He then came up with the suggestion that his friend should perhaps be taken to Doroshich as soon as possible . . . The kolkhoz village of Doroshich lies west of Kiev, near Zhitomir; there the authorities had set up a temporary typhoid hospital where the unfortunate victims were being sent from all over the Ukraine – there was an epidemic. They say no papers of any kind are asked for.

'Are you not afraid you will catch it from him?' asked Balázs Csillag.

'Who can know the dispensations of God on high, apart from God Himself?' and he made the sign of the cross in the Slav manner.

He had to beg two more carters to take on Dr Pista Kádas, and he needed constant support walking, until they reached the kolkhoz village of Doroshich. The sizeable but crumbling brick building bore a huge notice: QUARANTINE. The scene depressed him. This was no hospital; rather, some kind of isolation ward had been created not in the interests of the sick but of those who were still in good health. In various outhouses and farm buildings, even roofless sheds, lay the dying; many had no bed, or even a sack of straw, but just lay in the mud with eyes fixed upon the sky.

Balázs Csillag sought the reception office, but there wasn't one. A fat fellow in a leather apron was boiling injection sharps over an open fire, in a utensil that resembled a small cauldron. Balázs Csillag tried to explain why he was here; without hearing him out, the man jerked his thumb behind him and said: 'Number three.'

The barns and sheds had been given numbers. Balázs

Csillag slung Dr Pista Kádas over his shoulder and hauled him into number three. He passed a huge stables packed six feet high with dead bodies. He had to stop to vomit. In number three he found not a square inch of free space. The heaving smell of human bodies stung his nostrils, at last suppressing the smell of corpses. When he managed to lay Dr Pista Kádas between two others, he hunkered down by his feet, though he knew it would be wiser to flee this place before he took ill himself; but he had no strength to stand up. This is what life is, he thought. Through the gaps between the wooden roof-slats the freezing rain poured in, washing his face clean of the drops of sweat he had acquired while bringing in the patient. To have carried Dr Pista Kádas for so many kilometres only to end up in this ghastly hole . . . It was a pity to have made such an effort.

For the first time, here, his rock-solid faith faltered, his belief that he would get home, that there was a future, where in the house in Nepomuk Street the table would again be laid with the swishing damask tablecloth, the saffron-flavoured bouillon would bubble in the china dish, and the four male members of the family would in turn kiss Mama's hand (in this vision, Mama was still well), and then for a long time there would be heard only the music of the cutlery on the plates and the uninterrupted ticking of the grandfather clock.

He tried to work out where he might be in terms of undivided time, trying to add up in his mind the number of days they had spent wandering, and came to the conclusion that it was perhaps the 29th of April. The day after tomorrow is Mama's birthday, he thought. He almost burst into tears. A bald man with ulcers on his face offered him a piece of rag: 'Here!'

It was some time before it sank in that he was being addressed in Hungarian. He would gladly have embraced the man but then common sense prevailed and he did not

339

accept the rag; this was a typhoid hospital, after all. He asked if there were more Hungarians here.

'There were. Only the four of us left now.'

They had all come here from the same labour service division. The ulcerous man gave a detailed account of their calvary to this point, and must have been hoping that Balázs Csillag and his companion would reciprocate with their story, but Balázs's exhaustion exceeded even his hunger, and he fell asleep in mid-sentence.

He awoke to an ear-splitting shriek. Blinding white lights, chaotic red flashes, the smell of petrol fumes, desperate voices in at least five languages. In the chaos Balázs Csillag could clearly discern Hungarian words: 'Fire! They've set fire to the barn!'

Those able to get to their feet lunged like enraged animals at the side walls, though these were already ablaze with fiercely leaping flames. In one corner someone had managed to break loose a few planks and people were being passed through the hole one at a time. Balázs Csillag also fought his way through, fighting tooth and nail, but once he had managed to leave the blazing building behind, he was surprised to see that those running ahead of him were all falling down. Was the grass so slippery? – before he had an answer to this question, he heard the gun-blasts and felt the bullets hit his body: two machine-guns were chattering away from the courtyard, mowing down those who were fleeing like living torches. In his last moments before he lost consciousness, he understood: the bastards want to get rid of the contagious.

He lay, badly burnt, for three days, frozen in his own blood. He had taken two hits, one in the shoulder, the other in the stomach; the latter bullet had left through his back. When he came round again, it was early morning. He had time to consider what to do. He suspected that if he were found, it would be all over for him. They are hardly in need of an eyewitness. He should somehow drag himself as far as

340

the trees, in the direction from which he had come with poor Dr Pista Kádas. But he had too little strength left even to sit up. He decided to play dead until night fell again. This proved all the more easy to do, because he soon sunk into a deep faint. At first he would come to for a few minutes; later it would be for some hours. He saw that they had set fire to barns number two and four. The authorities had therefore decided it was time to liquidate the temporary typhoid hospital. No one is going to believe this.

The area around him seemed to be deserted. Perhaps there was no one apart from him who survived. But what about barns number one and five? Ach . . . it's all the same.

The following night he managed to drag himself to the trees. He found no human being; he had to rid himself of just a stray dog. He hid some six days among these fir trees, again living on the small fish in the stream and mosses on the trees. When he peeled off his clothing, he was horrified to see that in several places his skin and his clothes had fused. His eyebrows had been singed off, and some of the hair on his head, as well as on his chest and arms. His whole body was a festering wound and pain; in places, gangrene had set in. This is it, he thought. This is not something one can survive. His strength was fading fast, until he got to the point where he could not move at all. He allowed the grey shroud of helplessness to settle over him.

He came to on a makeshift bed, under blankets smelling of musk.

'Where am I?'

'In Tyeperov. Just sleep!' a woman's musical voice said in Russian.

He obeyed. In his feverish dreams he saw his father sing, in a clown's outfit, to an audience that was pretty much that of Lager 7149/2.

When he next recovered consciousness, the almond-eyed Armenian nurse told him he was in a camp hospital.

'How did I get here?'

'No idea.'

He never discovered who had had the kindness to save his life; all he knew was that he had been taken off the back of a truck in front of the camp hospital and put on an empty stretcher. The doctor was quite sure his recovery was nothing short of miraculous, since his body had been covered in second-degree burns. His back, chest and right calf had been left covered in pits and pockmarks as they healed, so that for the rest of his life he would not undress in the presence of another. On his face there remained only a scar the size of a matchbox to the left of his mouth, a scar that for years preserved the pain of the burning every time he moved his lips. This was one reason why he was disinclined to smile.

From the hospital he was transferred to a Lager again, this time to 189/13. From there he reached home in the spring of 1945. The most agonizing were the last three days, when the train seemed to spend hours motionless at Berehovo, Mukachevo and then on the border. In fact, they were told to leave the train there. Balázs Csillag did not hang around and promptly walked to Nyíregyháza. Compared with distances he had walked on foot in Russia and Ukraine, this should have been a pleasant little stroll, but because of the lasting injuries he had sustained, he now walked slowly and awkwardly.

At Nyíregyháza he boarded a freight train which took the whole day to struggle into the bombed-out East Station. The trains for Pécs left from the South Station, assuming there were trains at all. What could have happened to the others? He was tortured by forebodings. He did not feel he had the strength to continue his journey straight away.

The ruins of Budapest received him most unpleasantly, with biting winds and hostile-looking pedestrians who gave him a very wide berth, as if he were a leper. Balázs Csillag

342

thought they were repelled by the huge wounds on his hands and neck; it did not occur to him what kind of smell he might be giving off – the last time he had managed to wash was in Berehovo, at the station water-pump.

He tried to find one of Papa's friends, Uncle Roland, who had often visited them in Pécs. He was a piano-tuner who worked for the Opera, among others, and was fond of boasting of how many of the world-famous visiting artists had praised his work. Uncle Roland lived in Hajós Street, but when Balázs Csillag rang the bell on the corridor inside the block only a shrewish woman peeped out from behind the yellowing lace curtain, repeatedly squealing: 'He's not in!'

Balázs Csillag sat down in the corridor to wait. What can this hag have to do with Uncle Roland? The occupants of the flats in the block came and went, stepping over him. In the morning he awoke to find a dog licking his face. From the far end of the corridor, its owner shouted at the dog: 'Bundi, no! Naughty boy! Disgusting! Bundi, here, boy, at once!'

The dog, an indeterminate mix of several breeds, left him, giving a sharp whine. Balázs Csillag got up, dusted himself off, and abandoned Uncle Roland. He walked down to the South Station and waited for a freight train to Pécs, jumping onto the last carriage, which was carrying trestles and saw horses for use on building sites.

The house on Nepomuk Street was inhabited by complete strangers who would not even let him in. This house had been assigned to them by the authorities. They had no knowledge of any Csillags. Balázs Csillag was not inclined to argue and sat out in Széchenyi Square. There he was spotted by an old schoolmate, who put him up for a few days. This brief period was more painful than the time in the labour service battalion, in prison and the typhoid hospital all together: here he received the news. Of the entire family, he alone had returned. He had no parents, no brothers or

343

sisters, no grandparents, no aunts or uncles or nieces. None of his childhood friends had survived. Not even the chatterbox girl next door, Babushka, was there, with whom they were always playing Mummies and Daddies in the garden. Balázs Csillag had sworn that he would marry her. Looks like I shall remain unmarried, he thought.

Never mind marriage, it was hard enough to find reasons just to live. He moved into the hall of residence of the Calvinist secondary school, which had been converted into an emergency shelter. He lay on the bunk bed and stared at the ceiling. He was only two-thirds the weight he was before the war, but was quite unable to put any on. Of course, he had to eat more and better food. In the kitchen there was a hot meal once a day, but Balázs Csillag often did not even go down for that; kind folk would bring it up to him.

Then once again he took himself to the house in Nepomuk Street. On the firewall opposite he could still make out the remains of a poster from the Arrow Cross, the Hungarian Nazis, showing a triumphant Hungarian tank, with slogans above and below and a date. *One heart – one will! Forward to victory!* Balázs Csillag stared at it aghast. At the end of 1944 these wild animals were boasting of victory?

This time the door was opened by a shy girl with curly hair. She was in talkative mood. Her name was Mária Porubszky, a relative from Beremend; she was baby-sitting. The Varghas had gone to fetch food from Sikonda.

Balázs Csillag was unsure how to present what he had to say. 'Do you mind if I smoke?'

'Please don't, it isn't good for the little ones,' the girl said, showing him the Varghas' two children, one about two years old sleeping in the cot, the other, just a few months, still in the cradle. 'Aren't they sweet when they're asleep?'

Balázs Csillag just stood there, trying to bury his disfigured neck and hands in his shirt. He had forgotten, if ever he knew, how to address young women. Stork-like he shifted from one foot to the other. 'This house was ours. And there are some things here, if they are still here, that is . . . not valuable things, valuable only to me . . . a sort of family album . . .' and he made for the stairs, under which his father had had built a slim cupboard of sorts. In the old days that was where he kept his music. Later this lockable store was given to Balázs Csillag. The new owners of the house had forced it open and used it to store firewood. At the very bottom they had stuffed newspapers, presumably as firelighters. Among these he found, more or less intact, the volumes of the Books of Fathers. He had himself begun the last volume, a thick, hardbound, lined book, but it was empty, except for these words on the first page: *I hereby begin the latest volume of the Book of Fathers.* Nothing else. A few days later he had received the call-up papers.

He clutched his family's past to himself and wept, though the girl could not have seen any of this. His tear-ducts, too, had been damaged and he frequently needed eyedrops.

Mária Porubszky's index finger nudged his elbow. 'But you will tell me your name, won't you?'

He wanted to say: Does it matter? But then he said: 'Balázs Csillag. And what is yours?'

'Hey, you're not paying attention! I've introduced myself already: Mária Porubszky. But not for much longer.'

'What do you mean?'

'Because I'm going to be Mrs Balázs Csillag.'

'You are what!?'

'You heard me.'

'Mrs Balázs Csillag, my Mrs Csillag?'

'Yours.'

'Have you gone mad?'

'No, I was born mad!' her laughter rang out.

Her prediction, which she later admitted was no more than a bit of harmless fun, came true within a year. The wedding feast was held in the house of her parents in Beremend. Old Mr Porubszky was a carpenter, as all his ancestors had been.

Balázs Csillag went to the cathedral. He knew the priest, who had been a regular at Papa's restaurant. 'I want to sign up as a Catholic,' he declared.

'Why?'

'You are in the majority . . . aren't you?'

The reverend father knew what had happened to the Csillag family. He asked no further questions but sent him to theological classes. With ten-year-olds he listened to the lectures on the commandments, the martyrs, and the books of the Bible.

Soon he was able to look up the office of the Jewish community. In the archway there was a rusting plaque: SERVICES TO THE LEFT – OFFICE TO THE RIGHT. He turned right. He waited his turn and handed over to the old woman behind the desk the certificate he had obtained in the cathedral. She managed to work out what it said. Her face was covered with amazement. 'What is this?'

'I don't want to be a Jew.'

'I see . . . and so what am I supposed to do about it?'

'Make a note in the register.'

The old woman shrugged her shoulders, opened up the relevant volume, and wrote a few lines in the column headed ADDITIONAL REMARKS.

'Do you want a receipt as well?'

'I do.'

He received a piece of paper with a stamp on it which was proof that in the register of births maintained by the Jewish community the following amendment was made: *UB 238/1945. The above-named, on the basis of document number 67/1945 from the First Pécs Parish Office, has this day, 25th August 1945, converted from the Israelite religion to the Roman Catholic faith.*

Balázs Csillag slipped the piece of paper into his shirt pocket and went out into the street as if he had left something of himself behind. Since he had discovered what had happened to his loved ones he had done nothing but force himself not to think about how their lives had ended. But those images again and again came to the fore, together with the accompanying sounds and smells, and this was something that one could not bear and still remain of sound mind – he had to escape from them, at any price. If he was outdoors he would start to run and exert himself until he ran out of breath; if indoors, he went round and round taking tiny steps, like dogs chasing their own tails. He thought he would lose his mind if things carried on like this.

One or two of his old acquaintances looked him up, and he would be invited out; but then here, too, the conversation would come round to those they had lost, and he would just take himself off without ado. Only in the company of Mária Porubszky did peace descend on him: she never forced the conversation yet chattered away enough for two; when they were together they were like two plants growing in the meadow. He found it difficult to come to terms with the idea of marriage, having many concerns: 'Mária, if ever I dared undress, you will be horrified by the sight and will be revolted by me for a lifetime.'

'Well, now, dear Balázs, don't you know there are more important things than the body?'

They continued to address each other formally after their wedding. For Balázs Csillag his wedding night was as distressing as for many of his ancestors, and indeed he recalled them in those moments, until Mária Porubszky took him by the hand. 'Pay attention to me now, Balázs, and not to the past!'

This sentence proved to be a life-saving balm. 'I'm not going to attend to the past,' he repeated to himself in the voice of a naughty schoolboy. He closed his eyes and sighed deep sighs as his new bride gently traced with her fingers the wounded valleys of his body. He dissolved in the blindness of the love that Mária Porubszky, for reasons unknown to him, radiated in his direction.

The next morning, at dawn, in the kitchen garden at Beremend, he tore out from all the volumes of the Book of Fathers the somewhat musty pages, even the empty sheets in the volume that he had himself begun, and carefully burnt the pile of rubbish. Then he did the same to the covers. The first volume was the most unwilling to catch fire, although it was falling apart, especially at the spine, but he was unrelenting. 'I'm letting go of the past,' he muttered. 'I'm letting the past go to hell. I'm letting the past go. It is not necessary to remember . . .' Even that 'necessary' was inherited, and he corrected himself. 'I don't have to! I DON'T HAVE TO!' His voice rose to fever pitch.

The Porubszkys' house was close to the Israelite cemetery of Beremend. The caretaker had had to get up early to dig two new graves, since his assistant had not shown up for some days. He had enough problems. 'And you don't have to shout!' he shouted.

Da Nobis Domine Pacem.

The pencil drawing was of the WC in the room, where the inhabitants of the ward could attend to the call of nature; or, rather, those who were able to walk. In the background could be seen a double window, the corner bed, with the patient's case-sheet, and the bare leg of the patient lying there. Someone had just got up off the room WC – the person did not resemble any occupant in the drawing – and pointed with satisfied, rounded face at his steaming deposit.

That toilet had been made in the Thirties by the hospital carpenter, though the verb may be an exaggeration, since he had simply sawed a hole in the seat of a stool, into which the porcelain chamberpot had been inserted, to be changed in the Sixties for a container made of thick glass. The latter was somewhat loose in the hole and small accidents would result. By the time he drew this sketch on the back of a newsletter from the Lawyers' Association, Dr Balázs Csillag was no longer able to use the room WC; he even had difficulty clutching the bedpan. Under his masterpiece he had written the Latin prayer, but with the conviction that he had made a mistake in the grammar. Yet he was proud that for his whole life he well remembered what he had learnt about Greek and Latin in secondary school. The expression resounded in his head in the smoke-soaked tones of Mr Barlay. This knowledge was always available for drawing on in his head, he could whistle it up at any time, like a favourite watchdog. He spent many evenings with his favourite watchdog, reading the *Anthology of Greek and Latin Poets* which he had had published by Athenaeum Press. His wife Marchi could never understand this: 'How come he never gets bored with that same old book?'

'If you must choose between reading one volume a hundred times or a hundred volumes once, you will be better off with the former,' he said, quoting his teacher, Mr Barlay. To Marchi this was an alien way of thinking: she wanted everything at once, and if it could not be at once, then she wanted it even sooner.

Da Nobis Domine Pacem. Is that right? Sounds odd.

Sometimes his mind simply would not serve. This caused him more suffering than any physical pain. At first he could hardly wait for the visits of Marchi and his son; now he was not sorry if they came less often – it made him feel bad if they saw him in such dreadful shape. He lay on his bed all day long, his eyes closed.

It was getting on for twenty years since he had sworn to cut the Gordian knot of memories to liberate himself from all that he was unable to deal with. Now, nonetheless, in his

brain a spotlight was trained on the main paths and alley-
ways of his past, that is to say, of his life.

The cemetery at Beremend often came to mind; it lay
heavy on his conscience. His first job after the war was in
the transport department of Pécs Council, which was just
being reorganized; he had been recommended by Imre
Somogyi, the chief engineer on the railways. His father
before him had held a similar post: Imre Somogyi senior had
been a close friend of Nándor Csillag. He, too, had been
taken. Everybody had been taken. Very few came back.
During the reign of the Arrow Cross Imre Somogyi had
gone into hiding in the Mecsek Hills, where his training as
a scout had helped him survive. Pécs was liberated relatively rapidly, and there was still street-by-street fighting in
Budapest when the cafés reopened here. In Pécs's main
hotel, the Nádor, the women's orchestra had re-formed,
with gaps in their line-up and patches on their costumes,
but with enormous enthusiasm. That was where Balázs
Csillag had bumped into Imre Somogyi. He was just pondering whether to move to Beremend, to get further away
from Apáca and Nepomuk Streets and everything else that
reeked of the war.

The head of the transport department made it possible
for him – in fact, urged him – to enrol in the University of
Pécs. 'We shall have great need of qualified people!'

This was a pressing reason for staying in Pécs. They
rented a room by the month, opposite the cathedral. In the
morning he set off to earn his bread with egg-and-butter
sandwiches in his pocket. Marchi made a little on the side
with her lace embroidery. Balázs Csillag used to call her
Marchilla or My Marchillag in those days, which they both
found rather amusing.

At work Balázs Csillag came into contact with the transport section of the police. The police had just taken over
the old militia barracks, where they could ride in through

the back gate. The head of the section – another whose father had been one of the regulars in Nándor Csillag's restaurant – treated him as an old friend, and soon offered him employment. 'I have few men I can rely on, and even fewer whose heads are not cabbages. The old ones keep skipping off, afraid that they will be called to account.'

'Forgive me, but can you see me in uniform? Just look at me!'

'No one was born into a uniform. You'll get used to it.'

Marchi leapt at the chance and devoted all her considerable charms to persuading her husband to accept the offer, the clinching argument being not just the salary increase of almost 50 per cent (now in crisp forint notes, which had replaced the hyperinflated pengő), but the advantages of a service flat. How marvellous it must be to have a key to one's own flat and to be able to shut the door on the noises and rows of other people! If you have your own kitchen, you can cook whenever you like and don't have to worry about others raiding your larder. No hammering on one's own bathroom door just as one's soaking in the tub. This proved a particularly attractive argument for Balázs Csillag. As soon as they moved in, he got into the habit of reading the *Anthology of Greek and Latin Poets* while soaking in the bathtub.

He was given the rank of sub-lieutenant, and when a year later he was transferred to the administrative section as deputy head, he was promoted to first lieutenant, skipping one rank, which was rare. Initially he was involved with developing the general framework of the change-over to identity cards. He was at about this time prevailed upon to join the Party. After a six-month trial period, he received his little red booklet.

He was assigned tasks that required a great deal of circumspection: carrying out the nationalization of church schools, the monastic orders and the brothels. The greatest difficulties were caused by the last: it was necessary to use

351

force to remove the prostitutes from the four institutions comprising the town's red-light district and at two of them the policemen assigned to the task were pelted with rubbish, while at another site there were serious injuries.

If at all possible he gave the scenes of his childhood and adolescence a wide berth. He was not at all sorry that Apáca Street was renamed Eta Geisler Street. The house in Nepomuk Street was awaiting demolition, as the whole area was to be rebuilt with wider streets and roads.

The Minister of the Interior paid a surprise visit to the Pécs Police HQ. Balázs Csillag had the honour of being introduced: 'He will soon have his doctorate!'

The minister asked a few questions and inquired after his family circumstances. Balázs Csillag stood at (what his superiors considered not stiff enough) attention. 'Married, no children as yet.'

'Parents?'

'None.'

'Hm?'

'I have no wish to speak about this. May I be excused?' and he left without waiting for the answer.

Subsequently he heard that the minister had continued to express interest in him, believing he was concealing an Arrow Cross or a Horthyite father. A few weeks later he was summoned to Budapest to work at the Ministry. 'What happens if I refuse?' he asked his immediate superior.

'What happens is that that doesn't happen.'

He thought Marchilla would be devastated, but he was wrong. The woman clapped with joy. 'That's fantastic, Balázs dear, and you'll take me to the theatre? And to the movies? And to the opera?'

His final task in Pécs was to relocate the cemetery at Beremend. When the chief constable gave him the instructions, he thought he had not heard right. 'Relocate? A cemetery? What in God's name for?'

'Because it is to become the site of a power station. Industrialization is more important than the dead, that must be obvious.'

'And why does this require the use of police staff?'

'Because the cemetery is a Jewish one, Comrade Csillag. You get my meaning?' and the chief constable winked knowingly.

He's sending me because . . . someone's branded me a Jew, thought Balázs Csillag. He read the relevant file. The wrangling had been going on for a while. The Jewish community of Beremend and the Chief Rabbi of Pécs had launched an offensive, in their protests the mildest expression used being 'defiling the dead'. The Chief Rabbi had managed to secure the council's permission to transfer all the gravestones that remained intact to the Jewish Cemetery of Pécs. But as soon as two labourers arrived on the spot, half a dozen Jews from Beremend chased them off. According to the books, the police station at Beremend had a complement of four, but in the event only two men were available and they had requested reinforcements.

Balázs Csillag ordered the mounted police to Beremend, and this time he led them personally. By the time they reached the village, the gendarme saddle that he had polished to a shine had worn the trousers and the skin on his rear to shreds. The gates to the cemetery still gave shelter to a few unpeaceful descendants of those at peace within it. An old woman in a black headscarf, who somewhat resembled Ilse, shook her fist in front of Balázs Csillag's nose, whereupon he dismounted with great difficulty. 'What do you think you lot are doing, eh? Haven't you hounded us enough? No respect even for the dead, eh?'

The situation was complicated by the fact that Marchi's father and mother were both calling out the names of all the dead of the family who lay here. 'What sort of eternal rest is

353

this?' Then they suddenly noticed their son-in-law. They hesitated for a second, then decided to ignore him.

'So even they . . .' thought Balázs Csillag. I should have known. He tried to raise his hand to indicate he wanted to say something. It took a long time for them to calm down. Then he said: 'People, listen. Orders are orders. With your help, we can save every gravestone. Without it, we can save only as many as we can shift by the end of the day. The tractors are due tomorrow.'

'Of course,' shrieked the old crone reminiscent of Ilse, 'the stones yes, the dead bodies no?'

'Look, my good woman, what are we to do with the bodies? It's better for them where they are,' replied Balázs Csillag, quietly but firmly. He had witnessed enough scenes like this at the Front; he knew these people would give in.

'You're not a Jew, right? No idea what one is, eh?' the crone shrieked, stabbing the air with her gnarled fingers.

As the slabs left the ground one by one, each felt like a dull thud on his heart. He told himself off: it's all the same. *Your* loved ones don't even have a grave! He sauntered out of the cemetery, feeling that a cigarette would help him relax.

I shouldn't have smoked so much, he thought now, in his hospital bed. How many people had warned him, and how often! He had just waved them aside: 'You have to die of something sometime anyway.'

'True, my dear,' said Marchi, 'but it is not all the same when.'

There is a strong likelihood that it will be soon. Though Dr Salgó is quite upbeat: 'Now that we're controlling the embolism, we have every hope of positive developments.'

I would be happy with the positive development of getting up, he thought. He had difficulty in using the bedpan; he felt awkward that women slid it under his buttocks,

354

while they could glimpse his dried-up naked body as they lifted up the blanket, his manhood too, which, against his will, would curl out of the pyjama bottoms. He was ashamed all his life, not only of the ridges and craters of his burnt skin; in his youth he had been ashamed because he was so sickly, after the war because he had put on a lot of weight, and in recent years because he had become so shrivelled and shrunken. Only when he was in the upper years of secondary school had he had any success with women. Since then he had at most dared to stare at them, and if one happened to return his gaze, he would look away in confusion.

Now, sunken, incapable and unworthy on a hospital bed, he was troubled by the thought that he had not had enough female attention. There had been only three women in his life, not counting stolen kisses in school. The second he had married. The third – a silly affair at work – developed on a works outing and reached its climax in a clearing at Szilvásvárad. The reason he had so much enjoyed being with Iduska, who worked in accounts, was that he did not have to divest himself of his clothing and so had fewer inhibitions. There, in the grass, he realized that he had been quite seriously in error regarding the variety of ways in which a man and a woman may gratify each other. The thought of divorce flashed through his head, but Iduska poured cold water on it at once: 'You must be joking, my dear Balázs; we are both married with a raft of kids!'

'I have only one.'

'Well, I have three.'

The memories of Szilvásvárad again and again came to the fore, like a postcard that had lost none of its glossy sheen. Since he had vowed to rid himself of the family tradition of looking into the past, this was perhaps the first time that he allowed his thoughts to gambol about among the peaks of time, like giddy little goats. Initially, no further back than the years after the war.

When they moved up to the capital, they did not avail themselves of the tiny, two-room service flat on the newly built Ministry of the Interior estate in Kispest, because they were able to set themselves up in the family house in Terézváros, where the lower floors were occupied by Marchi's eighty-two-year-old widowed aunt; the upper floor was empty because this aunt's brother, a retired doctor, had received extraordinary permission to emigrate to Canada, where another sister lived. The Porubszkys were secretly hoping that if Captain Balázs Csillag moved in, the authorities would leave their property in peace. Marchi's aunt, Dr Lujza Harmath, always referred to the house as 'the villa' and to Hungary as 'The Balkans! My dear girl, these are the deepest Balkans!'

Balázs Csillag was irritated by the old lády's airs and graces and he took not one step to save the villa – in fact, a very modestly constructed and, after the 1944 bombing, rather poorly restored building; so it was, in due course, nationalized and Dr Lujza Harmath, as well as they themselves, became tenants.

'Let's just be glad that they aren't allocating some of the rooms to strangers!' opined Balázs Csillag. But the Porubszkys were not glad, and with this their contacts with the young couple came more or less to an end.

On the third day at work, the minister called him in. 'Strength and health the Hungarian says, Comrade Csillag. I hope you have settled in. I am glad to inform you that you will be working directly under me, drafting documents.'

'Understood, Minister.'

It soon became clear that Balázs Csillag was regarded by his minister, László Rajk, as a kind of personal secretary; he made him write his speeches, too. When he was made Foreign Minister he ensured that Dr Balázs Csillag was ('pro. tem.', he said with a wink) assigned to him, though formally he retained the rank of Major at the Ministry of the

Interior. He would often call him in for informal discussion. In their personal contacts – i.e. behind closed doors – he soon suggested that they drop the formalities, and they drank to this from the entertainment allowance cognac. He always appeared interested and understanding. He supported Balázs Csillag's request to continue his legal studies at the University of Budapest, and from time to time inquired about the topics he studied and the examinations. 'I'm envious. I'd much rather be at university.'

Balázs Csillag's feeling for László Rajk was unalloyed respect, perhaps even admiration of sorts. He could talk to no one of official matters, having been obliged to sign the Official Secrets Act, which extended the period of silence to ten years beyond the loss of his post for any reason, and he did not convey these sentiments about his boss even to Marchi. Comrade Rajk was a living legend, the hero of the Spanish Civil War, the youngest boy of the fairy tale, who had succeeded in scaling the highest peaks of the state machinery by his own efforts. He was a shining example to Balázs Csillag; for him he was prepared to work overtime, burning the midnight oil for nights on end, unremittingly poring over the text of the laws. He often sat on the edge of the bed, checking his texts and checking them again. Once his eyes strayed to the mirror mounted on the wardrobe door and he saw himself as he rocked to and fro, just like the orthodox Jews intone their prayers. 'Let the past go!' He ordered his upper body to be still, and from then on he checked his texts sitting bolt upright.

Marchi, on the far side of the bed, tossed and turned in her sleep, making a noise typical of her. She snored, a rough, noisy snore, like a man's. For a long time Balázs Csillag dared not bring it up, until one morning he decided to mention it. Marchi recoiled: 'The things you say, Balázs! How could I possibly snore – look at me!'

'Well, I suppose . . . to be sure . . .' It really did seem

357

impossible that this ethereal woman should snore. The topic never came up again.

At the degree ceremony, Marchi's face had a transcendent glow as she saw the applause from the other – mainly younger – graduates as Major Balázs Csillag received his doctorate in the maroon folder. He himself wondered what Comrade Rajk would say when he introduced himself as 'Doctor' and informed him that he had been awarded a red doctorate. Marchi bought him a richly engraved timepiece for the occasion and was a little disappointed that her husband's joy on receiving it was less than unalloyed.

Dr Balázs Csillag hurried back to the Ministry. On his desk lay an envelope. There was a minuscule gold pine-cone in it and a card with the words: *Well done! R.* The right leg of the letter curled away in a flourish and Dr Balázs Csillag was sure that it continued onto the enormous ministerial desk.

He could hardly wait to thank him for it in person. But R. was not in the office and in fact did not turn up that week at all. They however went on holiday, in the Ministry of the Interior's own complex in Siófok, on the southern shore of Lake Balaton. On the second morning the commandant of the complex, a repulsively obese lieutenant-colonel, summoned the holidaying cadres to an ad hoc meeting. He informed them of the situation in which socialist agriculture found itself: because of the inclement weather the harvest had been delayed this year and this could have the gravest consequences. The difficulties are of such seriousness that they, the cadres on holiday cannot pass over them without taking action. 'We shall therefore volunteer ourselves for unpaid social labour for four hours every morning at SFAC, the Siófok Farmers' Agricultural Cooperative. Coaches will depart from the main gate at eight o'clock.'

The announcement was met with an enervated silence. Dr Balázs Csillag raised an arm to speak. 'Comrade lieutenant-colonel, we have been building socialism for fifty weeks of the year, could we not be spared in those two weeks when we have been referred here to get some rest?'

'What's your name?' asked the lieutenant-colonel, puffing out his chest.

'Major Dr Balázs Csillag.'

'Stand to attention when you talk to me!'

'In a tracksuit? You must be joking.'

Faces in the audience reflected genuine panic. They are all shitting themselves, thought Dr Balázs Csillag. The lieutenant-colonel inflated like a puffball: 'This is by no means the end of the matter.'

'I certainly hope not.'

No one laughed. This was not the first time Dr Balázs Csillag found that not many people appreciated his sense of humour. The lieutenant-colonel ordered every adult cadre to assemble at the stated time and place, in light working clothes.

'Wives as well?'

The lieutenant-colonel was growing increasingly irritated by the clever-clever major. 'You heard me: every adult!'

'I'm afraid my wife is not in the employ of the Ministry of the Interior and therefore your orders do not apply to her.'

Despite Marchi's implorings, Dr Balázs Csillag insisted that she stay in the complex and she knew there was no appeal. So she spent her mornings on her own, basking in the sun on the stubby wooden pier in her lemon-yellow bathing suit, a magnet for male eyes. The other wives joined their husbands in hoeing, weeding and picking fruit. Oddly enough, they ended up with a deeper tan than Marchi.

The commandant of the holiday home minuted the insubordination of Major Csillag and sent it to the party personnel department of the Foreign Ministry. There, however, because of the complete breakdown of line management, it was shelved. R. had not been seen for weeks and it was rumoured that he had been arrested by the AVH, the secret police. Dr Balázs Csillag considered these rumours completely false and was convinced that R. had been entrusted with some secret assignment. He clung to this view until a circular informed the employees of the Ministry of the crimes perpetrated by R. and his accomplices.

Dr Balázs Csillag secured himself entry to the hearing, held in the HQ of the Iron- and Metalworkers' Union. It was September and the summer was bowing out with a burst of humidity. The building in Magdolna Street was ringed by Ministry of the Interior security personnel cleared at the highest level; this was the first time that his pass failed to secure him priority. His pass was the same as everyone else's. The hearing was set for nine in the morning, but the chamber filled up well before this. The silence was total; the little noises made by the official setting up the microphones were amplified to an unbearable squeak, particularly the shuffling of his rubber-soled shoes on a parquet floor waxed to a glinting shine.

When the accused were led in, Dr Balázs Csillag could barely recognize R.: the minister's skin had turned sallow and his hair was cut to recruit standard. Dr Balázs Csillag positioned himself at the end of the fifth row, ideal for catching R.'s attention, but try as he might, he could not. He was even unable to catch his eye, though they looked at each other more than once. Does he not recognize me, he wondered in shock.

In the dock he was surprised to see András Szalai, a man he knew from Pécs, whom he had at least as much difficulty imagining as a spy as he did László Rajk. Charges of a more fanciful nature were levelled at them, too. R. was supposed to have worked as an informant for the police while at university. His provocative actions were alleged to have brought about the imprisonment of several hundred building workers. He was a spy during the Spanish Civil War, then he became a Gestapo informant. Since the end of the war he had been recruited by the Yugoslav Spy Service, and he was also spying for the Americans. Recently he had been involved with carrying out Tito's plot to assassinate Comrades Rákosi, Gerő and Farkas, the triumvirate in charge of the country.

R. spoke very quietly and Dr Péter Jankó, president of the special council of the People's Court, had repeatedly to ask him to speak up.

'Do you understand the charge?'

'I do,' said R.

'Do you admit your guilt?'

'I do.'

'In every respect?'

'In every respect.'

Again he was murmuring; his tone of voice recalled for Dr Balázs Csillag his own during his cramming of the arcane language of the legal texts. This text was similarly arcane, yet R. was renowned for expressing himself with the utmost concision.

'He is mouthing a script he's been told to memorize,' groaned Dr Balázs Csillag that night in the kitchen.

'What?' Marchi had no idea where her husband had been that day.

'Nothing . . .'

'I have something important to tell you!' Marchi's face was radiant, her smile mysterious. When she divulged her secret, she felt the same sense of disappointment as when she had presented him with the watch. 'Aren't you pleased?'

'Of course I'm pleased,' said Dr Balázs Csillag somewhat mechanically. His head was filled with thoughts of R.: he must have been drugged. He had never seen him look so dead.

Now, in intensive care, he could see again, on the faces of

the patients at the end of their lives, the glassy stare that R. had worn at the hearing. It froze the spine to hear his last words:

> I declare unreservedly my view that whatever the verdict of the People's Court, I shall regard that verdict as just, because that verdict will indeed be just.

Such was the elaborate nonsense issuing from the mouth of R., famed for his succinct turn of phase and the sharpness of his thought.

The special tribunal of the People's Court announced its verdict at the end of September. Rajk, Szőnyi and Szalai received the death sentence; Brankov and Justus were given life imprisonment; and Ognenovich was jailed for nine years.

The executions were announced in mid-October in the newspaper *Szabad Nép*, 'Free Nation'. Dr Balázs Csillag could not get to sleep for a long time and when he did, he saw himself on the gallows and awoke howling and in a sweat. We've all been conned, he thought, just as they've conned each other . . . and everyone else. The whole thing's a fraud, lies, drivel; the crap about the peace front, the just fight, equality, brotherhood. It's nothing but a ruthless struggle for power, with the stronger always crushing the weak. There is nothing new under the sun.

He felt that with R. he, too, had died, now for the third time. The previous time had been when he found out how his father, mother, two brothers, grandmother, grandfather and all his other relatives had died. And the first time was in the typhoid hospital at Doroshich.

His howling went unheard; by then he had been sacked from the Ministry and was working as an unskilled labourer in a factory in Pest's industrial Angyalföld, permanently on the night shift. Such lowly work did not need a CV. By the time he got home, Marchi was up, though her pregnancy was a troubled one, and the doctor had ordered bed-rest. Dr Balázs Csillag made no attempt to find a better job; he knew that wherever he went, telephone calls would be made. He would be lucky if things got no worse. As soon as practicable, he enrolled on a retraining programme and obtained a qualification in machine tooling. With his brigade, in due course, he was awarded the Stakhanovite outstanding worker plaque.

Later, when he had progressed to shiftwork, their toddler once wandered into their bedroom in the middle of the night, sobbing. Dr Balázs Csillag, a lighter sleeper than his wife, woke up first: 'What's up, young man, what are you doing in here?'

'Mummy's noring, noring loud!' complained the little fellow.

By this time Marchi was up. 'What did you say I am doing?'

'Noring!'

'Now, now, young man, how can she possibly be snoring? Just look at her!' said Dr Balázs Csillag.

That sentence had a special resonance here in the hospital ward, where almost everyone snored, with the exception of Dr Balázs Csillag. But that was because he could not sleep. As long as the light was on he continued reading his *Anthology of Greek and Latin Poets*. If it was dark he continued to view the film of his life. The reels kept getting confused.

László Rajk and his coevals were rehabilitated and, on the first Saturday of October, reinterred with due ceremony in the Kerepesi Cemetery. After a long hiatus Dr Balázs Csillag met R.'s wife again, and his comrades of old, none of them any longer in work. As R.'s coffin was lowered into the ground to the sound of slow funeral music, Dr Balázs Csillag died for the fourth time. He withdrew completely into his shell, and neither Marchi nor his son could get through to him.

The fifth death occurred soon afterwards, on 4 November 1956. He was queuing for bread with his six-year-old son. Later he couldn't for the life of him understand how he could have taken the little boy with him out onto the post-invasion streets. A Russian FUG was passing by and sprayed bullets randomly into the crowd. People ran for their lives in all directions and in the confusion, for a few minutes, he lost track of his son. The boy turned blue with fear and had a stutter for some time thereafter.

He died for the sixth time having retired early one afternoon in autumn, while solving a crossword puzzle. He had lately got into the habit of passing the time in this way, filling the squares across and down at lightning speed, with the intense precision of someone preparing for the world cross-word championships. Suddenly he felt his heart swell up like a balloon, shattering everything around him; he lost consciousness at once, knocking his brow on the table, the pattern of the lace tablecloth impressing itself upon his skin. The paramedic managed to catch him in the final seconds before brain death set in and restarted his heart by pounding his fists on his chest. He cracked three of his ribs.

Six deaths are more than enough for one person, and he felt an even greater need to cling doggedly to his life-saving slogan: Let's leave the past! He could no longer live through the death by fire again, or the trial and execution of R., or those seconds that lasted for ever as he trembled in fear for his son's life. Still less did he have the strength for what had happened to his father, mother, brothers, grandparents and all his other relatives.

But now, as he felt the approach of his seventh death, he also felt the need to conjure up everything that he had inherited the capacity to see. He closed his eyes, and with the face of the first-born of nine generations, he awaited the kaleidoscope of images, the private view of the history of the Csillags, the Sterns, the Berdas and the Sternovszkys.

He detected only darkness under his eyelids, and sparkling circles of light.

It's not working. It's no longer working. I'm too rusty.

'Hello, Balázs my dearest! How are you?' came Marchi's voice, affecting cheerfulness. 'I've brought you lemons, fresh rolls, lemonade, and your puzzle magazines!'

'Thank you,' said Balázs Csillag without opening his eyes. In this new hospital, the presence of his wife was even more burdensome than before. Man is an ill-starred creature, expected to be loving even when he feels least like it. Marchi threw herself with military force into the care of her husband, and her over-attentive ministrations Dr Balázs Csillag found noisy and aggressive. In vain did he insist that two oranges would suffice; Marchi would pile six on his bedside table. There were even some left-over rolls from last time, and now here is the latest delivery, highlighting the distressing fact that he is unable to eat. I would be extremely grateful if you would kindly leave me alone, he thought.

In a short while his little boy ran in, covered in sweat – he was just as perspiration-prone as his father – and asked: 'How are you, Papa?'

'So-so,' he replied, unwilling to alarm him.

'And what does Dr Salgó say?'

'Slight improvement.'

This dialogue between them was repeated almost every time they met. There would then be a silence. Dr Balázs Csillag knew that his son would much prefer to get the hell out of there; it must pain him to see his father like this. He should tell him to buzz off. But he lacked the strength even for that. Never mind. You have to bear it when your father . . .

His life had not been a long one, and it had been filled with little joy and even less meaning. Once, he thought to himself, just once he should have taken the trouble to tell this to his son. He wondered if he was able to see anything of the past. He had never asked him.

Perhaps it was a mistake to remain silent about your parents and the others. Once you are better, you must certainly have a talk. You squeezed the past out of you but somehow it took the present with it . . . You didn't notice how you wasted the days and the years. Perhaps fate, heaven, God, or sod-all, will make sure your son fares better.

The next time he comes I really will make a start. A journey of a thousand miles begins with a single step.

That was the night death came knocking. The second day of January was two and a half hours old, so at least her husband did not pass away on New Year's Day, when they had celebrated his birthday on the ward. He was able to receive the cake, blow out the candles, drink a drop of champagne and open his presents, including the *Don Quixote* puzzle magazine's annual. He had made a start on the Giant Crossword. MOZART. BILLYGOAT. WAR AND PEACE. VOLGA. LIFE IS A DREAM. AMETHYST. BAKTAY ERVIN. PORRIDGE. INDIA. HEARTSEASE – this was as far as he had got.

In his final moments he saw himself standing in front of the Taj Mahal, as pictured on a black-and-white postcard he had been sent as a child. All his life he had longed to see it, though he knew he had no hope of doing so. According to the pathologist's notes his heart had swollen to twice the normal size because of the trials and tribulations of the life he had lived, and had encroached on the right side of the chest, pressing on the nearby organs, the lungs in particular. When the former colleague who gave the eulogy happened innocently to say 'He had a great heart!', Marchi burst into tears.

XI

AN EXHAUSTED LANDSCAPE BIDS WELCOME AS THE morning sunlight's shimmer tumbles down like corn into the dust from a ripped-open sack. The very slight rise in the temperature ruffles the shrunken torsos of the wayside acacias. The glass panes in the windows, left to their fate for months, reveal their need for a proper wash-down. Slushy humps of snow solidified on the pavement gradually begin to shrink. Ice weeps in the water butts, but the cold of the night brings frost to over-eager plants. The vortices of February's freezing air disperse the last traces of any mildness in the morning.

He was six when he had his tonsils removed. Until then Vilmos Csillag was so scrawny that the kindergarten nurse called him 'Thinbilly'. When he put on some weight, he was mocked as 'Tumbilly'. Only when he reached secondary school did he shoot up. He was slow to acknowledge the improvement in his looks.

He was in his first year at the secondary school when he heard two of the girls in his class talking in the ladies, which shared a ventilation shaft with the gents. Ági and Márti were smoking, despite a strict ban, as they discussed the boys in the class, where the girls were in the majority by 28 to 13. Only one of the boys passed muster, the gangling French-born Belmondo (real name: Claude Préfaut), who was a recent arrival and loath to divulge the complicated international history of his family.

'And what about Vili Csillag?' asked Márti.

'He's kind of . . .' Ági's voice became uncertain. 'A nice little boy.'

They giggled.

'Nice little boy, yes, you're right. A nice little boy!' Márti repeated the phrase like some new slogan.

'It's his eyes that are knockout.'

'Right! You've noticed, like a kaleidoscope?'

'Yes. Sometimes grey, sometimes green.'

'Even light brown, sometimes.'

The bell rang. Vilmos Csillag did not stir. He would never have dreamt that he would get the silver medal in class. He examined himself in the mirror. Just then, his eyes were river-green.

Almost a year later they were revising French in the flat of Ági's parents and exchanged a fleeting kiss over the kitchen table.

'You're not doing it right!' Ági protested.

'But that's how I usually do it,' Vilmos Csillag lied. In fact, it was his first time. The girl showed him how. Vilmos Csillag proved to be a quick learner. Of the girls in his class, Ági was fairly far down on the attractiveness scale as far as Vilmos Csillag was concerned, but she certainly rose a rung or two for finding him attractive. It was not the girl he wanted; it was the love.

Once it happened that only her older sister, Vera, was at home. She resembled her sister, but she was a fully grown woman, with substantial breasts, the mere sight of which made him break out in a sweat.

'Looking for Ági?'

'Isn't she in?'

'You can wait for her if you like.'

Vera attended the same school and was just taking her school leaving certificate. She complained that she had no chance of getting through maths. 'I just can't swot all these stupid formulae!'

'Make yourself a crib. And hide it in your . . .' He ground to a halt. He blinked unsteadily at the hem of the girl's tight skirt, where the darker band of her black stockings could be seen.

'All right, Willie dear, I'll make one,' she said, stroking his face; the red-painted nails travelled across the boy's field of vision like five burning aircraft. 'Listen . . . have you been with my sister?'

'You mean . . .'

'Yeah. Well?'

He blushed and made an uncertain gesture. 'I can't really . . . I don't want to.'

'So you haven't. I thought as much. She's just blabbing.'

'Is that . . . what she said?'

'Yeah.'

Vilmos Csillag had no idea how to behave in such an awkward situation, to maintain the self-respect of the male. He began to chew the corner of his mouth relentlessly. Vera's quick fingers hurried to the spot and separated mouth from teeth. 'Don't . . . Hey, your eyes have gone green.'

On another visit, he again found only Vera at home. They talked for a long time, about school, the summer holiday, teachers. Vera suddenly changed topic: 'You should grow your hair, Willie. It would suit you better.' She brought a brush, ruffled up the boy's somewhat curly hair and fashioned a Beatles cut for him. They took a look in the mirror in the hall. Vilmos Csillag knew that in the next few months he would not visit the barber's even on the headmaster's

369

orders – they were not allowed to wear the Beatles' mushroom-mop.

As Ági grew increasingly unreliable, so Vera became more willing to be a companion. Vilmos Csillag would never dare think of this tight-skirted, slickly made-up woman as one of the 'girls' at the school.

'What have you done to your hair, Willie?'

'I've combed it. And . . . I wet it!'

'You're such a sweetie!' Vera ruffled his hair. 'You arouse the animal in me!'

'What sort of animal?'

'A shark!' and she clacked her teeth as if to swallow him up.

Next time she came to the door she said: 'No Ági again, sorry.'

'Where is she?'

'Dunno. School play, I guess.'

'Ah.'

'Oh, OK, I'll tell you the truth. She's hanging out with Mishi. You get me?'

'What do you mean hanging out?'

'Going out with.'

'Going out?'

'Yeah. With.'

'But . . . I thought she was going out with me!'

'Typical. Can't spare the time to let you know that she isn't any longer.'

'I see.' He had to sit down on the laundry-basket in the hall. He tried to summon all his strength not to burst into tears, but one tear got away.

'Oh, my dear Willie . . .' Vera embraced him, her thumb wiping the tear from his eye. 'Come on!' and led him into her room. There she whispered: 'Party time!'

'Pardon?' The expression was new to him.

'My parents are away, in Parádsasvárad. Get it?'

When she began to take her clothes off, Vilmos Csillag was embarrassed and at first pretended not to see.

'You too!' Vera gave him a hand. Elsewhere, too.

Vilmos Csillag had imagined the scene a thousand, a million times, but always thought it would last a bit longer.

The girl gave a wry little smile as she rolled off and lay beside him. 'More practice needed.' She examined the refractory member, now shrunken and sleeping the sleep of a two-year-old. 'Hey, aren't you . . . ?'

Vilmos Csillag, after a long pause: 'Aren't I what?'

'Circumcised.'

'Why should I be?'

'Because that's the custom with your lot.'

'What do you mean, our lot?'

'Well, with Jews, OK?'

'I'm not Jewish!'

'I thought you were.'

'Where did you get that from?'

'Ági said. And you look it.'

'Come, come . . .' and he bit his lip as his father's turn of phrase slipped out.

Vera explained that on the basis of his looks, only someone who had never seen a Jew would not think him one. Soft lines, dark, wavy hair . . .

'My lines are soft?'

'Yeah.'

'Pity.'

'No worries, eh! We're Jews as well, it's no big deal!' She waited with a mischievous smile for the boy to laugh, but in vain.

'What makes Ági think I'm Jewish?'

'Oh come on, it's not cool. Perhaps you aren't after all . . . Those eyes, sea-green, they're suspect.'

'You suspect that I am or that I'm not?'

'Yeah, that you're not.'

371

Vilmos Csillag could hardly wait for his father to come home that evening. Papa just then was spending more time in hospital than at home, as the heart trouble that had been bothering him since the war had taken a turn for the worse. He rarely spoke to members of his family, so Vilmos Csillag, too, had lost the habit of sharing his thoughts with him.

The moment his father came through the door he gave a grunt and flung himself on the couch. Vilmos Csillag sighed. 'Could I have a word?'

His father was sweating profusely and kept wiping his brow. 'Sit down. What's up?'

'Just between the two us.'

'It is just the two of us, son. Your mother is in the kitchen.'

'But she might come in any moment.'

'Come, come.' There appeared on his father's face a look which was partly abstracted and partly blank; the look with which he shut out the outside world.

Vilmos Csillag knew he had only a small chance, but cut to the chase. 'How come that I know nothing of your past or how things were with your parents?'

'No. Not that.'

'Why?'

'It was a long time ago. It's of no interest.'

'But it is of interest.'

'End of story.'

Vilmos Csillag flew into a rage. 'And what about . . . is it true that you are Jewish?'

His father jumped up and hit him across the face with the back of his hand. Vilmos Csillag staggered to the bookshelf, for an instant unsure where he was. His lower lip started bleeding and the blood trailed onto his shirt collar. He heard the door squeak open and his mother scream: 'Jesus!'

'Leave Jesus out of it,' said his father, offering him a handkerchief.

Csillag Vilmos had never been beaten by his father – not that he ever gave much cause. At school he always managed to get marks that, if not the highest, were always good enough to put him into the bracket of 'good' students. But for his poor memory, he would be academically quite outstanding. Alas, often a day or two later he could not remember something he had learnt word for word. On the rare occasions that his mother gave him household chores, he washed up obediently, dried the dishes and went to the corner shop. He could recall only one big slap across the face and that had not been from his father. At the age of six he had got it into his head that he wanted a younger brother or sister and began to pester his parents about it relentlessly. His mother quickly disposed of him: 'Ask your father.'

Father had said: 'Don't stick your nose into grown-ups' business.'

But he was not to be shaken off like this and showered his parents with questions: why, when, how and why not. On one occasion during a three-hander he got so worked up that his voice began to sound like a dog howling and he yelled: 'And if you don't make me a little brother or sister, may you rot in hell!'

'Fine,' said his father.

'Now Willie dear, that's going too far!' exclaimed his mother, and let rip with a stinging slap across the face.

On that occasion there was no blood; now it would not stop. Sniffing, his mother brought the first-aid box and took out a little pillow of gauze to place on the split lip – she had done a first-aid course at her workplace. She wanted to know what had happened between the two men, but neither seemed inclined to tell her.

Hours later his father drew him to one side: 'Come out onto the balcony!'

Outside he lit a cigarette and offered his packet of Mátra cigarettes to his son: 'Want one?'

'Papa, I don't smoke, and anyway . . . you've forbidden me to!'

'Come, come . . . you really don't smoke?'

'No.'

'Clever lad.' For a while he puffed away without saying anything. 'My boy. Now listen carefully to what I'm going to say. This topic is taboo. Do you know what taboo means? Right. One hundred per cent taboo. One thousand per cent. There is no such thing as a Jew. There are only people. There are people who are shits, there are people who are good, there are people who are so-so. There are no Jews, no Gypsies, no nothing. Do you understand me?' and he grabbed his son by his shirt, so roughly that the top button popped out of its hole.

'Yes.' He was scared.

'So that's that cleared up.'

'But you haven't yet . . . you didn't . . .'

His father butted in: 'You are dismissed.'

For years Vilmos Csillag wondered why his father had used this military expression. He was constantly preparing to bring up the subject again. He was just waiting for a suitable opportunity. But his father communicated with him less and less, and with others, too.

Once he had the idea of writing him a letter. He spent weeks trying to find the best way of putting things, sketching his ideas in the big spiral-bound notebook. Here and there he decorated the draft. He planned to transfer, when he was ready, the text on to the magnolia-coloured writing paper he had received for his fourteenth birthday, but had not used a single sheet of the hundred in the set of stationery.

()()()()()()()()()()()()()()()()()

Dear Papa
Pap
My Dear Father
Dear Father

+ - + - + - + - + - + - + - + - + - + - + - + - + -

Father,
I am writing to you addressing you my Father *I am writing because I feel* in conversation *to have a conversation* I cannot you do not want you cannot *we cannot.*

It would be so good *I would so much like to talk, if we did not live like* complete strangers *two English gentlemen*, with *little in common* or to say to one another. *Why do you not want with me a normal* ordinary proper *relationship* human connection? *When I was small I seriously thought that every family behaved as we did, that is, everyone did his own thing and does not care about the others. I thought it was like this everywhere* they behaved like this. *I was open-mouthed when I saw at* Gidus's *at János Buda's they always have their evening meal together and tell each other in turn* what sort of day they've had *what their day was like*, so they share the good and the bad, like in the fairy tales, do you understand?!

X Y X Y X Y X Y X Y X Y X Y X Y X Y X

As long as
Since
Ever since I've been aware of things you have *always been more or less ill, and our life consists of leaving you alone dangling in peace, because any excitement is bad for you.* But *why does it count as excitement if* start talking *we have a conversation?* If

375

a father and a son If a father thinks of his son as *If there is mutual trust between father and son?* If they make each other feel *If they express* If they indicate *their love for one another?*

Where did we go wrong, Father?

When did it go wrong

What made it

Why

?!

I don't understand why this is *it has to be like this.* I would like to ask something. *Tell me, are you really* totally *not even a little interested in me?* Never *Nothing do you know about me and I know nothing about you. Perhaps you would not care you* would not be worried *if I just skipped school. Do you know how well I'm doing? What my favourite subjects are? (history, Hungarian literature). Do you even know what year I'm in?*

And why do you not want to share with me what you know? Why do you not ask how I'm doing with the girls? It's ridiculous but since I have been alive I can recall just one solely *no more than one serious* proper *conversation, and that happened because I humiliated you in front of your friends; I think you remember that. I couldn't have been six yet, when I heard some dirty words from some of the others and I asked right there in front of all the guests: Daddy, what does fuck mean. But you didn't laugh even then, not like the others, you just told me off, to be ashamed of myself, and locked me out; I hadn't the foggiest what was so awful about what I'd done. The next day you set about giving me the birds and the bees and mutual respect and love among human beings; I didn't get a single word of the whole business, but I was afraid in case I brought your anger down on my head* bring your wrath down on me *and when you ran out of examples from the world of fauna and avia was exhausted, I nodded that I had understood. Then Pityu Farkas lifted the veil on the whole big secret, at first I couldn't believe it, it sounded so revolting, I parroted back to him what you'd said about the birds and the bees and, among human beings, mutual love and respect, he laughed his head off so I kicked him in the groin; then he gave me a good hammering. You didn't even teach me how to fight; all I got from you was 'Don't let them get away with it.' That's easier said than done.*

The more
The moral
The more I write, the less it contains what I want I would
    like it to *the point.*

… ---- … ---- … ---- … ---- … ----- … ---- … ---- …

By the time, however, that this letter was ready to send, Dr Balázs Csillag was no longer in the land of the living. Vilmos Csillag did not stop writing. It might take months for him to add or delete a sentence. The point was not the text, but the thinking about it. The fragment of autobiography destined for a non-existent addressee took long years to write.

= =

You couldn't have known Gabi Kulin; we were thirds when he transferred from the Apáczai. Once, during form master's class, we were discussing the oldest Hungarian families, those that can trace themselves back to the seventeenth century, and silly old Boney picked on Gabi Kulin. He was a tall, well-built chap, with girlish locks.

*   I wonder what you would have said if I'd behaved like him: in vain did Boney and the head constantly go on at him about his hair; he didn't give a damn, until the head went ballistic and came in with a pair of hairclippers and cut a swathe lengthwise through his hair, saying, 'Now you will go and get a haircut!'*

Gabi Kulin did indeed go to the barbers' and had another swathe cut, crosswise! God, they almost threw him out.

But that's not what I wanted to say this time; in that class he eventually stood up and declared: as Sir seems to be so interested, I can reveal that my ancestors go back to the twelfth century, because we are descended from the Bán of Kulin, that's why my parents were sent into internal exile to Nagykáta. Boney was speechless and eventually said there must have been other reasons as well. Gabi Kulin snapped back: I am no liar, we had committed no crime and had only the patent of nobility, because the family fortune had been lost at the card tables. Boney ended the exchange saying: sit down, my boy, and don't answer me back.

I became good friends with Gabi Kulin; they lived out in Hidegkút and he had to change four times to get to school. I often went to see them; his mother made the best jam butties. I used often to ask him about his family, and he often answered with wonderful stories. When he asked about mine, I felt ashamed, as I didn't know anything about anyone.

When I ask Mama about her family, she gets everything mixed up. She confuses names and dates. She will not even tell me how the two of you met. I know from Uncle Marci that you were a secretary of Rajk's, but how did that come about? He mentioned that you walked home from labour service, and that the Nazis killed all your relatives. But nothing more. That's all I know about my history.

I feel I have come from nowhere and I suppose that someone who has come from nowhere is headed nowhere. Is that really and truly what you wanted?

Is that really how you wanted it?

Is it??

Father??

~ ~

*

Many things he never ever wrote down. Most importantly the fact that, over time, he did not miss his father less; on the contrary, he felt his absence more. The wound had perhaps healed over, but beneath the scab the infection had become permanent. In the time that remained at secondary school, he brought the house down with his rendering of Attila József's 'With a pure heart' at the poetry recitals. It was enough for him to say the first line – *I have no father, I have no mother* – for genuine tears to course down his cheeks, which students and staff alike regarded as unsurpassable proof of the reciter's skill.

As the years went by, his mother's tongue loosened dangerously; in fact, she could not stop talking. She was now prepared to speak of her late husband, but the picture she painted had no resemblance to reality. Dr Balász Csillag was apostrophized as a model husband with outstanding do-it-yourself skills, who was a leading figure of the antifascist movement during the War, who failed to receive his due only because his noble and sensitive character could not endure the compromises that necessarily had to be made in the course of a leader's life. Vilmos Csillag's modest interpolations ('Actually, it wasn't quite like that …') she rejected with a high hand and a loud voice: 'Come now, my dear Willie, what do you know about it? You know nothing!'

In this one respect Mama was probably right. Although … there were also things that she didn't know of. Vilmos Csillag well recalled his father's last month at home, when his health was still tolerably good and before he was caught in the hospital treadmill. He behaved like a pensioner who had taken early retirement: he rose late, went to bed early, spent all day on the balcony wrapped in a blanket, the crossword in his lap, taking occasional glances at it, when he would quickly insert letters, barely looking. Vilmos Csillag often went out to the balcony and watched as the thinning hair at the top of his father's head was pushed upright by the pillow behind his head. On one such occasion his father spoke. 'My boy.'

He was so surprised it took him some seconds to respond: 'Yes?'

'Tell me. What would you say if I were to move out?'

'I beg your pardon?'

'Your mother and I no longer get on. Marital relations have long ceased. I am a burden to her. I could move in with a former colleague. Start a new life. What do you think?'

Vilmos Csillag was quite thrown by these six fully-fledged sentences. He had already forgotten that his father was male and his mother female, if ever he had thought about it. He found it even more surprising that his father should start a new life when he was so close to ... well, everyone knew what he was close to. Such a turn is completely absurd for ... for such a short period. On the other hand, someone with only a few years (months? weeks? or who knows?) left is perhaps able to take more courageous decisions than lesser mortals.

His father was waiting for his answer, each deep furrow on his brow glistening with an amethyst-coloured drop of sweat.

'But ... why?' Vilmos Csillag asked.

'Long story.'

A dark judder went through Vilmos Csillag as he suddenly imagined his father should no longer be there, an arm's length away. 'Have you told Mama?'

'I've mentioned it.'

'And?'

'She laughed her head off.'

'Huh?'

'She doesn't think I'd dare.'

'Aha.'

'And you?'

'I think ... you'd dare.'

380

'I asked for your opinion.'

'For that I'd need to know why—'

His father broke in: 'I've told you: we no longer get on. What else do you need to know?'

'Well then . . . my opinion is . . . that it's not worth it as long as you are ill. It's better for you here at home, where you get first-class service from Mama, and I'm here too, if needed. When you're well again, you will have time to ponder the problem.'

'When I'm well again,' his father repeated matter-of-factly.

At that moment they both knew that Dr Balázs Csillag would never get well.

His father gave a sniff like a sniffer dog, then buried himself in the crossword on his lap. The conversation was over. Vilmos Csillag continued to watch for some time as Papa got into his stride and rapidly filled the square: whenever he managed to tease out the meaning of a clue, the flicker of a smile played about his lips.

This proved to be the most enduring image. Five years after the death of his father, Vilmos Csillag could summon up his face only with effort, and ten years later, in the man preserved on the black-and-white snapshots, he found it difficult to recognize his father. If he dreamt of him, it was frequently the terrace scene, where he was wrapped in a blanket, his thin hair, pushed skyward by the pillow, tousled gently by the wind, and around his lips that little almost-smile.

His father died before Vilmos Csilla finished secondary school, before he took his school leaving certificate – A*, A*, A*, A (French), A (Maths) – before his unsuccessful entrance exams, three years in succession, for the arts faculty, for law, for stage school, and for the teaching diploma; by which time he was resigned to not going into tertiary education and had to manage without.

About these things

Of such matters

Of all these matters you were unable to *could not know anything.* Nor of *my other lesser or greater achievements* of mine *in the university of hard knocks, in which you might have taken pride. Perhaps. With you it's always difficult to know. When I won the poetry recital competition at secondary school, with 'It's not yet enough', you said you were ashamed that I had read out such pseudo-patriotic poems. Was it my fault? It was a set text! Why did you never make* the stress *the effort to tell me that not all the poems in* that are found in *the textbooks are OK?*

I got no guidance from you, nothing to help me think, no framework or

It's difficult to . . .

You didn't hand on even what . . .

You didn't bring me up to know about life nor . . .

You did not spend time . . .

You did not care . . .

I did not count . . .

I am not reproaching you for anything, but what you don't get in your childhood, you will always miss, and that's not from me but from Jung. I guess you would never have imagined that I would read such books; as far as you knew I was a middling student in every respect. I wonder what you thought would become of me. Did you think about that at all?

I became a professional rock musician. I think that would surprise you, as in those days such a thing did not exist, there was only Studio 11, Mária Toldy, Kati Sárosi, and Marika Németh, who Mama said people loved soooo much, the way only Mama could say sooo much. Can you believe that four guys go on stage – three guitars and a drum, perhaps an electronic

organ – and this band can make ten or a hundred times more
noise than a symphony orchestra?

It's a pity that you can't now any longer by then
It would be so good to talk to you Papa.
FATHER
PAPA
FATHER DEAR
We should have talked.
It would have been good to have talked more.
Or ever
Never

, ,

Vilmos Csillag's visits to the cemetery were rare. In his view
his father was not to be found there: if he existed anywhere
at all, then it was in his, Vilmos's, memory, and it therefore
followed that it made not a whit of difference whether he
visited the area demarcated by others for mourning him. He
argued this view defiantly to his circle of friends and generally won them over.

'My dear little Willie, even the lowest peasant visits his
loved ones in the cemetery. You are the only person who
comes out with this pretentious guff!'

'Get off my back, Mama.'

'Well, you might at least drive me there. You don't have
to come in, you can walk up and down outside. I need no
more than ten minutes, or even less, five!'

This was the trap. You can't turn down your mother's desperate plea, but it would be absurd if, having reached the
arched wrought-iron gates of the cemetery, he were to just
hang around, obstinately clinging to his ideas, while Mama
placed a bouquet in the little marble vase affixed to Papa's
small marble plaque. If I'm going there . . . I'll go in with
her and do the honours.

Since the visit to the cemetery was unavoidable, he kept putting it off, with the wiliest tricks. By the time they got around to it, it was again February, windy and bitterly cold. Vilmos Csillag grumbled: 'We might as well wait for spring!'

His mother launched into a tirade: 'Have you any idea how long I have been begging you to take me? If it's too much of an effort for you, I'll go by tram, like the other peasants!'

This was Mama's trump card, the other peasants, down to whose level it is piteous yet sometimes inevitable to sink. Vilmos Csillag never understood where his mother got her invincible *hauteur*, which decreed that there are us, the cultured ones, all of us potential doctoral students of morality, manners and superiority, and there are, by contrast, other peasants, who have been vouchsafed little or nothing of this. His mother's father – and grandfather – were in all likelihood either unpretentious carpenters in the community of Beremend or perhaps tillers of the soil, in which light the 'the other peasants' tag seemed even more ludicrous. There was not an aristocrat or even an intellectual in genealogical sight, who might have had some genuine grounds for differentiating themselves from the uncouth plebs and country bumpkins.

Vilmos Csillag had no memory of his grandfather and only the very faintest of his grandmother, as if the negative of a photograph; by the time he was five they were both dead. Mama wanted to see their graves also. About the place of rest of the remaining relatives she told her son an unbelievable horror story. The village cemetery which had been the final resting place of the Porubszkys as far back as anyone could remember had been eliminated under socialism – 'sir-shelism', as she pronounced it – the gravestones that could be moved were transferred to Pécs, the bones remained in the ground, and some factory or power station had been built over the site. It sounded insane. Why would

384

anybody want to build a factory right where there was a cemetery? Vilmos Csillag added this story to the catalogue of his mother's mad tales. There were many of these, one more (or less) made little difference.

Sometimes his mother would come out with astonishing stories, and not always in connection with her late husband. The carpenter of Beremend rose to become the proprietor of a factory employing fifty, then a hundred people. By the time Vilmos Csillag grew up, the family home at Beremend had expanded from three rooms to twenty-two. The sand buggy soon acquired an elder brother, a six-horse carriage, which resembled the garish phaeton in Vilmos Csillag's favourite story-book, *77 Hungarian Folk Tales* – though that had belonged to the King of Prussia, not the Porubszkys of Beremend. Their original 2-hectare holding increased five-fold, to 20 Hungarian acres. Dashing hussars turned up, claiming to be related at great-grandfather level or beyond. Vilmos Csillag had only his own, unreliable, memory to draw on when he protested: 'Mama, in the old days you never told me this!'

'Come, come, what do you know about it, my dear Willie? You don't know anything, so it's better if you keep as quiet . . .'

'. . . as shit in the grass!' he completed another of his mother's favourite phrases.

'Exactly.'

Similar transformations were effected in Dr Balázs Csillag's career, in the level of affluence of his relatives in Pécs, and indeed in everything on which Mama gave little lectures. Her parents left Beremend for the capital in 1953, already burdened with serious illnesses. They died here so soon after their move, it seemed as if they had been destroyed by the sins of the metropolis. Vilmos Csillag occasionally felt the desire to find out something about the past, but if he asked his mother, he set off an inflation of the *temps perdu*, the exaggeration of the people who lived in the past, and he felt that he ended up knowing even less than before he put his questions. He could not understand what joy Mama could find in making such notorious overstatements – the most polite term that might be used for this activity.

The mustard-yellow Dacia came to a stop by the flower sellers' stands and he immediately took charge: choosing the flowers, paying for them, and gripping his mother's arm as if she were too frail to walk by herself.

The grave of the grandparents was covered by a modest slab itself covered in greenish lichen. Under it the text: DEUS MUNDUM GUVERNAT.

Once Vilmos Csillag asked: 'But weren't they Jewish?'

'Not very.'

'How can someone be not very Jewish?'

'You can if you don't want to be. They became practising Catholics after the war and paid regular visits to the Basilica. And I pay my tithe to the Church to this day.'

'Tithe? I had no idea there was such a thing.'

'There are many things of which you have no idea, my dear Willie.'

Vilmos Csillag had a sneaking suspicion that GUVERNAT should really have been written GUBERNAT. He wasn't sure. He never took Latin. He had studied Russian for eight years, but he did not consider himself competent to correct a Cyrillic notice. He had no talent for languages. What *did* he have a talent for? Good question.

In his own judgement he had not gone very far in life. In his mother's judgement, he had got nowhere at all. The Sputniks, a band which spent the summers doing gigs around Lake Balaton and in winter performed at shows organized by the state-managed National Organizing Office ORI, was difficult to take seriously, even though they

386

had a single released on the state label Qualiton, and the radio had recorded four of their own compositions, three of which were approved for broadcasting. Of these numbers 'The Pier at Szántód' reached the semi-finals of the 1972 Pop Festival, which is to say that television viewers had the opportunity to see and hear The Sputniks on two occasions. This was his tally at the age of 26. He had composed the music for 'The Pier at Szántód'. The first line of the chorus – 'What we lose on the swings, we get back on the roundabouts, yeh, yeh' – was, for a few months, on every teenager's lips. Mama was rather proud of her little Willie at this time, laughing as she received the congratulations of her friends. But in private she was none the less advising her son: 'Quit while you're at the top . . . I'm sure now you'd get into university – apply!'

'For what?'

'Arts, law, economics, does it matter which? The important thing is that you have a degree.'

'Why? Have you got one?'

'Oh my dear Willie . . . First of all, I'm a woman, and anyway we were at war when I might have gone to university, and then, on top of that, there were the restrictions, don't you know?'

'You mean the Jewish laws?'

'Come, come, why do you have to put everything so stridently?'

'I'm not putting it stridently, the matter is already strident. Were you Jewish, or weren't you?'

'You can't really put it like that.'

'Yes or no?' Vilmos Csillag had lost his patience.

'Why are yelling now? Is this what I deserve?' She was already in tears. The elaboration of the topic was again postponed. Vilmos Csillag didn't force the issue. He would have got no nearer to the truth if he had found his mother in one of her loquacious moods. When the kosher butcher in

Beremend happened to come up, he discovered that he was Mama's first cousin and had an exceptional singing voice. If, however, Vilmos Csillag pressed her on whether he sang in the synagogue, he got only small change: 'He sang wherever they let him.'

Once it turned out that, when things got very bad, Mama had taken shelter at her girlfriend Viki's.

'You went into hiding?'

'Oh my dear Willie, everyone was in hiding then! There were already air-raids!' and Mama would quote at length the radio announcer of the time and his announcements of the air-raids.

From the many tiny crumbs Vilmos Csillag eventually pieced together that old Porubszky must have been Slav (Serbian?) or some kind of *Mischung*, but his wife was perhaps entirely Jewish; her maiden name, Helen Ganzer, is suspect but not 100 per cent proof of Jewishness. How do we know she wasn't one of the Swabian German minority in Hungary? Either way, we can surmise that under the terms of the Nuremberg Laws, Mama might just as well have been deported in the same way as the whole of Papa's family. Including me, if . . . Of course, in real life there is no 'if'.

His mother speeded up when she saw the grey blocks of columbarium. From the back of an old phone-list, she read out his father's numerical address. Vilmos Csillag remembered only that the vast number of identical faux-marble blocks formed a square and his father's grave was somewhere in the top row.

And so it proved.

DR BALÁZS CSILLAG
(1921–1966)
REQUIESCAT IN PACE

*

The two dates were obscured by the small vase, the size of a man's fist, which Mama had paid for a year after the interment, though it took the unreliable monumental mason three months to attach it to the stone. Mama had fumed continually: 'Why in the name of the Virgin Mary does he keep promising if he's not going to do it! Why in the name of the Virgin Mary does he take my money if he can't manage to spit out when it will be ready? Does he think I can give him money in advance until doomsday? What does he think I am, the State Bank? What in the name of the Virgin Mary does he think he's doing!'

'Mother, can we leave the poor Virgin Mary out of this!'

'You have no say in the matter!' His mother was in one of her aggressive moods.

At such times, Vilmos Csillag kept well clear of his mother, like a frightened dog of a bullying one. My mother is a dog that bites as well as barks, he thought. And how! When Mama was in fighting mood, her mouth would not stop. Most often she spoke only to herself, but quite loud, her eyes half-closed and gesticulating wildly. 'If you think you can get the better of me, you have another think coming! You can't get the better of me, everyone who knows me knows that, no? I couldn't care less how long he has been manager in the Benczúr Street supermarket, I have been a customer there just as long, and that's what really matters. Don't you think?'

To those 'don't you think's only those who did not know Mama would have the temerity to reply. The pause for breath was too brief for a response and the torrent of words would resume without flagging, with a 'Do you think so?' inserted all too rarely. Vilmos Csillag, when a callow youth, was infuriated by these monologues of his mother's. He asked her once: 'Is this a conversation, or are you doing a solo?'

'I'll give you what for, young man! As if I didn't have

389

enough problems, all I need is that my son should sharpen his tongue on me! What do you mean you've run out of milk? You should order as much as is needed! Milk and bread are basics which it is your duty to guarantee to every citizen! Don't you think? Even if you're left with some over, that curdles or rots! Of course I have put it in writing in the complaints book – you shan't be sticking *that* in your shop window! I filled the page and more! It's an outrage! The customer has rights! Don't you think?'

Even at Papa's grave Mama began one of her rants when she noticed that someone – probably relatives of the man who rested below Papa – had stuck their three stems of roses *onto our vase*, the petals hung over Geyza Bányavári, born 1917, died 1966, mourned by his wife, son, daughter, and the others. This was fat in the fire for Mama, her eyes rotated in their sockets and with fingers splayed she stabbed the air: '*And the others*! Incredible! I'm surprised it doesn't say *Uncle Tom Cobbleigh and all*! But why don't *the others* buy themselves a vase, or his daughter, or son, or his wife? Why do they have to violate ours? Don't you think? What right have they? What grounds have they?' The wilting rose of Geyza Bányavári flew off, together with its wire clip, far away onto other slabs.

Vilmos Csillag was ashamed of himself for how little patience he had with his mother, and he promised himself countless times that he would hear her out patiently, lovingly even, because you can't hope ever to educate your mother. But when that next time came, he could not swallow the lump of anger that formed in his throat after sixty seconds of his mother's rant. They had monumental rows with Mama slamming the door and running off, even when they were in her flat. Shall I go after her? Shall I wait till she comes back? She'll come back anyway . . . Won't she? Don't you think? He bit his lip. Come, come, not you as well.

He was 22 when he moved out to Zugló on the Pest out-skirts, into a flat vacated by a musician friend, where the landlady was as deaf as a post, so that her restrictions – no women, no late nights, no ear-splitting yeah, yeah, yeahs – did not have to be taken seriously.

His mother took great offence when he announced the move, but tried to put a good complexion on the matter. 'Why should I object? This is the way of the world: the children grow up, fly out of the nest and build their own.'

Vilmos Csillag enjoyed thinking about how he would furnish his new residence, a room with its own front door and including a toilet, which he found unfurnished. He took it out on a long lease, as he saw no chance of ever buying a flat of his own. Perhaps when his mother . . . no . . . may God preserve her for many a year. He felt a pang of religion at such times, though this did not happen often. He was incapable of believing that there was someone in charge of his fate, or who even took a close interest in it. If he had had a guardian angel, she would doubtless have ensured that he did not end up as a crazy rock musician, in a risky, dead-end career.

Not for a long time had he been excited by anything as much as by the move. At first Mama was glad to help. But the cloven hoof soon showed through: not for a moment did she imagine that her son would take all his stuff and leave her alone in the 76 square metres that would all be hers. 'In fact . . . it would be more sensible if I took your flat. I don't need more space than that, then you could stay here . . . and sometimes you wouldn't mind if I stayed in the maid's room . . . don't you think?'

'Aha! Right! I move out so that we can still live under the same roof?'

'Spare me your sarcasm, my dear Willie, pretend I didn't say a word. Your will be done.'

Vilmos Csillag gave a roar of pain: 'On earth as it is in heaven, don't you think?'

His mother's eyes were like glass marbles: 'How come you know that, Willie dear?'

'Come, come . . . you made me go to RE in '56 . . . or have you forgotten?'

'Oh, that was so long ago, I thought you'd forgotten it all. I wanted to fulfil your dear grandmother's wish, may she rest in peace.'

Again and again she offered reasons why it was unnecessary for her son to move out. We've got a flat, she would gladly let him have the two big rooms, the maid's room off the kitchen was enough for her, she wouldn't use the bathroom as there was a washbasin in the smaller loo. Vilmos Csillag then asked why she had said before that she had no objections to him moving out. His mother at once beat a retreat: 'Fine, fine, let everything be as you wish, I shan't interfere.'

Don't you think? – added Vilmos Csillag to himself. Or do you think? When his bed, desk and bookshelf were being loaded into the band's minibus with the help of one of the roadies, she was dancing attendance around them, holding doors, suggesting how the furniture should be lined up, altogether as if the person moving was herself. But as soon as Vilmos Csillag took his seat by the roadie, she burst into tears and waved him off as if he were setting out for the Eastern Front. Vilmos Csillag felt awkward when he saw the passers-by. But there was no need: who cares what complete strangers think?

Shortly after this a three-man outfit invited Vilmos Csillag to join them as their fourth for a six-month trip to Scandinavia. Stockholm, Oslo, Bergen, playing on cruise ships. He hung fire. 'I . . . er . . . get seasick.'

'Seasick? You are brainsick, if you pass this up!' said the front man, who had worked out that they could each make enough for a second-hand car. 'A two-year-old VW, no sweat.'

Father,
I'm going away now and I don't know if I'll come back.

I've written this for you *to you during in the course of* over
the years.

If you get it, perhaps you will understand,

This will make it clear at least

That *I think of you*. More than you might imagine.

Ciao.

Ever,

Your son

Willie

Vilmos

. . . .

He put the sheets into a thick envelope which he sealed.
The day before his departure he took it out to the cemetery.
He had to wait a while until there was no one around the
block of columbariums. He put the letter on top.

He told his mother over the phone that he would not be
coming back. She had difficulty catching his drift. 'What do
you mean, my dear Willie, that you're staying out?'

'Oh mother . . . I'm sure you're the only person on earth
who needs a commentary.'

'All right, don't shout, but what happens when your exit-
visa runs out?'

'Sod the bloody exit-visa, I shall apply for asylum. I'll get
a Nansen pass.'

'Nan-sen?' She said it as though it were a swear word.

'That's what they call it, don't you think?'

'I see . . . but why won't you just come back?'

'Because it'll be better for me here. I'll earn loads, I'll
send you money, I don't know how you do it yet, but I'll

find out ... Don't worry, everything will be fine ... I've more or less settled in here, I'll soon have my own flat ... half the band is staying, that's to say me and another guy ...'

'Oh my God! What are you going to do there?'

'What we've been doing so far, playing music to drunken Norwegians.'

'But does that mean ... I'm not going to see you again? Is that it?'

'Come, come. You'll visit here first thing, I'll organize everything.'

'Oh my dear Willie, how lucky your dear father is no longer alive! This would be his death!'

'Of course it wouldn't, he would be delighted at his son's good fortune, that he's free and doing well ... believe me, Mama, everything will be just fine!'

'So ... you really ... really aren't coming back?'

They were both silent for a long time. At length the mother uttered the dark, sad sentence: 'So I shan't have a son ... or a grandson ...'

'Why shouldn't you have a grandson?'

This languid interpolation went unheard by his mother: 'You know you are the last of the Csillags?'

'All right, Mother! Don't cry. We'll speak again. Take care!'

When he put down the receiver, Vilmos Csillag felt that every part of his body was bathed in sweat. I have defected ... there are no more Csillags on Hungary. This ungrammatical phrase signalled the beginning of the decline of his knowledge of his mother tongue.

Eight years were to pass before his application for a visa to return to Hungary was granted. While he was still in Europe it never crossed his mind to apply. Anyone who left the Hungarian People's Republic was automatically treated as a traitor and villain.

394

Vilmos Csillag was unconcerned: for a long time he didn't even want to hear the word 'Hungary', never mind return.

From Scandinavia he went to Paris, then over the seas. In America he could not find work as a musician, with a repertoire of Anglo-Saxon classics that no one was interested in hearing with his accent. He worked as a waiter, then found a job with UPS, driving the cream-brown vans, delivering everything from the *Encyclopaedia Britannica* to Mayflower dishwashers.

He met his wife on his flight to the New World. Shea was half American-Hungarian and half American-Indian, born in Delhi, where her father had just set up a taxi company. The firm foundered as rapidly as the marriage, and Shea was taken back to the States by her mother, to the poorer part of Brooklyn where the grandparents, who had emigrated in '33, still lived. Shea was small, delicate and loud, and what Vilmos Csillag most liked about her was that loud mouth of hers, as she picked her way with balletic ease through the five languages that she spoke fluently, or the sixth, seventh or eighth, of which she knew only a few words. If they were in an Italian restaurant, she would converse with the waiter exchanging Verdi operas, in an inimitable Neapolitan accent. Even in the Chinese restaurant she could come out with a flawless sentence or two, bringing a happy grin to the face of the bowing staff. She could deploy a dozen words the way a resourceful housewife can in moments rustle up a tasty soup from leftovers in the larder when unexpected guests arrive.

Intellectually Vilmos Csillag felt like a dwarf by Shea's side, unable to master even the English language sufficiently to prevent the appearance, upon his very first words, in the corner of the Americans' mouths of that impersonal, tight smile they reserved for foreigners. Life with Shea was as frivolous as a stylish outing; it mattered little what the following day would bring. If ever they got hold of a bit of money, Shea at once found a way of spending it. She did not care for Vilmos Csillag's anxieties: 'We only live once. Don't you think?'

The musicality of her voice was an erotic stimulant for Vilmos Csillag, so for a long time he failed to realize that the girl was mocking his English pronunciation.

Their son was born so soon that perhaps Shea had fallen pregnant on the first flight they shared. In fact, then it was only their fingertips that did any wandering, under the light fake fur blanket of the Pan Am. Vilmos Csillag was in despair when she announced: 'I've got news for you. You can jump a generation.'

The penny took some time to drop. 'You mean ... You're ... ?'

'Oh yeah! Aren't you glad?'

'Oh dear ... I haven't even got my green card quite sorted out.'

'Don't you worry, I'll see to it. I'll see to everything. If I see to it, you'll be happy?'

Shea did in fact manage to see to everything, the only thing she couldn't see to was Vilmos Csillag himself. For him the USA remained enemy territory, where he dared move only with extreme care, lest he step on the little land-mines of everyday life. Such as any official document or printed matter, or telephone conversations with strangers. He never got as far as to listen without worry if someone turned to him unexpectedly in the street or a public place.

What was natural for Shea, always remained burdensome for him. In vain did Shea urge him to pay always by credit card; he preferred cash, because every time he handed his credit card to the assistant, waiter or checkout girl, his stomach would automatically contract, worried that perhaps they would take it and not bring it back.

They had endless discussions about the child's name. Ultrasound revealed that it would be a boy, of average weight. Shea longed for some exotic name, in tribute to her Indian side, but Vilmos Csillag had trouble imagining a son who might be called Raj after the famous actor, or Rabindranath, after the famous poet, or Ravi, after the famous sitar-player.

'Every male name in the US begins with "Ra"?' asked Vilmos Csillag.

'Don't be so sarcasatic! In Hungarian there's lots of *es*, so what?'

'Yes, but you have an American name.'

'Unfortunately. You should be proud of your origins.'

'And you don't think Rabindranath Csillag sounds idiotic?'

'I do. Because of the Csillag part. You should adopt a more sensible name . . .' though as she saw his eyebrows rise, she corrected herself: 'I mean, one that comes well, goes well here . . . Csillag is quite a tongue-twister for them, they say Chilleg or Kersilleg, do you want that? Why can't you be Vilmosh Star! William Star! That's fantastic, don't you think?'

The 'don't you think' still reminded him of Mama, still whimpering in 4 Márvány Street. With the exhibition of photographs on the chest of drawers. The wedding photo. Papa in uniform. Vilmos Csillag in the regulation photo of the Hungarian Album of Baby Smiles, tummy down on an obscured table, legs swimming in the air. Then the school-leaving photo. The promotional shot, stamp-size, of The Sputniks cut out of the *Radio and TV Times*, with the caption: 'Fresh talent in the semi-finals!'

If there is fresh talent, then there must be stagnant, dried-out, and even rotted talent, he thought; that's me now.

As for his son's first name, he immediately rejected 'Star' and, in line with his wife's principle that 'You should be proud of your ancestry' he also rejected the Indian forenames, after the briefest of considerations. 'And anyway, the child's three-quarters Hungarian and only a quarter Indian.'

Shea admitted this. They agreed that out of practical considerations they would choose a name that existed both in English and in Hungarian and furthermore was not too much of a tongue-twister for an Indian.

'What was your father called?'

'Balázs Csillag.'

'That's out, with that zh noise at the end. Grandfather?'

'Well . . . one I don't know, the other was I think . . . Mishka. Or Miksha!'

'You're crazy. You don't know the name of your grandfather?'

'That's the least of it. I know nothing about my clan.' The word sounded old-fashioned.

Shea laughed. 'Your *clan*? You mean your ancestors!'

'Nor them.'

'You're crazy! You're not even curious?'

'I'm not crazy. But there's no one to ask.'

He began to explain that only his mother was alive, and it was difficult to talk about such things with her; she would generally change the subject, saying: 'Come, come, my dear Willie, why rake over these ancient things!'

'But then maybe there's a skeleton in the cupboard!'

'You've been watching too many cop shows on TV.'

'How do you know? You may be war criminals!'

'You're crazy!' He quivered as he said: 'Us being Jews.'

'So?' Shea knew precious little of recent European history.

Shea continued to bring up the topic from time to time. She simply could not believe that Vilmos Csillag knew so little of his past.

'If you'd known my father you'd understand.'

Though even in adulthood he could not understand. How can you bring up a boy in such a cocoon of complete silence? 'I know nothing at all. I tried to work things out from the odd remark here and there; the results are meagre and confusing. I barely know the names of my father's parents, let alone those of his parents' parents. He never spoke of either. He was a broken man after labour service, I know, and then there was the Rajk show-trial, and the chronic, ever-worsening heart condition: these are reasons, but no excuse. This is not something he should have neglected. Perhaps if he had not died so soon . . . I was still wet behind the ears, didn't ask often enough, didn't suspect there was so little time left. Or rather, I did suspect, yet this was never on the agenda. As for Mama, well, she is much too scatter-brained to be a credible source.'

The more he went on, the less he understood it himself.

Henry Csillag came into the world at the Flatbush Medical Center in Brooklyn. His life hung in the balance as the umbilical cord twisted round his neck and almost strangled him; his skin turned blue, panicking the medical team.

For a long time Shea would not let her husband near her, claiming that the gynaecologist had said it would take time. In the end, she admitted she had lost her sexual desire for him. Vilmos Csillag was thunderstruck: 'What do you mean you've lost it? Where has it gone?'

'If only I knew! Believe you me, I don't understand it myself.'

'But then . . . what's going to become of us?'

She did not reply. Vilmos Csillag recalled a line from the desperate housing ads in the Budapest papers: 'Desperate: any and all solutions considered!'

But his wife did not read Budapest dailies. 'What do you want to consider? I move out? You move out?'

Vilmos Csillag realized that things were serious. Shea had stopped caring for the child. From time to time she exhibited the classic symptoms of a heart attack: sudden sweats, her right arm went numb, for several moments she would lose consciousness. They went the rounds of the men in white coats, from gynaecologist to psychiatrist: a lot of technical terms were tossed around, like vegetative neurosis, panic attacks, postnatal depression; she received any amount of medication and counselling; she was recommended sleeping cures, group therapy and courses in yoga. All in vain. Henry – his father insisted on calling him Henrik, the Hungarian form, often adding 'the Eighth' – was cared for by his father.

He was sacked from UPS for his notorious tardiness. About this time Shea landed in a New Hampshire sanatorium, only partly paid for by social security. Shea's mother offered to let her son-in-law and grandson live with her, though she was herself on welfare. Her tiny home was near La Guardia Airport, on the Brooklyn–Queens expressway, and the windows rattled day and night as the traffic rumbled by on the eight-lane highway.

For a long time Vilmos Csillag looked for, but failed to find, any work. He ended up at the airport, though not at La Guardia but at Newark, which it took him two hours to reach. His job was to stuff luggage into the bellies of the airplanes and to remove luggage from them. This was a sphere of activity that seemed particularly to attract exiles from Eastern Europe: there were two Poles, a Bulgarian, three Romanians, five Russians, a couple from East Germany and even an Albanian. No wonder I'll never learn English properly, thought Vilmos Csillag.

'Hungary!' the word popped into his head once after a particularly tough shift. Even Hungary has to be better than this.

He rang the Embassy, only to be told that he had to apply in person. The federal capital is half a day's journey from Brooklyn by car, though not in his twelve-year-old Impala, which two-thirds of the way there began to sound as if armed terrorists were firing from the radiator, and then gave up the ghost. The yellow AAA car soon rolled up behind him, but after one look under the hood, the AAA man slammed it down again. 'You can kiss this rust bucket goodbye.'

After several hours trying to thumb a lift, he was picked up by a truck carrying horses, but this took him no further than Delaware; here he exercised his arm in vain, until night fell. He walked on to the nearest rest area and spent the night on a bench. The next day he managed to reach the Hungarian Embassy, in a state that did little to inspire confidence. But that was not the only reason they treated him like a leper. The face of the lady clerk reminded him of burnt toast. A sourcunt, he decided, the long-dormant word bouncing around his head with a pleasant little buzz.

It turned out that his situation was not hopeless, because after his illegal departure from the Hungarian People's Republic the criminal proceedings normally pursued in such cases had not been issued and so – as the woman in the blue suit put it – he had 'no judgement' on his record. Even if there were, it would be theirs, not mine, he thought.

'But don't imagine, Comr . . . Mr Csillag, that you will be met by vestal virgins garlanded with flowers!' she said. 'And don't forget to obtain an American passport for Henry Csillag from the US authorities, as he is a US citizen.'

He was informed that the application for the child's passport had to be accompanied by the written consent of the mother, since Henry was a minor. Vilmos Csillag did not imagine this would be a problem, but Shea was adamant: 'You are not taking my child anywhere! You get me? I'd be insane to entrust him to a halfwit like you!'

'Insane pots and kettles!' he burst out, regretting it immediately. Shea began to rant and rave and, like the genuinely insane, her mouth filled with yellow froth, and brought two nurses running and a white-coat who held her down while she was given an injection in the arm. Shea changed to English and began to prattle at such a speed that

Vilmos Csillag could not make out a word. *She always does this when she wants to get the better of me.*

Every attempt to bring up this subject with his wife resulted in the same fit of rage. He had no choice but to admit defeat: US citizen Henry Csillag – who by then had learnt the capital letters not just of English, but also of Hungarian – could not be taken with him to the old country. This made him feel insecure and uncertain again. *Will they ever let me back into the US? If not, will I ever see my son again?*

To these questions the answers of the lady clerk with the burn-toast face were reassuring. 'Why shouldn't we let you go back to him? You're hardly a national treasure.'

Vilmos Csillag agreed.

'And anyway, those days are gone. The Hungarian People's Republic is no prison but quite a decent little socialist state, with human rights and everything!'

What might that 'and everything' be? Vilmos Csillag asked himself when, after a change of planes at Zurich, the Swissair flight landed at Budapest-Ferihegy. The captain thanked the passengers in both French and Hungarian for having chosen to fly Swissair and expressed his hope that they would soon be seeing them again on one of their flights. *Amen to that*, thought Vilmos Csillag.

Following this, they were not allowed off the plane for another forty-five minutes. Outside the sun rose ever higher, the temperature inside the plane rose even more rapidly, and sweat glands were in overdrive. It was May 1982, yet Budapest was receiving him with something like a summer heat-wave. His passport was subjected to thorough scrutiny by a border guard in a khaki jacket, then slipped into the latter's breast pocket, the flap buttoned. The guard stood up: 'Kindly follow me!'

He escorted him to a narrow room, where he was interrogated in considerable detail about the manner of his leaving

402

the country; based on his answers, the interrogator dictated the official record of the conversation to a typist who was fighting a constant battle to stay awake in the heat. All this took hours. Vilmos Csillag asked if he could have a word with his mother, who was sure to be waiting outside, but permission was refused. His passport was not returned; the official said this was likely to be a short-term retention, until his case was closed, and he would be given an official receipt.

He was allowed to go. He tottered out of the building, which compared with the airports in America seemed like a doll's house and was by now deserted – the arrival time of the next flight was not yet up on the arrivals board. His mother was not there. Not a taxi in sight. He sat down on his suitcase. He had a vague notion that there was a bus service to the MALÉV office in Vörösmarty Square in the centre of town, but he had no idea how to find it. At length a distinctly private-looking Skoda rolled up, and the driver offered to take him into town for a thousand forints.

As he climbed out of the car, he saw an old woman in the doorway of his block, who was shouting something and heading for the Skoda. It took him some time to register that it was his mother running towards him. They embraced and his mother covered him in sopping kisses and was already chattering away, saying how overjoyed she was and what a delicious meal she had cooked for her dear Willie. Her *s*s, *sh*s and *ch*s sounded odd. Goodness . . . Mama has false teeth.

In the evening at the dinner table, when Mama's dried fruit turned up on his plate – they had always been Mother's proud speciality – he began to feel that he had come home. His mother was convinced that pears or plums that had been expertly dried never go off; in fact, this is precisely what arctic explorers, mountain climbers and astronauts should take with them. 'And if there is a little white bloom here and there, that doesn't matter. It's not mould, just a little um . . . salt.'

The salt of life, thought Vilmos Csillag, popping a fruit in his mouth. But it isn't salty, it's sweet, crumbly, a bit tough. You have to keep trying to swallow if you want to get it down.

Next day they took the tram to the cemetery, this time at Vilmos Csillag's request. He would have ordered a taxi, but his mother said no: 'Oh my dear Willie, you're not going to waste your money on those thieves, they are out of their mind, they demand such a huge tip, and public transport here is fantastic, I know where we have to change trams, I've even bought you a ticket!' And Mama's will was done: they trundled along on the trams, riding into the gentle wind.

By the time they got off the last carriage, the sun had taken shelter behind the grey cotton-wool clouds. There was much lively buzzing of insects around the flower-sellers. Vilmos Csillag immediately felt at home and took the initiative as in the good old days, selecting a mini-bouquet for Mama's parents and short-stemmed roses (so that they would fit the little vase) for his father.

They had difficulty locating the Porubszkys' grave, it was so overgrown by moss. The gravestone itself had turned black and only someone who knew where to look would have been able to read the words DEUS MUNDUM GUVERNAT. His mother tore at the stems of the wild plants, panting, and regretting that she had not brought with her a little spade or even shears.

'Do you have a spade at home?' asked Vilmos Csillag.

'No, but I could borrow one.'

'Who from?'

His mother stared at him, her eyes clouding over. 'Just give me a hand, will you!'

They spent a long and awkward time there, with little result. In the end his mother gave up: we'll have to come again, properly armed. She placed the mini-bouquet in the middle, lit two candles, and began to pray. Vilmos Csillag could read her lips. Hail Mary. Our Father. Perhaps I should pray too, he thought, but it felt a little foolish to imitate his mother.

The site of his father's grave they missed entirely. Mama rocked her head to and fro helplessly: 'I don't understand it, it must be here, I swear!'

Vilmos Csillag's stomach was on the verge of exploding when he spotted the grave of Geyza Bányavári, born 1917, died 1966, mourned by his wife, son, daughter and the rest. Above – where he remembered his father being buried – now lay Dr Sombor Máva, 1955–1980. He had 25 years, Vilmos Csillag calculated, but only in order to delay the other, ghastly thought. Mama too had discovered Geyza Bányavári and began to hyperventilate: 'What is this? What's happened? How ... What on earth ... ??' Her breathing became irregular, and she crumpled by the columbarium, barely able to breathe, as her face turned the colour of blood.

One of the cemetery gardeners took them back to the main entrance on his little truck and offered to call an ambulance from the office, but Mama wanted to do something quite different in the office, and Vilmos Csillag had some difficulty preventing her from smashing the sheet of glass that separated the desks from Reception. She gave vent to a variety of inarticulate noises, and the girl in the sailor's blouse, who represented the state funeral company, attempted like a keen student to work out from the fragments she uttered what in fact Mama's problem was. Then she turned the pages in thick, black folders until she got to the bottom of the matter: 'Dr Balázs Csillag's urn contract expired on 2 January 1976, my good lady, because that was when the ten years expired.'

'But why wasn't I informed?'

'Do you have any idea how many cases like this we have to deal with? It is quite impossible to notify everyone by post; but we always put up a poster showing which individual graves or urns have expired. Even then there is a period of grace which may extend for between twelve and eighteen months. If during the period the relatives of the deceased fail to appear to sort the matter out and arrange an extension, the company can do little but vacate the unlawfully occupied places.'

'Expired! Vacate! Outrageous!' His mother shrugged off Vilmos Csillag's calming hand like a dog just out of water. 'Now they don't even leave the dead in peace! Some "eternal rest"!'

'I'm truly sorry, madam, there is nothing else I can say. I would imagine that someone who does not visit their dead for so long can be presumed, as far as the company is concerned, not to consider them important.'

'Why should it not be important? Just because recently I've been rather busy and have come more rarely, it . . .'

The girl in the sailor blouse lost her temper: 'Madam, your deceased was removed five and a half years after the expiry of the period of grace! And only now has it occurred to you to visit?'

'Five and a half years? Quite impossible!'

The girl felt she had the upper hand, and shrugged her shoulders: 'Minimum.'

'All right, all right. How much will it be to restore him to his place?' Mama pulled out her worn folder which she used as wallet and licence holder.

'Unfortunately, it is not in our power to do so.' The girl's lips stiffened into thin, parallel lines.

'And if I may be permitted to ask, why is it not in your power to do so?' A measured reply always whipped Mama to greater fury.

'Because the ashes from expired urns are placed in a

common grave, which is then thoroughly disinfected and covered with earth.'

Mama had to have the words repeated to her three times before she could take in their import. She was incapable of dropping the matter and screamed and yelled as she demanded to speak with the superior of the girl in the sailor blouse and then – having got nowhere with the stubby little fellow – the manager of the cemetery. Her wish could not have been granted, even if they had made an exception to the rule in her case, because the several hundred metal boxes taken from the urns and thrown into a common grave bore no markings of any kind, so no one could ever identify the remains of Dr Balázs Csillag. Mama's sobbing and the stabbing pains in her heart, and the holding up of all the staff at the cemetery, was all in vain: she had to come to terms with the fact that her late husband's ashes had ended up under the sandy grass of a plot in a place whose location could be given only approximately. She sat until closing time at the edge of the plot, on a broken-backed bench, continuously sniffling and blowing her nose.

Vilmos Csillag knew that she was inconsolable. He just stood behind her, his hands resting on her shoulders.

They were strap-hanging in the tram when he finally gathered the strength to ask her: 'Mama, how come you did not visit Papa for so many years?'

His mother's eyes were veiled in tears. 'It was constantly on my mind, I always meant to, and then something would always come up.' She was crying again. 'What a lazy, miserable wretch I am . . . Yet it is not right that he survived the War, the POW camp, the Rajk trial, only to end up in an unmarked grave like some criminal. This is not what this good man deserved of me, after so many happy, cloudless years together . . . ours was a model marriage, I tell you, model, everyone admired it.'

407

It was hard to let this pass. 'Come, come, Mother, you're not serious!'

'Why not, my dear Willie? A lot of bad things can be said of your dear father, but he was all his life a model husband and father.'

'Really? You think that a model father is one who practically never speaks to his son?'

'Yes, well, perhaps he was a bit taciturn, that's true.'

Vilmos Csillag's dander was up. 'Model husband, eh? Who when he was seriously ill was thinking that he would move out?'

His mother was thunderstruck: 'Where did you get that from?'

'From him! That's what he said!'

'You've made that up. To annoy me.'

He knew that for the rest of his life he would regret it but he had no mercy on his mother. He told her the whole story, sparing no detail.

His mother just listened, hooting frequently into her handkerchief. Vilmos Csillag's aggressive mood evaporated. Well now, what good did that do? he asked himself.

His mother said to him the following evening: 'You're angry with me for . . . losing Papa like this?'

He shook his head. We've lost everything else already anyway, he thought.

He felt he could not just sit at home all day and began to look for temporary work. He found some in the big covered market, where a schoolmate had a business dealing in live fish. Vilmos Csillag used a net to lift carp, catfish and zander from the glass aquaria; for a tip he would clean them and slice them up. He was constantly planning his return to the USA, and constantly postponing his departure. At first he exchanged letters weekly with Shea and his mother-in-law in Brooklyn, then the exchanges grew less frequent. His son on the photographs grew by leaps and bounds. He had begun to write a few childish lines himself. The forms of address and the closing formula would be in beginner's Magyar, the rest of the letter in English. He signed himself HENRYK.

Mischung, thought Vilmos Csillag.

The months went by. He longed to see his son again, though perhaps not strongly enough to take the necessary steps to do so. The illness that struck his mother out of the blue again wiped out the possibility of making the trip in the short term.

In the period of almost a year which it took for his mother to make the journey from the Kékgolyó Street clinic to the cemetery, Vilmos Csillag's hair had begun to turn grey. He hoped Henryk would turn up for the burial, but he sent only a telegram of sympathy, in which there was only one word of Hungarian, the family name of Vilmos Csillag. Shea and her mother are no doubt bringing the kid up to hate me.

Now he found it truly difficult to say why he was in Hungary. He sold the flat in Márvány Street and deposited the money in the Trade Bank, in an account from which, according to the current regulations, he could withdraw it in stipulated amounts when travelling abroad. No problem. I'll fetch Henryk and we'll have a holiday by the Balaton.

His plane landed at Kennedy Airport. He was not met, which did not surprise him. He was reluctant to spend money on a taxi and took the inter-airport shuttle bus. While he worked in Newark, the drivers had been prepared to stop for him on the corner of Northern Boulevard, only fifteen minutes' walk from Shea's mother. This time however the Sikh-turbaned driver would not make this illegal drop, so he had a walk of at least half an hour ahead of him when he dropped his two suitcases on the traffic island.

He remembered the area and knew that if he could get over Grand Central Parkway, he could make his walk much shorter. But the multi-lane expressway teemed and roared with vehicles, searing into his brain with the howl of

409

wounded wild animals. Without bags maybe he could have zigzagged across, but with two suitcases he had no chance. So it had to be the long way.

He walked along the ramp that led to the pedestrian bridge along an auto scrapyard. It was lighting up time, at least in theory; but in this part of the world it was the exception to find a working bulb in the streetlights – the street kids liked knocking them out with catapults.

Beyond the scrapyard the road, made of imperfect concrete blocks, turned down towards an oily garage entrance. In the building, half sunk into the ground, there were windows like those of the workshops in Vilmos Csillag's secondary school. In two places the broken panes had been replaced by ones that did not fit. This plot must have long ago gone bankrupt: the doors hung open and the name of the firm, KLINE & FOX, THE WIZARDS OF FORD, had broken off at one end and hung down in the wind, making a slight creaking noise. It was witty. He was pleased he understood the word play on 'The Wizard of Oz'. Abracadabra, just watch my hands, one, two, a Ford for you, air-conditioning, leather seats, power steering . . . He knew how to say 'power steering' only in Hungarian; it never needs to be said in English, because every car has it.

KLINE & FOX

He tried to get closer to the English pronunciation. Kline must have been Klein, the Fox perhaps Fuchs and then . . . more Jews . . . oh yeah. He imagined them. Béla Klein, no, Albert Klein, no, better: Miklós Klein, piano-maker. They fled here during the Great War from Kispest. Miklós Klein, starting out as a hawker, then vacuum-cleaner salesman, later office worker at Ford, meets Ödön Fuchs . . . Jenő Fuchs . . . Richárd Fuchs . . . Aha these Baradlays from Jókai's masterpiece, *The Sons of the Man with the Heart of Stone*. So it's Rezső Fuchs that Miklós Klein meets, and by then they've become Ray Fox and Mike Kline, and deciding to open a car showroom with a garage for servicing, they win Ford's approval, the business prospers, they go from strength to strength, right until the Crash, when . . .

No, they must have been flourishing here even last year, as the oil marks are quite fresh. He had left the scrapyard behind and was wheezing, so he put down his suitcases and sat down on them. When he continued on his way, he felt pitifully weak.

Is it possible that some grandfather or great-great-grandfather of mine also came to America?

He had to pause more and more often, his jacket and trousers were drenched; fat slugs of sweat lodged at the roots of his hair, stinging his scalp.

He was quite close to the Project, as the bleak housing estate where Shea's mother lived was known, built at the end of the Fifties as part of the comprehensive urban plan to help the poorer families of New York. Every inch of concrete surface had been painted some garish colour by hippies? addicts? the homeless? God knows who.

He could still hear the roar of Grand Central Parkway and the Brooklyn–Queens Expressway – it was the latter that made Shea's mother's life hell. The noise now reminded Vilmos Csillag of Niagara Falls. Like a million other Americans, that was where they had gone on their honeymoon. He would never forget the moment in the mountainous seas of the bay when the motorboat took them beneath the foaming torrent. Enhancing the visuals was the sound of a thousand billion drops of water cascading onto the agitated surface of the bay. Niagara Falls, Vilmos Csillag said, imitating his wife's accent not entirely successfully.

'Whassup?'

Two coloured men were kneeling on the concrete, by some burning rubbish, the acrid whiff of which just at that moment stung Vilmos Csillag's nostrils. He couldn't reply;

he had first to clear his throat. 'Just a minute,' he said in a whisper.

'Is this jug talkin' to us?' said one of them, in a worn-out black leather jacket, and trousers of similar stuff, which allowed strips of his knee to be seen.

Vilmos Csillag didn't understand the word 'jug': 'Whassup?'

'You mockin' me, shithead?' The other guy was somewhat younger, twenty to twenty-two, jeans but stripped to the waist. His chest, shoulders and arms were a riot of coloured tattoos.

Vilmos Csillag didn't understand this either. He was amazed at the way the designs on the man's skin merged into each other. He was still coughing.

'Git yo ass out of here fast!' said the leather jacket.

'Yo kin leave the stuff!' said the younger one.

Vilmos Csillag was not familiar with Bronx slang and clung to the handles of the suitcases in some uncertainty. From the tone of voice he understood aggressive intent of some sort, but didn't think that his insignificant goods or person could prompt anyone to act. As soon as he had caught his breath, he gave a sort of nod and said: 'Nice to meet you.' Then he walked on.

He had learnt that this was a harmless greeting. He did not for a moment suspect that the original sense of these words might, in this particular circumstance, be regarded as an act of aggression. Before he knew it the two black men had knocked him to the ground and begun to kick him. The one with the naked torso had a pair of Doc Martens, the other basketball shoes or trainers. Vilmos Csillag tried to roll towards the latter. He waited for them to stop; after all, what was the point of all this? A Hungarian sentence came to his lips: 'Enough already . . . I've nothing against negroes!'

'Nigger? Did you say nigger?'

A hail of heels and toecaps hit him in the groin, in the

412

eyes, on his nose, and when the Doc Martens got him in the testicles he lost consciousness. He saw again Niagara Falls – overexposed colour Polaroids taken by Shea, and black-and-white images shot by himself.

After a while the two men tired of battering the motion-less body.

'Is he still 'live?' asked the leather jacket.

'Look, he's still movin'.'

'Lessee his stuff.'

They took everything he had, sharing out his money and throwing his wallet and papers on the fire. The leather jacket wanted to keep his credit card, but the other took it from him and threw that too on the fire: too risky. They tore open the suitcases, but took only a pullover and a pair of shoes. The presents brought from Budapest all ended up on the fire, and the items that burned most fiercely were the matrioshkas that Vilmos Csillag had bought from an unshaven trader in the underpass by the Astoria Hotel. They opened the two small bottles of Tokay, but found it too sweet.

Vilmos Csillag came to at dawn. He felt his body weighed several tons and had been trodden into small pieces. Something dreadful had happened to him, yes; at first he was unable to recall what. He drifted in and out of con-sciousness. He saw what remained of his belongings: his favourite velvet jacket lay like a wet washrag in the dust.

As the evening cooled he finally managed to sit up. He was horrified to find, on touching his face, that there was an aching knot where his nose had been. A thin sound that must have been weeping seemed a miserable comment on his helplessness. He needed food, drink, a doctor, other-wise . . . He had lost his past and he was now very near to losing his future. I must stay conscious, he mumbled to himself. The sound bubbled out of his mouth unarticulated; he was missing four or five of his teeth.

He had a feeling that his cries for help would not be answered; at most he would attract the attention of figures like his attackers, if anyone. He crawled forward, in pain, on all fours, towards lights that shone more intensely. He saw jagged stars jumping around before his eyes.

Those lights came nearer only very, very slowly.

He did not notice that he had reached one of the open spaces near La Guardia, in the opposite direction to where he was originally headed. Large notices warning NO TRESPASSING indicated that strangers were not permitted here. Despite this, the local boys played baseball and football here on Sunday mornings, until the security guards chased them off. Vilmos Csillag himself had once played softball here with his fellow employees.

He reached a bushy patch and could only zigzag ahead. He was shivering with cold, though the first rays of the sun had begun to light up the land. I'll have a little rest, he thought, and sank to the ground. He lay on his side, in the position of the embryo in the womb; this was the way his vertebrae were least painful.

What will my son say if I turn up looking like this?

This was his final, his very final thought. He sank into a sleep from which he was never to awaken. Above his head blossomed the American version of the laburnum. It slowly let fall its blazing yellow blossom on Vilmos Csillag.

Two weeks later his body was found by three children who ran into the bush to pick up their frisbee. The sheriff of Great Neck visited the scene. At the end of the year the file was placed in a drawer marked 'unsolved'.

No prospect of further evidence coming to light.

Perpetrator or perpetrators unknown, victim unknown.

File closed.

XII

THE LONGER WINTER TAKES A-DYING, THE MORE spectacular will be the spring. On the last of the days of bitter cold, the land awakens to the morning chorus of the songbirds, and from the bottom of its heart yearns for the rebirth now approaching. There is not long to wait, soon we shall be welcoming the purest of colours, smells, tastes, forms and combinations, which may yet, in spite of everything, make the world a better place. At times like this it almost seems that nature is trespassing on the territory of art.

In Budapest everyone had a more favourable opinion of Henryk than he had of himself. His lanky form could have been quite manly if he had not been so hunched up and obviously lacking in self-confidence. When he spoke, a few uncertain errrm or hhhhh noises came out first, hopefully harbingers of more meaningful words. If he was excited he chewed his lips incessantly and tore the skin from the surface of his thumb until it bled, and sometimes beyond. Though he strove to speak his father-tongue flawlessly, he often, almost unconsciously, used English expressions in his Hungarian. Most of his statements ended up curling into questions, even if he was 100 per cent sure of what he was saying, which was rare.

In company he would sit in the corner, with an offended expression, eyeing those who managed to relax. Very common, that sort of behaviour, he said, or rather thought, though not very secretly he envied them. On his Macintosh Classic computer he opened a file in which he wrote diary-like notes, quite unsystematically, whenever the spirit seized him. In Hungary he did this in a Hungarian which was at first strewn with errors. He clung fiercely to his out-of-date computer, and if anyone suggested that he replace it, he would be shocked: 'But this is an industrial classic!' pointing out that one of the prototypes had been placed in the Museum of Science and Technology in Washington D.C.; he had seen it with his very own eyes. He had read three books about the rise of the Macintosh empire: he imagined the two teenagers as, in the garage of the parents of one of them, they put together the user-friendly computer, whose success had laid the foundations of the worldwide megacorporation.

This miraculous tale reminded him of the tales he had been told as a child. At night his father would sit by his bed and, eyes half shut, launch into 'once upon a time', and the littlest boy would set off into the wide, wide world to seek his fortune, a trusty stick in his hand and a satchel on his shoulder, always filled with the ash-baked scone. After exciting adventures he would be rewarded with half the kingdom and the hand of the princess, just as the Macintosh boys won fame and billions of dollars. So – it seems miracles can, and do, still happen.

Henryk was educated at undistinguished public schools. Flatbush Community School and Lee High School had barely any white students apart from himself. In the lower school, black was the typical skin colour; in the upper school, it was yellow. He was well versed in their talk, as fluent in black slang as in the nasal drone of the yellow-skinned population. The teachers were glad if they managed to survive the classes without fighting breaking out. Most of them carried weapons or defensive sprays in their pocket or bag.

It was thought that Henryk was a little weak in the head. When asked to solve a problem at the whiteboard he could often only croak; in vain did they chain the felt-tip to the board, someone always stole it. The more discerning teachers brought their own, the less discerning gave up using the whiteboard altogether. But the number of discerning teachers in those schools was few. Henryk had three times to endure the disgrace of repeating a year, but somehow, over twelve years, he managed to overcome the tribulations of compulsory school attendance. None of his teachers noticed that he was basically a lad with a good brain and it was only his memory that failed him. Even material he had crammed with utmost attention simply did not stick: by the time his turn came, the numbers and names had become hopelessly confused in his head, though he could remember with crystal clarity which page of the book the text in question occurred and in what type, colour and layout. He could see it; he just couldn't read it. At the age of ten he had been given spectacles which he had hoped would help, but they merely enlarged the lines of letters and figures – he still could not read them.

His absent-mindedness was already legend when he was very small. If his grandmother – whom he called Grammy, because of the prize – sent him down to the Chinese grocery, where their purchases were put on the slate, Henryk nearly always forgot what he was supposed to be buying. His requests to Mr Shi Chung, whose grandchildren were often his fellow students, were pure guesswork. If Grammy gave him a list, he would leave it at home or lose it. Once in school he had to fill in a form and he left both parents' names blank, as he could not recall them. His excuse – that they were long dead – was not accepted by Mrs Marber: 'A white Anglo-Saxon Protestant lad should always know of which family he is the scion!'

Henryk would have been glad if he had understood even the word 'scion', a Middle English word that his teacher had first encountered in Shakespeare. He blinked desperately behind his glasses, as he always did when an answer was expected of him. The unreliability of his memory did not improve with time; in fact, it worsened. He was too scared to utter the names of close acquaintances, lest he get them wrong. He was right; he often did. Even more insurmountable were the barriers presented by numbers. If he had to go to 82 Harvey Avenue, he was bound to ask at No. 28. In vain did he want to write everything down, because as soon as the figure 82 was uttered in his head it turned into 28 (or 39, or 173), and this was what came to the tip of his nib. He hated to make phone calls, because the integers he read out of his diary disintegrated the moment he lifted the receiver. He would look up the number again, but his memory, like a magnet without strength, dropped the number well before he had to dial. He had to prop the booklet open and lean it against the phone to ensure that he scanned the right line all the way to the number's end.

But he could remember images and tunes flawlessly; so he became the pillar of the mezzo section of the school choir. Grammy would have liked him to study music, but there was no money for tuition. The singing teacher at Lee High, Mr Mustin, sometimes took him in hand, and taught him to play the flute, but Henryk lacked the patience to read music. At the age of ten he scored quite a hit with his freehand drawings and in the pottery class of the high school his jugs and jars made a mark, but he gave up pottery quite soon after Miss Lobello remarked on his thick glasses. There was no denying that by the end of primary school he had reached pebble-glass stage: in the huge lenses his pupils looked like restless fish.

Despite Grammy's efforts, Henryk did not apply to university upon graduating from high school. He was sure his results would not get him into any but the most mediocre state universities, whose degrees were worth little more than toilet paper. He had two plans of action: 1. He would apply to join the Navy, where they take everyone who can take the strain; a career in the military is not so bad in peace time. 2. He would apply to work in the lawyer's office on Roosevelt Avenue (47, or was it 74?), where he liked the look of the well-endowed secretary. In summer he delivered pizzas for Domino Pizza, where the basic rule was that if they failed to deliver within 30 minutes of the order being placed, the customer got his pizza free. In the lawyer's office the secretary nearly always welcomed him with the words 'The thirty minutes are up!' – but she was usually joking. Henryk, however, invariably responded: 'In that case, your pizza is free . . . Enjoy your meal, ma'am.' And backed out of the premises, not for a moment lifting his gaze from the woman's ample cleavage. In his wet dreams he would nuzzle those warm peaks.

Plan A fell through quickly, his pebble glasses causing his rejection. Plan B seemed to be working, however: the secretary passed on his offer to her employer and the firm's owner called him in for a job interview. 'And why have you picked on us to apply to for work?'

'I am attracted by the truth.'

The square-built lawyer gave a nod and offered him the post of dispatch rider (bicycle), with effect from 15 September, on two months' trial, absurd weekly wages, and support of a very low order: 'Then we'll see.'

Henryk accepted. Grammy will be pleased that I've got a job, he thought. Anyway, there's a whole long exciting summer ahead.

He made friends with two boys at school: Koreans of small build, they barely came up to his chin. The two Koreans were planning a backpacking tour of Europe. Henryk worked on Grammy until she agreed to him taking out his savings from the bank, savings built up over several pizza summers, so that he could go with his friends. They crossed the pond on a charter run by a low-cost airline, a student-only flight on which they served neither food nor drink. The Koreans had brought large supplies of food, which they gladly shared with Henryk, though the overspiced dumplings gave him stomach cramps and he had to queue every half-hour for the toilet in the tail of the plane.

Their route was largely determined by the Youth Hostel Guide: they tried to visit towns where, on the basis of the youth hostel's price, location and cleanliness, the editors of this book gave a high number of points. Not a single hostel in Eastern Europe earned the maximum 10 points. The one in Prague was awarded 8, Budapest 7; the latter was available only in the summer, as the rest of the year it was a hall of residence. The two Koreans were not interested in Eastern Europe. 'Now that there is no Iron Curtain, it must be like Western Europe, only poorer,' said one of them.

Henryk told them that he was of Hungarian origin and would like to see the old country. When the other Korean heard this, he backed off, but in the end he saw that South Tyrol and Italy were also attractive. At this point they were still in Vienna and agreed to meet ten days later in Venice, which, though it lacked a good youth hostel, could not be missed out.

Henryk crossed the border from Austria into Hungary in the cab of a German lorry. He thought that he would feel a surge of emotion – but nothing happened. Undistinguished customs buildings, indifferent uniformed guards, similar to other crossing points in Europe; only the queues were longer. .

He had mixed fortunes hitchhiking to Budapest. This form of transport, which had been unknown to him, he had read about in Brooklyn Community Library, in a publication entitled *Europe on $25 a Day*. In the Netherlands he experienced for the first time how complete strangers would stop and actually give a lift to those giving a thumbs-up on the wayside. He loved it. He could not understand why aging hippies who were there alongside him thumbing, moaned that the golden days of hitchhiking were over, that drivers were now afraid of hitchhikers. It wasn't like that in the Seventies! The final leg he did in a car shaped rather like a brick, oddly rounded at the front and back, which gave off a terrible smell. The driver, T-shirted, perhaps only a little older than himself, could manage a few words of English. When Henryk asked about the car, he began to explain it was a Warburg. 'East German make.'

'But there is no East Germany now. Or is there?'

'Iz nat. Bat ven dis one made, still wars. Iz two . . . rhythm.'

'Rhythm?'

'Togeder cam benzin end oil.'

Henryk smiled and nodded vaguely, as if he understood.

When the sign for Budapest first appeared on the motorway, the driver asked him where he was headed. Henryk pointed to the address of the youth hostel in his book.

'Lucky. Heer vee are bifore it.'

The cement block of the hostel in Budaőrs reminded Henryk of the public hospital at Queens. The same day in the downstairs café he met a couple of dozen Americans. They took him to the brand-new pubs of the capital, where the punters spoke almost only English. 'This is the gold-rush time here,' explained Jeff McPherson, in a strong Irish accent. 'Pay a bit of attention and you can make your fortune here!'

Henryk paid a bit of attention. A week later he wrote to

Grammy to say he would be staying in Hungary until the end of the summer. He asked her to send him his Macintosh Classic by UPS, which had opened an office in Budapest.

It is fascinating for me to visit the land of my ancestors. I am sorry you are not here with me. Don't you feel like coming over now? I can send you a plane ticket.

It turns out my Hungarian is a lot better than I thought. Grammy, why don't we speak Hungarian together? After all, you're Hungarian too, aren't you?

Mama and Papa would be open-mouthed: now you can get almost anything here. In places they will even accept my credit card. It's a shame they never lived to see this.

He often thought of the two little Koreans, wondering how long they had waited for him in St Mark's Square by the arcades. He hoped it was not too long.

Grammy's long reply arrived with unusual speed.

My dear Henryk,
I'm glad you're enjoying yourself in Budapest. To me, you know, it's almost a foreign city, for as you know we hail from Szekszárd, in the south of the country, as I told you.

Szekszárd? He could have sworn that he had never heard this before. Is that still inside Hungary? He checked the map.

Szekszárd . . .

From somewhere in the dust-covered years of his early childhood a little ditty rose to the surface of his consciousness. Szekszárd's my birthplace, a stage-star's my lovegrace! – Papa used to say it to Mama when things were still OK. They would laugh at this appropriation of a line

422

from the poet Mihály Babits. He, Henryk, the toddler, tried to repeat after them: Sixard! Sixard! – which Papa liked so much that he would grab him and toss him in the air, with Henryk squealing, Mama squealing, even Grandma squealing, Papa would toss him up again and again, higher and higher as he rhythmically roared: Szek-szárd's my birth place, a stage-star's my lovegrace!

Only once did my parents take me up to Budapest, when I was ten, as they were trying to arrange my emigration papers. We stayed in the Hotel Hungária, by the Danube. Go and take a look, and think of me.

Henryk could not fulfil this request. He found no Hotel Hungária on the Danube: its place had been taken by the Forum Hotel and the Intercontinental.

My crazy husband always planned to take us on a grand tour of Europe, the high point of which would have been a trip to Hungary, taking in Szekszárd, which he pronounced Sixard, just as you did when you were small. But he was never able to realize his plan. Like most Indians, he lived in a dream world, not on the ground. I think you don't even know what he was called. Although I have told you before, you never pay attention. Am I right? You don't know, do you? Ganesh Kupar. That was his name – may the soil lie light upon him – when I met him in an eatery in Lee Avenue, Brooklyn. I was a dishwasher there and he a waiter. Yes, my dear little Henryk, that's how our life began. He was a restless man, continually driven by his hot blood, and I could not hold him back from doing anything he wanted to. Before I knew it we were in Delhi, flat broke, in a filthy alleyway, where 70 per cent of the inhabitants used the street both as toilet and bedroom. I had to get away from the danger that he signified, back to the US and to my parents. I never married again.

Henryk had a feeling that he had heard his grandfather was from India, but he had never put two and two together and thus realized that this meant he had Indian blood coursing in his veins and that was why his skin was so dark. Most of the cabbies in New York are Indian. Sikh, to be more precise: that is to say, from the military caste. Some even wear their turbans while driving. They are like . . . at the end of this train of thought the penny finally dropped: So, that's why . . . Some days before in a restaurant in Buda the fiddler had asked him: 'Are you a Rom?'

'I beg your pardon?'

The bulky fellow nodded significantly as he returned to his band: 'The bugger denies it.'

Henryk didn't know this word.

It's very kind of you to invite me to come, but I have no wish to stir up in my soul everything that I put the seal on long ago. I doubt if I could speak Hungarian. If Magyar words come into my head, each has some painful memory attached, so I would rather not force the issue. You wouldn't really understand. Have a good time over there, enjoy life, then come home!

By then Henryk was a salesman in the newly opened showroom of Macintosh Hungary. By August he had advanced to journalist, writing reports for the first English-language weekly, in the *Scenes from the Life of the Capital* column. Of the seven-man team, four were Americans, and of these he spoke the best Hungarian. The cultural column was in the hands of Ann (a blonde with legs reaching up to her armpits, she wrote nearly all the articles). She had two hobby-horses. She insisted on spelling her name without a final *e*, unlike most bearers of it; and she insisted with the same intensity on her American colleagues not behaving like dumb assholes in Hungary, but taking an interest in the

424

art, literature and customs of this small people. As soon as it became clear that Henryk was basically Magyar, she immediately regarded him as a fellow spirit and took him under her wing.

Since I have been living in Budapest, I have every reason to feel satisfied. Everything that did not succeed at home is working out here, better than I could have imagined. Here my shyness and unusual behaviour is accepted, including my less than perfect knowledge of the language. My finances are also in order. Without my having to make a particular effort, things are working out by themselves.

Ann crafted his application for a work permit, attaching the recommendation of the chief editor. She also got him a room to rent, though this soon proved superfluous, as he moved in with her. Ann lived out in the Csillaghegy area, renting the loft of a large detached house with a garden. The loft had been converted into a single large space with a gallery kitchen, with only the tiny bathroom hived off in one corner. When Henryk first climbed up the narrow hen-run-like ladder, he could not believe his eyes. While the lower two levels of the building looked very much like those of detached houses in the outer suburbs, in the loft space part of a Scottish castle had been constructed. In the generously sized fireplace, the U-shaped iron arms holding the logs, the bellows, the poker and the fire tongs could all have come straight from the time of Shakespeare. The oak-panelled, uneven walls were decorated with old firearms and country scenes. There was furniture to match, notably the dining table for twelve with ramrod-straight chairs.

The family whose hospitality Ann enjoyed had built their home by themselves, with their own bare hands, one might say, and when she rented their summer kitchen, there was as yet no roof on the house. The man had been broken down by the many years' effort he had put into the house, and had retired on health grounds. 'That is, he was forced to take early retirement.' Seeing their sad plight, Ann proposed that she would finish off the house, including the loft, in return for living there rent-free until she recouped her costs.

'So how long can you live here without having to pay?'

'Seventy or eighty years for sure.'

Ann's fellow lodger received Henryk with a warning rumble. The mongrel Bond (James Bond) was pitch-black and the size of a sheep.

'Don't worry, he won't hurt you!' Ann reassured him as the dog planted a heavy foreleg on each of Henryk's shoulders and panted directly in his face. She was right; the dog wanted only to be loved, its massive tail thumping the floor like a flail.

Henryk became fond of the creature, though he was not best pleased when Bond (James Bond) insisted on joining them in bed when they made love. 'I haven't the heart to chase him off. He was a stray, you know, and strays take everything to heart. He has no one apart from me.'

This sentence struck Henryk like a sharp arrow. I, too, am a stray dog, he thought.

In the company of Ann he set off to find the Hungária. But it turned out that Ann was thinking of the old Hungária Café, which was now called the New York. Henryk was resigned to this, but the tall blonde never gave up. In an English book on the history of Budapest she picked up the trail. She read it out to Henryk. 'The Hotel Hungária was one of the jewels on the Danube Corso, a much loved rendezvous for the local young people at the time. At the end of the war the Allies bombed it and the ruins were dismantled.'

426

Henryk did not want to send this news to his grand-mother, with whom he exchanged letters once a week. Grammy inquired when her little grandson was coming home, and he replied that he was planning to stay and it would make more sense for Grammy to come to Budapest.

They took Bond (James Bond) for walks by the Danube, and the enormous dog soon became well known on the Csillaghegy stretch of the river. Despite his intimidating appearance, he never troubled other dogs or animals, and was roused to anger only if he thought Ann was in danger. But then he would attack without further ado.

One evening, as they took three-quarters of an hour for their walk, Ann related the story of her parents' lightning divorce, since which she saw her father twice a year, at Thanksgiving and at Christmas. Her mother lived in Philadelphia; she was an illustrator of children's books. The actual stories were written by her father, in Florida. Once they had made a great team. Ann was herself the heroine of some of the stories, in her own name, which she enjoyed as a child but later found irritating and even offensive. Since her university years she had drifted away from her parents. Her mother's small-mindedness she found just as upsetting as her father's thick-headed stubbornness. Her mother's parents were Scots, her father's of Dutch origin; from her she inherited her freckled skin and maize-stalk hair, from him the surname that broke a thousand lips: Schouflakkee.

'So you're not really Ann Jagger?'
'Yes, I am now. I changed it.'
'Mick Jagger the inspiration?'
'Of course.'
'I would prefer to be Lennon. Henryk Lennon.'
'Go for it!'

427

When Ann asked him about his family background, Henryk told her the little he knew.

'Would you be interested in looking for your ancestors?'

'How?'

Ann explained that in Hungary it was now possible to go back through the parish registers up to about the middle of the nineteenth century. If you know when and where your father was born, you can find his birth certificate. That will contain some information about both parents, things like place and date of birth, perhaps their address at the time, maybe even their occupation. If you are sufficiently persistent, you can often find the grandparents' marriage records (you make a guess about the likely wedding date and rifle through those years), in which you can find information about the father and mother of both husband and wife. And so on. 'You only come to grief if you're stuck for the place, because you must look in the district where they were born or married.'

'How do you know all this?'

'I wrote an article about it. The Hungarians have gone crazy about their past. Hordes of them are having their family trees reconstructed, looking for their noble coat-of-arms and their old property deeds.'

Henryk first took the train to Szekszárd. Having the data about Grammy's birth to hand, he thought he had a pretty straightforward task. He had managed to make himself understood by the lady in the office, when it turned out that he did not know Grammy's maiden name. He decided to phone her. His grandmother gave a whoop of joy on hearing his voice. 'Henryk! So you are here!'

'No, not yet. Grammy, what was your maiden name?'

'Pardon?'

'Your maiden name! Can you hear me?'

'Yes. Don't shout.'

'All right, just tell me quickly, because my phonecard is

running . . .' The line went dead. He bought another in the shop. 'Grammy, please, before it runs . . .'

'What do you need it for?'

'Complicated. I'll tell you in a letter, just tell me what it was!'

'No . . . I'd rather not.'

'Why? Are you ashamed of it?'

'No . . . but . . .' Again they were cut off.

I was a little shocked to hear you asking about my maiden name. I am not a criminal to be hunted down *[his grandmother wrote in her next letter]*. To cap it all, I have told you this, too, many times. I was born Rachel Steuer.

'Your grandmother is either German or Jewish,' Ann opined. 'I thought as much.'

'Which did you think she was "as much"?'

'Jewish.'

'Why?'

'That's what they're like.'

'What are they like?'

The girl did not reply.

'You can't say that sort of thing! That's the beginning of fascism!'

'No, it's the beginning of your unbearable oversensitivity!'

'Even an elephant would be offended by this!'

'The shit it would!'

They had such a row that Henryk almost moved out.

On his next trip to Szekszárd he discovered that there had been no fewer than three Rachel Steuers born in Szekszárd on Grammy's day of birth. The girl in the office was surprised: 'Three Rachel Steuers on the same day in the same small town!' She had an access of communicativeness and told how she came from Paks, but her parents' house, where she had been born, was acquired by the state and razed to the ground. 'They needed the space, you know, for the Paks nuclear power station.'

Henryk did not know. He hurried to fax the photocopy of the appropriate page of the register to Grammy in Brooklyn, via the Roosevelt Avenue post office. His grandmother's reply was not long in coming.

As I've already told you, I have no interest in my past – thanks, but no thanks. But you were always as mad as a March hare. Have another look at my letter; what I wrote was Steiner – STEINER –, not Steuer!

Henryk was ashamed. In his computer he copied this odd-sounding name a hundred times, one under the other, in New York Bold type, half an inch high. Despite this, he was unable to remember it. 'Not Steuer, but Stouer!' he said, when Ann asked what his grandmother had written.

In Hungary it's always third time lucky. It's a folk saying, I heard it from the doorman. My third trip to Szekszárd had a resulting outcome. That is to say:
Rachel Steiner was born 3 July 1927, in Szekszárd at 6.30 in the morning. Father: Walter Steiner, farrier; mother Gabriella Duba. Both living at No. 18 Retek Street. Father R.C., mother's religion not stated.

On the mother's side this is as far as I have got.

Ann clapped her hands in joy: 'Farrier, that's fantastic! Congratulations! Put it in your CV.'

'What exactly is a farrier?' asked Henryk.

As soon as he was told, the scenario began to unfold before him: Walter Steiner, tall, muscular, bare-chested, the face of Marlon Brando, body like Arnold Schwarzenegger,

430

brings the gigantic iron hammer down on an anvil incandescent with heat, pauses a second to take breath, wipes the sweat from his brow, lowers the hammer, placing it by his feet, just like that statue Henryk saw on Dózsa György Way.

He was constantly sending his CV (in the end he did not put his farrier ancestor in) to Budapest branches of the large multinationals, because he soon grew bored with journalism. But that was not all he grew bored with. At first he was unwilling to admit it, but his ardour towards Ann was cooling; it was only Bond (James Bond) that he continued to adore.

As the leaves began to fall, Grammy acknowledged that her grandson would not be visiting Brooklyn in the near future. 'I'm arriving tomorrow,' she told him on the phone.

Henryk's heart welled up with love for his grandmother, which he seemed to have forgotten in the recent feverish weeks. 'Goody, goody, groovy Grammy's coming soon': he made up a little song as he danced around the loft flat.

Ann understood. 'She's coming here? You mean *here*?'

'Well . . .' he drooped. 'Where else is she going to go?'

'But this is my home, only I can invite her to stay.'

'Yeah? Well, invite her.'

'How can I invite somebody I have never even met?'

Henryk stared at her and for a while they looked each other steadily in the eyes. Then Henryk started to pack. He called Jeff McPherson. The fellow knew at once who was on the line. His characteristic Irish brogue resonated in the receiver. 'Hi Henryk, long time no see. What's new?'

'All sorts, Jeff. Jeff, would you put me up for a couple of nights?'

'Here's the address.'

Jeff lived on the winding road up to Buda Castle, on the top floor of a four-storey house, also a loft, or as the Americans liked to call it, a penthouse. Seems the Americans love these, thought Henryk as he hauled his gear up four flights, then another level, up the spiral staircase. No lift.

He enjoyed the welcome drink by the kitchen bar and apologetically confessed that tomorrow they would be joined by Grammy. 'Sorry!'

'No sweat! Perhaps she'll make us paprika chicken.'

'If she manages to climb up.'

'Hey, we'll bring her up ourselves!' Jeff's good mood was a ray of sunshine that lit up the darkest corners of life. By midnight Henryk knew that the flat was Jeff's own, as it was now possible for foreigners to buy property in Hungary. By two in the morning he had heard that Jeff bought and sold property, buying run-down houses, renovating them and selling them on at a hefty profit. By four in the morning, that Jeff preferred men, but there was no problem, he only went for men like Doug, his partner, who was on a business trip to Romania. 'He likes to travel, I don't. We make a good pair.'

Black-and-white photos of Doug were everywhere. Doug in the Palatinus lido. Doug in Venice. Doug at Lake Balaton. Doug in Ibiza. Generally in swimming trunks but at least half-naked. Henryk thought he looked like he imagined his farrier grandfather to be.

They drove out to meet Grammy in Jeff's ivy-green sports car. At the last minute Jeff managed to conjure up a cellophane-wrapped bouquet for the old girl. 'I can't help it, flowers are my fatal weakness.'

Grammy was bowled over by Jeff. 'A fine strapping fellow, your friend!' she whispered to him in Hungarian, so only he understood, from the dickey seat. Her sparse hair was tied in a girlish ponytail and fluttered in the slipstream.

'What does strapping mean?'

'Nice. Decent. Substantial. Don't they say that any more?'

Henryk didn't know.

Jeff made them dinner, Chinese. 'Canard laque!' he declared with some ceremony as he whipped the ornate lid off what looked like a silver dish.

Grammy was spellbound. 'And what do you do?' she asked Henryk. The conversation was in English.

'I'm in between jobs just now.'

'He's joining us,' said Jeff with an encouraging smile. 'We're in property, that's the going thing at the moment.'

Henryk's grandmother left after three weeks, secure in the knowledge that her grandson had rounded the corner. Jeff showed them the country house whose renovation was next on the agenda. The old lady burst into tears. The building reminded her of her childhood in Szekszárd. Jeff offered to drive her down to Szekszárd, especially as he had never been to the area, but Grammy declined. 'There is nothing left there of what's in here,' she said, tapping one temple.

Jeff insisted throughout that Henryk was a business partner. As Grammy's plane rose into the sky Henryk thanked him for this white lie. Jeff shook his head. 'No lie, sonny Jim, we need new blood . . . If it works out, you can have a share in the company . . . You'll be working for Doug.'

Henryk soon rose in status to partner with the right to vote in the limited liability company, whose name – originally JED (Jeff & Doug) – was for his benefit changed to HEJED, which came out almost as YOURPLACE in English. HEJED made successful property deals not only in Hungary but also in Transylvania and Slovakia. They were especially good at converting medium-size lodges and country houses. Doug, the Canadian giant, proved unequalled in resourcefulness in his dealings with builders and craftsmen, many of whom were scared of him. He bounded about the scaffolding like a mountain goat, in a white plastic helmet bearing the legend EASY.

Jeff negotiated with buyers and did the paperwork, while

Henryk's brief was the internal refurbishing. He bought period furniture on his trips around the villages, and had them restored either by experts or, sometimes, with his own hands. He had never derived as much pleasure from any job as came to him from this. He was particularly thrilled by fresh wood shavings and the smell of glue.

In the evening they would sit around at Jeff's (Henryk had moved into a flat of his own a couple of streets away) and drank historic Hungarian wines as they browsed through books and albums of art history. Henryk acquired serious specialist knowledge of furniture, carpets, and especially lamp styles; in the Lamp Museum at Zsámbék he was the only regular visitor. The nouveaux riches treated the phone number of HEJED Ltd as if it were the password to enter the circle of the top hundred thousand.

Henryk's first car in Hungary was a ten-year-old ATV, a Cherokee Jeep, bought from one of Jeff's drinking pals. He gave it a test drive to Pécs. In the county archives he was received much more cordially than he expected; they accepted his solemn word that he wanted to carry out scholarly research and gave him a temporary reader's ticket. In the place which seemed like a school hall, an elderly archivist attended to the researchers' requests. Henryk confessed to him that he was searching for his ancestors.

'What is the name of the family?'

'Csillag.'

'*Echt* Pécs folk?'

Henryk did not understand the word *echt*, and nodded uncertainly.

'What was their line of business?'

'Unfortunately, I don't know.'

A few weeks earlier he had visited the state registry in Budapest and on the basis of the date of birth they were able to supply him with a document about his father. *Vilmos Csillag, b. 5 Feb. 1950. Father: Dr Balázs Csillag (1921),*

Mother: Mrs Balázs Csillag, née Mária Porubszky (1929). Both resident in Pécs.

It was this trail that had led him to Pécs. He showed the document to the archivist. He read it carefully and then suggested: 'Choose one name, and on the basis of the year of birth, start looking at the year.'

'Which should I choose?'

'I would try Dr Balázs Csillag.'

Nothing. Henryk thumbed through 1920 and 1922 as well, just in case . . . His hands turned black, but in vain. No sign of grandfather. Or grandmother.

'Are you sure they were born in Pécs?'

'No.'

'Because if they were, they must be here. Ah, just a minute, could it be . . .' and he leaned closer, almost whispering, 'that they were Jews?'

'Yes. Could be.'

'You don't know.' It sounded like a statement, not a question.

'They have all been dead for many years.'

'Fortunately, we hold a certified copy of the Jewish registers, from '49 onwards.'

In the Jewish register Henryk at once found Dr Balázs Csillag – he was born on New Year's Day. Nice, he thought. Every new year they could drink to the memory of grandfather as well. In the OTHER REMARKS column he found the following note: *UB 238/1945. The above-named, on the basis of document number 67/1945 from the First Pécs Parish Office, has this day, 25th August 1945, converted from the Israelite religion to the Roman Catholic faith.*

He read it over four times, word by word, before he managed to fully grasp its meaning. The old archivist leaned over from the far side of the narrow table, their heads almost meeting above the brick of a book. He lowered his wizened finger onto the rubric. 'To be quite honest, I have never seen such a note in a register of births.'

'So this means my grandfather was a Jew at first, but then later he . . .' He did not complete the sentence.

'The family suffered a lot in the hard times, didn't they?'

'That's just it . . . I don't know. I don't know anything about it! Let me try Mária Porubszky.'

'Go ahead.'

No Mária Porubszky.

'It seems she was born elsewhere,' said the archivist.

'So that's it, is it?'

Henryk's American accent made the old archivist smile. This hurt Henryk and so he did not ask his questions, though to some of them he might have received a reply. The archivist suspected that the young man should head for the Jewish cemetery, for if a family is from Pécs, there is a chance of finding an uncle or two or a great-grandparent, and if he were to return with a year found engraved on the gravestone, he might have more luck in his search. But in America Henryk had been brought up to do things himself and he did not ask for advice. He managed to reach the Jewish Cemetery anyway, though he had set off for the main cemetery. At the office there he was told that they could check the old registers for his Csillags only if he knew the exact dates of death.

'Take a look in the Jewish Cemetery!' suggested one of the officials.

He had trouble finding it and twice drove past it in his Cherokee Jeep. The entrance was up a narrow side street: an iron gate painted black in the middle of a yellow brick fence with a handwritten sign in pencil: RING LONG AND HARD! He did so, but no one came. He returned some hours later to find the gate wide open.

Dr Balázs Csillag, Mária Porubszky, he kept repeating the words to himself, like the first line of a prayer. Will they be here?

436

My grandfather was a Jew but he did not want to be. Because the Jews were persecuted here during the war. But the war ended on 25 August 1945. What is the point of becoming a Roman Catholic then, if he remained a Jew all the way through the dangerous times? I don't understand.

Another question presents itself. Does this mean my father was a Jew? And that I am a Jew as well? At the Jewish Community office they said that it was the mother that counts. My mother was half Indian, half Hungarian. Jeff says Grammy is highly suspect, a Steiner, particularly a Rachel, is obviously Jewish. Grammy says no, she says a farrier could not be Jewish and was more likely to be a Swabian, that is to say, a German settled in Hungary. But then why would a German family have to flee from here? I don't understand this either.

According to the archivist, just because someone was a Roman Catholic, he or she could easily have been a Jew. Confusing. He says those who converted were none the less hounded by the Arrow Cross (Nazis). So in the end what am I, with all these ancestors? Indian, Swabian, certainly Jewish, perhaps Jewish, converted Jewish, and of course America is in there too . . . A cocktail. A genuine, proper, thoroughly shaken cocktail.

How great it would be to know what happened when I was not yet born. How great it would be if once, just once, I could look into the past. How great it would be if I could fly back on the 'Back to the Future' time machine! But it cannot be, everyday life is not like Hollywood.

But it's truly a tale of adventure, this disappearance of my father without a trace. All that's certain is that he flew back to the US, as they found his name on a Swissair passenger list. And that's all. At the Federal Bureau of Investigation they said that he probably left for a new life in another state, perhaps in another country, Mexico, or somewhere in South America, presumably under another name, so he would be impossible to trace.

It's a shame and thoroughly reprehensible that my father took the entire history of our family with him, into the void. He lost it. I'd like to find it. I've opened a new file, with the name 'Father et cetera', and I'm copying into it everything that I can find out about our family. I will print out several copies. At least what little we know should not be lost. So that if I ever have a child, I can hand it to him. Or her. He (or she) should not have to start from scratch.

Pécs cemetery seemed neglected, with most of the grave-stones standing at drunken angles. Henryk was not sure if it was appropriate to enter in jeans, Teva sandals and Ray-Bans, and he went in timidly. He tried to read the German (Yiddish) and Hungarian inscriptions, the Hebrew characters he could only caress. Isn't there some office here, with someone to help? The building next to the entrance, several storeys high, had all its doors closed. The steps at the back suggested a flat: a baby's bath and a rocking horse indicated that there were small children here. What can it be like to grow up in a cemetery – a Jewish cemetery?

He set off at random down one of the rows. He knew that Dr Balázs Csillag was born in 1921 and his wife Mária Porubszky in 1929. The question was: when did they die?

He paused at those graves where he could read the names.

Ignác Koller and his wife Hédy.

Béla Weiss. Robert Weiss. Alexander Weiss. Izabella Weiss. Vilma Weiss.

Albert Weiss and his wife Aranka Skorka.

Lipót Stern.

Mihály Stern.

József Stern.

Dr Jenő Schweizer and Judit Wieser.

Imre Walser.

Máté Rotj.

Mojzes Roth and Eszter Holatschek.

Ernő Moohr.

Miksa Straub.

Ottó Rusitschka.

And . . . his head was reeling . . . the vault of the Csillag family!

Two structures the size of phone booths rose high above all the others, with a cupola recalling the Turkish dome of the church in the main square of Pécs. Unbelievable! . . . These are my ancestors! he thought. He began to perspire.

Here lay Dr Antal Csillag, who died in 1933, Dr Bencze Csillag, died 1904, Dr Ervin Csillag, died 1877.

Heavens! Here they are! His knees shook. It was plain that Dr Antal Csillag was the father of Dr Balázs Csillag, Antal's father was Dr Bencze Csillag, and the latter's father was Dr Ervin Csillag. Fantastic! He scribbled down the names. Doctors? Or lawyers, like grandfather? And where are the wives? Perhaps all will be revealed in the archives.

Only as he was leaving did he notice a grassy area, the size of a small garden in the corner by the entrance, where a row of grey gravestones of uniform size and shape stood, leaning against the fence. They seemed very old: the wind, the rain, the snow had all but worn them smooth. By the side there was a metal plate, like a road sign: BEREMEND. He had no idea what that could mean. I'll ask someone. He wrote it down, otherwise he'd forget. He stood a long time on the parched grass. The afternoon began to smell ever more sweet. The buzzing of the wild bees tickled his eardrums.

'You staying?'

An old woman, brightly dressed, was standing behind

439

him, a faded muslin kerchief tied about her head, a worn pair of clogs on her feet. Henryk did not understand.

'Excuse me?'

'Because I would like to lock up.'

'Oh, right . . .' and he moved to go.

'No rush, mind!' said the old woman barring his way. 'Stay as long as you like.'

'Please could you tell me what is Beremend?'

'Beremend?' The old woman blinked fiercely as if caught out doing something naughty.

Henryk pointed to the metal sign.

'Ah, Beremend! That's a village, not far from Pécs, further down.'

'What's the sign doing here?'

'Dunno really. I was doing them a favour . . . They left the key with me while they all went off to a wedding in Baja.'

'Well, thank you,' said Henryk and went out into the street.

The old woman followed him and immediately locked the iron gate from outside. 'Farewell.'

He hurried back to the archives but there was no trace in the parish registers of Dr Antal Csillag, or of Dr Bencze Csillag, or of Dr Ervin Csillag.

'Doesn't prove anything,' said the archivist. 'There are always documents gone astray. If I were you, I'd believe the gravestones.'

From Pécs Henryk drove to a little village in County Somogy, where Jeff and Doug were waiting for him in a camper van, with a celebratory meal. They ate in the open air. Henryk gave a detailed account of how far he had got.

The HEJED Co. had bought two run-down properties in County Somogy. Jeff had already secured firm buyers for them. In Somogyvámos it seemed virtually impossible to imagine that in place of the ruins heavily used by the cooperative there could arise a country house similar to that of the original owners, the Windisch family, in the eighteenth century. This family of Austrian nobles had put down roots in several areas of Hungary; in Somogyvámos there lived one of the more impoverished branches. What remained of their shrinking lands had been taken over in 1950 by the Red Star Agricultural Cooperative: the grander rooms were used as offices, while the outhouses became grain stores. Since the dissolution of the cooperative it had stood derelict, the weeds waist-high in almost every room.

Henryk had not lost any of the impetus he had gained in Pécs and early in the evening he walked to the village cemetery. He passed under the rusting curlicues of the sign RESURREXIT! and began to examine the crosses and the gravestones. The better-off families had had monuments raised to them here that he thought were large enough to live in. Mechanically, his ran his eyes over the names. The most monumental crypt, almost a mausoleum, housed the dead of the Counts Windisch and the family Illés.

As the sun disappeared behind the hills, the air turned gradually colder. Henryk had the curious notion that he would lie down on one of the bed-shaped crypts to see if he could sense the presence of the dead at rest beneath him, or the presence of death itself. Newly planted trees lined the path, their branches arching over him. As the evening breeze brushed through the trees their leaves touched and sighed. Woolly clouds flitted across the sky. Henryk closed his eyes and not for the first time felt how the majesty and beauty of nature could actually hurt. He imagined what it might be like when you could not experience even this. If you cease to exist in this world. What becomes of you? Where do you go? If anywhere . . .

'Bíró?' queried a woman's voice, obviously pleased.

Henryk opened his eyes. A blonde though greying woman with a broad face was staring down at him, a metal

441

watering-can in her hand. She smiled as if he were an old acquaintance.

'Excuse me, but . . .' Henryk sat up.

'Bíró?' the woman repeated, with a beatific smile. 'Jóska Bíró!'

Henryk cleared his throat. He noticed, now, that the grave on which he lay was the resting place of Mihály Bíró and his wife, mourned eternally by their adoring sons and daughters. He stood up and shamefacedly dusted himself down.

'Oh, it's such a long time since we've seen you in these parts!' the woman said, shaking him vigorously by the hand.

'Actually . . .'

'Yes, I know how busy it must be in Pécel too.'

'In Pécel?'

'Or have you moved on?'

Henryk found it more and more difficult to own up. But he was spared this, as the woman unexpectedly gave a shriek:

'Oh no, what am I saying? You're not Jóska Bíró at all, you're the other one, his friend, who stayed just for the summer, . . . little Vilmos . . . Vilmos Csillag! What brings you to these parts?'

'You knew my dad? Vilmos Csillag was my dad . . .'

'Heaven preserve us!' The woman clapped her hand to her face, which bore many signs of having worked in the fields. 'Of course . . . How could I have . . . it's been so long! But it feels like it was yesterday.'

Art is rarely able to surpass life. It was sheer chance that I lay down on a grave in Somogyvár Cemetery which turned out to be the final resting place of Mihály Bíró. Who would believe that just then there appears old Mrs Palóznaki, maiden name Ági Mandell, who was a childhood friend of Mihály Bíró's son. It was with these Bírós that Papa stayed in the Fifties, because they

442

*offered country holidays to city children for payment, taking in
as many as three or four at a time. Ági Mandell said Papa was
the only one to come back year after year.*

Absolutely incredible!

*I asked her to describe what sort of a child Papa was. She
said delicate. He was reclusive, not as loud-mouthed as the
village kids. She also recalls that the colour of his eyes changed
all the time, depending on his mood: sometimes it was grey,
at others green, or even light brown. I thought I could detect
that Ági Mandell had a soft spot for Papa, but she denied
it – she had fallen for Jóska Bíró ('head over heels', as she
put it).*

*I discovered that the Arrow Cross had taken Mihály Bíró
because he was Jewish; he returned from one of the German
Lagers and became a corn exchanger. Since their village did not
have a mill of its own, the peasants would take the corn to
Mihály Bíró, who would exchange it for flour using a complicated formula that factored in weight and quality; he would then
take the corn to the nearest mill himself. That was how he made
his living. Until serious illness (cancer) forced him to give up.
After his death the children sold his house, which became the
agricultural cooperative's nursery. Now it stands empty. Jóska
Bíró became a stonemason and to the best of Ági Mandell's
knowledge he moved to Pécel.*

*My grandfather was supposedly in the Ministry of the Interior
as a 'backroom boy' (Ági Mandell's phrase). The minister was
László Rajk, who was hanged. What happened to my grandfather she does not know. I wrote down her address and the phone
number of the bakery where she works in the office, and I gave her
my details too.*

Henryk spent several weeks in the village, during which
Ági Mandell invited him over for dinner more than once.
Her roast pork was so succulent that Henryk had thirds, not
just seconds. He was under the weather for days afterwards,

but still considered that he had never in his life eaten anything so delicious.

The Somogyvámos estate had been sold to a distant kinsman of the Windisches, a Viennese business lady called Frau Rosa Windisch. She was rising forty, but the turkey-like wattle under her chin made her seem much older. This not especially attractive part of her body she assiduously tried to conceal with chains of silver and gold and rows of pearls, which therefore constantly drew attention to it. Frau Rose Windisch spoke English with a dog-like bark and was never happy with anything. She strode up and down the half-ready building with eyebrows arched and head continually shaking: 'I can't believe this!' Her intonation was a tribute to the meticulousness of the Berlitz method.

'What is it now that she can't believe?' Jeff asked Henryk, quietly.

'She'll let you know, don't worry.'

Frau Rosa Windisch wanted to establish a stud-farm here, with a Gasthof for Austrian and German visitors, the main attraction to be daily horse-riding. She thought that the quality represented by the HEJED Co. did not come up to Western standards. But it soon turned out that hers did not either: her taste was that of the petty bourgeois Austrian, and she would have much preferred brand-new garden gnomes to the nineteenth-century reliefs which Jeff and his team were restoring with such care.

The three of them could hardly wait to be rid of the testy lady, and could not be bothered to take her on for retaining 10 per cent of the contractually agreed price on the grounds of alleged shortcomings in quality.

'Good riddance!' said Jeff.

They left the estate in Henryk's Jeep. Stopping at the sign that marked the end of the village, they took great satisfaction jointly and severally in urinating on it.

Jeff and Doug took two weeks off and went on holiday to Malta. Henryk went into the office quite often – it now consisted of three interconnected rooms on the Bem Quay, by the Danube – and chatted with the office girls and the bookkeeper. Having no work, he realised how lonely he was. He tinkered with the 'Papa et cetera' file. He gathered what information he had into a family tree on the computer, printed it out on the all-in-one used for photocopying the blueprints of the HEJED Co. and pinned it up on the wall of his flat.

I'll add to it, as and when I have something to add, he thought.

He often thought of Ann and even more often of Bond (James Bond). These were two rare examples of names that he remembered even in his dreams, perhaps because they often featured in them. He had to remind himself how luke-warm his feelings for Ann had become by the end. But Bond (James Bond) he loved unreservedly (the last person he embraced with the keenness he felt for this sheep-sized dog had been his mother). Bond (James Bond) generously tolerated this and would sometimes lick Henryk's face, his tongue rough, warm and wet.

Maybe I should get myself a dog . . . a big one.

In the absence of his two friends, however, he decided that what he needed was a two-legged friend. Though he was quite certain he was not interested in men, in his heart of hearts he was not quite so certain that he was interested in women. However intimate he came to be with Ann, they had never come close to that melting into one another he had read about in novels. He hadn't ever, so far, felt anything like that. Which was to say that he had never been in love. That, or the novelists were pulling a fast one.

His evenings would generally begin in restaurants and end in nightclubs, mostly in the ZanziBar, frequented by a lot of English-speakers, chiefly Brits, on account of the

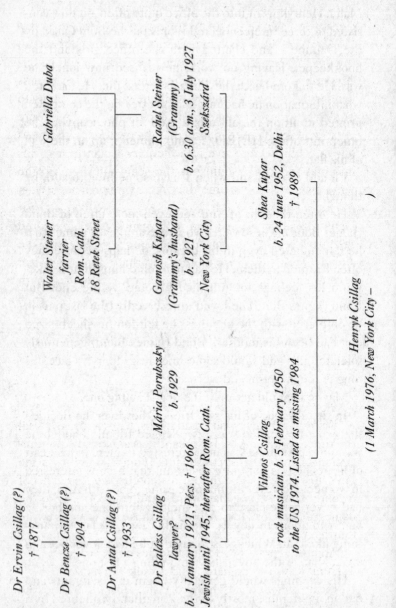

Dr Ervin Csillag (?)
† 1877

Dr Bencze Csillag (?)
† 1904

Dr Antal Csillag (?)
† 1933

Walter Steiner
farrier
Rom. Cath.
18 Retek Street

Gabriella Duba

Dr Balázs Csillag
lawyer?
b. 1 January 1921, Pécs. † 1966
Jewish until 1945, thereafter Rom. Cath.

Mária Porubszky
b. 1929

Gamosh Kupar
(Grammy's husband)
b. 1921
New York City

Rachel Steiner
(Grammy)
b. 6.30 a.m, 3 July 1927
Szekszárd

Vilmos Csillag
rock musician. b. 5 February 1950
to the US 1974. Listed as missing 1984

Shea Kupar
b. 24 June 1952, Delhi
† 1989

Henryk Csillag
(1 March 1976, New York City –)

wide selection of beers on offer. Henryk never got drunk, but a couple of pints of Guinness loosened his limbs sufficiently for the stroll to his house, which was near by. Dog-walkers often walked past, and Henryk would eye up the dogs no less than the women. The dogs would generally amble over to him, pressing and sniffing, their tails windscreen-wiping furiously, while he was always happy to hunker down and stroke their backs. He would inquire after the dog's name, age, breed, if the owner or walker was not in a hurry. His sieve-like memory instantly lost this information, so he would put the same questions to the same owner the next time they met. The bigger the dog, the more Henryk liked it. Not far away there lived a Great Dane that always made him melt inside. And he greeted the four black Labradors with the same joy every time; he already knew they were mother and three pups, the latter seven-months-old males who had already caught up with their mother in size.

'What are they called?'

'They're still called Milady, Athos, Porthos and Aramis,' said the brunette holding the four leads not in her hand but wound round her neck.

'Sorry, but those are strange names.'

'Haven't you read *The Three Musketeers*?'

'I'm American, we don't read books, we just watch TV all the time,' said Henryk. He meant it as a joke. His pronunciation of the Magyar consonants brought a smile to the girl's lips. Henryk brought out his notebook with his list of recently learnt Hungarian words, and started to write the names down: 'Milady, Athos, Porthos ... what was the fourth one?'

'Aramis.' The girl had faint freckles on her cheeks.

Henryk swallowed hard. 'May I walk you home?'

'Easily done. I live right here. Ciao!' The girl herded the black Labradors through the gate. Henryk could not take his eyes off the muscular legs, hidden by her skirt to mid-calf.

The following evening he hung about that part of the road, in the hope of bumping into the girl and the dogs again, but in vain. The third day he decided he would wait around by the gate until they turned up. Ten minutes later the girl and the dogs came down. 'Waiting for us?'

'How did you know?'

'Saw you from the window.'

Henryk introduced himself. The girl's name was Mária Zenthe. Her hand shook Henryk's firmly. He asked if they could meet on purpose, as it were. Mária gave him a long look. 'Difficult.'

'Because of someone?'

'Yes.' She pointed to the dogs. 'Because of them.' She explained that they could not be left alone for any length of time, as the pups would certainly trash the flat.

They were quickly on first-name terms. Henryk suggested a weekend trip north to the Danube Bend. Mária was hesitant: this number of dogs is too many for a car. Henryk insisted that there was plenty of room in the Cherokee Jeep.

They set out for Szentendre, towards the Danube Bend. The girl spread some old towels on the back seat and gave the dogs the signal 'in you go!' and they obediently hopped in. Henryk could see in the rear-view mirror that they were looking round with faintly bored expressions, like Madison Avenue ladies in their limos.

Mária joked that she was a rag-and-bone woman. The bone referred to the dogs, but the rag was genuine: she designed, sewed and wove carpets, curtains, wall-hangings and cushions. She had recently graduated in applied arts. She was a native of Hódmezővásárhely and had come up to Budapest to take her degree. She had had a serious relationship and was now poring over its ruins. Milady had originally belonged to her ex, József, but she was so fond of Mária that after the split they agreed Milady would be hers. József was a sculptor in metal. They lived in his workshop-cum-flat. Mária could stay until she found a flat of her own and make a living, that was the agreement. József had meanwhile moved back to his mother's. Hardly had he removed himself from her life, then Milady became pregnant and gave birth to eight pups from a father unknown, which Mária had seen only from a distance, a German Shepherd possibly, or a cross of some sort. When József heard of the mésalliance he seemed to turn on Milady. Since then he had taken no interest in her at all. The newborn pups had looked like little black rats; five she managed to give away, three remained with her. 'I don't mind. I've grown very fond of them.'

'I can see why,' he said, the hot breath of the four dogs on his neck.

It was as they were passing the new estate at Békásmegyer that there was the first sign of problems. Aramis started quietly to retch, his head and neck in spasm.

'Whoa!' said Mária. 'Better stop, he's going to throw up.'

Henryk however could not move over in time, and Aramis emptied the contents of his stomach on the seat and the car floor, with plenty left for Henryk's back. Mária was all profuse apology as she tried to limit the damage with Kleenex. As soon as they set off again, it was the turn of Porthos to vomit. And so it went on. The dogs threw up steadily, one after the other, and the inside of the Cherokee Jeep was pervaded by the acrid smell of the acid from the dogs' stomachs. Mária tried desperately to calm the dogs down, pleading with them and shouting at them by turns, but they just stared at her balefully, as if all their sad, dark pupils reflected the same thought: Sorry, but we have no choice but to submit to the call of nature.

Mária would gladly have turned back but Henryk said it

was a shame to let this spoil their day. 'Anyway, I don't think there can be anything left to bring up now.'

In Szentendre and then in Visegrád they made quite a stir with the four black dogs. Henryk behaved as if he were the owner. They got back about ten in the evening, the dogs asleep on the back seat.

'Thanks for everything,' said Mária. 'Wait a moment. I'll just take the herd up and then I'll come down to help clean up the car.'

'Come, come . . . I'll see to it tomorrow. But do come back . . . for at least an hour or so.'

The four dogs stayed locked in the workshop until three in the morning and chewed up everything that they could sink their teeth into. Henryk saw Mária up to the flat. She surveyed the battlefield but did not despair. 'Well, it's time for a spring-clean anyway.'

Henryk stayed. When Jeff and Doug came back, he introduced Mária as his fiancée.

'Indeed?' Mária seemed dubious.

'I don't get it,' said Jeff, thought Doug. Henryk repeated: 'My fiancée.'

'Are you sure about this?' asked Mária again.

'Congratulations!' said Doug, nodded Jeff.

Mária later pointed out that he might have discussed the matter with her first.

'Well . . . I'm sorry. So what do you think?'

'Not so fast. First we have to get to know each other better.'

'But I've got to know you already!'

Mária shook her head. 'There are many things about me that you don't know. Important things.'

'So tell me.'

'I can't do it just like that. In due course. All in good time.'

Henryk had to resign himself to a wait.

Dear Grammy,

I'm still doing fine. The firm HEJED Co. continues to expand, but this time I want to write about something else. I think that perhaps this is my HEJEM, my place, for ever.

I have met someone, a girl, and if it were up to me we would get married tomorrow. I'd be delighted if you could meet her. Could you not come over again? Let me send you a ticket!

His grandmother telephoned at once. 'I will come, but let's wait with this a little. Don't rush things. First you should really get to know each other well.'

'That's what she said, too.'

'Clever girl.'

These were busy times for Mária. She was making wall-hangings, an insurance company having ordered four large ones. She sat at her loom from the crack of dawn and stopped only to take the dogs out the regulation three times a day. If Henryk wanted to see her, it was during these walks that he could do so. They went on the wider pave-ment of the upper quayside, following the frisky little herd and apologising to the more easily frightened pedestrians.

'Tell me, do you believe in reincarnation?' asked Mária.

Henryk was at a loss. He had never asked himself this question and so had no answer. When he was small he had attended church, and his grandmother would certainly have liked him to become a proper White Anglo-Saxon Protestant, but as no one around him took God seriously, he too thought religion was just empty ceremonial which he gave up as soon as he could, just as he did the scouts.

Reincarnation was the cornerstone of Mária's view of the world. Death is also, simultaneously, birth or rebirth. After the decay of the body, the soul lingers on for about a century and a half, following various paths by way of purification; only after this can it begin its next life. Someone who was born a man in a previous life generally becomes a woman, and vice versa.

For Henryk the prospect that after his death his soul could have a second helping in another being was new, exciting and tempting; nevertheless he found it difficult to believe.

'You don't have to believe it,' said Mária. 'When the time comes you will find it as natural as the fact that the sky is blue.'

Henryk was not convinced that this would happen, much as he might long for it. In the course of further conversations he discovered that Mária shared the views of a German philosopher called Rudolf Steiner, who was well known at the beginning of the century. 'He was a spiritual visionary. There are people possessed of the ability to see on a higher plane, that is to say, they can see things that others can't. They say you can be born with this ability, but it can also be achieved by self-education. In our time, the path of self-education is more common. Man today has lost his ability to see within. We possess what are called spiritual senses, but these cannot operate of themselves and have to be developed by the individual. I have many books on this; if you're interested I can lend them to you.'

The vast majority of the books were, however, in German. Henryk knew no foreign languages; he had English as his mother tongue and Hungarian as his father tongue.

Spiritual vision and self-education: so many unknown spheres. Just as hard to believe as reincarnation and at the same time just as attractive.

It turned out that Mária spoke English, German and French very well, and even some Danish. A lover of opera, she could also manage some Italian.

It's true, thought Henryk, I really don't know her well.

452

'Why did you never go to college?' asked Mária.

'I came here instead. This is my university.'

'Aha. So you didn't have the courage to take on a degree.'

'That's not what I said.'

'But it's true anyway, isn't it?'

Henryk thought about it a while and then admitted it was. 'How did you know?'

'It's typical of Pisces.'

'Pie seas?'

'The astrological sign. You are Pisces, aren't you?'

Henryk had no idea. Mária asked when he was born and when she heard the date, nodded: 'Yes, that's Pisces.'

Mária was well versed in the art of casting a horoscope, something she had learnt from her grandmother. She cast one for everyone she came into contact with and who gave their permission.

'You ask for permission?'

'Of course. It's a very intimate matter. Things can be revealed which the natives . . . the person concerned won't perhaps be happy about. Or they won't be happy that I'm the one to have revealed them. So . . . can I cast yours?'

'Yes.'

'Do you know the exact time of your birth? Hours and minutes. I need it for the ascendant.'

'I've no idea.'

He called his grandmother to ask, but Grammy did not know. 'In those days we were not on smiling terms.'

'Smiling terms?'

'Yes. You know, we were not very pleased that she had married your father . . . In fact, not in the least pleased.'

'And why have you never mentioned this before?'

'Did you ask about it?'

'How can I ask about something which I have no idea about?'

453

There was silence at the other end of the line, then a quiet sniff or two.

Henryk changed the subject. 'You haven't asked about Mária . . .'

'How can I ask about somebody I know nothing about?'

They both put down the receiver offended.

Mária said that she could calculate the ascendant only on the basis of the exact place, day, hour and minute of the birth, though she had heard of astrologers who were somehow able to calculate it from the subject's most important life-events. She wrote to such an astrologer in Szeged, giving her the dates of the death of Henryk's mother, the disappearance of his father, his arrival in Hungary, and the date the two of them had first met. She was not satisfied with the answer (which had cost an astrological ten thousand forints). 'She says your ascendant is Aries. But I see nothing of Aries in you. Aries are fiery, liable to set their home ablaze, repeatedly dashing their heads against brick walls. Of course, you may be Aries none the less, but the planets in the twelve houses are so arranged that your ascendant is less typical of you than your Sun, that is, Pisces.'

'Well, now, is that good or bad?'

'I can't put it like that. How interested are you in this?'

'Very.'

Mária nodded and launched into a detailed explanation. She did not tell fortunes from the stars, she only drew conclusions about the subject's personality. That is, certain basic traits, with which the subject can do what they wish and are able to. In her view one's horoscope influences the nature of one's fate no more than some 25 per cent; the rest is down to genes, family background, upbringing and self-development. Be that as it may, those born under the sign of Pisces have some difficulty in negotiating the boundary between themselves and the world. They are often lonely.

Being the twelfth sign, the most complex, it yields the most sophisticated personalities. Pisces generally evince some sensitivity to art, perhaps even some artistic ability; there are, for example, many musicians among them. 'They put on the pounds easily . . . though you show no sign of that yet. Have you heard of Enrico Caruso?'

'No.'

'He was a world-famous opera-singer. Some say the greatest tenor of all time. He is Pisces. I mean his Sun is. Then there is Elizabeth Taylor. Or Zorán. Have you heard of him?'

'No.'

'He's a Hungarian rock singer. Then there is, let me see, Sharon Stone. You must know who she is.'

'How come you know so many people's sign?'

'I've looked them up in *Who's Who*. These days I can sometimes tell just from the face. Especially Scorpios, Virgos and Geminis.'

Henryk took extensive notes from Dane Rudhyar's *The Astrology of Personality*, which he found on Mária's bookshelves. He still found it easier to read English than Hungarian. Astrology was again something which he revelled in, which made his spine tingle, though his doubts were never allayed. How can one claim that a person's character could, even in part, depend on where and when he was born? Well . . . surely you can't. At the same time it was beyond doubt that the Moon is implicated in the movement of the tides and the menstrual cycle, yet it is one of the smallest planet-like objects of all. Can one then say for certain that the heavenly bodies do *not* have any influence over us? Well . . . surely you can't.

He tried hard to memorize the order of the signs of the zodiac, to master them like a poem: Aries, Taurus, Gemini, Cancer . . . Here he always got stuck and had to sneak a look at his notes to continue: Leo, Virgo, Libra, Scorpio . . . Again he needed help: Sagittarius, Capricorn, Aquarius, Pisces. He could not understand why he was unable to hammer into his brain these twelve words, let alone the dates of each. He envied Mária and her memory of cast iron: whatever that girl once set eyes on, or heard, or experienced, it was for ever seared on her brain. Before the sculptor József, Mária had been in love with a Danish boy and had learnt Danish for his sake – in effect in two months (the list of rarer verb forms was still pinned to the toilet door). Henryk failed to make any inroads even on the Magyar vocabulary he targeted.

'If you are so troubled by your poor memory, why don't you develop it?' asked Mária. 'You can improve every aspect of yourself, it's just a question of willpower.'

On her instructions, Henryk started by memorizing lists of numbers, and then progressed to names. He began to feel he was making some headway.

Mária did not move in with him, nor did she let him share the workshop-cum-flat with her. 'It would be a bad omen.'

'Amen?'

'Omen. Sign, premonition. I think it's Greek. Or Latin.'

'But surely we know each other now!'

'Not well enough. I still don't know what the most important thing in life is for you.'

'You.'

'Don't be silly! I'm serious.'

'Only you could ask a question like that. And right away you make me feel like some stupid toddler.'

'A toddler would be able to answer on his or her level. Think about it.'

Eventually what I came up with was that you should be happy. Whereupon she says: who is the 'you'? I replied: 'Me.' Whereupon she: 'A selfish view, but OK. So what is needed to make you happy?'

This again was a typical Mária question. I gave her the list:

456

'Money, then good health, a secure family background, I guess that's about it. Now what about you?'

She looked grave. Because we don't agree on anything. The things I mentioned are, in her view, cliché ideals of petty bourgeois life. Health is like the air: it doesn't make you happy as long as you can breathe it, in fact you barely notice it. She would not put a secure family background here either, because in the end you must count on yourself.

In her view it's not these sorts of thing that you need for happiness, but abstract things, for example: firm and consistently followed moral principles, then knowledge, willpower, endurance. And good fortune. She was sorry that I hadn't learned even that much yet. She could hardly marry me.

When she said this to my face, I ran home and wept. I knew she was right, in a way. But I also knew I wanted her as much as I ever wanted anything or anyone. I turned on my heels and went back. I bounded up to the fifth floor to knock on the workshop door. I knew what I wanted to say to her.

'If I have not learnt enough, teach me; if I am not perfect, love me!' Henryk practised the words as the black iron door opened.

Mária let him in.

'Now do you know me well enough to . . . ?' Henryk asked at breakfast.

'Maybe. But you don't know me well enough yet. You idealize me, although I have many bad qualities.'

'For instance?'

'Excessive self-assurance. The firm conviction that I must continually educate everyone. A degree of pedantry. Poor time-management. But I am an Aquarius, not very practical, as you know.'

Henryk loved Mária's faults, too, even if these sometimes annoyed him. He had occasion to discover that Mária's bad qualities were just the same as her good ones.

457

The self-assurance was handy when it came to dealing with officials and businesses. Her enthusiasm for teaching people was what made it possible for Henryk to learn from her. Pedantry and knowledge were fruits of the same tree. With the lack of practicality came the purity of her soul.

Following this train of thought he came to realize that probably everyone's faults are the same as their virtues. He tried to look at himself in this light. He was relatively slow (i.e. thorough and determined). His self-confidence was low (i.e. modest and careful). He was not well educated (i.e. had a thirst for knowledge). His memory was rubbish (i.e. quick to forgive).

He felt his relationship to Mária was growing ever closer, despite the fact that she continued to keep him very much at arm's length. Most worryingly, Mária insisted on spending two nights out of four, on average, in her workshop-flat, and on those nights Henryk had to sadly tramp home alone. At the mere mention of the word marriage her eyes flashed fire: 'No. Not yet.'

Once, in bed, Henryk asked her: 'If you became pregnant, would you marry me?'

'It would guarantee that I wouldn't.'

'Oh, my . . . Now that I really don't get!'

'But it's simple. If we have a child and are married, in case of divorce we would fight over the child. If we are not married, it can't happen. You could not do anything to me.'

'But why would I want to do anything to you?'

'In your case, that's really hairy. You might one day decide to go back to America, you'd take the child with you . . .'

'Oh, Mária, what a weird view you have of things!'

'A realistic view. It may be hard to imagine now, but all my girlfriends are divorced and I have seen how it reduces people to the level of animals.'

'But look at the many pluses of marriage: the security, the

sharing of everything we have; even in the case of divorce, under Hungarian law half of everything is yours!'

'I told you I am not materialistic.'

Henryk thought his head would burst, like an over-inflated football. What a set-up! Every girl longs to get married, the only exception being the girl whom fate had brought him together with. He guessed it would be point-less to argue; he would just bounce off Mária's iron will. There was nothing for it but to accept her as she was.

The ease with which Mária gave birth to my son almost sug-gested she had been practising. Konrád Csillag came into the world on 14 April 1996, weighing two and a half kilos and measuring 48 centimetres in length. In the MÁV (Railwaymen's) Hospital the consultant thought it would be advisable to place him in an incubator. But Mária refused her consent, saying it was unnecessary. She was right. Little Konrád flourished and ten days later we were allowed to take him home. By then Grammy had safely arrived and joyfully embraced her great-grandson, admitting that she had not thought she would live to see this day.

We notified Mária's parents, too, but they did not come. They are as angry with Mária for not getting married as I am. Although I am no longer angry. I have accepted that nothing involving her is straightforward. Only her grandmother Erzsi came up from Hódmezővásárhely. Grammy was still with us. I thought they would get on well, but they avoided each other in some hostility. Erzsi was constantly checking my son's horoscope (Aries, with Taurus in the ascendant); she perhaps devoted more time to this than to little Konrád.

By then they were living in Üröm, in a detached house that was three-quarters ready. Mária's studio was to be in the loft, Henryk's office in the basement, but these were still at the blueprint stage. The regulars of HEJED Co.

were supposed to finish the work in the house, but the firm was so inundated with work that work on their home was continually put back. On the ground-floor lounge Henryk built a fireplace of undressed stone, a carbon copy of the one in Mária's flat. He thought he would not be able to get hold of a genuine bellows, poker and fire-tongs in Hungary, but was amazed to spot a set at Budapest's Ecseri flea-market. Some enterprising Hungarian was (re)producing them by the dozen.

The colder half of the year was nearly over, but Henryk was glad to light a fire in the evenings. It pleased him to show Mária how well the flue was working. He could watch for hours as the flames encroached upon the logs of crackling wood. A joyful end, to turn into light and warmth, he reflected.

The dogs took possession of the garden, digging out and chewing up the flora. Mária was not bothered too much. 'We'll sort out the garden when we have time.'

But they didn't have time for quite a while, as the newcomer took up their every moment. For the moment, Henryk neglected HEJED Co., but Jeff and Doug took it in their stride. They preferred to throw a few one-liners at him: 'When we have a child, neither of us will come in to work for a bit!'

Mária wanted Konrád baptised. Henryk did not understand. 'But you are constantly on at the church!'

'Doesn't mean he should be denied holy water.'

'What's the point?'

'What's the point of brushing your teeth?'

Again, Henryk gave up on this debate. But he insisted that either Jeff or Doug should be his godfather. Mária raised no objection. 'But which of them?'

'Let them decide.'

'Both of us!' Jeff decided.

So my son had two godfathers in the persons of my dear friends
and business partners. As for a godmother, we asked Mária's
childhood friend Olga to do the honours.

The business did not languish while I was employed as a
father full-time; on the contrary! Doug had done some sniffing
around and discovered that state grants were now available for
refurbishing the old castles of Hungary, and we were successful
in applying for some.

At present we are working on five sites, in Hungary and in
Transylvania. I never imagined it was possible to make money
out of something you enjoyed doing. As a result of our work, the
past is recreated in stone and wood, so that it continues to
endure.

The faraway USA becomes an increasingly faint memory.
Sometimes I feel as if I had only dreamt those years, that is to
say, in effect the whole of my childhood and youth. And now I
can be certain that I am going to live here, as long as God, Fate,
fortune, heaven, and all the stars allow it . . . or? Here was
born my son; when the time comes, let him bury me here, in the
land of my fathers.

Konrád was called Tapshi by his mother and sometimes
Flopsy by his father, which means almost the same. Konrád
did indeed resemble a little rabbit, especially in the way he
blinked. His legs tended towards an O-shape, and during
nappy-changes he joyfully kicked out into the air, like some
battery-driven toy.

He began to roll about, crawl, speak and walk much
earlier than the books suggested. Henryk was seized by an
uncontrollable urge to record every moment. He photo-
graphed, videoed, sound-recorded and also made notes
in his 'Papa et cetera' file. Hence it is possible to know
that the first coherent sentence uttered by his son was 'We
goin ford and back!', a fair analysis of the motion of his
pram.

He was soon amazing his parents. At a year and a half, he was able to recall and recite stories he had heard, word for word. Poems heard a few times also came out exactly as the originals, and again and again. Numbers stayed in his memory just like words. He certainly hasn't taken after me, thought Henryk.

Konrád was also a sensation at the nursery. He solved jigsaws and puzzles with ease; he proved an ace with buttons and shoelaces. In the nursery he was always the one who recited the poem or sang the song at special events and occasions. His drawings graced the walls.

He was not yet three when one afternoon he was found in the basement – by then Henryk's office had been finally completed – sitting in front of the computer, pressing the keys on the keyboard.

'What are you doing?' asked Henryk.

'Dwawing.'

He was indeed using a drawing program: on the screen a square house was taking shape.

'Have they got a computer in the nursery?' Henryk used the English word.

'No.'

'But then . . . how do you know how to do this?'

'You know how!'

The parents could hardly believe it. Konrád had watched them start the computer, and this was not the first time he was amusing himself with it. When Henryk reported this to Jeff and Doug, Jeff nodded and said: 'Soon as he's out of the nursery, he's got a place on the board!'

The square house was repeatedly drawn by Konrád and began to resemble a fortress.

'What is this?' asked Henryk.

'Fortwess.'

'What?'

'Fortwess. Wot owd people wivd in.'

'Where did you see such a thing?'

Konrád put his index finger to his brow.

Jeff and Doug are right, thought Henryk, he's going to be an architect.

That summer, as he entered his fourth year, Konrád learned the shapes of the capital letters all by himself. From his mother he got a little notebook with a tiny lock. On the first page he wrote, in red, green and blue crayon:

PAPA MEIK HOUS.
MAMA MEIK KAPET.
END I REIT.

These three lines were endlessly quoted by his parents to each other and to their friends.

On the cover he later wrote in drunken letters:

BOOK OFFTEIRS

'What do you mean, Book of Tears?'

'Book of Fathers!' Konrád corrected him and what he had written on the book: BOOK OFFATEIRS.

'But why?'

'I want. Like you have "Papa et cetera".'

Henryk blanched. 'How do you know that?'

'In the machine.'

'You've read it?!'

'Oh, Papa, donno no small letters!'

It did not occur to Henryk that at the touch of a key, every text in the computer can be made all-capitals.

This was a time when Mária's life was totally dominated by the approaching solar eclipse. She read everything she could about it. She was determined to travel to Siófok on the Balaton, because the astronomers had worked out that there would be the best view. 'If we miss it, the next opportunity won't be until 2081, and we shan't live to see that.'

Konrád might, thought Henryk, and the thought somehow dampened his spirits.

Mária felt that great things were in the making. She quoted Nostradamus, who had foretold this event, too. Henryk could not understand how the eclipse could be what was foretold in the quatrain which Mária translated as follows:

> In the sixth month of 1999,
> The Great Mongol king will descend from the sky.
> This Terrible Ruler will have his say,
> Afore power comes under Mars's sway.

But he too had been gripped by the thrill of the mystical: what will happen if strange events should indeed be set in train on the 14th of August? He bought the special tinted glasses recommended by the Radiation Physics Institute and rented a house in Siofók for a week.

On the night before the eclipse there was gridlock on the Balaton highway, the cars inching along painfully slowly. The dogs were uncomfortable and whined and dribbled, but as they had not been given supper had nothing to throw up. Konrád was sitting between them in the back, tirelessly stroking them and wiping their jaws with a wet rag.

'If it's cloudy tomorrow, I am going to have a heart-attack,' grumbled Henryk.

But the dawn woke them with a translucent light. They had a hearty breakfast and sat out on the veranda, so as not to miss anything. Henryk had a notepad and pen, Konrád his notebook and coloured pencils. The dogs chased each other round the garden.

Konrád was doodling. Henryk sneaked a look. There was a fantastic scene of steep hillsides, a battlefield and five or six Suns in the sky, though they could have been exploding shots from a cannon.

Below were three words in red.

CAVE   WATCH   BEGINNING

'Why did you write that?' asked Henryk.

Konrád shrugged.

Mária looked at the sun with concern. 'Isn't it time to put the glasses on?'

'It's too soon.'

The dogs became increasingly agitated. They can sense that something extraordinary is happening, all three of them thought.

The spectacle in the sky lasted from 11.24 until 12.46.

Henryk tried to write down everything as accurately as possible. He did not suspect that his ancestor Kornél Csillag had, too, though it is true he had done so from memory, in old age, recalling what he had witnessed as a child. Those sentences can no longer be read by anyone, ever. They have vanished into thin air.

The Gypsies working on my land told the story that when the Sun darkens over it is the giant Gryphon that embraces the Sun. Its urine falls as a harmful dew that brings plague and pestilence; that be the reason for covering over the wells at the eclipse. Merely superstition for the simple folk? Or is it really so? Were I to know the answer, verily would I inscribe it below.

I was myself but simple in those days, suspecting nought of the miracle to come. To me the darkness was but the evening falling sooner. Then I beheld the change in the colour of the clouds, they and the land turned a deep shade of green. The air did cool apace. As the darkness thickened, so did the fright of the birds and the

465

insects grow. They flew hither and yon and some fell dead on the ground. The dog with me howled a piteous howl. I was frighted unto death.

As the final sliver of the Sun darkened over, the stars of the night were seen of a sudden in the firmament. Thus far do I recall, then I lost hold of my mind. Meseemed my end was nigh, and that of the world also. Yet my story had hardly begun.

Later I heard from others what a magical sight I had missed: a diamond flame inwrapt the Sun, like unto a halo. They can rejoice, in whose sky the Lord has conjured such glory.

When this too had passed, it was said there came quickly a dawn, for the second time on that day. The affrighted beasts and folk rejoiced and bid welcome to the light reborn.

AUTHOR'S NOTE

The publisher has asked me to say a few words about the historical background to the novel. Though I don't really think it is essential to know anything about Hungary or its history to make sense of the novel, some readers may want to know a little of the broader context.

Some personal history first. The Hungarian original of this book was my twentieth publication in Hungary and my ninth novel. An earlier novel was about my mother, whose character, for me, was similar to that of the socialism that dominated our country for four decades. She was tyrannical, unfair, cruel and unpredictable – but at the same time rather amusing. (I was born in 1950 and so grew up in a 'softer' kind of socialism, which was not without its humorous side.) Some years later, I felt as though I owed it to my father to write a novel about him, too. Unfortunately, he was a man of few, if any, words. He had died when I was nineteen, and I didn't know much about him.

So I decided to do some research. I went down to Pécs, in the south of Hungary, where my father had been born and his family lived. The archives revealed some enigmatic facts: my father had had two brothers, and his father had also been called Miklós Vámos. That Miklós, my grandfather, came from Nagyvárad (now Oradea, just inside Romania). He had owned a substantial shoeshop in Pécs. His father, Mendel Weissberger, had owned a distillery in Budapest, but had himself been born in Homonna (now Humenné in the Slovak Republic). How had my great-grandfather come to own a distillery in Budapest, while his son had been born in Nagyvárad? And how had my grandfather ended up with a shoe-shop in Pécs? And what became of the distillery? I found no answers to these questions.

My father spent longer fighting in the Second World War than it actually lasted. He had been called up for manoeuvres even before the war, targeting former territories of the Hungarian kingdom that had been swallowed up by neighbouring countries after the First World War. During the war itself, he was a regular soldier until the enforcement of the Jewish Laws, when he became a member of one of the unarmed Jewish forced-labour brigades, sent ahead of German troops to sweep the minefields 'clean' for them as they advanced on Moscow. He was one of the very few to survive. When the front collapsed, he fled with some others and was captured by Soviet troops, becoming a prisoner of war. He escaped with a friend, and it took him several months to walk home to Pécs. He arrived to find that his whole family had been killed by the Nazis.

I had not even known that I was a Jew. When in elementary school my classmates expressed anti-Semitic sentiments, I followed their example, believing 'Jew' to be no worse than any other rude word. In high school, a girlfriend asked me if I was a Jew. I answered that I was not. I mentioned this to my father, adding that I knew we had nothing to do with the Jews. My father adjusted his glasses, and then said, 'Well, I'm not so sure.' There was no further explanation. And that was how I learned I was a Jew. (I do not speak Hebrew or Yiddish; I don't know the customs, the rules, the prayers. Nevertheless, whenever I hear of anti-Semitism, I *know* I am a Jew.)

Back to my father. Somehow he became a secretary to a minister, László Rajk, who was the victim of a showcase trial and executed. My father was fortunate to escape prosecution. He worked for seven years in a factory before he fell ill and, after a long period during which he was in and out of hospital, died. That's all I could find out about him – hardly enough for a novel.

What was I going to do? If I couldn't write a novel about my

468

father, why didn't I write one about every Hungarian father? I picked one hundred of them, famous and unknown men, and started to collect their biographies. But that seemed a little boring. I decided to choose twelve of them who would represent the twelve astrological signs – they would stand in for every Hungarian male. In the original text, in each chapter the first name of the central character starts with the same letter as his sign. The 'vignettes' that introduce the chapters try to create the mood of the relevant sign: the sentences were collected from old Hungarian calendars and yearbooks.

The novel describes the lives of twelve first-born sons in a single family, each the father of the next. This provided a solid and straightforward structure, and I sincerely hope the reader has no problem following the story, even if it is complicated in places. Please note that the Jewish name of the family is Stern and the Hungarian is Csillag – both mean 'star'. I knew the final scene would have to be the solar eclipse of 11 August 1999, since that was about the most beautiful sight I have ever seen. I tried to discover if there had been one roughly three centuries earlier and when I found that there had, the time-frame of the novel was in place; and that is how it became a Hungarian family saga.

Many readers in Hungary, and some in Germany, have written to say how envious they are that I know the story of my ancestors so well. I wish that were true. As must be clear by now, I know virtually nothing. I have made up a family because I lost my real one. But I am not unhappy if readers think they are getting the story of my forebears.

It may also help the reader to know that the Hungarian nobility and those who counted as the intellectuals of Hungary spoke French and German until the beginning of the nineteenth century. Only the poor used Hungarian, and the Hungarian language of the time lacked a great deal of vocabulary. One of the happiest chapters in the history of Hungarian culture is the period of intense language renewal towards the end of the eighteenth and in the first half of the nineteenth centuries. Writers, poets and linguists came together to create a modern Hungarian language and did so primarily by creating a large number of new words. I thought it would be interesting if in each chapter I used the words and grammar of the period in question. In the first three chapters, which take the story up to about 1800, I tried to use only words that existed at this time. I am aware that this is not something that can be easily recreated in translations into Indo-European languages, but I hope it is apparent that the language of the novel gradually becomes 'younger' as we approach the present.

A Few Notes on Hungarian History

One well-known fact is that Hungary and the Hungarians have lost every important war and revolution since the time of the Renaissance king Matthias Corvinus. He occupied Vienna and became Prince of Austria. He died in 1490. Since then, the nation and its heroes can be found only on the losing side.

A famous, if hoary, joke is instructive.

A Hungarian enters a small shop in New York and wants to buy a hat. But he doesn't have enough dollars on him, so he asks whether he could pay in forints, the Hungarian currency.

'I've never seen any forints,' the owner of the shop says. 'Show me some.'

So the Hungarian shows him a ten-forint note.

'Who's this guy here?' asks the owner.

'This is Sándor Petőfi, the brightest star of Hungarian poetry. He lived in the nineteenth century. He was one of the March Youth who launched the 1848–49 War of Independence. He was killed in a battle at Segesvár when the war was crushed by the Austrians and the Russians.'

'Oh my God, what an awful story . . . And who is this guy on the twenty-forint bill?'

'This is György Dózsa, who led a peasant uprising in the sixteenth century. It was crushed and he was executed – actually, he was burned on a throne of fire—'

'OK, OK. And who is that, on the fifty?'

470

'That's Ferenc Rákóczi II, leader of another war of independence, crushed by the Habsburgs. He was forced to spend his life in exile in Turkey.'

'I should have guessed. And on the one hundred?'

'That's Lajos Kossuth, leader of the 1848–49 War of Independence, you know. After it was crushed, he had to flee—'

The owner stops him again. 'OK, you poor man, just go – you can have the hat for free.'

(Note: these banknotes are no longer in circulation, owing to the ravages of inflation.)

The Eighteenth Century

Towards the end of the seventeenth century, the Wesselényi–Zrínyi conspiracy to overthrow the Habsburgs was quickly and bloodily put down. Some of the participants, like the grandfather and his family in the first chapter, were able to flee abroad. Only the Treaty of Karlowitz in 1699 ended this chaotic period, finally sweeping the Turks out of Hungary and Transylvania (in fact, the Turks controlled more of present-day Hungary than the Habsburgs) after a period of occupation that it had seemed would never end, and in fact lasted one hundred and fifty years. The period of Austrian rule that followed was even longer. Hungary was more or less a colony until the First World War.

But the revolts and plots against the rulers continued. The so-called Kuruc ('vagabond') guerrillas proved a major irritant to the Habsburgs. The Kuruc were led initially by Thököly and later by Ferenc Rákóczi II, who was very nearly successful. When the rebellion failed, as we saw above, he and some of his commanders took refuge in Turkey, and the country endured the Habsburgs' bloody revenge. For centuries, the term 'Kuruc' referred to anyone opposed to the Habsburgs, or any tyrant. Supporters of the Austrians were called 'Labanc' ('tousled'), a term used for collaborators and reactionaries. Both nouns are found in Hungarian poetry.

The movement for the linguistic renewal has already been mentioned. It also had an anti-Habsburg angle, because people who spoke Hungarian, rather than German, were thereby rejecting the official language of the monarchy. The outstanding anti-Habsburg event of this period was undoubtedly the 1848 Revolution and the War of Independence. For the best part of two years, the nation genuinely believed that it could oust the Austrians and gain its long-deserved independence. The rebels under Lajos Kossuth and an independent army *almost* succeeded – only the assistance of the Russian Tsar and his Cossacks finally tipped the scales in favour of the Austrians. The retaliation was even more brutal than usual. A number of martyrs were created in a few months: you will find their names on street signs in Budapest and other Hungarian cities.

A period of the bleakest silence and suffering ensued. A new era of conciliation began only in 1867, thanks to Ferenc Deák, a middle-of-the-road politician (who has a walk-on part in the novel). He was the leading figure among those who thought that while the past should not be forgotten, the future lay in a settlement with the Austrians. The pact was called the Ausgleich ('Settlement'), and the Dual (Austro-Hungarian) Monarchy was born. It was known locally as '*K. u. K.*', abbreviating '*Kaiserlich und Königlich*' ('Imperial and Royal'), because the Habsburg on the throne became both Emperor of Austria and King of Hungary. Though there were common ministries, the most important offices remained in Austrian hands.

In 1896, the Hungarian nation celebrated a thousand years of existence with much fanfare. Some historians claimed that the actual year of the country's founding was 895, but that the authorities had needed more time to organize the pomp and circumstance. If this is true, it is another typically Hungarian tale.

The Twentieth Century

For Jews living in Hungary, life had never been easy. Down the centuries they were not allowed to own anything, including land.

The situation varied somewhat according to region and city, but their equal rights were first enshrined only at the end of the 1848 Revolution and War of Independence, in which a great number of Jews participated. (Most of them wanted to be Hungarians and behaved accordingly.)

After the First World War the Paris Peace Treaties were unkind to Hungary. The country lost approximately two-thirds of its territory and about half of its population. In the new, smaller Hungary, the proportion of Jews, especially in the professions, now appeared very high. This fostered a crude anti-Semitism. For example, a regulation, *numerus clausus*, restricted the proportion of Jews allowed to attend university to their proportion in the population as a whole. My father was able to obtain his law degree in spite of this rule, but he was unable to work as a lawyer when more restrictive anti-Jewish laws came into force in the 1940s.

Having been on the losing side in the First World War, Hungary wanted to be among the winners after the next one. They curried favour with Germany and Hitler, who seemed willing to help with the restitution of the lost territories – another example of the far-sightedness of the Hungarians ... By 1945, Hungary had lost two armies and almost a tenth of its citizens, including roughly half of its Jewish population.

Socialism was no easy ride either. The new rulers of the country eliminated each other in accordance with the Soviet dictum that it is essential to try your best comrades on trumped-up charges and execute them. And if a dictator lives long enough, he can rebury and rehabilitate those who have been killed. This is what happened to László Rajk. He was reburied in 1956, just before the Revolution that *almost* shook the Soviet empire. Soviet tanks crushed it in a matter of days. More martyrs were created. The prime minister of the revolutionary government, Imre Nagy, was among those hanged.

He, and others, were reburied with full honours in 1989, the year socialism collapsed. János Kádár, who had reigned since 1956 and was considered the murderer of Imre Nagy and many other freedom fighters, was ousted. I had never dared hope I would live to see the end of socialism. I happened to be in the USA in 1989

473

and when I read in the *New York Times* what was going on in Hungary, I could hardly believe my eyes. I thought Western journalists were exaggerating events and I was constantly waiting for the bad news: that the Russians were invading Hungary again, as they always did. Thus the humble author is shown to be useless at foreseeing the future, unlike many of the characters in this novel. Literature has its uses, even if it is Hungarian.

Miklós Vámos
December 2005